# The Great Deception

Also by Syd Moore

*The Witching Hour (formerly The Drowning Pool)*
*Witch Hunt*
*Strange Magic*
*Strange Sight*
*Strange Fascination*
*The Strange Casebook*
*Strange Tombs*
*Strange Tricks*
*The Twelve Strange Days of Christmas*
*The Twelve Even Stranger Days of Christmas*
*The Grand Illusion*

# THE GREAT DECEPTION

## SYD MOORE

MAGPIE
BOOKS

A Magpie Book

First published in the United Kingdom, United States of
America, Republic of Ireland and Australia
by Magpie Books, an imprint of Oneworld Publications Ltd, 2025

Copyright © Syd Moore, 2025

The moral right of Syd Moore to be identified as the
Author of this work has been asserted by her in accordance
with the Copyright, Designs and Patents Act 1988

All rights reserved
Copyright under Berne Convention
A CIP record for this title is available from the British Library

ISBN 978-0-86154-965-8
eISBN 978-0-86154-163-8

Typeset in Dante by Hewer Text UK Ltd, Edinburgh
Printed and bound in Great Britain by Clays Ltd, Elcograf S.p.A.

This book is a work of fiction. Names, characters, businesses,
organisations, places and events are either the product of the author's
imagination or are used fictitiously. Any resemblance to actual
persons, living or dead, events or locales is entirely coincidental.

No part of this publication may be reproduced, stored in a retrieval system, or
transmitted, in any form or by any means, electronic, mechanical, photocopying,
recording or otherwise, or used in any manner for the purpose of training artificial
intelligence technologies or systems, without the prior permission of the publishers.

The authorised representative in the EEA is eucomply OÜ,
Pärnu mnt 139b–14, 11317 Tallinn, Estonia
(email: hello@eucompliancepartner.com / phone: +33757690241).

Oneworld Publications Ltd
10 Bloomsbury Street
London WC1B 3SR
England

Stay up to date with the latest books,
special offers, and exclusive content from
Oneworld with our newsletter

Sign up on our website
oneworld-publications.com

MIX
Paper | Supporting
responsible forestry
FSC® C018072

For Jools

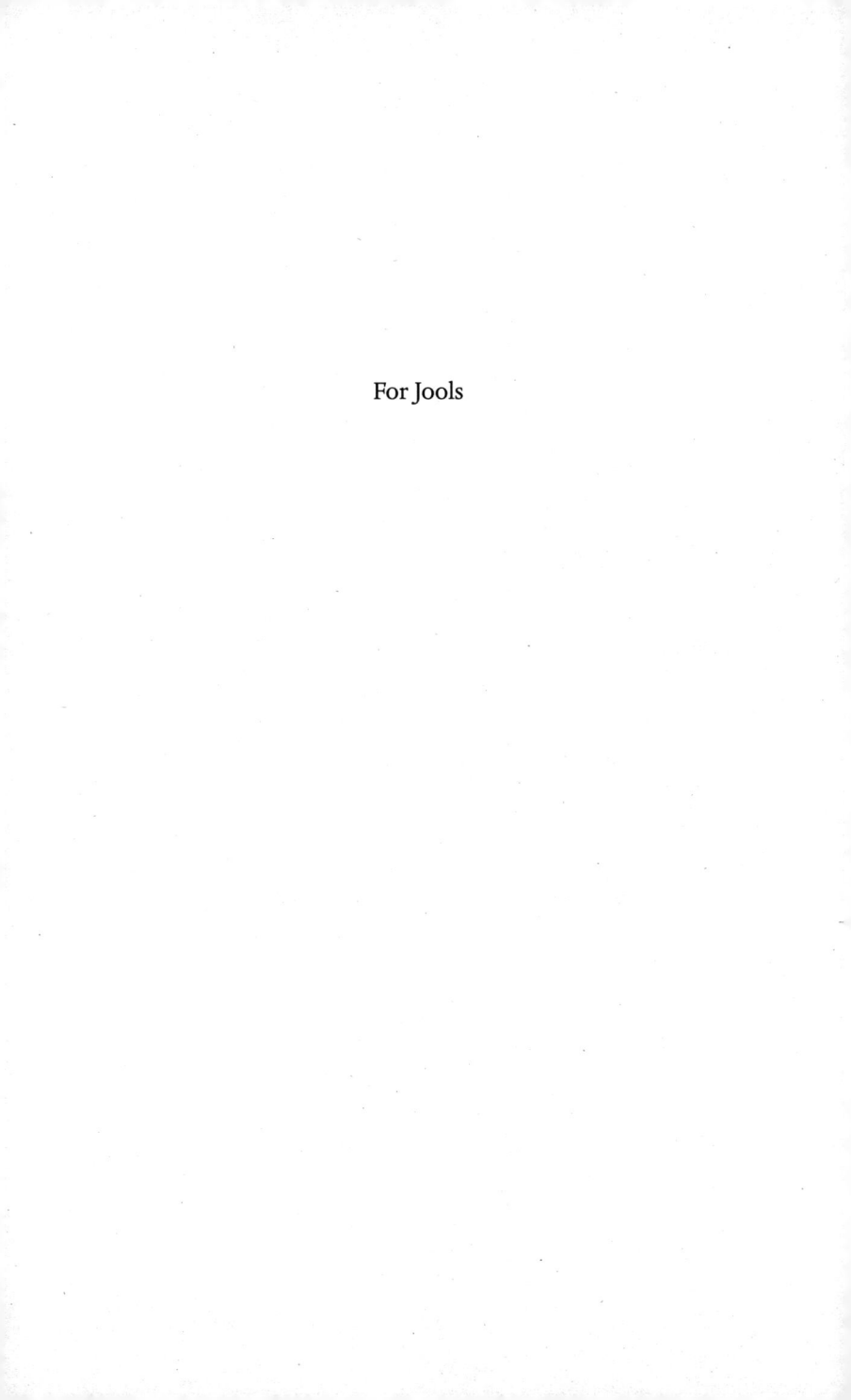

10 MAY 1940

*The commander does not wish to impart this news. Who can tell the mood of his superior? His ultimate superior. Although the commander has announced his presence, the man with the moustache continues to sit in his chair on the far side of the desk, back to the visitor.*

*On the mantelpiece the clock marks the hour: three chimes. The commander notes the papers spread out upon the desk, the blotter with ink spatters on the leather, the globe beside it.*

*The Führer's presence dominates the atmosphere like a thundercloud that has not yet broken. An electric current radiates from him in waves.*

*Waves, thinks the commander. His throat grows dryer and at once the study seems to shrink around him. The air leaves the room. The Führer does not change position as he speaks. 'What is it then, that cannot wait?'*

*Stumbling over his words, the commander thinks of the fate of messengers. 'My Führer. The news is b— not good.' His words tumble and catch, so he gathers himself. But in this, the briefest of pauses, the man with the moustache leaps to his feet.*

*In one move he has spun around to face the commander, who notices his superior's features are strangely impassive. This belies the energy building, throbbing through him, causing the room to vibrate with the increased pulse of his heart.*

*The supreme leader stands like a monolith.*

*Silence.*

*Faltering, the commander continues. He must get this announcement out then leave as quickly as possible. 'The British . . .'*

*A muscle in the Führer's jaw begins to flicker.*

*'The British,' the commander continues, 'have crossed the North Atlantic. And taken Iceland.'*

*At first there is no reaction. Then his superior clenches one fist. With a sudden movement, he punches the globe on the desk, sending it flying across the room.*

*A moment of confusion then, propelled by conventional good manners, the commander rushes after it. The globe spins against the skirting board in the corner. Bending over, he sees the blow from his superior has split its surface. A fracture has opened up in Iceland, from Reykjavík to Borðeyri.*

*As he picks it up, the world falls apart in his hands.*

## TWELVE HOURS EARLIER

The rock is like a giant's fist pushing up through the waves. Upon it, all is quiet. Even the falcons. They flapped in after the last trawler, diving over the wake for spoils, and returned full-bellied to their black nests at the uppermost point of the cliffs.

In their bunks the islanders sleep. Exhausted, wrapped in blankets and isolation.

Dawn breaks at one minute past three. It is the change of season on the island and the beginning of long summer days and midnight sun.

In the skies above Reykjavík a Walrus seaplane circles. The pilot and his crew sweep the bay with their eyes. They have been told the enemy are everywhere and must spot any tell-tale signs of periscopes or snorkels outside the harbour. But the sun has not yet climbed over the easterly mountains and the waters below are dark and impenetrable.

Out in the North Atlantic, in the control tower of HMS *Berwick*, Colonel Robert Sturges awaits their verdict. The commanding officer of Operation Fork, he is responsible for the men aboard the two destroyers in this convoy, HMS *Fearless* and HMS *Fortune*, and a cruiser, HMS *Glasgow*. In his charge are 40 officers and 746 Royal Marines: Force Alabaster. A small intelligence detachment and a diplomatic mission are also readying to disembark. The young marines, who have not yet finished their training, hold onto their rifles tightly. Fifty of them have never fired a gun in their lives. One, full of fear, having written a farewell letter to his mother, slips underneath a tarpaulin and fires the only shot of the day.

The rare sound of an aircraft wakes some of the islanders from their slumber. Curtains are twitched. A handful of people get up and, curious, make their way to the harbour.

The Icelandic authorities are informed of warships approaching their land. They assume it is the new ambassador arriving from Great Britain.

Also alerted by the aircraft is Herr Werner Gerlach, the German Consul. A personal friend of Hermann Göring and Heinrich Himmler, he was removed from his last appointment in Basel at the request of the Swiss government, for 'subversive political activities'. In Germany he had proved his loyalty by informing on doctors who treated Jewish patients. Since his appointment to Iceland, he has welcomed many German citizens to Reykjavík and helped them obtain good positions in a variety of Icelandic industries.

When Gerlach is told about the approaching vessels he telephones contacts across the country, then rushes to fetch secret documents and begins burning them in his bathtub. He will be apprehended in this act later and will protest the neutrality of Iceland. The arresting British officer will remind him that Denmark too had been neutral until his countrymen attacked. The flames will be subdued quickly by a standard-issue British Forces fire-extinguisher.

Meanwhile, a man in the north of the island hides stolen treasure.

At 3.40 a.m. the British ships can be sighted by the naked eye. The biplane continues to circle the city. A night watchman alerts the chief of police to the crowd of people gathering at the harbour.

Troops are trans-shipped ready for disembarkation.

At 4.36 a.m. dawn breaks over Germany. Its armies begin their assault on the Netherlands, Belgium, Luxembourg and France.

Just before 5 a.m. HMS *Fearless* begins sailing towards Reykjavík harbour.

In the home of the departing British Consul, five guides assembled hours ago under the pretence of holding a cocktail party to celebrate a birth. Not a drop of liquor passes anyone's lips. The night hours have been busy with intense preparations: where might they seize houses and land to accommodate British officers and men? Who should be arrested? Now Consul Shepherd leads them to Reykjavík harbour so they may assist the troops as they arrive.

At 6.20 a.m. the marines reach harbour and disembark under the quizzical gaze of the Icelanders.

Concerned by the numbers who are gathering, Shepherd turns to a police officer.

'Would you mind asking the crowd to stand back a bit, please?' he asks. 'So that the troops can get off the destroyer.'

It is a polite request but delivered by the consul of an invading force. However, the response is equanimous. 'Certainly, sir,' the policeman replies.

As the marines file down onto the quayside and pass along the dock, one of the Icelanders snatches a rifle from a young man and stuffs his cigarette into its muzzle. The crowd collectively holds its breath and considers the invading troops, awaiting their response. The soldiers have been briefed on establishing good relations with Icelanders – treating them with the greatest courtesy and respect – so do nothing. Remembering that he is relieved it is the British and not the Germans who have landed, the Icelander throws the rifle back. The men of the infantry division breathe out and continue on their way into the alien landscape. The next foreign beach they will tread upon will be in Normandy, if indeed they make landfall, so many of them becoming ghosts that their regiment will be disbanded.

Marines follow, handing copies of a hastily translated leaflet to the crowd at the harbourside. 'Tilkynning' it is headed. 'Announcement' in English. The Icelandic is poorly worded and, to the troops' surprise, elicits giggles and laughter from the recipients. The military personnel take this as an odd but positive response and continue distribution with smiles on their lips.

Meeting no resistance, the British guides identify themselves and lead off five separate groups.

Consul Shepherd welcomes Major Spike, who heads up the intelligence team. They seize the German Consulate.

Others occupy the telephone exchange and the broadcasting station. They knock on the doors before breaking them down and apologise profusely to the buildings' caretakers, promising to reimburse them for damage caused. Another group requisitions weaponry shops and the post office. Buses, lorries, trucks and taxis are commandeered or hired, used to ferry troops around the city and to the camp that is set up in a large, open space to the south of the city. Three roads leading in and out of Reykjavík are secured by sentries posted at junctions.

German citizens are dragged from their homes. Some will never return.

At 10 a.m. the Icelandic government meets.

An hour later the British contingent, headed up by the newly appointed Ambassador Smith, are ushered into the Cabinet Room. The ambassador is accompanied by the head of trade, Consul Shepherd, Colonel Sturges and Lionel Fortescue. The latter was not only responsible for the badly translated 'announcement' leaflet but has also been successful in establishing a ring of forty spies and contacts on the island.

Hermann Jónasson, the prime minister, vigorously protests the invasion, then insists that the Icelandic people will cooperate with the occupying force, as they believe they have come in the spirit of goodwill.

Rooms, empty houses and buildings are quickly rented. Hotels fill to capacity. The best, Hotel Borg, is requisitioned for officers.

Colonel Sturges tours the capital with the chief of police, Agnar Kofoed-Hansen. The latter is unaware that the British suspect him of pro-Nazi sympathies, knowing that he was trained in Germany. Not knowing he stayed there as a personal guest of Himmler.

By late afternoon Herr Gerlach and his staff, along with the records that have escaped incineration, are aboard the cruiser HMS *Glasgow* bound for England. Gerlach will later be exchanged for some of the British Embassy staff in Belgium. Much to the annoyance of the Secret Intelligence Service.

About the same time in London, Neville Chamberlain offers his resignation to the king.

At 6 p.m. Hermann Jónasson telephones London to issue a formal protest. The rest of his government are attending a relaxed meeting at Hotel Borg with Charles Howard Smith, the new British Ambassador, and a couple of bottles of good Scotch whisky he brought over with him.

Winston Churchill is sent to 'kiss hands' with the king and becomes prime minister.

Hermann Jónasson broadcasts a radio address to the nation, announcing the appointment of Ambassador Smith and the British occupation of the island. He reiterates that the occupiers have no intention of interfering with parliament and that their action has been taken to protect the country from German invasion. These declarations, he says, 'are undeniably rays of sunshine in the dark days that have come upon us.' He asks his people to respect the British soldiers as guests and to show them 'courtesy everywhere'.

Tents are erected for the soldiers to sleep in. The school holidays have started and local children help to pitch camp, thrilled by the arrival of the British soldiers.

When the sun goes down on the streets of Reykjavík, young people, especially girls, come out and surround the troops, keen to see what the foreigners are like.

Darkness falls across Europe.

It is 10 May 1940.

Lives, lots of them, are about to change forever.

# Tilkynning

Brezkur herliðsafli er kominn snemma í dag á herskipum og er núna í borginni. Þessar rádstafanir hafa verið gerðar bara til þess að taka sem fyrst nokkrar stádur og verða á undan Þjóðverjum.

Við Englendingar aetlum að gera ekkert á móti Íslensku landstjórninni og Íslenska fólkinu, en við viljum verja Íelandi orl"og, sem Danmörk og Norvegur urðu fyrir. Þessvegna bidjum við yður að fá okkur vinsamlegar viðtókur og að hjálpa okkur.

Á meðan við erum að fást við Þjóðverja, sem eru í Reykjavík eða annarsstaðar á Íslandi, verður um stundar sakir bannað
(1) að útvarpa, að senda símskeyti, að fá símtól.
(2) að koma inn í borgina eða fara út úr henni fyr nokkra klukkantíma.

Okkur þykir leiðinlegt að gera þetta ónaeði, við biðjumst afsokunar á því og vonum að það endist sem fyrst.

R. G. Sturges, yfirforingi.

## Tilkynning – Announcement

The British military force arrived today on warships and is now in the city. These measures have been taken to secure the place and be ahead of the Germans.

We Englishmen have no intentions against the Icelandic national government or the Icelandic people, but we want to protect Iceland from the fate that overtook Denmark and Norway. For this reason we ask you for a friendly reception and to help us.

While we are dealing with Germans who are in Reykjavík or elsewhere in Iceland, it will be temporarily forbidden to

(1) transmit by radio, send telegrams or get a telephone.
(2) enter the city or leave it for some hours.

It is regrettable to cause this inconvenience, we apologise and hope that this will end as soon as possible.

R. G. Sturges, Supreme Chief

CHAPTER ONE

Night presses down on the rooftops. Streetlights are sparse. In the centre of the city, despite the fact there is no blackout, the sky seems infinitely darker. Within it, sparkles of eerie brightness. Starlight is cold. Everything is.

She was told to expect the temperature of a crisp Christmas Day. But it is bitter here, like a bad February, gale-tossed with frosted pavements despite the fact it is not yet mid-autumn.

At this point Daphne is still alive though she knows she must be careful when she walks.

So careful.

Skidding is out of the question. One errant move and the blades concealed in her heels might click out and spark on contact with metal. Or cut through flesh. Not that there are many people in her proximity. For a capital city, the streets are rather empty. This entire island has a smaller population than Southend-on-Sea.

Daphne Devine, aka Dione-Smith, has read the troops' briefing document. She is no longer expecting the population to be comprised of Eskimos, or to be eaten by a ferocious white bear:

```
Iceland is the second-largest island in
Europe and approximately the size of
Ireland. It is something of a desert. Hot
springs and volcanoes exist in great
numbers and the latter are why you will find
```

> the country covered with boulders and rocks
> that have been spewed out by their erup-
> tions. These are covered with a variety of
> grasses, Arctic flowers and lichen. It is
> not always covered in snow, though there
> are thirteen glaciers. Polar bears do not,
> as some believe, hunt the Icelanders. Nor
> do the natives hunt them. The last polar
> bear sighted on the island arrived upon an
> ice floe that had broken off and floated down
> from the Arctic Circle.
>
> The people are European in appearance.
> They do not live in igloos and eat blubber.
> In fact, there is a rich heritage and
> literary history to the island, which was
> settled in 874 Anno Domini. Icelanders
> boast the oldest parliament in the world.
> These natives are very cultured. A good
> percentage of the Reykjavík population
> speaks English.

Her Icelandic contact, she has been told, is fluent. For which she will be grateful.

Certainly, she hopes the journalist she is to liaise with here will be more affable than the prickly major she reported to yesterday. Responsible for intelligence and relations with the islanders, Major Spike was very much as his name suggested. Below a pale, domed skull, his moustache was waxed into two honed spears as if to underline his rigidity. They pointed down to his mouth, which even in repose conveyed terse disapproval.

Entering his office, she had passed a young man sitting patiently on a chair by the window. After introductions were offered between herself and the major, she gestured to the young man. It would be rude not to acknowledge his presence. Despite the onset of war some habits persist, which cannot easily be surrendered. Good manners are important.

'Oh,' said Major Spike. 'My interpreter.' He waved a hand at him. 'Jóhannes, you may leave. I can understand this one.'

The young man rose. He did not salute but hesitated, then bowed to her before he left the room, leaving Daphne mildly amused.

'Is English not your first language, sir?' she asked by way of conversation.

He glowered, jowls quivering lightly. 'The calibre of new British recruits is not what it should be. I cannot understand the dialect of the lower classes. Jóhannes is able to translate both Icelandic and peasant. That boy will go far.'

Uneasy under his scrutiny, Daphne fought an urge to curtsey, to appease this big man, and felt, for the briefest of moments, relieved she did not have to answer directly to the major. 'I'm glad you find my accent comprehensible, sir,' she said.

But he was not interested in any niceties she had to offer and was already speeding on, his manner that of an overburdened typist with work to get through. 'Look, I'm not particularly happy about you waltzing round the city. A woman, unchaperoned,' he said, rifling through papers strewn across his desk. 'Where's that report from Commander Fleet?'

'I'm not aware of him, sir. My commanding superior is Hugh Devereaux.' And in her mind she pictured the man with the white hair and charismatic voice who had recruited her.

'Hugh!' The major dropped his hands briefly onto the desktop and sat back a little in his chair. 'Knew him at school. Excellent chess man. Your divisional head, is he? Not surprised. Not at all.' And he returned to shuffling the files. 'Excellent chess man.'

Finding the right document at last, Spike searched the text. 'Yes, right here. It says a certain Septimus Strange will arrive to guide you in four days' time, am I right?'

'Yes, sir. Mr Strange will—'

'That would suggest you are conducting initial reconnaissance. Good. I cannot recall the details of your target. Presumably of minor interest if a woman is involved in the operation. Some kind of performer, is that so?'

For a moment Daphne was not sure if he was referring to her own status or that of the man she was tasked with investigating. She plumped for the former. 'Yes, sir. I have previously been employed in the theatre myself and so was considered suitable for this job. Our target is a—'

But the major was not interested in such fripperies. He fluttered his fingers, signalling she should shut up. 'As long as it doesn't interfere with my duties. All messages through me, you understand?'

'Yes, sir.'

'Quite. Well, dismissed then.' He snapped his fingers. 'Look lively, girl. I've got work to do.'

And she was ejected.

On the one hand she was grateful that the meeting had taken so little of her time. On the other, slightly concerned: he had not asked for any details about her accommodation or the timescale for the mission. Though she did not welcome intrusion, she would feel safer in the knowledge that her presence here was at least officially registered, her address logged. So that if she disappeared, someone might notice her absence. As a woman working alone, she appreciated the freedom, but it was laced with jeopardy.

Still, she thought, perhaps Spike was already privy to the information.

She hoped so.

Less daunting was the meeting arranged for tonight, though there was still much at stake. It was vital that Daphne should earn the trust of one of their best contacts on the island, a female journalist. She would be dependent on her for cover, local insight and new intelligence.

---

The night is so cold as she click-clacks through the streets. Frost pinches her nose. Her lips are chapping. She is very aware of the lipstick in her bag, which will not offer any relief. Such a petite, dainty object, innocuously nodding to female vanity and yet, just like her, deceptive, potentially lethal. Who could have dreamed up such a thing? She has not yet fired the disguised pistol at another human being and wonders if she will be up to the task should the need arise.

Beneath her overcoat she wears a suit designed and put together by the couturier Vivien Steiner, which is chic and warm though the lapels chill her. She can feel them through the fabric of her blouse. The knives concealed within have absorbed the icy night air, as has the blade hidden in her belt. It is not just the temperature that causes her to shiver. She is a walking fortress. A death machine.

But it is better not to linger on these thoughts.

A sharp breath in to dispel them.

The air here smells sulphuric, eggy. She must have wrinkled her nose because, beside her, the landlady's son chuckles throatily and says, 'You will get used to it.'

She lifts her head and pitches towards him. Her walk becomes momentarily shambolic as she rights herself. The heels of her shoes are much heavier than any she has worn before – even the ones in her mother's blocky Charleston slippers, which she was occasionally allowed to borrow on Sunday afternoons. *If* Carabella was feeling generously disposed towards her boisterous daughter. In that second, a mental image comes to her: she is dancing, kicking her feet around, hands swinging wildly from side to side, while her parents sit laughing in the living room. But that was before war came, before her family was scattered across the globe.

'The water is better here,' the man says, and she tries to gauge his expression to see if he is being antagonistic. Is this an assertion of Icelandic superiority? Should she apologise for her reaction to the distinctive odour? But his face is cast into shadow and she cannot read it; the Reykjavík sky recedes to the moon.

Björn has been volunteered as a guide by his mother, Daphne's landlady. Hospitable to a tee, Guðrún Gunnarsdóttir has a comforting presence. She looks just the way a landlady should, with blue eyes the colour of forget-me-nots, tidy grey hair gathered into a bun on the back of her head and clad in a traditional dark frock. 'Of course,' Guðrún had announced with a kind and matronly smile that offset the note of command in her tone, 'the lady must not walk through the city alone. This is no slur on your conduct, Miss Daphne. Our newspapers are full of assaults committed by occupying soldiers. Young ladies must exercise caution out there.' Then, as a full stop to the conversation, delivered with an expression that brooked no dissent, she said, 'Björn will accompany you. A woman needs a man.'

And Björn, Daphne's escort, is a broad, strapping lad with pale eyes, lighter than his mother's, and the firm jaw that she has started to notice is a feature of his countrymen. A fisherman by trade, as many others here appear to be according to her briefing:

> Fisheries are regarded as Iceland's chief industry. They are a major driver of the economy and employ a significant portion of the workforce.

Navigating past a shelter made of sandbags, he indicates that they must round the corner into a wider road.

For a moment she is stunned. It is the high street. Shops and cafés are brightly illuminated, the air filled with the competing sounds of conversations and motorcars.

People are going about their usual business, *freely*.

Such a stark contrast to London, whose inhabitants must grope their way past boarded-up pubs and blacked-out department-store windows, that she is suddenly overwhelmed by a surge of inconvenient feelings: dismay, vexation, envy. Though occupied by a foreign force, albeit a friendly one, the Icelanders have more liberty than her friends and family back home.

There are many more shoppers, more workers, more pedestrians here than on the outskirts. Though it appears some are unable to walk in a brisk fashion.

As they approach a group of merchant seamen, one of them steps aside, allowing her to pass. But he misjudges his footing, freewheeling off the kerb into the road, landing with a grunt on his backside. The rest of the men hoot wildly. Daphne halts, unsure whether to ignore the fallen man or lend a hand.

But Björn urges her on. 'Black Death,' he whispers. 'A spirit. It damages your brain. There is nail varnish in it. Can send you crazy. Never accept a drink of Black Death. Never.'

'Oh,' she says, as they leave the seamen to it. 'Thank you. I didn't know. It wasn't . . .' Then she halts the easy flow of words. She was about to say *in the briefing* and is shocked by her own lack of discretion. He cannot know that she is not Daphne Dione-Smith, a journalist despatched by *The Times* newspaper to cover a local sensation. He cannot know that she is acting for the British Security Service.

If indeed she is.

Everyone has been so vague about which department she belongs to. Though she has been privy to the meetings of Section W, others have told her it doesn't exist. But she *knows*.

It matters not either way. She is tasked with a mission and will do her utmost to deliver. 'A matter of national security,' was how Hugh Devereaux put it. 'In Iceland.'

Of all places.

It is so different from anywhere she has visited before. The mountains that surround the city are huge and dark. They rise out of the ground like the shoulders of great blackened giants. It is not hard to see why the native mythology tells of trolls striding out from the camouflage of this otherworldly landscape. The scale of the scenery is huge. Yet the city is so small.

She is mildly surprised by the sight of a man on horseback clip-clopping down the centre of the street. No one else raises an eyebrow.

'Here,' says Björn. 'Where you are to meet your friend.'

He has stopped by a small café apparently built from corrugated iron with windows overlooking the street.

'When shall I collect you?' Björn asks.

Collect me? Daphne thinks. As if I am a parcel! She immediately softens her reaction. Perhaps it is only a quirk of translation: she must remember to be generous to her hosts. 'No need,' she says. 'I will be dropped back at your house later.'

It is a lie.

However, Björn should not be privy to her every movement. She must push back to gain independence. This is vital.

His hesitation is apparent in the lines that crease his forehead. She wonders if he is used to encountering dissent from women.

A long pause, then he shrugs. 'As you wish.' He bobs his head to her. 'See you later.'

She waves and watches him walk back down the street until he has turned the corner and is out of sight.

Immediately she retraces her steps then heads for another road nearby. At last she reaches a different café whose windows have fortuitously steamed up.

She looks behind her then enters.

CHAPTER TWO

The interior of this café is cosier than she expected from the austere, utilitarian frontage. Wooden planks line the walls. They are varnished and hung with pictures: small landscapes and embroidered verses. Windows are decorated with lace panels at the top. Lots of small tables and chairs pack the space. Not one of them is empty.

The journalist is not at the specified table by the counter.

For a moment Daphne stands in the entrance and assesses the room, removing her gloves while discreetly surveying the tables. She has been told to look for a tall woman with blonde hair. There are many of them in here, all paying no attention to her.

Now she has stopped hurrying, she finds herself hot and sticky. Sweat beads on her upper lip, but she will not shed her coat until she has found the reporter. A brief quickening of panic begins to surge through her veins. She reminds herself to hold her nerve. That's all that panic is – a testing of resolve – and she has been selected for this mission precisely because she has demonstrated excellence in that particular field.

Someone waves to her from a corner.

The woman makes eye contact then looks purposefully at the empty chair opposite hers. It is draped with a fur coat.

Daphne makes her way across the café.

'Anna Tómasdóttir?' she asks, feeling a little vulnerable. What if this woman is just being friendly or has mistaken her for someone else?

'Sit down,' the blonde instructs, and Daphne obeys. The other woman has authority in her voice. Just like Daphne's landlady.

Do all female Icelanders speak in such a way?

'Best not to be so conspicuous,' she tells Daphne. The Icelander's wardrobe is not dissimilar to her own, though the blouse is made of thicker fabric than those manufactured back home. Perhaps rationing has not yet hit the native clothing industry. 'This city is small,' says the woman. 'People notice each other. Strangers stand out.'

Daphne permits herself a wry smile. Excellent – confirmation: this *is* her contact. Thank goodness she has made the right call. 'Even though', she says, responding to Anna Tómasdóttir's assertion, 'the population has just been swollen by thousands of foreign troops?'

'Even though,' Anna repeats, her lips curving by return. The smile softens her features, which are gloriously Nordic. Her face is fine-boned, the planes of her cheeks high over a narrow chin. Full lips are painted the same shade as the lipstick that swings heavily in Daphne's pocket: Blood Red.

'There are some foreign nurses stationed here,' says Anna. 'But not many women overall.'

Daphne removes her hat, then realises she hasn't introduced herself. Though certain formalities have gone out of the window with the onset of war, old habits persist. 'I'm Daphne Dione-Smith.'

The reporter's sharp eyes widen slightly. They are blue, not as bright as Daphne's landlady's but threaded with glacier-grey, and give an impression of steely intelligence. 'I know,' she says. 'I have seen your picture. They sent me a leaflet from your show.'

Daphne is quick to scan the reporter's face to see if there is any sign of disparagement there. But it appears that Anna is unphased by Daphne's previous life as a stage magician's assistant. War both warps some conventions and eases others simultaneously.

'You are a journalist now, I understand?' Anna's English is admirable. Her accent brightens and lengthens the vowels, contracting some of the consonants.

'Yes. With *The Times.*'

'We met at a conference in Versailles?' Anna's jaw does not move much as she speaks, hinting at an innate conservatism.

Behind her, Daphne hears the bell above the door tinkle to announce a new customer. Outside air blows in, lowering the temperature briefly. Anna's eyes stray to the newcomer as Daphne replies, 'Two years ago, before the outbreak of war, I am led to believe.'

'Fine,' says Anna, switching her attention back to her guest. 'We shouldn't have much trouble with that story.' Daphne hears the way her 'r's roll on the last word. It is not unattractive.

'The international press have visited us,' Anna continues, eyes sweeping over the interior of the café, suggesting some of them may even be in here now, 'to cover the invasion.' Again, Daphne watches for signs of discomposure or resentment and finds none.

As if reading her thoughts, Anna nods and says, 'Luckily, you'll encounter less hostility here as a woman, British men are sometimes viewed with suspicion and jealousy.'

A diner or waitress drops a plate behind Daphne and she breaks off their conversation to turn around, realises she is being rude, so turns back to Anna who has paid the interruption no attention. 'Oh, yes? Why is that?'

'This invasion has been not only of soldiers but a generation of bachelors.' The journalist smiles and tosses her head. Hair the colour of undyed satin brushes her shoulders. 'My male compatriots now find themselves competing for the attention of the female population.'

'Ah,' says Daphne. She had not thought about that. There is clearly much to be learned from this woman. She will make an efficient guide in this strange land.

'We have both British and Canadians stationed here,' Anna continues. 'The latter are deemed far more interesting by local girls.'

Daphne can't help but say, 'Well, I know how they feel.' And for the second time Anna smiles, though it is now merely a crease of her lips. She does not probe further. However, Daphne relaxes a little: they are starting to find a feminine empathy.

Unprompted, an image of the man she left back home flits across Daphne's mental screen: Jack, the Canadian engineer seconded to her last mission. Voice of honey, physique of Adonis no less. Currently stationed up north in Britain and not seen for two months. When will they meet again?

She stubs the thought out like a cigarette. *Must focus on this meeting.* Though it is hard, in these days of uncertainty, to banish any notion that brings with it a scrap of hope, however foolish that seems.

'You'll have coffee,' says Anna. Is it a question or another instruction? Daphne wonders. Then the journalist continues, 'The coffee here does not have that dreadful chicory added to it. Most of the rations, I can put up with. But not that. Or would you like Indian tea? I know you British are fond of it.'

It is important to blend in, so Daphne says, 'Coffee is fine.' Though it is quite late in the day for it.

Anna raises her hand to the waitress but addresses Daphne. 'It is good that you found the place. I wondered if the directions were sufficient.'

'Fortunately, I was escorted by my landlady's son.'

Anna's eyes pop. She withdraws her hand. 'Björn Haraldsson?'

The Icelandic naming system is still a bit of a mystery to Daphne. 'The landlady's name is Guðrún Gunnarsdóttir,' she begins.

'Yes, her son.' Anna is already on her feet. 'Then we must leave at once.'

'No,' says Daphne, realising her mistake. 'I meant he walked me to Café Hilmar. I left him there, and then came here when he was out of sight.'

But this does not reassure Anna. 'Nobody should see us together. I have not yet laid the groundwork.' Her eyes strain towards the front door. 'Nor do we know if he followed you, or who might be watching.'

This confuses Daphne. 'We're just two journalists meeting to discuss a feature.'

'I do not think it is wise for us to let Björn Haraldsson and his friends know where we are. I am not familiar with his circle but there are Nazi sympathisers in the capital, and I would imagine they would be very interested to learn what a civilian Englishwoman in Reykjavík is up to. And that is for us to disclose only when we are ready.'

Although she thinks Anna is over-reacting, Daphne understands the importance of establishing trust, so carefully gets to her feet. As the waitress approaches, Anna stoops, cups her hand and whispers in her ear. Taller than Daphne had supposed, now she is standing up, Anna towers at least six inches over the young girl.

The journalist bends her lean frame and picks her coat off the chair. All those pelts must be heavy though she makes light work of it. As her hair falls back and she slips the fur over her shoulders, Daphne recognises something of the Hollywood star Carole Lombard in the high-arched eyebrows that frame the Icelander's large, expressive eyes. 'This way, quick!' Anna ducks round the counter and disappears into the kitchen.

Daphne follows, passing a middle-aged man and an older woman with hair wrapped up in a scarf, tending to bubbling stockpots that reek of fish. They look at her but do not comment or smile.

The rear exit leads into a small courtyard. Anna crosses it and opens a gate. 'Out here. We'll go to my office.' And they zigzag through the back streets and across several unmade roads until they reach a square block of a building cast from concrete, sombre and severe.

In the unlit doorway Anna fumbles with her key. Then the door opens and they climb a narrow staircase.

The room into which she is led is warm from the stove in one corner, not still hot but not cold either. Daphne goes straight to it and warms her hands. Though they have been outside perhaps only twenty minutes, the temperature has plummeted.

Smouldering red embers in the grate are the only light source: Anna has not flicked the switch by the door. Instead, she brings down an oil lamp from a shelf and sets it by the typewriter on her desk, strikes a match. Soon the flame is dancing upon the wick. 'I don't want to advertise our presence. There will be other staff about. Downstairs with the printers.'

Daphne nods and unbuttons her coat, taking the chair opposite.

Already Anna is at a filing cabinet. As her fingers skip over the files she says, 'The British government fears that there is a fifth column in our country. '

'At home too,' says Daphne, and her mind roams back to her nasty encounter there with two German agents. She wonders now, as she has done ever since, if they managed to make contact with anyone else: sleeping agents or subversives. The thought that there could be British collaborators at home, hiding in plain sight, ready to aid the enemy or destabilise the country when the balloon goes up, is eminently chilling. As someone who has spent all her working life, prior to the war, jumping out of boxes, being sawn in half or shot at, she has relied heavily on her faith in the skills and dexterity of her boss and friend, Jonty Trevelyan aka The Grand Mystique. It is the incaution of trust that she finds one of the most disturbing things about these troubled times; and she wonders how they will rebuild such bonds when this bloody war ends.

Anna has selected a file and brought it back to lay upon the desk. 'I do not think it is as bad as the British believe.'

'But there are some?' asks Daphne.

'There will always be *some*,' Anna says, her emphasis asserting it as an unassailable fact.

Yes, Daphne thinks, and says: 'You are correct, Anna. Not everyone at home agrees with Churchill. Some believe the Germans have got it right.' She hears herself sigh. A democracy, by its very nature, must allow different views to coexist. One must fight for the right for others to disagree. But utilising this right in order to destroy democracy is unconscionable. Germany has become a monoculture characterised by the madman at its helm. 'Am I correct in thinking,' she says, not wishing to dwell on this thought, 'that you believe this spiritualist we are to investigate to be one of these?' Daphne watches her select a page from the file: a newssheet.

'Spiritualist, clairvoyant, medium, call him what you will. Sindri Karlsson is his name,' says Anna. She unfolds a piece of paper and hands it over.

It doesn't answer Daphne's question but she knows she would not be here now if there were no doubts about the man. 'He attended university in Copenhagen, the musical academy or what you would call a conservatoire. Studying piano. As a youth he had high hopes of joining the National Orchestra but his talents were not up to scratch and he was reduced to performing in theatres.'

Heaven forbid! thinks Daphne, and watches to see if the journalist is aware of the slight she has just delivered.

But no, Anna steams ahead. 'At some point he developed the ability to communicate with spirits and see into the future.'

Daphne deflects the impulse to feel slighted – there is no point finding offence where none was intended – and focuses on the clipping taken from Anna's newspaper. However, when she tries to read it, she sees the text on the page is typed in the strange Icelandic alphabet, scattered with dots and accents. Though, above the column, there are photographs of Karlsson that need no explanation. One shows him onstage in a dinner jacket and wing collar, chin lifted towards the gallery, arms outstretched as if summoning energy, or perhaps basking in appreciation. The other is a close-up. His portly stature may well be ageing but she would put him only in his mid to late thirties. A large, doughy face is fringed on top by dark hair, so uniform it may be artificially coloured. Parted in the centre, it is greased back past his ears. A moustache curls over plump lips. Beneath, a pronounced double chin. However, it is the eyes that instantly draw her in. They are mesmerising, full of energy. Something about them holds the onlooker's gaze.

Pulling her own away with some effort, she finds herself asking Anna, 'Are you a believer?'

Is that a smirk on the reporter's face? Suddenly, Daphne worries she sounds naïve and foolish.

But Anna's expression softens. 'Visitors here often ask that question. Usually with regards to the Huldufólk.' Daphne's blank expression has her translating the term. 'The Hidden People.' When Miss Dione-Smith's eyebrows crinkle, Anna cocks her head to one side and offers, 'Elves?'

'Oh, I, well . . .' Blundering through her response, Daphne has a sense that she has caused offence.

'We are a superstitious people,' the journalist responds. 'Some traditions continue to exert a strong hold over the Icelandic population. Even to this day new roads cannot be built in a straight line if they intrude on a site sacred to Huldufólk – an elf church – or rocks they are known to live in.'

Thinking it a joke Daphne laughs, then notes the serious expression on Anna's face.

'Many Icelanders say they do not *not* believe in them. Just in case the elf folk really exist and cast misfortune upon them.' Now she is openly grinning.

'Oh,' says Daphne again. She is not sure what to make of any of it.

'This is a land,' Anna continues, extending one arm towards the window, dark and opaque, 'where the ground can tremble and the wind can blow you off your feet. Where geysers gurgle and larva surges from the earth without warning.'

'Yes,' says Daphne, getting her drift. 'Unseen forces all around, I suppose.'

'Correct,' says Anna, clipping the consonants. 'And anyway, the elves are just as invisible as God, aren't they? But many believe in Him.'

It is a fair point but doesn't really answer Daphne's question – is Anna a woman of faith?

The journalist leans over and taps the photograph on the clipping that Daphne has spread out upon the desk. 'He, though, I am not so sure about. Do I believe in Sindri Karlsson?' she asks herself rhetorically. 'He exists, this is true. Do I believe he has powers?' She fixes her eyes on Daphne. 'Some of his predictions have been strangely accurate.'

Daphne leans in, her attention fully commanded. 'Like what?'

'Some say he predicted the fall of Denmark in April. Certainly, he arrived back home from there to Reykjavík at the beginning of that month.'

Daphne nods, extrapolating Anna's line of thinking. 'And Germany invaded Denmark and Norway on the ninth. Though he could have seen it coming – politically.'

'Or he might have been tipped off,' Anna adds.

Daphne takes some time to process this. 'Ah, I see. That, of course, is a theory, certainly. But one cannot assume everyone who returned had inside knowledge. The outbreak of war in neighbouring countries seeds widespread anxiety. Icelanders may well seek the comfort of a home that is cut off and far away from the fighting.' She is pleased with her logic, though doubts that a return to Iceland in advance of Denmark's occupation is the only suspicious thing Sindri Karlsson has done.

'I agree,' Anna says.

'There is more?'

'Of course there is.' It sounds cutting, but Daphne doesn't think that Anna is being discourteous, just pragmatic and unemotive. 'In late summer,' the journalist continues, 'I attended one of Karlsson's performances or meetings. A woman in the audience asked about the safety of her son. He is a fisherman and she was worried about attacks off the coast. She told Karlsson that the young man fished off the east, towards the Faroe Islands. His words to her were, "I see that way danger lies. Avoid it. Tell all his men to avoid that sea." And she passed on this information. Later I learned that a British ship was laying a row of mines there, stretching across to the Orkneys.'

Daphne's eyebrows rise.

'To prevent the German fleet from gaining access to Iceland's south coast,' says Anna.

'So he had prior knowledge of the manoeuvre?'

'It is a possibility. Or else he genuinely has psychic powers. That particular stretch of coast was certainly dangerous at the time. He was right to warn her.'

'And he was announcing it to the public too. Interesting,' Daphne ruminates. 'I think I probably need to see him for myself.'

'I'd say so,' says Anna. Then she runs her eyes over her guest again. 'Have you had experience of this before – clairvoyants, mediums?'

'A little,' Daphne returns. The light on the lamp splutters. She sees an emotion flicker over Anna's face but cannot read it properly. Since they have been in the office the fire has diminished to barely a smoulder. Daphne realises she is straining her eyes to study the other woman.

Anna cocks her head to one side again, which Daphne understands now is a gesture she makes when she is questioning or rather probing a source.

In response Daphne explains, 'I have worked in the theatre, with a magician. Much of his magic is sleight of hand and illusion. Our skill lies in making the audience believe it is real. But during my time there, I have seen psychics, and fortune tellers too, and I would say much of their work is of the same ilk. Very entertaining. And most people go along to such shows in search of entertainment. Not all, I know. But many.'

'So,' says Anna, 'you are not a believer? In the supernatural and such?'

Daphne considers this for a moment. 'I think it is possible to give an impression of psychic ability. Though recent experience prompts me to state, in the name of cooperation and transparency, that I also do not *not* believe in it.'

'Ah,' says Anna. 'Like us and the Huldufólk?'

'Like you, yes. Not from any fear of retribution,' Daphne adds, to be clear. 'But because . . . I can't really explain it. Not yet.'

This goes down well with Anna, who shrugs as if to say: Me too – I know what you mean. She stabs a finger at the clipping on her desk. 'I see. Well, our medium is appearing at the old picture house tomorrow, so you can make your own mind up. I'll meet you there before the show. Take this. Some bedtime reading. I have translated what you need to see.' She slides a cream-coloured folder over the polished surface.

One last ember splutters in the stove. The light dies and the room is plunged into darkness.

Time to go.

*Leave now*, says a voice in Daphne's mind.

But it is only the child in her being silly, the impulsive, fearful part that does not heed reason.

Isn't it?

### Successful Clairvoyant to Appear in Reykjavík

It is not so long since the inventor and scientist Thomas Edison announced plans to create a 'spirit phone', a device that he believed would be able to communicate with those no longer living. Unfortunately, death claimed Mr Edison before he was able to create such a mechanism. But now here, in Reykjavík, we are offered the opportunity to witness a man who claims to be able to do such a thing.

Sindri Karlsson reports that his unusual skill came upon him suddenly when he was working as a musician in an orchestra in Denmark. 'I was walking home from a performance,' he told this reporter, 'late one evening last year, and happened to slip on a faulty pavement. The fall occasioned a bump to the head and mild concussion. Later that night, I was awoken by someone shaking me. When I came to my senses, I found I was alone.'

### Voices

The clairvoyant said that it was the next evening, whilst he was accompanying a theatrical performance on piano, that he heard the voice 'of a woman, whispering in my ear. She was telling me to speak to a man in the audience with a burgundy cravat. I could not hear everything but distinctly made out the words "ring" and "Bible", which she repeated with great emphasis. After the show, I visited the theatre bar and fortuitously the man was there. It took some courage to introduce myself to him and even more to relay the curious message. When I did, the man developed a ghastly pallor. He told me his wife had passed away recently and his finances were badly hit. I offered my condolences and left. Can you imagine my surprise when, the very next night, this man greeted me as I made to step outside the stage door? He told me that he had looked in the family Bible and found his wife's jewellery hidden in a hollow carved out of its pages. Although his grief was not assuaged, he was able to sell the gems, pay off his debts and look after his family.'

Since then the spirits of the departed have visited Mr Karlsson regularly to send messages to those left behind, and sometimes to caution them about dangers of which they appear to have a prescience which we mortals do not.

'Returning to the home of my birth,' said Mr Karlsson, 'I feel it is my moral duty to offer the same assistance to my countrymen who need guidance now more than ever.'

Sindri Karlsson will be performing on the second Wednesday of every month at the Reykjavík Picture House.

Contact the box office for more details.

## CHAPTER THREE

The news feature was devoid of the scepticism that Anna had expressed during their meeting. Daphne attributed that to the objective reportage style that newspapers used to cover certain subjects and issues. Those not concerning the current war.

Amongst the paperwork were several photographs of the clairvoyant that had not been selected for print. These shots showed the man in context. One had caught Anna on the edge of the frame, notebook in one hand, pen poised in the other. Her gaze was angled down, for the medium was not as imposing as Daphne had imagined. The journalist's frame towered above Karlsson's. Daphne deduced he stood a few inches higher than herself, perhaps five feet six, which was several inches shorter than Anna.

There was something in Karlsson's bearing that came across as arrogant or aloof. Though, as a seasoned performer herself, she was aware that one's onstage persona could be markedly different from what is left when the greasepaint comes off. She had seen any number of outlandishly confident actors shattered by bad reviews and heckling. Many sought to work in the theatre to find the appreciation and validation they had yet to experience in real life. Nonetheless, it was a strange contradiction of the profession that while it attracted those who ardently wished to step into the spotlight and feel the gaze of hundreds of pairs of eyes, a great many of them were predisposed to chronic vulnerabilities and possessed very thin skins.

Magicians and stage assistants seemed not as flawed in this respect. Perhaps because their focus was on technical skill and trickery, sleight of hand. If a performance was not well received by the audience, it was likely down to a poor rehearsal or faulty equipment. And these could all be learned from, and the performance thus bettered. Jonty Trevelyan, The Grand Mystique, had never taken criticism too much to heart and had advised her to do the same. She had followed his lead quite happily. By contrast, she had once seen a Shakespearean actor reduced to tears after his Hamlet was deemed 'foppish and unmanly' by a critic. Despite the consolation she offered, Daphne had privately agreed and thought those qualities the strongest point of his portrayal: for surely the slaughter of a weak old man and his servants was hardly the benchmark of 'masculine nobility'?

Although she was hesitant to pre-judge, she also thought there something foppish about Karlsson. Perhaps it was the sash he wore around his waist, or the bejewelled cufflinks? Though, of course, this was his costume for the show. She would have liked to see what his workaday wear comprised. Thoughtfully, Anna had enclosed the address of his lodgings, which Daphne resolved to visit in the morning.

And here it is – one of those Reykjavík builds with corrugated iron fixed to the outside. Well kept. Echoes of what she would call Swiss chalet-style are to be found in the pointy gables. There is a balcony on the first floor upon which stands an urn of milk and sack of potatoes. It is being used as a larder, which she thinks quite resourceful. She likes the way the Icelanders have painted their homes in different colours: navy blue, mustard yellow, aspidistra green. Cheerful, it must help with the dour climate and long nights. Today the air is boisterous and blows hard against her, as if trying to snatch the ground from under her feet.

She has found shelter behind a tree. A rare sight in Iceland. There are few in the city. Hardly any in the gardens. This one, she thinks, might be a birch or mountain ash. What foliage remains clings to its spindly branches. The leaves have mostly turned from red to watery copper. She shifts position. There is little shadow to sink into: today's sky is cloudy and grey. This wind is northerly, bringing ice crystals from the Arctic, which smart upon her nose.

Soon she will have to walk around the block again or else her loitering may attract attention. For ninety minutes she has been observing the house from different angles. So far no one has come out.

Stooping to retie a lace on her shoe, a red leaf catches on her shoulder. She picks it off and holds it in her hand for a moment before releasing it to the wind. It is a little like the maple on the Canadian flag. Jack is not on her mind as much lately. Which is a blessing and also a worry: if she is thinking less often of him, it is only to be expected that his memories of their time together are fading too.

A door slams nearby. Leaning forward, she peers round the tree trunk.

At last! It is Karlsson, wrapping a scarf around his neck as he marches down the road, his gait suggesting he is in a hurry. She inches back, completes the bow on her shoe, then stands and looks at her watch. Keeping to her side of the street, she begins to follow.

When he reaches the junction, his coat flaps open. As he stops to rebutton it, she slows. He veers right and is lost behind the building on the corner. Approaching the crossroads, she sees he has walked down a little way and crossed into a narrow street. She will have to be careful there – it is empty of bodies that might give her some cover.

She pauses to admire a small park with swings for children. Despite the inclement weather a few are romping around. These conditions, she realises, aren't inclement for them. It is what they expect for this time of year and their parents have prepared them accordingly. All of them are bundled up in jackets, woollen hats and thick gloves.

Karlsson moves on, turning right again. She leaves the children to it and walks briskly after him. The road he has gone into is wider, with a sprinkling of shops and cafés. At the bottom is a large hotel. She wonders if this is his destination, but he pauses only to check his reflection in the picture windows and then takes a left turn. This new road passes the lake in the city, which she has memorised from the map given to her at her briefing. Tjörnin, 'The Pond', is one of Reykjavík's central landmarks and helps to orientate her. The buildings around it are bigger – municipal offices and halls.

Left, right, left, right. The streets thicken with people and begin to incline steeply. Karlsson is not quick, which is just as well as by now she too is panting slightly. At last, he stops before a café with large front windows. These have not steamed up and Karlsson peers in. Before she can duck behind anything, he spins on his heel and inspects the pedestrians to either side.

Damn.

Daphne is forced to make a split-second decision and continues walking past the clairvoyant. Although she wants to turn and check if he has noticed her, she fixes her eyes on the street ahead. There is a small chapel or church. She makes for it.

The door is open. Inside a few pews, bare white walls. The sounds of the street recede. It is a little pool of tranquillity. Silence laps within as she pauses for a moment to collect herself. The sight of the simple cross behind the altar stops her and she finds herself genuflecting, an old spiritual muscle-memory. Though her parents are no longer practising, her father converted to Catholicism to marry her mother, Carabella. Previously Lutheran, the conversion was perfunctory. Like most men, he, his father, uncles and family acquaintances, came out of the Great War profoundly changed. Those who returned from the front were often maimed or confused, guilty to find themselves back in the embrace of their loved ones when their brothers-in-arms lay rotting in a foreign soil, many without tombs or gravestones to say they were ever there at all. That they had ever existed at all. These cataclysmic absences, whether of the body or the mind, or entire living, breathing people, deeply affected the belief in a God who could allow such suffering and destruction.

The war to end all wars, she scoffs silently. What did The Fallen make of their sacrifice now that a new conflict had broken out? Though she has not discussed it with him, she wonders if her father seeks out God in the dark corners of his life. She suspects not, though you never know. In times of upheaval and crisis people cling to hope, and if that comes in the form of faith, well, she will not cast the first stone.

While not as affected as some, her family has suffered already since the outbreak, with Uncle Giuseppe deported to Australia (but at least alive), and her mother interned on the Isle of Man. Though her release may well be imminent if Daphne succeeds in her mission. Her mission! And her brain snaps back to the present. She cannot linger and returns to the church door, the words of Hugh Devereaux resonating through her mind: 'Top priority. Reports of German agents landing in the east of Iceland have come to the attention of Intelligence. Something is afoot. The Garrison is preparing for an Axis counterattack. We cannot let enemy agents or sympathisers help them from within. Carry out surveillance on Karlsson, identify his associates, evaluate his performance. Prepare a statement for Septimus Strange when he arrives.'

She bustles out and into the tunnel of wind created by the buildings to either side of the street, heart quickening.

There is a shop directly opposite the café where her target stopped. She hurries to it and, once inside, gains a position with an uninterrupted view of the premises that Karlsson has now entered. She pretends to browse the items in the shop window. To her dismay, she finds it is filled with fishing paraphernalia. She has been on small fishing boats, back home in Leigh-on-Sea, but has never taken up a line. The equipment is odd, curiously fascinating. Bright feathers tied upon hooks; things that look like bobbins.

'Má ég hjálpa þér, fröken?' a voice says behind her.

It is the shopkeeper, an older man with questioning eyes and thinning silver hair.

'Sorry,' she says, then curses herself: she must exude confidence and not apologise for stumbling into a man's world. 'I am looking for a gift to take home to my father?' She is glad that he has been on her mind as the lie flows out with ease.

Although now she has her back to the café and does not know if Karlsson is still there. She cannot lose him.

'English.' The shopkeeper presents it as a statement. 'Nurse?' He looks at her head, which is covered by a felt hat. All military personnel are required to wear uniform when out in the city.

'No,' she says. 'Newspaper reporter.'

He seems to accept this with a slight roll of the eyes. The initial bemusement of the Icelanders is slowly giving way to a more natural reaction from the inhabitants of a city whose numbers have been almost doubled by belligerent overseas forces. 'What fishing does your father like? It is excellent here. We have salmon, very fresh, and in the sea – abundance.'

Her back is itching with the impulse to turn round. Is Karlsson still there? Or has he left? Has she slipped up already on this, her first real task? 'I don't know,' she stutters.

A smile crosses his face. 'Our women here fish too,' he says, asserting his nation's superiority in the matter and simultaneously chastising her lack of experience.

She is becoming hot and fears the appearance of sweat on her forehead. Bodies have a language all their own and can scream and holler though their lips remain closed. She is not as accomplished in reading their signals as her boss, The Grand Mystique, but will put what she has learned from him into practice when she watches Karlsson tonight. She must not, however, let this shopkeeper find her out. 'Do you have a catalogue I can take with me?'

He shakes his head as if this is a churlish request.

'Then I will return when I have found out more,' Daphne says, and with that she leaves and crosses directly to the café.

She had not intended to go inside but finds herself opening the door. Thankfully there is no bell. Still, her entrance draws the eyes of a few customers. She swerves and dodges her way through the narrow gap between the tightly packed tables, sighting Karlsson at the back, sitting with two men. Taking up position six feet away, she sits with her back to them. It is a strategic move.

She removes her coat and brings her handbag onto the table. Then she takes out a powder compact and makes as if to check her reflection in the mirror. But it is angled so that she can see over her shoulder. She pats her hair whilst observing the man next to Karlsson. He is young, perhaps early twenties. White-blond wisps escape from a woollen cap as he hunches over a mug, watching the steam rise in syrupy curls and listening. His angular face is devoid of surplus fat, suggesting he is lean or thin. When the man opposite says something, he looks up sharply at him, and then at Daphne. She snaps the compact shut.

No. She should not have done that. It was too reactive. Though she has every right to check her appearance like any other woman here. Instead, she takes a lipstick from her bag, double-checking it is not the concealed pistol; though she knows that is safely stowed in a pouch sewn into her pocket, it is better to be safe than sorry. She flicks the mirror open again. At the back of the café, the men's eyes are directed towards the tabletop. Judging from the shape of his shoulders, it looks like the man with the trilby hat has pushed something across the surface. His body blocks her line of vision so she cannot see what it is. Perhaps if she lifts the mirror?

As she raises it to change angle, she sees the waiter by her table is watching her. How long has he been there? Can't be that long, can it? A few seconds. Maybe half a minute? He does not ask what she would like, so she says, 'Coffee, please.'

He regards her coolly with dark eyes. 'We do not serve fish and chips. Near the British camp is a place called Mama's. You can get it there.'

What is this? A dismissal? Or is he merely offering information, assuming the English consume fish and chips all the time, his helpfulness obscured by the same flat Icelandic reserve that Anna displayed?

Or does his tone convey banishment – has he seen her looking through her mirror? Surely not. She stands firm and says, 'Just the coffee then.'

He nods curtly and withdraws behind the counter.

I will have to up my game, she tells herself. Trust no one. But can the island really be full of sympathisers and agents, watching her every move? Anna said the fifth columnists were few in number, not so many as the British assume. Undoubtedly the Icelandic government has its own eyes about the town, keeping track of foreign nationals. Who knows which residents may be on their payroll? This is a small café but central and, judging from the number of customers in and out of the door, popular. The turnover is swift, which makes it a good place to see who is in the capital and what company they keep.

In the distance bells ring the hour. A chair squeaks on the lino flooring as a diner gets up from their place. The waiter returns with her order, pausing a moment to stand back and allow someone to pass. It is Karlsson. His coat sweeps against her table and knocks the salt cellar on its side. To avoid his apology, and his gaze, she peers down into her handbag on the pretext of finding her purse. But Karlsson does not stop. When she looks up, Icelandic króna in her hand, he is already halfway out of the door.

She accepts the drink and pays the waiter. As she sips patiently, the man in the trilby hat appears in her sightline. Average height, average build. Nothing distinctive about him other than the suit trousers, which she sees beneath his long overcoat. He wears shoes rather than boots, which look more appropriate for an office than the rutted Reykjavík roads. Behind him trundles the blond man. His garb suggests physical labour – there is mud spattered across the bottom of his trousers, dark-grey smudges on his jacket sleeves. She watches them go out of the door and then leave in different directions.

Above the rooftops clouds are moving faster, turning darker. What time is it? Could twilight be coming so soon? She has not yet acclimatised to the rhythms of Icelandic life and was thrown this morning when the sun did not rise until after half-past nine.

The hour hand on her watch points to three. Later than she thought.

She has half a mind to leave her coffee undrunk and go after her target. However, the waiter's eyes are still keen. Instead, she takes out a sheaf of paper and pretends to write a letter home. 'Dear Father,' she pens, 'all good in Iceland. The weather is bracing.' She writes a little about the boarding house, then describes the landlady as if she was the man in the trilby and the blond as if he was her son. The notes will help her commit the men to memory before she is able to relay the details to Anna at the theatre tonight. Where she will scrutinise Karlsson as he reaches over the abyss and opens his mind to the dead and undead still walking the earth.

For a moment, she shivers.

*The dead and undead.*

Though she does not know it yet, soon they will be all around her.

## CHAPTER FOUR

'Mmm,' says Anna. 'I do not know them. Although maybe the younger one, with blond hair.' Then pauses and asks, '*Is* he younger?'

'Couldn't tell for sure.' Daphne thinks back. 'He looked stronger, shorter but thick- set.' That or his clothes were better padded. Possibly both. 'Walked more slowly. Had something directionless about him.'

'Could be Sigmundur Gunnarsson,' says Anna to herself. 'An active communist—' She stops talking as they both stand to let a large woman in a wet coat pass along the row. Once she has reached her place, they sit down again and the scent of aged wood and dust is dispelled into the atmosphere. Daphne fleetingly wonders how long the show will be. The theatre chairs back home have similarly stiff backs but there the seats are cushioned for comfort.

Anna lowers her voice. 'Keep your eyes peeled. Perhaps they will be in the audience tonight.'

Instinctively, Daphne's eyes stray over the rows in front. She and Anna have taken seats at the rear to be discreet, and Daphne can only see the backs of heads. However, one can learn a lot from hair – how old a man is, by the extent of grey or white. Though it is different for women, who may colour their curls, the quality of the shine achieved can correlate with the level of care taken. The use of good hair products, hairdressers and sharp shears indicates disposable income. Or the lack of. Collars and grime can speak volumes, as can superior fabric. The assembled audience seems to have come from a variety of backgrounds.

Sitting in the row in front is an old woman in a long black dress with a V-shaped lace collar, which Anna has told her is an outfit the English call 'Sunday Best'. It reminds Daphne of Greek widows. Not that she has met any, though she has seen photographs in the Sunday pictorials.

There are others similarly attired and of comparable age. She supposes the older you get, the more ghosts fill your life, and finds herself relieved, tonight, that she does not have too many of her own to worry about. Grandfather Gunter died eight years ago. Though he was happy to go and 'meet my Lotte'. She wonders, suddenly, if he will make an appearance but thinks it highly unlikely that his spirit would roam the earth. The night he died, he went up to bed and laid his gold watch (which he did not wear as a rule) on the desk in his room, beside the Bible. When they found him in the morning, he had a smile on his face she thought serene and was wearing a dress shirt and clean trousers, as if he had *known*. Though she was only fourteen she had thought that her grandfather, who always seemed to know what to do, had decided it was the right moment for him to leave the land of the living and pained. She missed him terribly but is glad now that he did not live to see another conflict break out. And for the second time today she thinks of the dead in their shallow graves on the Somme. Was it worth it? Is it ever worth it?

Will it be worth it for her?

It is true that her situation is not, by any measure, as bad as that of men on the front line. And now those at home are suffering too. Even Buckingham Palace has been hit. Bombs have no respect for rank or status. All lives should matter. However, a perverse tally exists: one life taken here is a victory over there.

One lost there is celebrated in Old Blighty. How did we come to this? A death cult, competing for annihilation? Is this the price that must be paid for standing up to evil?

Though the last thought sounds hyperbolic, she knows it is no exaggeration: her division has evidence that members of the German High Command are proponents of Luciferianism, worshippers of the Antichrist himself. Their aims of swallowing up the world, imposing a new order on it and inverting Christian values are terrifying. Hitler must be stopped. And she is resolved to do whatever is needed to help the Allied campaign.

Despite this determination, Daphne is not unaware of her own vulnerability. Major Spike's words may have annoyed her, 'a woman, unchaperoned', however it is fair to say that she *has* encountered perilous situations and knows only too well that it is possible to be overpowered by men. It has happened in the past and may do so again. Of course, men can be matched by women in skill and dexterity, but when it comes down to basic physicality, brawn always overpowers the brawn-free. The trick is to utilise deception and appear frailer than is in fact true. This, she can do. This, she has done numerous times on the stage. Nevertheless, she feels in her pocket for her lipstick. Not the real one.

There are men in the picture house audience tonight, though their numbers are not as great. Some are old, some of working age. A couple of soldiers have come along. One British, one Canadian, seated together on the front row. They appear to know each other. She still does not understand how everything fits together here. There are troops all over the island. From her briefing notes she understands that one company controls Reykjavík while another has gone twenty miles north to Hvalfjörður, which is a fjord – like a loch back home. Though this one is very deep and a natural harbour for boats, and submarines, and whales. Another squadron has occupied the landing grounds at Kaldadharnes, south of the city, and two other areas, one of which is a seaplane station in the southwest. She remembers all of this, but as yet cannot orientate herself on the ground. Perhaps she should ask Anna's help with that.

When she leans towards the journalist, she notices a scowl cloud over her face, and a feeling of uncertainty catches her. What is Anna? Agent? Friend? No, Daphne thinks, she is a contact and must have been vetted. Perhaps she is one of the circle of sympathisers established on the island before Force Alabaster arrived.

Daphne feels it is all right to ask her, 'Where is Kaldadharnes exactly?'

But Anna puts a finger to her lips and says, 'Shhh,' then nods her head forward, sliding the notes and descriptions of the diners at the café into her pocket. When Daphne looks to the stage, she sees a slim man in a dinner suit walking into the spotlight.

The house lights dim. A murmur runs through the audience. The men put their cigarettes out.

A hush falls.

The show is beginning.

'Welcome,' the man onstage intones. 'It gives me great pleasure as the manager of this fine establishment to greet you tonight. I know that many of you have battled against the rain to be here, to see a man whose gifts can only be compared to those of the American clairvoyant Edgar Cayce.' A couple of women in front of them let out an 'Ooh.' Even Daphne has heard the name. Cayce has set up institutions, libraries and associations committed to furthering the understanding of psychic phenomena. His pedigree is impressive.

'The astonishing gifts tonight's medium possesses impressed me greatly on his first visit here' says the manager, as a ripple of excited applause breaks out in the front rows. 'So I have invited him back for, what I hope may be, the first of many more performances. Ladies and gentlemen, I give you: Sindri Karlsson and Jessamine.' He bows and then disappears into the wings.

Behind him the deep crimson curtains glide open.

The stage is dark, empty but for a microphone in the centre and a desk further back on the right, upon which a candle burns. It flickers, casting nebulous shadows. A small but well-chosen prop that adds to the eerie atmosphere, Daphne thinks. Cheap too.

Gradually a blue, wavy light illuminates two silhouettes at the back by a screen. The colour brightens from navy to turquoise. Bubbles seem to rise up the screen behind the figures and disperse into the heavens. The illusion makes it appear that they are standing at the bottom of the ocean.

Stage lights flicker. A silvery spotlight bathes the desk. The shorter of the two figures, a woman, steps into it. This must be Jessamine, the assistant, clothed in a flowing robe. Her long black hair reveals a streak of pure white, which runs from above her left eyebrow down the entire length of her glossy mane. Daphne hasn't seen anyone like this in Reykjavík and thinks she looks wildly exotic.

Jessamine stands for a moment and gazes at the crowd, as if seeing beyond them. 'Tonight,' she says, 'we dance on the edges of time, where past, present and future converge.'

A violin starts up in the orchestra pit. The unseen musician glides his bow across the strings. The sound sends tingles down Daphne's spine.

'There are energies here I must banish,' Jessamine continues, her speech heavily accented. 'Evil may lurk in the corners. Yes, even here.' Instinctively the audience, discomfited, looks around the theatre. 'The mischievous must leave before the master opens himself to the spirit world.' She takes the blue candle from the desk and begins to twirl around on the spot. Chiffon layers and scarves in shades of blue and white, sewn into her costume, swirl out as she spins to the front, her arms undulating and serpent-like, her wrists curled, so she looks like some strange human representation of a whirlwind with a flame at its centre. When she reaches the apron she touches her candle to the floorboards, head bowed, then whips round with startling swiftness, spinning to each side of the stage. An oboe joins the violin.

It is a good act – the low notes in this lilting melody evoke feelings both mournful and unsettling. The woman's sorrowful expression underlines the mood.

Her moves are precise as she touches the flame to each wing of the stage and then swirls her way around its entire circumference. At times she looks as ethereal as an air sprite, then ripples like a watery elemental.

When she reaches the desk again, she halts. Slowly, she replaces the candlestick. As soon as its base touches the wooden surface the music stops and the stage is plunged into darkness.

An expectant pause.

Then a spotlight hits the microphone at the front of the stage to reveal Karlsson standing there. Gasps of surprise echo through the stalls. It is as if he has travelled there by willpower alone, without moving his limbs.

The master's face a mask, he stands still for a moment then extends his arms, palms up, and the room hushes once more.

Next he drops his hands to grip the mic. 'Welcome, seekers of the unknown.' His voice is powerful – booming all the way to the back seats. 'Please be introduced to my spirit-sister, Jessamine.' The woman by the desk bows her head and then sits down and takes up a large feathery quill. Daphne sees a sheaf of paper set beside it.

Then Karlsson reclaims the audience's attention. 'All I need, for you who are drawn here tonight to find answers to life's enigmas, is your open minds. The success of this evening lies in your hands.'

He pauses. The audience stirs. A moment of silence before he speaks again. 'People of Reykjavík,' he says in a voice that has become much deeper, 'let us initiate ourselves into the ethereal realms of the spirits. Please close your eyes.'

Another hush falls over the audience as they comply. Daphne, however, keeps her eyes open until the woman in the next seat glares at her. When she lowers her head she notices that Anna is taking notes – well, she is writing in squiggles across a pad on her lap.

'Shorthand,' she whispers to Daphne.

She has heard of it but never seen it before. It looks like hieroglyphs.

'Yes!' Karlsson's voice rings out from the stage. 'You have opened yourselves. Awake. Awake, ye undead who still walk the earth.' Heads snap up.

Karlsson's hands are in the air. 'Thank you, I feel your consent come to me across the aether. Let the mysteries reveal themselves.'

The master's hands strengthen their grip on the mic. He closes his eyes. His lids flutter. 'Yes, come to us, spirits, to this land of fire and ice. This is a nation of resilience, where the spectres of our forefathers continue to whisper in the wind, where the threads of fate are woven in the loom of time.'

He pauses, letting the words settle. Some of the audience exchange glances. Then his hands begin to move, drawing invisible symbols in the air. A light shines on him from the orchestra pit so that shadows dance upon the screen behind him. If Daphne was not so versed in theatre arts, she might think the spirits were manifesting.

'I can feel this place is now charged. Charged with a mystic energy. O, souls, send us painted visions of our futures waiting to unfold. I see you gather.' He looks at the audience, and then, glancing briefly to one side, says, 'There are many here. I will do my best to voice them. Though they draw on me, I shall try to convey their messages. To reveal their truths. But we shall see whether that takes three turns, four or seven. It is – oh, how it is! – my duty to serve.' He bows then stretches out his arms, this time to the audience. 'I see your destinies. The phantoms speak of challenges, but also of endurance. And freedom.' Pointing to the back of the theatre, he says, in a voice that shakes slightly, 'But wait – I see a man. A soldier.'

Some members of the audience turn around to see if they too can glimpse the ghost but are disappointed.

Karlsson's eyes grow wide. 'He wears the uniform of a Canadian and holds something in his hands.'

There is a stirring at the front where the soldiers are sitting.

'Quiet!' Karlsson tilts his head as if listening. 'There is a name coming through. No.' He holds his hands up as if to stop someone. 'Not a name – a place.' The master squints, concentrating hard. 'France. I see the French flag.'

A woman a few rows ahead of them starts fidgeting in her seat. 'My brother,' she exclaims. Those around urge her to stand.

'What's that?' Karlsson blinks into the lights. 'Is there someone who recognises this spirit form?'

A woman wearing a simple tea dress, her brown hair threaded with strands of grey, gets to her feet. 'My brother,' she says, voice faltering, heavy with unspent emotion. 'Ragnar fought in the last war. For the Royal Canadian Horse Artillery.'

'Ah,' says Karlsson and nods as though everything suddenly makes sense. 'So those long leathery straps that he is holding in his hands . . .?'

'Reins,' says the woman to herself, then louder, tilting her face to the clairvoyant, 'They're reins!'

The audience gasps, marvelling at the accuracy of his vision.

'Yes!' says the woman, losing her self-consciousness. 'He loved the ponies, trained them on our farm!'

Again, an awed murmur ripples through the stalls.

Karlsson holds one finger in the air and smiles. 'Ragnar's telling me that he has found someone who was searching for him. He's telling me . . . I think it is a name. A name beginning with "B" . . .'

Behind him Jessamine scribbles on a piece of a paper. When she holds it up, Daphne sees she has written a capital B on it. For a moment the assistant holds the paper above her head, then twirls down to the front of the stage and shows it to the audience. It reminds Daphne of the black-magic routine that she and Jonty used to perform. It was she, the assistant, who worked the hardest to direct and misdirect the audience, while The Grand Mystique reaped the reward of applause. But that is the way for women: always creating a situation that enables the men to shine and claim the glory. However, the memory forces her to pay closer attention to Jessamine, who has returned to her desk and laid down the paper upon it. Daphne watches her hands for signals.

'Yes – the letter B,' says Karlsson, again wresting back attention to himself. 'Not for a man. For . . . let me see.' He laughs, as if he is sharing a joke with the deceased. 'Is it for . . . a pony?'

'Brúnn!' the woman suddenly shouts. 'Brúnn was one of our horses! Ragnar loved him very much.'

'Yes, he did,' said Karlsson. His voice becomes gentle. 'And Ragnar wants you to know that he and Brúnn are reunited. That although your brother rests on a foreign shore, both he and Brúnn are at peace and together now.'

'Oh.' The woman covers her face with a handkerchief, but everyone can see she has started to cry. She sits down abruptly and is comforted by the friend sitting next to her. 'Thank you,' she whispers.

Jessamine twirls into mid-stage. 'They may rest now.'

In the pit the violin starts again.

'Another voice I hear. Strong in presence.' Karlsson has closed his eyes. For a minute nothing but the notes of the violin fill the air. Then, 'Isak – his name is Isak.'

Two hands shoot up. One at the rear, another towards the front.

Karlsson's eyes open but he ignores them. 'A – a farmer.'

One sad hand flops down.

Karlsson shifts his attention to the owner of the remaining hand. 'Stand if you will, my dear.'

It is a middle-aged man who gets to his feet. 'This sounds like my father,' he grunts. 'He passed last year.'

'Ah,' says Karlsson and dips his head in a show of respect. 'That is why his voice is so clear. He mentions a clock.'

'Yes,' says the man, his excitement evident in the sudden tension of his body. 'He had a favourite cuckoo clock. It stopped working before he died. Then after the funeral, when we came back, it started chiming and wouldn't stop! We had to take the weights off.'

'I know,' says Karlsson, and a rumble of appreciation resonates through the auditorium. 'He is telling me that was his sign to you that all is well with him.'

The older man nods. 'Will you send him my love?' he says through strangulated vocal cords.

'Isak knows this, my dear sir. He—' Karlsson's words are interrupted by a violent jerk of his shoulders and he begins to cough. Hand clamped over his mouth, he turns to Jessamine who quickly fetches him a glass. When the paroxysm has begun to subside, he takes a mouthful and finds relief. 'Thank you for the water. The water is good tonight.

Refreshing and calming. They,' his hands undulate into the air, 'feel it too.'

Another sip, then once he has completely recovered himself, he looks back at his audience and apologises. 'They are draining me. When the spirits manifest, they use my vitality to connect to the world of the living. Forgive me.'

A wave of concern goes through the picture-house patrons. Someone starts clapping. Others, in a show of support, join in and soon the entire theatre is applauding. Daphne too. Even Anna puts down her pen.

Karlsson's hands come up – halt! – and the applause stops. 'This may be my last visitor of the night,' he announces.

The woman next to Daphne mutters, 'Skiljanlegt.'

Daphne doesn't understand but senses the spectator is sympathising with Karlsson and acknowledges this with a polite smile.

Onstage, the clairvoyant has angled his face slightly to the left. 'They are not saying their name,' he says. Then he laughs and calls to the empty space above the heads of the audience, 'Slow down, I will get it to them.' He looks to Jessamine and makes a shape with his fingers, then back at the audience. 'I see "W". Jessamine, please.' His assistant has drawn the letter on another piece of paper and shows it to the audience.

'Is there a Wilhelm or a Walter here tonight?'

A shuffling in the audience, then two men, rows apart, stand up.

Karlsson lets his gaze pass over them both. 'The spirit is in a hurry and has not said his name. A fisherman, I think. Or someone who worked with fish.' He wrinkles his face as if he can smell the stench around him. The audience chuckles. He has them in the palm of his hand.

'I think this is for me, sir,' says one of the men, a young one. 'Wilhelm. My father worked in the harbour.'

'Yes,' says Karlsson as the other man sits back down. 'And so does another member of your family.'

'My brother Jón,' says Wilhelm, eyes widening.

'Your father wants to send him this message.' The medium looks down and takes a deep breath. 'Jón's fate is entwined with the elements. He must embrace the storms that are soon to come for they shall bring him great sustenance. Great sustenance for many. And, and – I hear him say – this will shape his character.'

But the young man standing before them says, 'I don't understand. What does that mean?'

A slight flicker of the eyelids – annoyance? – then the medium bows his head and clasps his hands across his stomach. 'These words are not mine.' He directs his gaze to the young man and eyeballs him. 'They are not for you. But from your father to Jón. He will understand.'

The young man, Jón's brother, frowns. Someone beside him tugs on his jacket and he sits down, though reluctantly. Daphne thinks he is not sold.

Letting out an audible sigh that reaches those in the back seats, Karlsson moves one hand up over his heart. Fluttering like a butterfly, Jessamine appears at his shoulder and they swap places so that she has the mic. 'Our time is up, the master weakens,' she announces. 'But please join us on Friday when, if the auspices are right, he will manifest a spirit itself in this very theatre.'

She picks up his hand and holds it high, as if he is a winning boxer who has gone three rounds in the ring.

They are just about to bow when a piercing scream rings out through the theatre. 'I see someone.' It is the woman the clairvoyant had spoken with earlier, the horseman's sister. 'They are standing behind you.' Her hand is outstretched, pointing at the two people onstage. The mask of professionalism has slipped and Jessamine looks bewildered. She starts and spins to look behind her.

'An angel!' the woman cries out and clasps one hand over her mouth.

Whispered exclamations sweep across the auditorium.

Karlsson is stepping back, with quick, sharp glances into the prompt corner from whence the manager charges onto the stage, clipping the edge of the desk as he hurries to the front.

Again, the woman speaks. 'He is unfolding, the móri.' She holds her hands out at her sides. 'Spreading his wings.'

Daphne whispers in Anna's ear, 'What's a móri?'

'Ghost,' she says, eyes fixed on the drama developing before them.

Centre-stage now, beside Jessamine and Karlsson, the manager booms, 'Thank you very much for a wonderful evening.' He begins to clap, urging the audience to follow his lead.

But now, up on her feet, the woman is yelling, 'His wings!'

Many in the audience are clearly confused, unsure if this is part of the act, unwilling to comply and leave should they miss something spectacular.

'They smoke,' says the woman in a voice that falters. They all watch as she clasps her hands to her face. 'Oh, God, he is falling.'

Daphne covers her mouth with her hand. 'Lucifer!' The Antichrist has been on her mind all day. Is this why?

Anna turns to her. 'What?' Then she jerks back, eyes round, startled. 'Oh, no,' she says and gestures to Daphne's face.

Detecting wetness above her lips, Daphne pulls her fingers away and sees scarlet splashed on them, but her mind is still fixed on the woman's exclamation. 'Lucifer is the Fallen Angel,' she explains to Anna, while fumbling for a handkerchief to stem the nosebleed. 'That woman. She says she can see the Devil in here.'

Someone else, near to them, yells 'Fire!' and they look up at the stage. The candle has been knocked over and set light to the papers on the desk.

'Out!' the manager bellows. 'Out now.'

There is a crack, then a swish.

The curtains come down.

## CHAPTER FIVE

Anna has got hold of Daphne's arm and is steering her round the side of the picture house. They nudge past other audience members who seem unsure whether to be horrified or delighted by the turn of events. There is an enormous amount of babbling going on.

'This way,' says Anna, and guides her to a door at the rear. 'I have arranged for you to meet him.'

'But won't they be evacuating the place now?' Daphne asks.

'It was a small fire. Someone will put it out.' Anna shrugs and Daphne marvels at her cool demeanour. Nothing, it seems, ruffles this woman. And Daphne wonders if she should be pleased by this or worried.

It is not a stage door, more of a tradesmen's entrance. Anna knocks five times.

'It was a strange show,' says Daphne as they wait. She spits on her hanky and tries to wipe the blood spots out of her blouse.

'That spectacle at the end did not happen before,' Anna says. Then, when Daphne does not respond, adds, 'The woman who screamed – perhaps she is part of their crew?'

Daphne pats and wipes around her face. 'Is it all gone?' she asks Anna, who nods.

Stowing her hanky in her pocket, Daphne responds, 'Some acts use plants in the audience, but I'm not sure that was one of them. Karlsson and Jessamine appeared too surprised.'

Anna's face screws up. The term is alien to her.

'Oh,' says Daphne, realising her error. 'It means someone who has been planted,' she makes a gesture as if she is digging up soil and placing a vegetable in the hole, 'in the audience.'

'I see,' says Anna. 'Is that common in Britain?'

'Not common. But a few acts tend to do it – Vaudeville mostly. It's tricky, if you forgive the pun: should the audience suspect you of using a stooge – that is, *a plant* – then your reputation will soon be in tatters.'

She is prevented from giving an example by the rattling of the door, which is opened by a young lad. He recognises Anna and bids them both enter.

In front of them stretches a narrow corridor. They are ushered down it and wait outside a door. The young man puts his ear to it, knocks and is told to come in.

The dressing room in which they find the clairvoyant and his assistant is bigger than the one Daphne uses at the Oriental Theatre but just as sparingly furnished. She experiences a pang of nostalgia when she sees Jessamine at the dressing table, removing her wig, and is disappointed to see that her locks are false. Daphne had thought them magnificent. The hair underneath is flattened down, a light colour like a fawn's hide.

Karlsson, who has got to his feet in the presence of ladies, greets Anna warmly, not with a hug but a double-handed handshake. Afterwards his left hand rests for slightly longer than is usual upon her arm.

Anna frees herself in two deft moves, gesticulating to her left. 'This is Daphne Dione-Smith from *The Times* of London.'

Karlsson's eyes widen greedily. 'Oh, my,' he says, bows, picks up her hand and kisses it. His lips are moist against her cold flesh and when he raises his head she feels their oily imprint on her skin. 'Such a prestigious paper to be interested in someone as lowly as me.' He releases her and cracks the lipstick pasted onto his smile. 'I am flattered.'

Daphne is mildly shocked by the kiss, but supposes it is a theatrical gesture and pours as much charm as she can find into her response. 'I too am delighted to make your acquaintance, Mr Karlsson.' And adds a nod to Jessamine in as friendly a manner as possible. The assistant smiles but it does not reach her eyes.

'Please sit,' says Karlsson and indicates the empty armchair in the corner, which Anna immediately commands.

Jessamine hurries to fetch a stool, for which Daphne thanks her and then perches upon it.

'Thank you for seeing us, Sindri,' says Anna.

'Not at all, not at all.' He sits down again in the seat he had vacated.

Jessamine settles on the edge of her dressing table and watches them. She is nowhere near as imposing without her wig. In fact, there is a little of the sparrow in her lean frame and colouring and the darting movements she makes.

'I must apologise,' says Karlsson, when they are all seated. 'For the coughing paroxysm that overtook me.'

Daphne and Anna demur.

'This old picture house is full of dust. They are building a new theatre, but it has been requisitioned by the British for the occupation. As soon as it opens, we will move there.'

Anna rolls her eyes. 'I doubt it will be soon.'

If he heard this, Karlsson does not acknowledge her pessimism. Daphne makes a mental note – the war, he thinks, will not last long and presently Germany is winning. Though he appears, like many performers she knows, to be narcissistic. Perhaps his optimism is born out of a desire for more luxurious surroundings. He continues like a raconteur reaching the climax of a story: 'And of course the crazy woman at the end . . .'

'Oh,' says Daphne. 'Was she not one of yours?'

'Mine?' asks Karlsson. He takes a breath and stands back with his hand upon his chest.

'Part of the act?' Daphne adds and realises it is possible that she has insulted him.

Indeed this question brings about a change in the medium. 'Act!' he says with outrage. 'No, she is *not* part of,' he spits out the next words as if they are contaminated, 'the act! Probably some copy-cat who wants to set up in competition.' His head is wobbling from side to side as he speaks, the pitch of his voice rising to a squeak. 'I do not have an *act*. My visions, my communications, are authentic. As real as you and I!'

Oh, dear. She must come in now and play the pretty, blundering fool. He does not know that she has trodden the boards herself and practised 'telepathy' in front of an audience. What he does know is that she is a reporter for a quality newspaper, with the expertise that must accompany such a role – resourcefulness, writing skills and a nose for investigation – which may have put him on the defensive. *If* he has anything to hide.

'So sorry,' Daphne says, lowering her head a little in a pose of meek submission and looking up at him through her eyelashes. 'I didn't mean to offend. It was so,' she sifts through words and selects one she thinks he may approve of, 'so *thrilling* and unusual. I have never seen anything like it before.'

This appears to soften him a little. 'Yes, I suppose it was.' He taps his chin, as if thinking about the potential of such a display.

Without any knock to announce a new arrival, the door opens. It is the stage manager, evidently surprised to see Anna and Daphne in the dressing room.

Up close now, she thinks there is something familiar about him. Though perhaps it is because he has just been onstage. Karlsson says something to him in Icelandic, but the manager shakes his head and the exchange continues, becoming more heated: consonants parry back and forth. Jessamine deliberately rotates her body a full ninety degrees to the mirror and smothers her face in cold cream.

Anna gets to her feet. 'Daphne, we should leave. It seems they must discuss the fire.'

'Understood,' she says and launches herself off the stool.

But Karlsson is right there before her, hand outstretched. 'I think you need to see more of me,' he says with a leer.

She laughs and tries to make it sound tinkling, despite the heavy lurch of her stomach. A voice in her head tells her it is a good thing – he has forgiven her indiscretion.

Then, leaning closer so that she can smell his cabbage breath, he murmurs, 'I have a private consultation coming up on Saturday. A séance.'

This time Daphne's reaction is real. 'Gosh, really?' A séance! The word conjures peculiar images in her head: candles in a circle, darkness, ectoplasm.

He takes a step back, delivers a shallow bow this time. 'I will enquire if you may come along. Then you will see this is no "act". Where are you staying, my dear? I can let you know once I speak to the hosts.'

But Anna slides between them and grabs Daphne by the elbow. Steering her towards the door, she calls to Karlsson, 'Get a message to my office. You know where that is.'

And then they are out.

Close to the centre, they walk through the streets of the night-city until they come to a large square. In the middle is a statue of a man in Victorian clothing. Daphne can see it quite well with streetlights on, which again feel like something of a luxury. Why is there no blackout here? The island's isolation must be a factor. Although, she reminds herself, one must be alert to enemy invaders who may come from the sea or skies. She looks up and sees the night is clear, which is likely why it is so cold. Her scarf is on the chair in her room at her lodgings where she left it. The part of her neck from her collar to her chin feels the touch of the air's raw fingers. Wind-riding spirits abound, she thinks. Then for a moment, out of nowhere, she imagines real hands there, squeezing her throat.

The unbidden image forces a shiver.

Anna has noticed and says, 'We'll go into the Hotel Borg. It will be warm and it will be open.'

There on the corner is the large hotel, five or six storeys high, whose windows Karlsson admired himself in. Anna makes for its white walls and high-arched windows. She leads Daphne through a porch with the hotel's name emblazoned across the floor. The door ahead is painted with a picture of what Daphne at first thinks is a castle with the sun rising behind it. They push against the glass and come through into a lobby. On the wall opposite is the same image, and Daphne realises what she had taken for a castle is an artist's impression of the letters H and B – Hotel Borg – fashioned into the form of a tall building. Its windows are glassless and the shape reminds her of bombed-out churches back home, which she is sure was not intended. For her surroundings are most definitely *not* derelict nor church-like. Quite the opposite. The walls are painted gold, the floors polished. Strains of a band playing somewhere nearby.

Anna pushes through another great arched doorway and they click-clack their heels into a bustling bar. At once Daphne is overcome by the sounds, smells and heat. She takes off her coat, so she will feel the benefit, and immediately her cheeks begin to flush.

It is extraordinary in here – another world. The walls are painted with murals of people dancing. Every table is packed.

Gleaming beneath her feet, the wooden floor is criss-crossed with darker, thinner inlays to resemble a chequerboard.

From the ceiling, tiled in a white material, perhaps marble, embellished with gold flourishes, hang two great chandeliers. Such lavish style and flashy design seem quite at odds with the modest city outside.

As Daphne reaches the large serving area at the back, a set of double doors at the nearest side of the room opens. A British officer and two young ladies tumble out, laughing, accompanied by a staccato blast of trumpets.

It really is *quite* the thing, almost like being in the West End again.

Her whole frame relaxes and she realises that she misses London. Not the one she has just left behind. The one before that, before the bombs and permanently hunched shoulders and charcoal nights. As her former tutor, Miss Sabine, might have coined it: London's previous incarnation.

But here she is. In a glimmer of something that is as it once was. And in Reykjavík of all places.

Anna has already put in an order for drinks. She points to a corner of the bar by a door. 'Come!' The little nook is made up of padded seats covered in green plush, set around a small table. At the moment it is being used as a repository for coats that have not made it into the cloakroom, either because of the ticket price or limited capacity. Anna, ever resourceful, pushes them up and over the seat backs so they can both squeeze in and sit down.

It is quite snug but Daphne is the most comfortable she has been all night.

Taking in the expression on her face, Anna smiles. 'Not what you expected to find in our city?'

'Oh,' says Daphne as she unpins her hat, 'I am glad of it. A little life.'

'Better than death and ghosts,' Anna agrees. 'Hotel Borg accommodates the British officers,' she goes on, looking around. 'So, if you wish, I can try and get you a beer.'

'A beer!' cries Daphne. Does she look like the type of woman who drinks beer?

'It is banned here,' adds Anna.

But that makes no sense. 'They have banned beer but the officers can drink it? Why has the army banned beer?'

'No. Our government did. A few years ago. All alcohol at first, like in America: prohibited.'

'Oh,' says Daphne. 'Yes, prohibition.' Her eyes drift to the drinkers at the bar, some of whom clutch pint glasses yet still manage to look rather raffish and alluring.

She runs her fingers through her hair and feels it tumble past her shoulders. Tonight she has worn it long, as the Icelandic girls do, though has pinned it up at the sides. There is never any time to get a wash and set but she still wishes to look well-styled and neat. 'Are only officers allowed to drink the beer? Not the soldiers?'

Again Anna smiles. 'The English, we have observed, allow certain social classes privileges not extended to the rest. The officers are paid more. Though the troops do the hard work, they have fewer krónur in their pockets.'

Goodness, thinks Daphne, her companion is brazen. Her eyes dart from side to side, checking no British gentlemen are within earshot. Thank goodness the coast is clear. Even so, Daphne wonders if she should caution Anna: such talk reeks of socialism!

Gently, Anna removes her own hat. 'It wasn't long till red wine became legal,' she says, and extracts a long pin with a pearl on the end. A silken lock of hair tumbles down. 'Then spirits.'

'They are much stronger than beer,' says Daphne, admiring the satiny sheen of Anna's hair. It must be the Reykjavík water that lends all the women here such sleek tresses.

'Prohibition was . . . is . . . political. By the way, I ordered you a Scottish whisky and water. If you don't want it, I'll have it.'

'That's fine,' says Daphne, though she has not yet tried hard liquor. 'I'm glad it's not banned.' She is trying to sound worldly.

Anna grins. She really is defrosting, thinks Daphne.

A waiter arrives with their drinks on a golden tray – tumblers nearly half-full of rich, golden liquid are accompanied by a small jug of water. No ice. They help themselves.

Anna waits for the waiter to leave then takes a long sip and throws back her head. Her eyes are a crystal blue and become wider, twinkling under the light of the chandelier. She is very attractive when she smiles and loses that dour demeanour. Cradling the glass in her hands, she leans across the table to Daphne and whispers: 'What did you make of the show? Of Karlsson?'

Daphne is ready to talk about it and feels she can be honest. 'It was odd,' she says, leaning forward, and lowers her voice. 'I was surprised to hear that woman who saw the Devil—'

Anna interrupts, 'Who *said* she saw him.'

'Yes, yes,' says Daphne and pours a measure of water into her glass, despite the fact Anna is drinking her whisky undiluted.

The doors to the adjoining room hosting the band swing open and let out a blast of loud music and laughter. Daphne inches closer. 'That woman wasn't a plant.'

'Ah, yes,' says Anna, sticking out her chin and puffing up her chest. 'This is not an act!' She has lowered her voice to mimic Karlsson and thumps the table to add drama. It makes Daphne laugh in earnest. Perhaps for the first time since she set foot on foreign soil. It is a relief.

When she has recovered, she says, 'I'm not so sure of *that*.'

'You are referring to what he said. His messages?' Anna asks.

'Actually, I wasn't. I meant that the whole performance *is* an act of some sort, isn't it? There is an audience who have bought tickets to see an entertainment. How authentic Karlsson is, I cannot yet say. However, you are right – the messages are worthy of further scrutiny. Can we go through them? You'll have to translate your shorthand for me.'

'Of course.' Anna nods with efficiency. 'But of which makes you uncertain?'

The strange syntax reminds Daphne that English is not the journalist's first language. And this, in turn, prompts her to think upon another thing that has been playing on her mind. 'Does he always speak in English?'

Anna stretches out her hand, picks up a pen and gives the top a slow, deliberate twist. 'The audience is international now, since the Allied occupation. Troops and diplomatic staff are not so well versed in Icelandic.'

'Ah,' says Daphne. 'I did see two Allied soldiers there. A fair point. But one may presume that German agents might not be fluent in the native tongue either.'

This seems to impress Anna. 'That is also true.' She looks down and taps the open notebook with her pen. 'Jessamine is a new addition since the last time.'

'Is she?' says Daphne. 'I can see why. She brings a certain glamour to the stage, for sure. Her dancing stretches the running time to that usually required for a solo performance. But I always think that a man who needs an assistant, needs a decoy.'

'I see,' Anna says, drawing out the 's'. 'Jessamine, you are suggesting, does more than enhance the drama?'

Daphne keeps her face neutral. 'Of course, she is visually appealing and brings a dynamism to the spectacle. In magic acts, assistants draw the audience's attention *away* from the magician at crucial moments. But I do not believe that is solely the case here.'

'And why is that?'

'It is obvious. Think of it – if communication with the dead were real then you would not need to dress up a miracle. Why would you need an assistant, a dance? Wouldn't the phenomenon itself be enough?'

'This is true,' says Anna. 'And yet some of his messages, his predictions, have proved to be right.'

'So I hear.' There are many who profess the ability to communicate with the spirit world and with all the bereaved who fill the present landscape; there is certainly an appetite to believe it is a true phenomenon. However, Karlsson's accuracy is unsettling.

Anna fidgets in her seat and brings it closer to Daphne's. 'Jessamine takes down notes for those the spirits come to, I saw.'

'Surely, though, they would remember what they heard themselves?'

'In the shock of the moment, perhaps not,' Anna says thoughtfully, and Daphne wonders what shocks she has had to be so knowledgeable. She herself has endured some. And not so long ago. Indeed, she finds her memory of what happened to her, deep in a forest in the West Country, has substantially deteriorated. Was shock at work then? Is that what prevents her from recalling details?

Anna's eyes are on her face, examining every feature. But now Daphne can't remember what she asked.

'What about the letters Jessamine wrote down and held up?' she presses on. 'That seemed unnecessary.'

'Ah,' says Anna. 'Wilhelm is not a traditional Icelandic name. "W" is not in our alphabet. I can see the logic in that.'

'Fair point.' Daphne knows Anna is sceptical, though her last answer seems to contradict that position. 'But the props were so flamboyant,' Daphne finds herself bleating, as if on the defensive. 'The robes, the large feathery quill, the candle . . .'

Anna shrugs. 'Atmosphere? To create the right conditions.'

Feeling uneasy, Daphne replies pointedly, 'You are being most generous.' It comes out as churlish and she bites her lip, angry that she has not been more restrained. Sometimes she says things before her mind has managed to pull up the brake handle.

But Anna grins again. So many of them tonight. Perhaps it is the whisky loosening her. 'I am being an advocate of the Devil.'

Daphne smiles at this little quirk of translation. However, another mention of the Antichrist has her reaching for the tumbler of whisky. She thinks again of the inversion of Christian ideology that the Third Reich embraces. Anna cannot mean she is advocating for that, can she? 'What struck me,' she says, pushing the thought away for now and swirling the liquid in her glass so that it blends, focusing on what she wanted to say before, 'was the eloquence of the things he said, the poetry of the messages.'

'Yes! There is something in that, I think.'

'Anna!' a woman shrieks.

Daphne looks up at the bar, where the voice has come from. Someone is waving at their table.

A fair-haired woman, *another* fair-haired woman, breathless and flushed, is weaving her way through the tables towards them. 'Anna!' she squeals. 'Anna Tómasdóttir?'

The journalist mutters something in Icelandic under her breath. Her face drops then readjusts itself, her lips curve upwards. Though the smile is forced: Anna's eyes do not crinkle at the corners. 'Ah, Kolbrún Kristjánsdóttir.'

Whispering to Daphne, she explains, 'She was a friend of my brother's.'

Daphne notes the past tense. Although she does not mention it, she wonders what drew Anna to investigate Karlsson in the first place. God is not the only entity who works in mysterious ways. Grief, she has seen, moves its hosts to act out a range of peculiarities. The Grand Mystique, Jonty, had become both tight-lipped and loose-tongued at different hours of the day after he lost his Mrs Trevelyan. Despite his expertise in the tricks of the trade used by most travelling showmen, her boss spent long hours in the dressing room of old Madam Yolande and her crystal ball. Time may heal, but hope is what keeps the heart pumping. And it can be cruel.

Kolbrún leans against the back of their padded corner seat. Her blouse is clinging to her, damp patches visible around the armpits. Her cheeks are rosy, either with warmth or drink, and exude healthy vitality. Rotating her hand in quick impatient circles, she beckons Anna to move further up and nimbly slips into the gap.

Daphne squashes herself against the bundled coats.

'I thought I saw you earlier!' Kolbrún trills, as if she has just solved a puzzle. 'Watching Sindri Karlsson! I follow you in the paper, Anna. Read the article you wrote on him. Are you writing another? It was your feature that made me go and see him for myself.' Her lips are tinted russet and do not match her pink cheeks. She has a broad face, her skin pulled taut across the bones like canvas over tent poles.

'I'm not,' she says and gestures to Daphne. Introductions are now required. 'Daphne Dione-Smith is here from *The Times*, English newspaper.'

'Oh, hello,' says Kolbrún, wiping wet strands of hair from her forehead. 'How marvellous! So Sindri's fame has spread?'

Daphne nods, feeling that she is entering uncharted waters. 'That it has,' she says, and before Kolbrún can grill her about the particulars of the job, asks her, 'What was your impression?' To add weight to her cover identity, she reaches for her handbag and takes out a small notepad with a pencil fastened into the spine.

Kolbrún glows with excitement.

'Sorry,' says Daphne. 'How do you spell your name? May I quote you in my feature? Always good to get audience feedback.'

'Ja hérna!' says Kolbrún. Her eyes widen and she breaks into a large-lipped smile before spelling out both names. Anna arches her eyebrows and nods minutely at Daphne – she approves.

'Well, I thought he was brilliant,' says Kolbrún. 'That story he told the young man, about his father and the cuckoo clock! He couldn't have known that, could he?'

Daphne nods in a non-committal way. Her recall is better than Kolbrún's: it was the son who volunteered the story not Karlsson. The medium only mentioned a favoured clock. It was the young man who filled in the rest. She finds it interesting the way that Kolbrún's memory has chosen to reinterpret her experience to confirm the extraordinary.

'Then the lady at the end.' Kolbrún points at the wall. Daphne briefly squints at it, then realises Kolbrún's mind is back in the picture house. 'And the fire. What a sensation! I could not tell if it was meant to happen?' She looks to Anna for an answer.

Her friend shrugs.

'I don't think so,' says Daphne, remembering Karlsson's protestations in the dressing room about a potential rival.

'Then what does it mean?' asks Kolbrún. 'That the Devil is amongst us?' Despite her evident warmth, she wraps her arms around her middle and gives herself a hug.

'I wouldn't give it too much thought,' says Daphne, feeling the need to soothe.

Kolbrún is not dampened by Daphne's words but wide-eyed with the thrill and excitement of the evening. 'You know, there are rumours about Sindri Karlsson,' she says, and curls her index finger, bidding them come closer.

Daphne shares a glance with Anna, who slides her elbows onto the table. 'Oh, yes?' she says, feigning mild interest.

Daphne's pen has stilled on the page. Her face, fixed into her vacant performance grin, turns back to Kolbrún.

'Yes.' Now the girl is nodding her head and peering around as if she is about to confide a great secret. 'It is said that he has access to a powerful book. A grimoire from which he learned his skills of' – her voice sinks to a conspiratorial whisper – 'galdrar.'

Daphne shoots a glance at Anna, who interprets: 'Sorcery.'

It is a raw term that makes Daphne's spine begin to tingle. 'Galdrar,' she repeats to herself, and adds 'grimoire' to the list of words on the page. She has heard it before recently but can't remember where.

Kolbrún is trying to say something else now. This time the word seems to catch in her throat, as if some greater force does not want the young woman to release it into the world. 'Ne– necro—' She pulls down a gulp of air, and then it is out. 'Necromancy.'

Laced tightly with associations of dark magic, the word causes Daphne to shiver, as would any girl with a penchant for Saturday Night Shockers at the Hammersmith Palais: necromancy is the art of communicating with the dead. In her mind tattered corpses clamber muddily from their graves. Ugh! For a moment, she wants to snap her notebook shut, fetch her coat, get on the next boat back to Scotland and put as many miles as possible between herself and this dark isle, full of sorcery, spirits and whispers.

But she doesn't. She reaches for her glass and lets the flow of fiery whisky burn her tongue and fill her chest with warmth. Unexpectedly, it takes her breath with it. She begins to cough. The back of her throat is on fire. What is this stuff?

The fit doesn't stop until Kolbrún, who has sprung to her feet, slaps her on the back. Anna fills a spare tumbler with water and passes it to Daphne.

The cool liquid runs down her throat and helps to alleviate the inflammation. When she is able, she splutters an apology and watches Kolbrún retake her seat.

'I'm not used to it,' says Daphne and points to the glass.

Catching the eye of the waiter, Kolbrún orders a drink for herself. 'For Anna?' she asks her.

Anna mouths, 'Same,' and holds up her empty glass.

'For Daphne?'

'No, no, I'm fine, thank you.'

Kolbrún takes this as an excuse born from pecuniary constraints. No doubt it is expensive in here. 'It is all right,' she says to Daphne. 'The man there will pay.' And she sends a smile over to a dapper lieutenant at the bar, who is talking to a very tall and very thin naval officer. The former looks over and raises his glass to the three of them, a smile blooming under his moustache.

'You must be careful,' says Anna, observing the interaction. 'There are some who are not happy about us fraternising with foreigners.' Then she feels Daphne start and adds, 'Of the male variety.'

'They are just jealous,' Kolbrún returns, with a dismissive flap of her hand.

'Not all of them,' Anna warns. 'There are those who think Icelandic morality is being compromised.'

At this Kolbrún lets out a laugh. 'Not you, I hope?'

Anna, however, does not smile. 'Of course not. However, there are some things that I'm privy to that the common man is not. As you know.'

Kolbrún's curiosity is piqued. 'Oh, yes? You *must* tell me.'

Daphne stifles a sigh. The conversation is charging off on a tangent. She suspects that this is where Kolbrún's interest is truly centred. Certainly, it will not now be possible to talk to Anna about Sindri Karlsson's performance tonight. Not in the detail that is required. 'I must go,' she says, leaning over Kolbrún and grabbing her coat.

'Oh,' says the woman. 'Not for me, please.'

Interpreting this as 'not on my account', Daphne shakes her head. 'No, I'm tired,' she says. Which is a lie.

'I'll see you tomorrow then,' says Anna, though they have arranged nothing.

Quick on the uptake, Daphne tilts her head. 'Yes, four o'clock, wasn't it?'

'Half-past,' says Anna. 'At the paper.' She nods and then turns back to Kolbrún. 'There are observers,' she begins.

Daphne fastens her coat and leaves the noise and warmth behind her, aware that her night is not over yet.

# LOOSE LIPS

# Sink Ships

*Careless talk costs lives*

CHAPTER SIX

A brief interval at her lodging house. Just enough time to change her clothes and pick up a bundle of uniforms and socks, wrapped in a laundry bag.

Then she is back on the streets again.

This time she heads away from the centre, aiming for the south of the city, where one of the army bases has been established.

The night has grown colder still. She pulls in her coat and hefts the bag over her shoulder. It is uncomfortable, but necessary. Local women take in washing from the soldiers for a fee, and this is how she must access the camp. Enemy eyes may be anywhere, everywhere, and morality seems to be an issue. What good reason would a British reporter have to visit a camp full of men at night? She would not wish to attract more attention.

The outfit and washing have been provided for use in such a situation. She does not know by whom. They were simply there when she arrived, as she knew they would be. Though her briefing was not detailed, there is enough intelligence to steer her through this part of her mission.

She is exceedingly grateful for her journalist guide, who adds vital local information. Of course, Daphne must trust no one, and this should extend to her new friend. No, not her friend – her contact. Though she can't help but warm to the enigmatic Icelander. Anna puts her in mind somewhat of Brigit Harkness, with whom she trained, now in the south of England helping the Home Guard with their camouflage techniques as they prepare for the German invasion. She hopes dearly these will never be put to the test. Although the country is now on a far better footing than it was in the summer, she is not sure that it will be able to defeat the German war machine, which is monstrous in its efficiency. Monstrous, she thinks. And, again, her mind revisits the picture house. The image of the Devil invoked by the woman in the stalls has unsettled her. For Daphne too saw smoke. Though it must have originated from the paper on Jessamine's desk catching the candle flame. However, the symbolism of Lucifer is not lost on her. She has been privy to intelligence kept from the British public and knows that the Führer and his cronies may have adopted the fallen angel: the god without a heart who operates a subverted moral compass. The enemy excels in perversity and has overturned all traditional concepts of war. Hitler has given his word on several occasions to respect the neutrality of countries like Denmark and Norway, who were subsequently invaded. Iceland too was promised its freedom. Which is why she is here.

This invasion has been covered in the BBC broadcasts and newspapers but not to the same extent as the Battle of France and the Low Countries. And now, at home, this isolated northern isle does not command much attention: all eyes are on the skies, and the fire and destruction that rain down from them each night. Who knew this war would spit out its rage above their heads? That the Englishman's house would become not his castle but his coffin? That the stink, dust and soot of the Underground would signify relief, sanctuary?

The world has turned upside down, she thinks. No wonder Lucifer is manifesting into it. He must feel quite at home.

And yet Reykjavík, she decides, as she trudges out on the muddy road, despite its sulky, brooding weather, is a refuge of sorts. Far away from the bombs, though there remains the threat of imminent attack, life here feels more, well, ordinary. There have been no air raids, no sirens since she arrived, and no drills. She still carries her gasmask everywhere – some habits are hard to break – but she has noticed the locals do not. They are less tightly wound: so far war has been conducted over *there*. It did not touch these shores till the British arrived and brought it to them. No wonder there is resentment. Though how long the strategic island would have remained unoccupied is anyone's guess. The country's neutrality arrangement with Germany was a deal with the Devil. And, going by his track record, he was never going to honour it.

And then, with her mind on the Devil again, she suddenly remembers where she has heard the word 'grimoire' before. It is a magic book full of spells. Jonty sometimes pretended to read from one when they performed The Disappearing Man. The book had nothing in it but a script, of course, and a few back-up 'spells' they could use should they need to abandon an illusion mid-act. The grimoire's jacket was made of thick, tanned leather carved with magical symbols, runic staves, and bound together by a leather strap. And so Karlsson is rumoured to have access to a real one, is he?

'Who goes there?'

So preoccupied by her thoughts, she has not noticed the sentry post in the shadows. Stammering, she gives the password.

A shadow detaches itself from the darkness of the checkpoint and a sentry emerges into the half-light cast by the high midnight moon: his helmet shines at the crown. She cannot see his face beneath the rim but has the impression he is scrutinising her intently. Despite the disciplined authority in his voice, she can tell he is both young and shivering. His baggy uniform does not look warm enough for an Arctic winter. Wool-serge trouser legs are tucked into his boots. The uniform is one left over from the Great War. She has seen it in photographs, newspapers, and would recognise that outline anywhere.

He does not speak for a long minute then says, 'Essex?'

Expecting some sort of challenge, this throws her. 'Yes,' she says meekly.

'My uncle lives there,' he says. '*Lived* there. Once. Southend. I've ridden the donkeys.'

An error has been made in confirming his guess, she realises. Though it is too late now to pretend she is local. Perhaps she should feel concerned, but the guard's fleeting reminiscence is like a hot potato in the hand. She finds it warms her.

'Ah, yes,' she says, picturing the donkeys, with their colourful harnesses and badges, plodding steadily across the beach by the pier. 'And I hope you got a stick of rock too.'

'The heck I did! He's tight as a gnat's arse, that one.'

The language, though raw, eases the tension round her shoulders. She swings the laundry, which has grown heavy, to the rough ground. 'Is that a Yorkshire accent?' she asks.

He stands there like a rook or a skinny crow, peering. 'Scarborough. What's an Essex girl doing all the way over here, then?'

'Can't say, of course.'

He knows this, knows she cannot say more, but does not move, keeps looking at her, not stepping forward, not letting her pass.

A cloud inks out the moon and the world becomes momentarily darker.

She is becoming attuned to the lack of noise. All she can hear is the shriek of the wind, nagging a hill in the distance that is shaped like a coolie's hat. She can't see it but she knows it is there. A landmark by which to steer towards this gale-battered spot.

Is she, she wonders for a moment, all alone out here with this soldier?

She still has her deadly lipstick in her pocket but her suit, with its concealed blades, is at her lodging house, in the wardrobe.

The sentry continues to stand guard. She hears him breathing and swallows unexpectedly, her throat dry.

'A'right,' he says at last, and lets her through. 'You know where you're going?'

'I do.'

'Then goodnight to you, Miss Essex.'

She navigates her way round the camp, following the map she has memorised. Though things have changed since it was drawn up and she finds herself stumbling towards a latrine block, which must have been built recently. The stink of it is bracing.

How much of her has the sentry taken in? Her hair is folded atop her head and concealed under a hat. Her clothes are those of a washerwoman, well-used, patched in places and torn at the seams. The cold comes in under her armpits when she hoists the laundry bag. On her feet she wears men's boots. *Boy's* boots. She does not look like a London-based reporter. She does not look like a stage magician's assistant. She does not look like a Security Service operative. But her presence here is as unusual as her accent. The Infantry have come mostly from the north of England: Scarborough, Calderdale, York. Though she does not think her accent particularly strong, she notes that she should make some effort to rationalise it a little, to pronounce certain words in the Queen's English. Previously she has resisted such homogenisation, but now understands it creates a curtain around oneself that may usefully limit perception. Such deception has its advantages, as well she knows.

There is another guard outside the Signals post. Again, she repeats the password she has been given for today: 'It is a fine night for a promenade on the harbour, under the stars.'

It isn't, she thinks as she says it. It is far too icy. And briefly her rogue mind sends her an image: strolling with Jack under the gaze of the mountains, laughing as the water laps at their heels.

Silly. The harbour is sandbagged and the pavement's a good few feet above the sea. And Jack is hundreds, if not thousands, of miles south of here. Probably tucked up in bed. Probably warm.

This guard does not challenge her. Weary and impassive, he opens the door and lets her in. His eyes are baggy, his nose red. He is practically falling asleep on his legs.

Down the corridor. Knock, knock, pause, knock, knock.

The bolt is drawn. She pushes the door and comes into a small room with a barrel-shaped ceiling. Two signalmen are on duty. One, about her age, asks, 'What is it: phone call or telegram? Or is it urgent?'

They both have mugs of coffee before them and she experiences an impulse to ask for one. There is a stove in the corner, which she goes to and warms her hands. They are freezing. She has forgotten her gloves.

If one of them offers her a mug she will take it. But they don't. The man her age says again, 'Well, what will it be?'

'It's not urgent,' she says, and he hands her a piece of paper with blue lines printed across it and a pen.

'In capitals, please,' he says.

'Of course.' Her fingers have become red and stiff. She closes and uncloses them. Then, looking round for a seat, 'Can I use this?'

The younger man has not acknowledged her. He has a headset on and is writing down words on paper that is a different colour, frowning as his pen scratches across the page.

She takes the form and the pen and sits at the spare desk, presumably belonging to the other soldier. It has black equipment on it and a nest of wires. After breathing on her hands to warm them up, when some of the feeling has returned, she smooths out the crinkled sheet and writes: 'Subject to enquiries the coat is not an exact fit. Further examinations necessary.' As an afterthought she adds, 'Tailor has a fitting guide (Icelandic – 'grimoire') in the north country. End'

When he reads the words on the form the signalman almost scoffs. Almost. Nothing that passes through this post can be taken at face value. He makes a big show of exasperation and sighs, 'You haven't written where you want it sent.'

She hasn't been asked. However, Daphne can sense this one might be keen to cause her trouble if she lets him, so puts a finger on her lips and giggles, 'Oh, silly me. I do apologise.'

This time the signalman smiles.

That's better, thinks Daphne, and smiles back.

She writes the HQ comms unit's identifier across the top of the sheet and hands it back.

'Urgent?' the signaller asks.

'No. But it is expected.'

'As you wish,' he says rather politely. Which seems to surprise them both.

She leaves the camp strangely comforted by the darkness of the night, which swallows her whole. The silhouettes of the mountains remind her of the great blue whales she has been told visit this place. And she is momentarily captured by a Sunday-school memory of Jonah, gulped down by one, staying in its belly for three days and three nights, then spat out on a foreign shore. Why was that? Why was he eaten?

Then she remembers: he refused a command.

Lucifer the Lord of Misrule would no doubt celebrate that, she thinks. And the thought becomes fascinating to her. The next moment she worries that she too is being infected. Can evil so easily contaminate?

When she gets into her bed, she makes things worse by getting angry that these thoughts cannot resolve themselves, but only ignite further questions. Why, she asks herself, why has Italy become allied to the Nazis? The Third Reich has so blatantly nailed its Antichristian colours to the mast, their allegiance to dark powers, and yet Italy is a Catholic country. Her mother Carabella, a native, is always blessing Pope Pius XII. What does this pope make of the country's new German friends and their idols? How does Mussolini, devoutly Catholic, feel about his diabolic partners? If fascism means that one must worship the nation over the self, does it also mean that the nation usurps God? Does religion take a backseat when there are foreign lands to be gained? Should it not come to the fore when one is experiencing the dark impulses of greed and avarice? Is that not what Jesus railed against when he turned the tables in the temple? When he chided the moneychangers and merchants and the dove sellers?

Her mind catches on the last image. And she remembers again the priest's voice on a rare morning at Sunday school, when she had asked why they were selling the doves in the temple. 'Those birds were slaughtered by the poor as they could not afford grander sacrifices.'

She thinks about sacrificing doves and how that might look. Then, just before her thoughts sail into dreamland, she sees Jesus overturning tables, scattering merchants and money, cages opening, birds flying high into the sky.

One of them, she sees, flaps burning wings.

**British Officer Assaults School Pupil**
*Occupation soldiers menace college students.*
Underhanded actions and behaviour by local collaborators with the British have aroused considerable anger in the town. Citizens have recounted how, not long ago, a majority of the Municipal Council agreed to loan the occupying army the Town Hall for a dance, and thereby support unnatural and unnecessary fraternisation between the occupiers and the town's inhabitants.

Yesterday evening the occupying army took advantage of the council's generosity and held the dance. Invitations went to the town's 'better citizens' and 'friends' of the army.

A list of those attending was made by schoolboys from the local grammar school who stood by the doors. One of the invaders, of officer rank, took objection to his companion's name being noted. When challenged, the noble pupil stood firm. With a shocking lack of restraint, the officer removed his glove and slapped the poor young man on the face! Protests have been made to the highest level. We, as proud Icelanders, will not give in to such bullying intimidation.

It is right therefore that this newspaper – for the instruction of its readers – should reveal the names of those who accepted the invitation and fraternised with the occupiers. Please be aware they are as follows:

Miss Nanna Sigurjónsdóttir, headmistress
Örlygur Jessen, and child of the same man

Miss Brynja Baldvinsdóttir, teacher
Mrs Valgerður Sigurðard
Miss O. Jensdóttir, launderer
Viggó Sigurðsson, doctor, and wife
Dr Kristinn Thorkelsson and wife (adjudicator of damages caused by the British)
Miss Bryndís Þorsteinsdóttir, shop worker (also seen at Hotel Borg with occupiers)
Sverrir Halldórsson, college teacher, and wife
Miss Ida Björnsdóttir, seamstress (also seen in British cars and at Hotel Borg)
Miss Áslaug Friðriksdóttir (Hotel Borg)
Örn Snorrason, schoolteacher
Miss Dagmar Hallgrímsdóttir (Continued on page 4)

CHAPTER SEVEN

There is a man in the dining room. A captain. A British captain.

Daphne has busied herself with a newspaper but is sure he is intending to come over and say something. It will be difficult to ignore him. The room is not like a breakfast room in a guest house or hotel. There are no separate tables. Mrs Gunnarsdóttir, the landlady, or Guðrún as she insists on being called (addressing elders and superiors by their first names is not deemed improper here), has turned her home over to the use of naval and army officers. Visitor accommodation on the island is scarce and this house is well built, insulated and spacious. Now that Guðrún's two daughters have married, their old rooms, the attic and the parlour are put to use for a fair rent.

The dining room has a sideboard at one end upon which stands an oil lamp with a brass base and a huge white globe-shade. It is always on and never runs out of fuel. Underneath it is a lace doily that remains white and spotless. A lamp in that corner is well placed as the walls are panelled with wood painted deep red. Somehow the colour sucks daylight from the room. The long table and the chairs ranged around it are heavy, fashioned from a deep rose-tinted wood. By the window is a chaise-longue covered in expensive fabric. Guðrún's late husband has not been mentioned but Daphne thinks he may have been a merchant, exports or imports: the furniture is good quality and has a Danish appearance.

The captain is staring at the tureen of porridge. It was quite glutinous when Daphne helped herself fifteen minutes ago and beginning to form a slimy membrane. Though it probably just needs a good stir. The pot has been placed on a metal grille, beneath which a candle burns to keep it warm. Or burn it.

She decides that if he makes for the porridge, she will find it in her heart to be pleasant. If he calls for the landlady and requests something else then she will give him the cold shoulder.

Just at that moment, Guðrún herself comes through the door that leads into the kitchen. 'Captain Armstrong, Captain Armstrong! Please sit down. I will bring it to you with some syrup.'

The captain jumps back as if he has been caught doing something untoward. 'Oh, yes, yes.'

He looks at the table and puts his hands in his pockets and rocks back on his heels, his gaze on Daphne. Then he sidles closer and points to the chair opposite hers. 'May I?'

'Please do,' she says, gliding her eyes up from the page and onto him. Tall, the physique of a sportsman. Not rugby though – perhaps tennis or cricket. He fills out his uniform. The cut looks bespoke. They do that, the officer class, get their uniforms tailored for them.

Guðrún bustles over and takes her empty bowl. 'More, Daphne?' She nods to the captain and says, 'Miss Daphne,' by way of introduction.

'I'm fine, thank you, Guðrún,' she says. She is a good eater and has learned to consume victuals, whatever their flavour, whenever she can. One never knows if one will be called away on another task before having the opportunity to refuel.

Captain Armstrong seats himself and points at her newspaper. 'You're a reporter, Miss Daphne, I hear. Is that your newspaper?'

'Oh,' says Daphne, folding it away – she is clearly not going to be able to read anymore. 'No, this is a local publication.'

'Reykjavík?' His eyes are inquisitive. He wears a neat, though thin, moustache, and has dark eyebrows and hair swept into a side parting. She puts him in his mid-thirties.

'It's a forces paper, the *Midnight Sun*.'

'Any good news?' he asks as Guðrún returns to him with a small mountain of gloop in a bowl.

'Um,' Daphne says. 'Not really, no.'

'Must be something,' he says.

'Parliament is to be prolonged. Because of the war.'

He takes a spoonful of porridge, which instantly stops his mouth moving. His eyes tear up. Daphne looks away and opens the paper again to hide her face, for fear of laughing. 'The British have made a tremendous impression on the Americans, it seems, by the way they are coping with the bombing at home.'

'That's good,' she hears him say, in a clogged voice. He is still acclimatising to Guðrún's unique culinary style.

'The Germans are starting day bombing.'

'Oh,' he says, mournfully, through another mouthful.

The kitchen door swings to and fro: Guðrún disappears, hurrying back to the sink with the dirty crockery.

Daphne reads on. 'There is resistance to the Nazis in Norway.'

'I'm glad. I heard that the Quislings did not represent the majority of the population.'

'That's right,' she says. It is encouraging to read that the Norwegian traitors, who opened the doors to the Germans, have been shunned by their fellow countrymen, those who did not welcome the fascist invaders.

The captain picks up on her limited response, assuming (correctly) she does not want a lengthy discussion on the matter. 'Anything else?' he asks.

'Someone has sent in three ecclesiastical limericks, which the editors have published. Would you like me to read one out? "There were two young ladies of Birmingham, / And this is the story concerning 'em . . ."'

'No, please,' he says, laughing now. 'I don't think I can cope with more turgid slop.'

Thankfully, Guðrún has not reappeared to overhear this last remark. Daphne puts down the paper and finds herself pleasantly surprised by his broad grin. Some captains she has met have been stuffy and superior. A few downright rude. She has not previously met one who has such an easy manner, has not made her feel distinctly subordinate. But then again, she is a reporter, isn't she? Not a recruit. Still, this officer is at least friendly.

She eyes the porridge and says, 'Best to get down early. Before it, er, thickens.'

'I'll remember that,' he says. 'Which paper do you report to?' he asks. The question is casually aimed, apparently for conversation.

'*The Times.*'

'Oh,' he says, looking impressed. 'I know the editor . . .'

'I'm so sorry,' she says speedily, offering him the newspaper. 'But I must run. I have someone to meet at the harbour.'

'Thank you,' he says and asks no more.

Their fingers touch as she gives him the paper and she notices that his are exceptionally cold. He does not look robust. She hopes he will adapt and wonders if she has been rude in not asking for more details of his posting. But this is war. They are on the clock. Normal etiquette is suspended.

'Another time,' he says.

She waves and leaves the room, grateful that she has not had to lie. Not about everything.

\*    \*    \*

Outside the wind is bracing. She hurries down the road, past the other houses in their funny shades of blue and yellow.

The air is full of sleet, which irritates her eyes. Dots of it are melting on her face. They pop on her skin then trickle down into the scarf she has wrapped round her chin. It is becoming soggy.

She takes the left turn onto the main road that runs along the waterfront. Briefly she thinks of her fantasy, yesterday: she and Jack walking hand in hand. In her head there had been a sunset colouring the sky in orange, peach and pink. Today it is dark and grey and heavy with frosted water. She laughs at herself and notices a bitterness that has not been there before. Where has that come from? What does it mean?

Perhaps, she thinks, she is growing up. Abandoning girlish fantasy for the stark reality of working for her country. Of losing her autonomy. If young women ever have any to surrender in the first place. She scoffs aloud again and finds herself disquieted by the sound. It is not patriotic to be cynical.

Her scarf catches the wind and flies up around her face. She is glad she has not worn lipstick or else it would be all over her jaw. Vanity is not compatible with practical clothing. Though she has seen that the Icelandic girls manage to make the most of it, she has not picked up their style yet.

There are soldiers up ahead on the quay. Infantrymen no doubt waiting for the ship due in, which will bring with it more supplies, more weapons. Hopefully, warmer clothes for the troops. They will be tasked with hauling the cranes, attaching the chains that dangle overhead, steadying the loads, distributing the cargo wherever it needs to go. Right now, they are at ease, stamping their feet, leaning against trucks, lighting cigarettes.

She finds a space to stand and, like everyone else gathered there, watches the silhouettes on the horizon becoming more distinct.

A young boy wearing a cloth cap pushes past her and circles the soldiers. 'Heil Hitler!' he shouts with mischievous glee, till one of the men raises a fist to him. It is an empty threat: the occupiers have been cautioned on maintaining good relations with the natives. The boy will not be cuffed. And he knows it: the knowledge emboldens him.

As he runs away, back to a group of rosy-cheeked children, she sees that his expression is victorious. He does not know what his words mean, only that they irritate the soldiers. And for that, she sees, he has won a sweet from the other boys who have egged him on. Bravery is contextual.

When her attention is drawn back to the sea, the ship is closer. Slowing. Foamy white clouds of water cluster round the prow. It slices through them, steering starboard, towards the harbour.

On the quay a sergeant major barks out orders, readying the troops for action. They are standing to attention now, not a cigarette to be seen, only butts that smoulder near their feet.

She moves closer to the water. The ship is docking. A gargantuan crash as the gangplank hits the stone of the harbour wall. Everyone jumps. She hears the children behind her laugh, and then there is more pushing as they clamber forward to see what new drama will unfold.

The gangplank slides over frosted walls. An officer directs two soldiers to fasten it. They grab onto the rails. One of them does not have gloves and lets go immediately. The steel must be freezing. She has heard of men losing skin to iced metal and looks anxiously at his commanding officer, who does not flinch. Does not say anything to withdraw the ungloved soldier, who grabs, then releases, grabs, then releases the frost-cloaked machinery. The other is doing his best to manoeuvre the gangplank into place, taking as much of its weight as he can. At last, two more men are dispatched to rope the apparatus down. On its rail a pink sliver glistens. The gloveless soldier stands to attention. His face is grey. Sweat sheens his forehead.

Another man of superior rank, she does not know which, wearing a well-padded winter coat, walks ceremoniously to the top of the gangplank where a uniformed officer, who she thinks must be an admiral, stands and salutes. Words are exchanged. There is nodding of heads. Then the man of rank coasts down the plank, gripping onto the rails. His hands, she sees, are sheathed in leather gloves.

There is a commotion on the decks. Soldiers are lining up. When they fall still, an order is shouted and they begin to march down the gangplank, filing onto the harbourside. Some of them wobble as their feet touch the quay.

Daphne and the other bystanders are told to stand back, to make way.

Of course, she complies. Though she does not cede her place to the children or the inquisitive locals who have lingered to see who is coming now. She keeps her eyes on the troops, finding herself impressed by their synchronicity, dozens of arms and legs moving in time as if they belong to one huge caterpillar. This is a disciplined and organised army, she thinks. Hopefully the Icelanders will see that too.

It takes a good hour for the troops to disembark. She worries that she has missed him and spends long minutes looking round. Has he already come ashore? Is he lost in the crowd?

And then, on deck, she spies him, a suitcase in one hand and briefcase in the other. For a moment she feels almost maternal: that coat will not keep him properly warm.

Then he is on the quay, looking around. She waves at him, but there are too many people taller than she is so she takes off her hat and holds it in the air.

'There you are!' says Septimus, his face appearing over a small group of young ladies out to eye the fresh blood, two children pushing along at waist-height beside them. They part to let the noisy boys through and Septimus approach. He takes a step towards Daphne, then stops when he sees the young lads and leans back, politely allowing them room to pass. 'I'm so pleased you made it,' he calls to Daphne.

She is not sure what he means – made it to Iceland? Made it to the harbour? Why would she not? Though she does not articulate these thoughts. Not here on the open quay, with the cold numbing her toes. Taking Septimus's damp elbow, she steers him away from the throng.

He sways slightly, reminding her fleetingly of Jonty and their nocturnal strolls home from the dive bars of Soho.

'Not yet got my land legs,' he says, eyes darting over the skyline and off to the black hills. Fuzzy wreaths of white cloud deck them today like a fur stole the island has put on 'specially to greet its visitors. The snow-caps glint above them, diamonds in a tiara.

'Ah, yes,' says Daphne. 'I had that problem too. Won't take long to adjust. Now, what would you like to do?' she asks. 'Go straight to our lodgings, which are about a twenty- minute walk away, or warm up and refresh ourselves somewhere closer?'

'Warmth,' he says, with emphasis. 'And I would like something to eat that hasn't come out of a tin.'

'Hotel Borg,' she says and is astonished by the authority with which she expresses herself. 'Follow me.'

Half an hour later they are back in the bar she left last night, though the difference is striking. Far more sedate and only half-full. Waiters survey the tables. Everyone is dining. No one stands at the bar. There is no jazz, no band, no wildness in the air though a gramophone is playing quietly in the corner. It lays a cushion of sound across the conversations taking place in here, so at least they will not be overheard.

Septimus has plumped for a table by the window, which she thinks is not ideal. He is keen to take in the view. Though, conversely, she is aware this means those outside will have a good view of them. There are trees and bushes about the square that may provide cover for interested observers. Undoubtedly there will be some, especially here. She remembers Anna's warning to her friend – not everyone is happy about foreigners arriving.

'I need to orientate myself,' Septimus says as the waiter brings them menus. 'Is this the main square?'

'It is. Austurvöllur. That is the parliament building over there.' She points to the stern, charcoal-grey rectangle at the southern end, which dominates the square. Surprising really as it stands next to the main cathedral. Such holy buildings, she always thought, were meant to tower over everything else, reminding all citizens of the eyes of God upon them. Though this cathedral is the size of a parish church. Everything here is smaller. Except for the landscape, which is giant-sized. 'It is called the Alþingishús and is equivalent to our Houses of Commons and Lords,' she tells him. She has absorbed so much from trudging round the streets and is a more valuable guide than she had realised. It is a delightful surprise.

'Such a forbidding-looking building,' remarks Septimus. 'Its darkness puts me in mind of some of the municipal offices in Sheffield,' he says absently.

'Those are probably blackened by soot though, aren't they? Factories, furnaces, smithies and the like?' Daphne suggests, swivelling round to view the assembly rooms.

'Of course,' says Septimus and smiles. 'Coal: the by-product of our formidable Industrial Revolution.'

'Well,' she says. 'You must look at the Alþingishús in a different way. The blocks used to construct it were hewn from the native rock. To me they reflect this landscape.'

'Magma, you mean,' says Septimus.

'The country is full of volcanoes, did you know?'

'Yes, that's right,' he says, wagging a finger at her but looking past her eyes, into a memory. 'I read that. It really is fascinating, isn't it? So cold on the surface and yet so fiery underneath!'

'Sounds like you are describing a person,' says Daphne and laughs.

'I suppose so.'

Just as she brings her eyes back to him, they catch the orange flare of a match in the hollow of a palm. Someone is lighting a cigarette in the shadows of the trees opposite. The match-flame whips up and down then loses the battle for life and is extinguished. All she can see now is the cigarette's glowing tip, bobbing above the chin of someone whose build indicates they are masculine. She wishes the sun were out so she could get a better view. Then remembers, at this time, it would have dropped behind the high roofs of the buildings opposite. They have entered the island's prolonged twilight.

Perhaps she should speak to Septimus about the risks inherent in being so easily seen from the street. Difficult though – he is superior to her in age, sex and, most importantly, rank. She is still unsure of his job title. So much is left unsaid in her new line of work. Ranks and roles are not rigorously stratified as in the armed forces. Section W is looser, more flexible, expansive. All the better to see you with, she thinks, and looks out into the square again.

Whoever it was there under the trees has gone now. Conceivably they had just stopped for a moment to catch their breath or draw on a snout, maybe have a break. Not everyone is interested in her and Septimus. Lots of people are carrying on with life as normal. It is only she and the man she must report to who are aware of the difference that a few days has made to their lives and environment.

A pot of tea is brought to their table together with two portions of salt fish and potatoes.

Septimus is clearly ravenous. He leans over the steaming plate and inhales deeply.

'Was your journey over good?' she asks. The food was evidently not up to much.

'It's all a matter of perspective, isn't it?' he asks in a manner that does not expect an answer. 'It wasn't a first-class cruise liner. But it got me here, didn't it? Which is its function. Though I must say, I am very glad to be in Reykjavík.'

She waits to see if he will expand but has the impression that he wants to get on with other things. So she says, 'I have been in attendance on the target and, I have to say, there is —'

A fork with a potato speared on one end waves in front of her. 'No,' Septimus says, then munches and swallows before he adds, 'Nothing, please. Not yet.'

She stops and stares at him. What does he mean?

Her blank expression makes him smile. 'I am sure you have your own ideas about . . . "the target". And I am aware that Hugh selected you because of your background in the theatre, your experience with performers and the like.'

'I . . . Well, yes,' she stammers. 'I have seen many acts like—'

He cuts her off again. 'I don't wish either of us to use the term "act" until I have had first-hand experience of the man himself. "Act" insinuates inauthenticity, entertainment, pretence. It is a prejudgement.'

She acquiesces; he has his reasons, she's sure, and so cuts into her fish. It is indeed very salty. She wishes there was some vinegar on the table to souse it. When she has finished her mouthful and digested Septimus's statement, she puts down her cutlery and takes a sip of tea. 'Am I right in thinking that you believe, then, it is possible for some people to commune with the dead?'

Septimus is still chewing on his fish, which she thinks may be drier than her own for it takes him a good while. 'I'm not suggesting that this man,' he says, once he is able, 'that he, Karlsson,' he adds loudly, too loudly in Daphne's view, 'can or does. I am ensuring that we remain open-minded on the matter. What is the point of investigation if you have already made your decision, know the conclusion? Why come all this way?'

'I'm not saying I've already made my mind up,' Daphne protests. 'I merely thought you would want to hear my report.' She makes sure her last sentence finishes in a whisper, to emphasise the need for caution in such a public arena.

Septimus lowers his own voice accordingly. 'If you tell me what you have learned then I will become biased to your point of view. Hard as I may try not to.'

'I see. Have you met someone . . .' She pauses, unsure of how to phrase her question. 'Have you encountered a claimant who also credibly professes to speak to the dead? Or to hear them?'

His eyes narrow. 'That is not the question you should be asking, Daphne. Have you heard of the Akashic Records?'

She shakes her head.

'Miss Sabine never mentioned them?'

Ah, she thinks. It is to do with the spirit realm. Miss Sabine had been her tutor in the summer. A Rosicrucian, Daphne believes, although nothing was specifically said.

'The Akashic Records are a permanent record of all thoughts, feelings and actions.'

Really? she thinks. This seems a bold claim. 'According to who?'

'According to esotericists and mystics and some academics.'

Daphne lifts her eyebrows and makes a soft 'oh' sound.

'They are believed to be stored in a psychic vault, as it were,' Septimus continues, 'that exists outside of space and outside of time, and they play an important role in Theosophy, a religion that attracts many German followers. Elements of it are racialist: Blavatsky, co-founder of the Theosophical Society, taught that humanity evolved from different "root races". Aryans, of course, are at the top of the tree.' He rolls his eyes briefly. 'The leaders of the movement are Mahatmas, mystical people who oversee the spiritual growth of civilisations. Blavatsky said she communicated with them telepathically.'

Daphne finds this incredible and is unable to muffle a snort.

Septimus flicks his cold grey eyes over her. 'I don't think that is particularly funny.'

Is he chastising her or merely stating an opinion?

'You may well smirk,' he says, though she does not think she is. Not really. 'But I have a very great respect for certain belief systems. Science is one of them. And who is to say that all the energy that goes on in here' – he taps his forehead and fastens his grey eyes on her – 'is contained by a layer of bone? Doesn't electricity pass through bone?'

Is he asking her? She is not sure so stays quiet.

He nods and pops another potato in his mouth. She waits for him to swallow.

'Well, I'll tell you,' he says. 'It is a semi-conductive. Who's to say the electricity that comprises someone's thoughts, images, words, can't leap out and be shared by anyone who is receptive?'

Now Daphne is sure he is waiting for an answer. But is unsure of what to say. Is she walking into an intellectual trap?

Taking her silence for ignorance, she assumes, he tells her, 'No one can rule this out because I don't think we've developed the technology to measure or test it yet. But we have *all* experienced times when we have been with someone close and said the same thing.'

She thinks of her father. That happened with them sometimes, when they were sitting around the dining table. Sunday lunches mostly. Along the lines of 'Please pass the potatoes, Daphne/Father.'

As if catching her memory, he agrees. 'My brother Sixtus and I bought each other identical Christmas cards two years running, for instance. But I digress. Regarding the Akashic Records, some psychics, clairvoyants and other intuitives have confessed to being able to "read" them. If the accessing of such information is possible it has huge implications for operational wartime strategies.'

Daphne processes this. She wants to tell him that Karlsson is quite convincing in certain respects. But she can't, so she says, 'Our target is performing tonight at the picture house. I have drawn you a map of how to get there.'

'Excellent,' says Septimus. 'This is the sort of thing I've been waiting for.'

He lays his fork beside his knife and dabs the corners of his mouth with the napkin provided.

Daphne stares at him, unable to read his expression. Rather than resume their esoteric conversation, she plumps for logistics. 'The picture house is not far from here – the Hotel Borg,' she clarifies. 'Some of the audience pop in for a drink afterwards. British officers frequent this place.'

'I can see that,' he says, looking around. Then a different expression comes over his face. 'And have you met Major Spike yet?'

'Yes,' she says but as she does, remembers that she failed to do something he had ordered. 'Oh, dear. I've just had a thought.'

'What's that?'

'He said he wants all communications to go through him.'

'Did he now?' says Septimus.

'I forgot and sent a telegram to Mr Devereaux last night. He was expecting it, though.'

'Hugh?' Septimus cocks his head to one side. 'My orders are to answer to Commander Fleet.'

Daphne thinks back to the briefing room on her first visit to Section W. Was Fleet present? In the low-ceilinged room in the basement of Wormwood Scrubs, an eclectic group had been put together. Though it was difficult to tell who was who: most had been wearing civilian clothes to avoid the detection of military personnel in the prison. Just as in Iceland, there were spies everywhere. And the Germans were ruthless. If they were to find out such meetings were taking place in the prison it would undoubtedly become a priority target.

The wireless in Guðrún's dining room crackles nightly with reports of bombing raids on Kent, Liverpool and Birmingham. London, of course, has suffered greatly already. Only last week Waterloo station went up: a bomb destroyed the signalling system and telephone exchange. The *Midnight Sun*, which she was reading at breakfast, described how a handful of inexperienced station staff and nearby soldiers kept trains moving using only flags. Bravo to them, she thinks, then recalls the reporter admitting that the Luftwaffe were proving to be highly competent adversaries: 'coming in large or small formations or in streams, splitting up and then rejoining, feinting, weaving, employing every last ruse and even using the clouds as camouflage to confuse our brave defenders.' British pilots are going down every day, day after day. Though the Luftwaffe suffer heavy losses too. More so even.

And despite the fact she knows she should pay close attention to Septimus, her mind wanders briefly to Roy Dalton, a young man who once proposed to her. Mortifying. She was far too young for a start. Though he was a nice enough chap, but simply not for her. *Is*, she thinks, *is* a nice enough chap. Her use of the past tense makes her feel serious and superstitious. She does not want to jinx him. He has signed up for the RAF. As if her thoughts could impact on who is killed and who is not. Silly! Though Septimus's talk of the Akashic Records would suggest everything is already decided and written down in the books of fate. Which suddenly makes the outlook seem doubly glum. Predestination. What was the point of anything if the future was already laid out, just like the past, and we humans nothing more than monkeys or automatons, juddering through life to the organ grinder's tune?

'Daphne!'

She jumps. Septimus is looking at her, his head tilted to one side. 'I said, "Did you meet him before you left?"'

'Who?' she says.

'Commander Fleet! The new secondment. Oxford man. Has some very interesting ideas.' His eyes dance and he shakes his head. 'Off with the fairies then, weren't you?'

He is too sharp to lie to, so she says, 'Actually it's elves here and they are called the Hidden People.'

'Elves?' He smiles.

She thinks he is patronising her, so says, 'Not like our elves. These aren't little people. Gudrun, my landlady . . . *our* landlady, told me they are like human beings. Taller in fact. They act like humans too and are highly intelligent. Just not visible unless you have the gift of second sight.'

'Fascinating,' says Septimus in earnest. 'I intend to spend some time exploring Icelandic folklore. Is there any talk of elves and second sight in connection to,' he leans forwards and says under his breath, 'Mr K?'

Ah, she thinks, so now it is permissible to allude to Karlsson. 'No, not that I'm aware. Not yet. But further investigation is required. Indeed, we should make a move. Time is getting on. This performance tonight – you should go without me. I have been invited to a private session tomorrow, which I will attend with Anna, our contact here.'

'That sounds well organised,' he says. 'Thank you.'

She is not used to people expressing gratitude for her work and is touched by his good manners. 'I am happy to escort you to our lodgings,' she tells him, aware she will be cutting it fine before her meeting with Anna.

He accepts and waves to the waiter for the bill, for which Daphne is also much obliged. Iceland is as cold as a diamond and just as expensive.

## CHAPTER EIGHT

Anna is waiting for her, sitting on the gloomy stairs just inside the entrance to the newspaper's offices. She wears a soft grey suit with a light-blue silk scarf tied at the neck and looks unaccountably sultry. Scarlet lipstick plumps her lips so that they stand out against the milky whiteness of her skin. Strawberries and cream, Daphne thinks.

Behind her light floods in from a streetlamp and hits Anna's irises so that they shine and flash: like twin gemstones or the eyes in a peacock's tail. Tonight she looks, Daphne sees, like a femme fatale.

'Oof,' says her contact and stands up, brushing dust from her hands. 'Close it! Close it!' The illusion of sophistication disappears as she puts her shoulder against the door and forcibly pushes it shut. 'Brrrr,' she says and shakes herself. 'Open – quick. Close – quick. Here we learn to keep warmth in.'

'Sorry,' says Daphne, though she didn't think she'd been lingering.

'The boss wants to see you. I've tried to put him off but he's a persistent fifl.'

Daphne is not sure what that last word means but thinks it is probably not flattering, as Anna's mouth screws up with disgust when she says it. 'Then,' she says, 'I want to talk to you about those messages we heard last night.'

'Of course,' says Daphne, following her up the stairs. 'Several things have been bothering me.'

Anna reaches the top and waits for her. 'Good,' she says. 'Then both of us feel the same.'

Daphne falls in step with her as they move down a corridor with doors leading off to either side. At the end they press through double doors into a large communal workspace. Half a dozen newspaper employees are in here. To the right there are typesetters and layout men. To the left reporters at desks with typewriters and piles of paper on them. At the far end a typist, the only other female present, is talking on the phone. Her desk blocks the entrance to another office with wraparound windows, allowing the occupant to look out over his workforce. The glass door has words printed across it. **Ritstjóri: Örn Andrésson**.

Anna catches the typist's eye and she waves them into the inner room.

A middle-aged man sits at a large oak desk, smoking a cigar, reading a newspaper and, judging by the sharp aroma in the room, drinking some sort of liquor. 'Ah,' he says, looking up. 'Anna. Come, come.'

They are already on their way.

He is not clean-shaven but has a moustache and beard. Dark hair threaded with grey. Round glasses over striking eyes the colour of polished mahogany. Though he has the appearance of a gentleman scholar, his build is large and brawny. He points to the chairs opposite his, which they take. 'And you must be Daphne Dione-Smith.' He says it as if finishing an argument with a statement that precludes further discussion.

If only he knew, Daphne thinks, and is tempted to say no, just to puncture his self-confidence. She cannot tell if she would like to work with him or not. Likely he is, what her father calls, 'A man who is immensely pleased to be who he is.'

She nods in assent.

'I hope Anna has been treating you well,' he asks, and puts the cigar to his mouth.

'She has been,' Daphne says. She was going to add 'very informative' but thinks twice. It could be taken the wrong way, and she supposes he is unaware of the real reason for her presence.

However, the burly Icelander is already saying something else. 'I won her in a bet, you know.' He blows out a long, satisfying plume of smoke.

'Oh?' she says and glances at Anna who raises her eyebrows: she has heard this too many times already.

'With my father,' she explains. 'They are good friends.' Then to her boss, 'Best decision you never made, Örn.'

'She's right there,' he says and smooths his whiskers down. 'How is the medium article progressing?'

'Very interesting,' Daphne says. 'Coming on nicely.'

'I'd like to read it before you go, if I may?'

Cheek! thinks Daphne, but she says, 'Of course. Thank you for your interest.'

Anna slaps her hands onto her knees. 'Which is why you are here, isn't it, Daphne? We have notes to compare. Please excuse us, Örn. Work to do.'

The editor casts one last appraising glance over Daphne then picks up his glass and goes back to his reading without saying goodbye.

Anna switches on the light in her office this time. The stove is alight in one corner. A pot bubbles on top of it, filling the air with a nutty, resinous aroma.

'Coffee?' asks Anna and makes straight for it.

'Yes, please.'

'Look on my desk. There's a photo. Have you observed the man on the far left?'

Daphne examines the photograph. It is a black-and-white image of men at work, raking over soil. In the distance she can see a Nissen hut. She looks more closely at the man Anna has indicated. He is standing, leaning on a rake, with the posture of one who has just wiped his face clean of sweat. Indeed, in his hand he has what she thinks is a rag, but on closer inspection sees is a cap. The hair is light and the clothes familiar. 'I think,' she says, 'that it could be one of the two men Karlsson met in the café.'

'As I thought.' Anna nods and purses her lips. 'Sigmundur Gunnarsson. An active communist. He is working with the British, helping to clear the land for the new airfield.'

'Gosh,' says Daphne. 'Don't we vet the workers?'

'Of course,' says Anna. 'But he would not have disclosed his political allegiance, I think. And other Icelanders would be reluctant to inform the authorities. Sigmundur has unhealthy friends.'

For a moment Daphne wonders if she means sickly but then Anna adds, 'Violent,' and she realises that the meaning is 'unwholesome'.

'Russia is allied with the Germans,' Daphne says, more to herself than her contact.

'It is an uneasy alliance,' says Anna. 'However, these allegiances do currently stand.'

Daphne hears a clattering of tin mugs on the stove top. But she is still inspecting the photograph. Could this man be working somehow with Karlsson? They look like they would move in very different social circles.

'Other news: we have been sent formal invitations for tomorrow's séance,' says Anna. 'We must attend and pay close attention. Torfi Birgisson, a well-known shipping magnate, will be there and also his wife. With people like that in the audience, we can expect a good performance. However, first I would like to go over what was said yesterday evening.' She pours out two steaming measures of coffee. 'Milk?'

'And one lump, please.'

Daphne hears Anna drop sugar in the mug and give it a stir. 'I've typed up my notes. There's a copy for you on the desk. Green folder.'

Anna is very well organised, thinks Daphne as she takes the file. Her notes are typed out on duplicating paper with a paperclip to keep the pages together. Flimsy and thin between her fingers, they fall forward over themselves, so she lays them on the desk, side by side. Resting on her elbows, she settles in to read.

It is odd to see the evening laid out before her like a script. She skims over the introductions, the 'awakening' and 'opening of the minds', until she comes to the section that gives her pause. Now that she sees the words typed out in black and white, she realises that they have been circling the back of her mind since last night.

'Ah, yes,' says Anna, reading over her shoulder. She sets down a cup on the desk for Daphne. 'I wondered if you had noticed that.'

Returning to her own side, the journalist picks up her set of notes and shuffles them till she comes to the passage that has held Daphne's attention. 'Is it normal, in the theatre, to set out how long you will go on for?'

Lifting her head, still keeping her chin in her hands, Daphne shrugs. 'I'm not sure that there is a "normal" with regards to clairvoyants, psychics, mentalists and the like. But no, I haven't seen the time set out like that before. Not sure what the purpose would be really. Perhaps it adds a sense of value and makes the audience feel that they are honoured, that the clairvoyant's time is precious?'

Anna neither agrees nor disagrees. So Daphne touches her fingers to the typed lines, then reads them out loud: '"I will do my best to voice them . . . I shall try to convey their messages . . . their truths. But we shall see whether that takes three turns, four or seven."'

After taking another long sip of her coffee, Anna nods. The stove in the corner spits and crackles. 'And then he is talking about seeing a soldier,' she says. 'An Icelander in Canadian uniform.' She puts the mug down on the desk and cocks her head at Daphne, as if weighing her up. 'Some of our men did fight for Canada in the First World War. The Canadians know this. Our country has connections to Newfoundland. It is plausible that a number of those recruits fell in France. But that he saw an Icelander in Canadian uniform seems to me more than a lucky guess.'

Daphne purses her lips then relaxes them. She must be careful as she makes her statement, so as not to undermine her contact. 'An impressive start,' she agrees. 'But he did not say that the man was an Icelander. Not at first. He said he could see a man in a Canadian uniform and there were two soldiers in the front rows. The Canadian was in his uniform. Karlsson was likely to have spotted them from the stage. I wondered myself if the Canadian chap might pipe up. He could have had family who fought and died in that war.'

'And yet,' says Anna, 'it is the sister of the man Ragnar who stands up. What are the chances of that?'

'She had lost her brother. Many bereaved people attend psychic audiences. So many men died during the last war that the grieving number many, many millions. More than the dead even. Every fatality was a son, father, uncle, cousin – or indeed a brother. These ripples extend further than we can know and those left behind are often possessed of a desire to reach beyond the veil of mortality, to speak to their loved ones, to seek answers. So many died too young. Such a frustrating waste of potential – all those lives cut short. Not lived.'

'It was a world war. There are many grieving in Iceland,' says Anna. Her voice wavers slightly. Daphne looks to her but her face is obscured. A glossy curtain of hair hangs down, touching the pages she has spread across the desk.

So instead Daphne sends her mind back again to the theatre and the young soldiers they had noticed there. She taps the transcript. 'The Canadian may have thought the spirit was native to Iceland and been waiting for further information. But before any came, the woman announced it was her brother.'

Anna breathes heavily enough for Daphne to hear her, then says, 'She *wanted* it to be him.' Her voice is low, almost a whisper. Daphne is curious to see if she will say more but she doesn't, so Daphne picks up her coffee and tests it with her tongue. It is still hot and strong. And delicious.

After a moment Anna remarks, 'I thought it interesting that Karlsson asked "Are those long leathery straps that he is holding in his hands?"' At last she glances at Daphne again, cheeks pinched, muscles taut around the mouth. 'And the sister confirmed what they were. Karlsson *saw* something in his hands. Quite exceptional in a performance of this kind, don't you think?'

There is something defiant in Anna's gaze. Her nose looks moist and red. Daphne notes this but doesn't let it sink in as she is already disagreeing with the words that have come from Anna's mouth. 'I am not as convinced,' she says. 'If a medium suggests that they can see the someone, *anyone* who is dead, people will search their minds for relatives who have passed over. If further pronouncements resonate with a mourner, then they might well agree and volunteer more information. So when Karlsson said he saw the apparition with something in their hands, the relative agreed. Most people are desperate for illusions to be true,' she says, then finishes with, 'believe me, I know.'

'And yet,' says Anna, coolly, 'if you refer back to my notes you will see that Karlsson mentioned the reins first. Before the sister. He could not possibly know the minds of all the audience members. Unless he possessed an astonishing gift.'

'But of what kind?' Daphne wonders aloud. When Anna narrows her eyes, she feels the need to explain. 'He may be very good at understanding the language of the body, of correctly interpreting the feelings that are manifesting from within. There are clues in the words a recipient uses and the way they speak to the medium – he may excel at interpreting tells like that.'

'You're right, of course,' says Anna, now more upright in her seat. 'I think we can assume that a large part of the audience comes in the hope that they will be chosen to have a message relayed to them. Or else, if you are completely sceptical, why bother coming at all? You would not want to waste your time or money. Though I still can't quite understand what you mean about the reins in the spirit's hands.'

'All right,' says Daphne. 'Imagine that your boss has passed over.'

'If only,' says Anna and rolls her eyes.

But Daphne can tell she doesn't mean it. She continues to speak, holding out her hands, mimicking Karlsson onstage. 'I see someone there. What's that? Oh, he says his name is Örn. "Ah, yes," you say, "that was my employer, a newspaper editor." Now you've given him a clue to the spirit's earthly occupation, it's easy for him to build a more convincing character. "Would that be a pen in his hand?" You would probably agree, wouldn't you?

'And,' Daphne flicks to the part of the exchange that supports her theory, 'look, although she hadn't mentioned reins specifically, the sister said he had lived on a farm and raised the ponies there.'

'I see now what you mean,' Anna agrees. 'If he was attending to the ponies then he was likely to be seen about the farm with reins in his hand.' She bends her head and neatens the papers on the desk. 'The animal's name was Brúnn. Very common for horses in Iceland: it means brown.'

Daphne wonders if Anna has been playing devil's advocate up to this point. Now she is conceding. 'Curious,' Daphne says, remembering a particular part of the show, 'that it was Jessamine who wrote down the letter B and held it up.'

'Is it?' Anna asks.

But Daphne's eyes are back on the script. 'What about the next "ghost" he hears? Isak?'

'This also is not an uncommon name,' says Anna.

'According to your notes, it was at this moment that Karlsson began coughing. He said in his dressing room it was because of dust. But I remember onstage he took a glass of water and said' – she reads from Anna's notes – '"The water is good tonight. Refreshing and calming." I thought at the time that was a peculiar thing to say.' She glances at Anna, who is still focussed on the transcript. 'Then,' Daphne goes on, 'he announced the next turn would be his last.'

'Presumably because of the coughing fit, which he found exhausting.' Anna is nodding. 'He said the spirits drained him.'

Dust or spirits – does it matter? Daphne sees a 'W' on the notes, underlined. 'Then we have Wilhelm or Walter. A fisherman. The young man identifies him as Wilhelm.' For a moment, unaccountably, she has a vision of Jonty, The Grand Mystique, onstage back at the Oriental Theatre, brandishing a gun in his hand. But the thought does not stay long as Anna is speaking and draws Daphne's attention.

'That's right.' She pokes the notes. 'Then Karlsson goes on to say Wilhelm's brother does the same work.'

Putting a finger to her chin, Daphne clears her mind and thinks. 'Don't these sorts of jobs or industries run in families?'

'Yes, many businesses here are family-run.'

'So it could be a logical deduction on Karlsson's part?'

'It could be.'

'He relays,' says Daphne, 'the message that Wilhelm wanted to send to Jón, his other son.'

'Yes,' says Anna, and stares at her blankly.

So Daphne elaborates. 'But why not "speak" to the man in the audience who has bothered to turn up?'

'He did not want to talk to him,' says Anna simply.

'You mean the spirit did not want to talk to his son or that Karlsson did not want to?'

Anna laughs lightly. 'Perhaps you lose earthbound etiquette when you die?'

She hadn't realised it before but now Daphne is relieved that Anna has made the joke. The atmosphere between them becomes less taut. 'Let us assume for a moment,' she says tapping her pencil on the transcript, 'that it might not be an authentic visitation.'

'Yes?' says Anna and waits for her to continue.

Daphne is starting to wonder if her reserve is not typical Scandinavian behaviour but an individual eccentricity. She looks down at the script Anna has typed out and quotes the words written there: 'Jón's fate is entwined with the elements. He must embrace the storms that are soon to come for they shall bring him great sustenance. Great sustenance for many. And, and – I hear him say – this will shape his character.'

'And this is coming from Wilhelm,' says Anna, then adds, 'W.'

Anna articulating the letter has jogged Daphne's memory back to the scene at the theatre. She sees Jessamine holding up the card with the letter written on it.

The visual memory starts a cog turning inside her brain and now she sees the letter W drawn onto the board in the Wild West trick she'd helped to perform just two months ago. During this sequence she'd pretended to be afraid while tied to a board.

Then The Grand Mystique shot a bullet (blank) just above her head towards a target. Beneath it was a large painted letter N. The board was designed to resemble a gold prospector's compass. A switch to dislodge the piece of paper covering a pre-made bullet-hole was concealed in the letter W just by her right hand. N E S W. North, east, south, west.

In her mind, a bell rings and she makes the connection, turning back to last night's message. 'Storms coming. Great sustenance and storms,' says Daphne again, thinking out loud. 'It's got to be!' She sits up straight as the mystery starts to reveal itself. '"W" is not for Wilhelm. It's for west.

'"Tonight the water is calming."' She looks up at Anna. '"Storms coming", spoken while Jessamine is holding up a W – "Storms will be coming in from the west."' It is starting to make sense. 'This message is for Jón. Could he be . . .? Is it possible that Karlsson is giving out weather forecasts to enemy contacts?'

Anna's face tilts towards her, eyes widening. 'Djöfulsins!' she says and slaps the desktop as if it had been rude to her.

'Or,' says Daphne starting to feel breathless, 'are we seeing patterns where none exist?'

She must exercise control, not get carried away. 'Is the weather forecast even significant?' But even as the words fall from her lips, she remembers the officers, on her voyage over, discussing high winds and quiet seas, the need to land at low tide when transporting troops from vessels to shore, to deliver cargoes and essential supplies when the water is calm.

Anna starts in her seat and spears Daphne with her eyes. 'You must know,' she says, 'that *all* warfare is dependent on weather.' She points over her shoulder through the uncurtained window behind her. 'Air operations need clear skies. Fighters, bombers and other aircraft can be grounded by fog. We have much of it. And clouds can hide targets.'

'Yes,' says Daphne, recalling her training. 'Operations

conducted at night should be executed under a full moon. For good visibility.'

'Detailed weather reports are of vital importance on this island.' The journalist jerks her head for emphasis again, her frame filling with tension so she is entirely straight-backed. 'The Germans have been desperate to get hold of them. The British, your major, has sent Icelanders to England simply for owning short-wave radios. All radios on our fishing fleet are set to a single frequency – and it was difficult to get approval for that. But the fishermen need to be warned about turbulence and from which direction the wind is coming in.'

'Storms come,' says Daphne again, 'and Jessamine holds up a W. "Tell Jón." It all seems so clear now. "Whether that takes three turns . . ."'

'Or four or seven,' Anna adds.

'But he didn't get to those because of the coughing fit. "The water is good tonight. Refreshing and calming." More reporting on meteorology.'

'My God!' Anna exclaims. 'He practically announced it.'

Daphne pauses as a new thought hits her. She leafs back through the transcript. 'Sustenance,' she says. '"For they shall bring him great sustenance." Sustenance – supplies? I wonder if there is a shipment coming here from America? From the west? Septimus Stra—' She corrects herself. 'I collected someone from a ship this very morning. But that came from the east.'

'Shipments from the west though. Can you find out about those?'

'I can't ask. It will be top secret. But I know a man who can.'

# CHAPTER NINE

Major Spike is not there. Despite her correct use of today's password Daphne has been curtly dismissed.

Frustration is becoming a familiar feeling. It is, after all, the way of the world to discourage young women from their enthusiasms. However, she believes they are on to something here and, if Karlsson has given out information to enemy agents about a convoy, many lives are at stake. She wonders how many have been lost to hierarchy and bureaucracy.

Then her thoughts, driven by doubt, cycle back on themselves: what if the clairvoyant has not given out information? What if he is genuine in what he sees and hears? Or could he be making it all up to sensationalise his stage show and they have made something of nothing? What if it is all a coincidence?

Jonty had once told her that the human mind has a way of recognising incidents and words that result from chaos, but which acquire meaning from one's own preoccupations. Both she and Anna have been observing Karlsson to see if there is an intelligence leak. What if that has made them find meaning in random proclamations? It could cause the medium great harm. And the British authorities here are trigger-happy in deporting anyone who may appear subversive. Even if, as Anna says, they merely own a wireless.

Oh, dear, she thinks. Oh dear, oh dear. Am I right? Is this enough to condemn a man?

She cannot come out on one side or the other. As this realisation seeps in she stumbles and feels once more the steel in her shoes. The weight of them, of everything, makes her suddenly gasp and her breath crystallises in the sharp night air. It is too easy here to make mistakes, slip up and wound.

And this last notion brings her back to her surroundings. Thick layers of cloud have blocked out the moon so she cannot see much at all. Streetlights here are spread wide apart, their globes of light dim, casting long shadows. But they do not overlap, so large patches of darkness stretch between them.

It is late and the citizens of Reykjavík are tucked up in their beds. The roads are deserted. If I fall, she thinks, no one will hear me. No one will help me. A feeling of dread starts to touch her as she walks out of the thin circle of light from one streetlight into the murky gloom ahead.

It is a fair way back to Guðrún's boarding house. She pulls her coat tightly around her and focuses on the sounds she can hear, which are few: a car slowing its engine, the distant sea crashing against harbour walls, the shriek of a bird objecting to the breeze, her breathing – in then out, the rhythmic click of her weighted heels. And then, another sound. Indistinct but also regular. She tunes her ears to it like a bat. Not up ahead but behind her. Thud, thud, thud.

Footsteps. Heavier, far heavier than her own. Though muffled.

She darts a glance over her shoulder. Is that . . .? Did she see a shadow disappearing into the blackspot between the lights?

Hastening her pace, her own breathing starts to stall, then comes in quicker as she speeds her gait.

A spluttering sneeze behind her. Perhaps ten, fifteen yards. A workman making his way home from a night shift, no doubt.

She takes the next right. Though it will make her route slightly longer, she wishes to lose the shadow behind.

Up the residential road. One streetlamp only. Darkness.

And then, she hears the footsteps quicken.

Nearer.

Nearer.

He is right behind her.

She spins

And sees

a man: tall, broad-shouldered. Face obscured by a thick scarf and hat.

He stops, as if surprised, and then turns to a gate, lifts the latch, fumbles with his keys.

And she breathes out a great sigh of relief.

Which frosts the air.

The enemy may be over here, but they are not *everywhere*.

Her mind is too locked up in war and conspiracy.

Some people are just people. Getting on with their life, going through their daily routine, thinking about their supper.

She wonders if she will ever be just a girl, free from steel blades and care.

*He did not know whether to feel contempt or pity so allowed himself neither. It was wrong to give in to such weakness: compassion was a defective impulse. The duty of the strong was to dominate the feeble.*

*In one way their stubbornness was almost admirable, a loyalty of sorts. They, of course, would soon come to see that their refusal to accept the authority of the state was inevitably life-limiting. Though some must know this and yet it seemed not to deter them: life, they believed, was not strictly temporal.*

*For all his outward observances and professions, he preferred not to put his own beliefs to the test. What if the High Command was wrong?*

*Though this lot were adamant that a better world awaited them, they did not speed to it. However, none so far had attempted escape or challenged the guards like some of the other triangles. This predisposition made them more acceptable in many ways. Which was probably why he had heard of other officers taking them as domestic servants. Less trouble.*

*Last year, he had passed through Plötzensee Prison when one was being punished. Refused to sign up for military service, damn' fool. The man was very clearly unfit; he need only have gone through the physical examination to be cast out, rejected, released. Insisted though, didn't he? That war violated the commandment: Thou shalt not to kill.*

*They sliced his head clean off with the guillotine.*

*Silly man.*

*Now he watched the purple triangles bob around as the men – are they men? – formed into lines.*

*He couldn't understand why they didn't rise up. Why become these human doormats? Then a thought occurred to him, impish but amusing. And there wasn't a great deal of joy around.*

*'Get them to put out their arms, like that,' he called across the castle courtyard to the young man herding them out. The junior officer immediately complied, barking out the order.*

*'Tell them to lie down,' he commanded.*

*And so the young man did. Strange that as soon as the words left the junior's mouth the prisoners were on the floor, hunched together, a stripy carpet, albeit a tatty one.*

*'Walk on them,' he shouted.*

*This time the young officer hesitated.*

*'I said: WALK ON THEM.'*

*And the young man obeyed.*

*He could hear the cracks and punctures as the hobnail boots stomped across the ribcages and shoulder blades, yet none of them resisted.*

*'All right, all right,' he said to the officer. 'You've had your fun. Now get them up. There is work to be done.'*

*Confounding that they could be like this.*

*If there was a shred of empathy left in him, the docile acceptance of his caprice has dispelled it.*

*They bring it on themselves, he decided.*

CHAPTER TEN

Dreams. Odd. Disconcerting. She is reluctant to dismiss them. Entirely. Since childhood, she has guessed that some fears which haunt dreams do, in fact, come true. Though she has fought against this sentiment. An obedient child, it was not acceptable to ignore the entreaties of parents: 'It's only a dream, a nightmare.' But she *knew*.

One, for instance, took place in a forest. Mossy, encircling pines. She remembers it well. Close to the very same witch's cottage that Hansel and Gretel stumbled into. In their shady circumference, the surrounding trees hid a monster. One made of flesh, albeit a different sort to her own. Dark flesh, cold flesh. She could 'see', without actually setting eyes on it, that its huge pointy head contained long jaws full of black teeth, more glittery than granite and harder than steel. Those fangs dripped gore over claws so sharp they could slice though dark flesh, cold flesh, and warm flesh like hers. It sniffed the air to scent her.

'But it's not real,' said her mother. 'It's only a dream,' cooed father.

Then, a school trip. The museum. And there it was: a dinosaur. Perhaps a tyrannosaurus rex. Maybe another species. She didn't know. But she recognised it from her dream. She had 'seen' it. Even before the diagrams and the artists' impressions and the long explanations about extinction.

In the same way she knows that in some place, right now, someone's nightmare is coming true.

But what is the point of dwelling on the night's deformed spectres? That will do more damage than good. Some things *should* be shut in dark cupboards at the back of the mind. And locked away there.

She gets up, shakes herself. Goes to the jug and bowl on the chest of drawers and pours out a measure, splashes water on her cheeks, washes her armpits with a lardy brick of soap. This helps.

The window is misty. Condensation slips down the long rectangular panes of glass transforming it into a foggy mirror. She cannot see the rain outside, but just as in her dreams, knows it is there. Some things you don't have to see to know that they are real.

Downstairs in the dining room Septimus is fully revived after the voyage. How can he be so transparent? How can he reveal naked anticipation in this way? It is verging on recklessness.

'Think of what can be *achieved*,' he trills.

'I hear what you are saying,' says the captain with a wink at Daphne as she surveys the buffet table.

'Nothing,' Septimus continues, 'is what it seems.'

Impatiently Daphne waits for a break in conversation, but Septimus cannot contain his excitement. She thinks he is being rash and goes over to the window, which is clearer down here, though also fog-stained. It is still dark outside. A cold wintry morning that blocks out the world. She knows what is on the other side of the street: a house, small. A block of concrete covered with corrugated iron, windows presented either side of the door in symmetry. One solitary, stunted and bare tree in the garden. She cannot see it but she knows that it is there.

The captain says, 'Miss Daphne, are you joining us?' and she has no other option than to take her place at the breakfast table.

She loads a small bowl with the lumpy porridge, dribbles syrup onto it and some extra milk. The latter feels a little too extravagant, so she stirs it in before returning to her place.

Then waits with a prickly energy racing through her. She does not like the way she fears the judgement of men, though acknowledges the fact it has been bred into her.

'Oh, yes,' says Septimus as she sits down. 'You two must already be acquainted.'

'We are,' says Daphne. The captain wears a smile on his lips that she has not seen before. His eyes are shining. She is not sure where this internal light comes from. Perhaps Septimus is suggesting something untoward has occurred? She counters defensively: 'There is only one table at Guðrún Gunnarsdóttir's house. The captain and I have taken breakfast together here and also shared a newspaper.' There is no warmth in her voice. In fact, her bloodless tone occasions a questioning glance from Septimus.

Yet the captain continues to be gracious. 'Indeed,' he says. 'Thank you. Would you like it back?'

'No, it's fine.' She knows she sounds priggish but somehow can't stop herself.

'I have just finished this,' he says and hands over a salmon-pink slip of paper. 'Not of the same calibre as your own publication, of course.'

The reference to her cover has her wobbling mentally, worrying if he has delved any deeper into her background and fake references. She takes the paper. It is thin, only two folded sheets, like most of the English-language newspapers here. 'Thank you,' she says, attempting to look professional. 'Anything I should note?'

'Apparently we Brits shall be keeping summertime all through the winter,' he says.

'Oh, splendid!' Septimus lightly claps his hands. He seems rather boyish this morning. Lighter in his mood than she has experienced so far. 'I do so hate turning the clocks back in autumn,' he says. 'Those dark winter nights.'

Each one of them falls into a moment of contemplation – pondering, she assumes, the darker ones that they are enduring in Iceland. Daphne thinks briefly of the deadly dim patches between the streetlights and last night's tramping footsteps.

Whatever the captain is thinking of, it brings a slight blush to his cheeks.

'Do excuse me,' he says and suddenly bows like a Russian courtier.

The gesture is oddly charming and softens Daphne towards him.

I must try to be nicer, she decides.

Septimus fetches another cup of coffee from the sideboard. 'I have asked Guðrún if we may have the room to ourselves after breakfast. Which, as I believe we are the only three guests at present, means now.'

She has not yet finished her porridge but scoops a final spoonful into her mouth.

'I will just fetch my notes,' says Septimus and sets his coffee cup down at the place opposite. 'If you write them up then I will submit a report to Major Spike when I see him.'

'As you wish,' says Daphne. Now she finally has her chance to expound upon the theory she and Anna talked through last night. 'I would like to talk to you about—'

But Septimus has gone already.

Gathering the utensils and crockery, she carries them into the kitchen, where Guðrún is sweeping the floor.

'No, no,' says the landlady, waving the broom at her. 'I will do that.' She relieves Daphne of her load.

'It's fine,' says Daphne, noticing these words sound much warmer than when she used them to address the captain. Why is that? It is not just his closeness to the editor of *The Times* that unnerves her.

'I will come in soon and clear,' says Guðrún, returning to the broom. A wisp of hair separates itself from the bun on the back of her head.

'Mr Strange would like us to have the room to ourselves. I think he has asked for that?'

'Yes, yes.' Guðrún does not appear aggrieved though there is something pursed about her mouth when she confirms it.

'For my newspaper work,' Daphne adds.

This effects a change. 'Ah, yes,' says Guðrún, wagging a finger at her temple and touching it slightly. 'Newspaper woman.' She smiles broadly, as if she is proud of her lodger, and puts her hands into the pockets of her pinny.

Daphne's not sure what to make of this but decides to try and flatter her hostess. 'I need to file my copy soon. And I'll certainly be mentioning your wonderful Icelandic hospitality. We are so grateful, Guðrún. Would you mind making sure that we aren't interrupted? And if it's all the same to you, I'd like to close the door?'

'I will make the fire up first,' says the landlady, her bright blue eyes blinking atop cheeks which are becoming prettily pinker.

Daphne thinks about declining the offer, if it is an offer not a statement, but also appreciates the warmth that will fill the room. 'Thank you,' she says, and ignoring her landlady's protestations, decides to speed things up by ferrying the tureen and the syrup pot back into the kitchen. Guðrún finishes sweeping the kitchen and comes into the dining room to take up the white embroidered tablecloth from the table. The oak underneath is gleaming. Guðrún runs a damp cloth over it. 'I will polish later,' she says.

'It is rather gorgeous,' Daphne says.

Guðrún's chest plumps out like a delighted pigeon's and she squirms with pleasure at Daphne's words. 'A wedding present,' she explains.

Septimus has now returned with armfuls of notepads and pens and lays them on the surface. Guðrún nods, seemingly pleased by the evidence of 'paperwork'. There is coffee to be had on the stove, she tells them, then opens its door and adds fuel to the fire. They thank her and at once get to work.

Septimus dictates his observations on Karlsson's latest performance.

It seems that he is less convinced the medium is a fraud than the women are. Judging by the responses from the audience, he has calculated that the man has a sixty percent accuracy rate, which is, apparently, above average. Although Karlsson had a coughing fit last night too. 'Perhaps he has weak lungs or is suffering from a seasonal cold,' Septimus remarks. 'Or nerves. Next line,' he tells Daphne. 'The manifestation of an ancient guildsman of Reykjavík, I suspect may well have been cheesecloth regurgitated from the stomach. An unpleasant smell tainted the air afterwards, which was probably due to digestive acids.'

Daphne turns her nose up.

'No, it wasn't pleasant,' says Septimus but does not linger on it. 'The spirit warned the population of an impending disaster on the water. Lead was mentioned.'

Feeling this may be her chance, she asks, 'Did his assistant hold up a card with a letter on it?'

Septimus pauses. 'His assistant? He performed alone.'

'Oh,' says Daphne. 'But did he mention a direction, east or west?'

Septimus takes a moment to look through his notes. 'No, not at all. Though he certainly hit home with a message to a young man. Absolutely right about his mother, apparently. Next line.

The mention of a female spirit by the name of . . .' When he sees Daphne has not moved, he stops dictating. 'What is it?'

She is trying to add it up. 'Yesterday my contact Anna and I reviewed his previous performance, line by line. We think he may be giving out weather information and alerting spies to any convoy on its way.'

Septimus's lower lip drops. He sits back and places his hands palm down on the table. 'That is quite an accusation to make, my dear. He did not refer to any such thing in my presence.'

'Let me get you the transcript,' she tells him, then remembers that she has left it at the newspaper office. 'Oh, confound it! I can fetch it from Anna for you to read.'

'I have to see Major Spike in ninety minutes,' he says.

That will not give her enough time to get the transcript and return. 'I'll bring it home tonight.'

'Are you not observing a séance?'

She nods. 'Indeed I am.'

'Very well. I also have a matter to attend to this evening, but I will meet you back here later and we can discuss it then.'

'But,' says Daphne, feeling the window of opportunity close, 'if we're right then we should alert the authorities so they can take action.'

'*If* you are right,' says Septimus. He steeples his hands and puts them under his chin, thinking. Then rubs his forehead as if trying to suppress an irksome thought. 'Daphne,' he begins. The way he says it does not sound good. It puts her in mind of her father's tone when she has done something wrong. 'I know you have been fast-tracked through the ranks, and yes, that is impressive as far as it goes. However, you do not, I believe, have the years of experience and training in these matters that fit you to draw conclusions such as this on your own.'

But, she thinks, she wasn't on her own. Anna agreed with her. 'Only,' she begins, aware any further assertions might infuriate him further, 'if our conclusions are correct, then there are lives at stake.' And adds 'sir' in an attempt to mollify.

Septimus frowns. She can feel his displeasure cool the air between them, as if an icy draft has come through the window. It chills her.

Up goes his chin. The index finger on his right hand appears to want to point at her, but he withdraws it, controlling the impulse, and instead clenches his fist. 'You, Miss Daphne,' he says, 'are not seeing the bigger picture. Karlsson clearly enjoys popularity here. How do you think the local people will feel if they see one of their own arrested by the British on the evidence of two young girls? One British, one a reporter.' He spits out the 't' and drags over the 'er', so that it sounds more like an insult than a job. 'No, no, no, we must be careful. We must investigate thoroughly before we act. Greater minds than yours will take the decisions on this.'

She can't stop herself, however. 'And the men at sea, on the convoy at risk? How will their families feel if they drown in the Atlantic? Particularly if they learned that there was prior warning of an attack.' She knows she has spoken out of turn with the allusion to leaked intelligence, but there is no stopping her now. 'And that the authorities did nothing?'

His expression neutralises. All emotion is wiped away; a shutter has come down over his face. He is clearly not used to being challenged by a 'young girl'. 'Do you know how many people a convoy involves?'

She thinks he is being rhetorical so says nothing. He persists. 'Do you? How many ranks of command, admirals and members of the war cabinet would be required to take time out of their busy schedules to consider evasive action? How many troops and marines would be affected?'

Now he expects an answer. She has no idea so shakes her head.

'Hundreds, if not thousands! Now would you like me to go and tell them that Daphne Devine, magician's *assistant*, would like them to change their strategy because she and her girlfriend have visited a clairvoyant?'

Her cheeks are burning. Now he has put it like that she feels deep shame. Though there is still that thing inside her, that nub of defiance her parents and teachers were always warning would get her into trouble, which rears up now. 'But surely this *is* intelligence?'

He sighs and bends across the table, taking the paper she has written on. 'I will finish this myself.' Then he gets up and walks across the room. Just before he opens the door, he pauses and says, 'You are not the only agent we have on the island, you know. Some have been here for years. Not days.'

He turns the doorknob and she hears him mutter. She is not sure what he says but thinks it is something like 'Silly little girl.'

## CHAPTER ELEVEN

Anna has dressed up for tonight's séance. She has scarlet lipstick coating her mouth and her lashes are not fair like her hair but dark.

'It is to be hosted by Olga Jónsdóttir,' she says as Daphne falls in step with her. 'A widow of great wealth.'

The night is clear and cold, but the wind is whipping up anything that is not fastened down. Daphne glimpses a stray length of fabric – blue satin – peep from Anna's heavy coat.

She feels her own coat weighing upon her like armour. Underneath it, her suit. Though of pale pink with a decorative thread running through, tonight she wonders if it will appear too ordinary, lacking in elegance and style. However, it will protect her, should that be necessary. A few triggers, and levers manipulated at speed, and she will be armed. The thought of such deadly transformation wearies her.

'I am not dressed in eveningwear,' she says.

'You need not be,' Anna replies in her stony voice. 'You are here as a professional observer.' Then, before she can reply, 'Were you able to speak with Major Spike?'

'No,' says Daphne. At this Anna stops in her tracks. Daphne continues a few steps more then turns back.

Anna's face is impassive apart from a deep line that hangs horizontally above her eyebrows.

'Sorry,' says Daphne. 'He wasn't there.'

Moving again, her friends eyebrows hoist up her forehead replacing the frown. An explanation is expected.

'I tried,' Daphne bleats.

'What about this Severus? The person you collected from the ship?' In other circumstances the clumsy translation might have made Daphne smile, but she feels Anna's disappointment sharply and cannot raise herself up.

'I spoke with him. He is not convinced.' She doesn't say why, wishing to protect her friend from her superior's scathing criticism. 'More evidence needs to be gathered before we can pass on the intelligence to . . .' She pauses. Who would it go to? She can't think so says, 'The higher-ups.' And points stupidly into the air.

Anna's breath comes out like angry smoke. 'Surely it must be passed up the chain of command at once and they can decide? The commanders are paid good money to make such judgements.'

'It's a matter of persuading them,' Daphne urges her. 'All actions have consequences.'

She is thinking of diplomatic relations on the island and the reaction of the ranks Septimus detailed. But Anna says, 'Yes – young men will die. Be blown apart!'

'I know. I know.' The reporter is articulating Daphne's own misgivings. She feels sheepish as she explains, 'This is war. There are so many different areas of activity, we are just a small part of huge and complex operations. We cannot move forward on guesswork alone. We need to be certain, have solid information.'

She cannot see Anna's face as she barges past and thunders on ahead, but she hears what she says: 'Then we will get it tonight.'

And suddenly, as if she was shaking out a bed sheet with her mother, billowing it up and down before pegging it to the line, doubt rushes upon her like an updraft: why is Anna so intent on this? They cannot be absolutely certain they are right. Not yet.

False allegations and disinformation may work very well for the other side. It makes her question why Anna is so determined to get this message through. Where does that willpower come from? Is it rooted in good faith?

The night becomes chillier as they walk on in darkness. Anna does not speak and Daphne does not wish to be spoken to. Disordered emotions whirl within: frustration, confusion, dismay and something else. Something darker that tumbles around like a raven's feather caught in a cross-breeze. She does not like it.

Thankfully there is no time to think on it for they have arrived outside the address where the séance will be held. It is a very large house with a balustrade on the first floor and a turret on the third. For a moment Daphne is besieged by images of castles and fairytales. Then the front door opens, silhouetting a man standing before it. He steps over the threshold and into the light and Daphne recognises the build and the trilby hat of the stranger Karlsson met in the café she followed him into.

'Come,' says Anna, when she sees Daphne staring, and they both hurry up the steps to the grand front door, which is painted red like letterboxes at home and has leaded glass in the transom. A servant in a frilled apron, perhaps the housekeeper, stands just inside the hall, taking the coat and trilby from the man. As he turns to thank her, the light falls on his face and Daphne recognises him: it is the picture house manager.

Of course, it would be perfectly reasonable for him to meet a performer, and she questions once more her conviction that Karlsson is guilty. Yet the manager would also know who had bought tickets to the show and those details might prove exceedingly helpful to the medium in some of his revelations.

Though that is fraud, not espionage. If anything, information on such a matter should be given to the Reykjavík Police to deal with.

She hands her coat, like Anna does, to the housekeeper, who shuffles them towards a fine dining room, or is it a parlour? Or perhaps it is both for two large rooms have been opened into one. At the far end, in front of a great bow window, curtained against the night by green velvet, there is a circular table dressed in satin and lace cloths reaching down to the floor. Upon it, candles. Only one is lit.

In one corner there is a lamp. In another a fire burns in a hearth. She enters the parlour and sees it has a window seat and several armchairs, only one of which is being used. Instead, the guests are standing with their drinks, making small talk. Anna immediately walks up to a man in a dinner suit. He is deep in conversation with a matronly woman whose large bulk is contained in a black-and-white embroidered dress.

But before she can follow Daphne is intercepted. A man steps in front of her. Karlsson's hair glistens. She can smell his cloying cologne, which is almost overpowering and makes the back of her throat smart.

'Good evening, Daphne Dione-Smith.' The clairvoyant executes a low, theatrical bow. Daphne stands stock still and forces her cheeks to lift and contract, squeezes out a smile. When he rights himself, he takes her hand and kisses it. 'The scribe from overseas,' he says.

She laughs as if this is nothing, as if she is used to men kissing her hand and flirting with her.

Lowering her eyelids, she flutters her lashes. 'Good evening, Mr Karlsson.' Tonight his face seems more moon-shaped and paler than ever.

'Please,' he says, 'Sindri. So delighted you were able to make it.' He lets go of her hand with performative reluctance.

She feels the skin where he has kissed her. Once more his lips have left a residue of cold saliva, yet she cannot wipe it off. To do so would be an affront.

Taking her elbow, he guides her towards the nearest group.

Anna sees them and steps back a little to let them into the circle. Daphne steals a look at the older woman in the armchair who must surely be the owner of the house. But Karlsson moves her past Anna to a middle-aged woman with dark hair streaked with white, who is smoking a cigarette.

'Olga,' he says to her, 'may I present Miss Daphne Dione-Smith.'

'Ah,' says their hostess. Glossy beading is threaded through her dress, which is fringed with black tassels. It is all so glittery that even when she does not move, the light winks and catches on her, giving the impression of a roiling sea reflecting constellations above. Her very large bosom supports rows and rows of pearls. Daphne sees them rise as the woman's gaze strays over her. Under this inspection she becomes aware of her suit, worn for days now. *Too ordinary.* Then Olga's face creases and she receives a smile. 'Please make yourself comfortable, Daphne. A drink?'

'Yes, please,' she says, hoping Karlsson will let go of her arm. Olga beckons to a young maid in the corner, holding a tray of drinks. On her mistress's instruction, she steps forward to offer a glass of champagne. Daphne's surprise at encountering such an exotic and pricey drink is evident for Olga laughs. 'We may be at the end of the world here but we are still *of* the world, my dear.'

A little colour flames Daphne's cheeks. She immediately transforms her face into a mask of mild delight – the corners of her mouth twitch, enhancing the Cupid's bow shape of her lips. Her deep-green eyes widen. She tilts her head in the direction of her hostess and says, 'Oh, just marvellous, marvellous.' She knows from experience this simpering and gauche performance works wonders on both women and men three or more decades her senior. It is part of the arsenal of tricks derived from the theatre, and put to good use outside of it.

She is performing now as she raises her glass in a toast to Olga, who is pleased to have cut a sophisticated figure before her young guest.

Karlsson has disappeared.

Daphne leans forward to clink glasses with her hostess.

'This house is haunted,' says a loud voice in her ear. She turns and sees a man who is definitely three decades her senior. If she had been quick enough she would have brought out the simper again. However, his proximity and words cause her to shudder. This time she camouflages her reaction with a twist of her shoulders and a little titter. In case anyone has been quick enough to sight the involuntary shiver, she puts her hand over her mouth in a coquettish pose. It is a gesture that Jonty has told her is indicative of shyness and puts others at ease. Although, at the same time, it is fair enough surely to be squeamish about hauntings. Or is it that if one attends a séance one should be inured to fear of the supernatural?

The man with the golden moustache and matching slicked-back hair adds a chuckle in time with Daphne's giggle. 'Oh, yes,' he says and leans in ever-closer. 'My wife thinks it's a dog.'

Daphne cannot stop herself from inching away from him: he is far closer than common decency allows. Rather, than British decency allows. Perhaps the Icelanders don't mind so much. He sidles yet closer. 'I had the impression,' he says with a wink, 'the phantom was a small child.'

She is not sure if Olga senses her discomfort, but the older woman wiggles her fingers in front of his nose and says, 'Torfi, do stop teasing the poor girl.' Oh, thinks Daphne – Torfi. This must be the shipping magnate. The hostess steadily elbows the man back and in a stage whisper, as if confiding in Daphne, says, 'He is an awful wag, you know.'

'Guilty as charged,' Torfi says, now at least four very welcome feet away. He raises his free hand in surrender. In the other he holds a glass of champagne, three-quarters drained.

'Torfi, allow me to present Daphne Dione-Smith of the *New York Times*.' Olga dips her head graciously as she makes the introduction.

'Oh, my,' says Torfi and drops a brief bow. 'Brains *and* beauty. *Very* pleased to meet *you*.'

'The pleasure is mine,' says Daphne, squirming under his roving eye. 'Although I am in fact only a reporter for the London *Times*. We are separate publications.' She hopes she has got that right.

He holds his glass up to her in a toast. 'From either institution, you are most welcome here.' Then he finishes his champagne. 'Please come and meet my wife, Greta.' He takes her arm firmly and pulls. Daphne sees him nod to the maid, who intercepts them with the tray of drinks. He pauses to swap his empty for a fresh one then guides Daphne towards another woman, about the age of their hostess, who is sitting in the armchair by the window. 'Your youth and vitality will cheer her.'

Although of the same generation, Torfi's wife could not be more different. Instead of Olga's glamorous dress, she wears the outfit that Anna had described as Sunday Best. True, her black jacket and long skirt are made of fine fabrics: silk damask with velvet cuffs. Over her white hair, which is long and hangs down her back, a velvet cap is pinned. Ivory silk is wrapped around her neck and tied at the front in a bow.

Torfi introduces her as 'My beloved Greta'. The woman's eyes are so glazed that for a moment Daphne wonders if she is blind. But then the pupils contract and roam over Daphne's face. The woman barely registers the presence of another human being. Greta's lips move but no words come out. She moves her hand to her heart and croaks, faintly – oh, so faintly – 'Forgive me.'

With a jolt Daphne realises the woman's face is unlined. Her snow-white locks, evident frailty and sluggish movements suggest someone much older yet her skin is testament to the fact that she can't be more than forty. Perhaps younger.

'Oh, excuse me,' says Torfi. 'There's Jón, just arrived. Olga's cousin. I must speak to him.'

And he turns, leaving Daphne standing in front of this pale marble statue of a woman, feeling marooned. Her stomach plummets and for a moment she thinks Greta is glaring at her, then she realises her gaze stretches way beyond anything in this room, into a realm only she can see. Sighing, she lets her head swing down again, as if she has not the energy to hold it upright. Is she staring at her feet? Daphne wonders. For a moment she worries that her own shoes are too shabby for such palatial surroundings. The intensity of Greta's focus makes her uncomfortable. She shifts her feet together so they, at least, are neat.

The movement prompts Greta to look up. As if seeing her for the first time, her eyes widen and she asks, 'Have you lost someone, dear?' And Daphne realises that the parasite sucking the life out of this poor lost woman is grief.

Her instinct is to say no, for it has been a while, but that would also denigrate the relationship, so she tells the truth and says, 'Yes.'

'That's what I thought,' says Greta.

Cold fingers slide round Daphne's wrist.

'Yes, I thought so,' Greta says again, her voice becoming stronger. 'You can tell, can't you?'

The woman tugs her. 'And have you made contact?' she asks greedily. Her eyes are no longer hazy but flickering with animation. 'Have you?' She moves her other hand and grips onto

Daphne's arm so that for a moment she is a little afraid, as if Greta is a drowning woman who may pull her under.

Trying to extricate herself, Daphne shakes her head. 'No, I haven't,' she says, knowing she will find finger-shaped bruises there when she undresses tonight. 'Not yet.'

These final two words provoke an immediate change in the woman, who lets her go.

Desperation is replaced by a beatific smile. 'That's why you are here. That's why we are *all* here,' says Greta and lolls back in her chair, resuming her semi-reclining position. Daphne watches her expression slide into vacancy again. Greta's eyes lose their focus, as if a dark cloud has settled over her face.

'There you are.' It is Olga this time who scoops Daphne's arm under hers. 'I see you have met Greta. Let me introduce you to the others.' And she leads her back to the main group. 'I'm sorry about Torfi's wife,' she says. 'Come, meet Kári Abelsson and June. June has lost her brother but she wears it much more lightly. A son, of course, is a greater loss, but Greta can put a dampener on these soirées. She's quite terrible in her grief.'

Terrible, Daphne thinks. Why is some grief more socially acceptable than others? Though it is quite ill-mannered to speak of Greta's burden in such a way, she does not want to be brought low by *terribleness,* and the thought that it could be contagious flashes through her mind.

As they weave through the small crowd, a young man in evening dress intercepts them.

'It won't be long now, will it?' he asks.

'No,' says Olga, and comes to a halt beside him. 'This is Jón Jakobsson, my cousin. And a doctor,' she says proudly.

They shake hands. Younger than Olga, his moustache is fine and shaped with wax. His hands have long elegant fingers. 'I do need to get on tonight,' he says.

'Have a drink,' says Olga and points him in the direction of the maid. Then she pushes Daphne towards a couple who have seated themselves by the fire.

'Hello to you.' The woman who has been introduced as June shines brightly in the lamplight. From the way in which she pronounces English it seems that her underlying accent may be different from the other guests'. Her hair is dark, worn coiled on her head in a fashionable style; her skin darker than Daphne has come across in Iceland so far, and she wears eye makeup too. 'My husband Kári,' she says, extending a hand with varnished nails towards a stout man in evening dress. He flicks a lighter and attends to her cigarette.

Puffing on it, June breathes out smoke as she asks, 'How are you finding Reykjavík?'

'Oh,' Daphne says. 'Different to London, of course. But I'm enjoying it very much.'

'Are you covering the occupation?'

Before she can answer, Olga's voice rings out and she says something in Icelandic for everyone to hear.

'You'll have to tell me later,' June tells Daphne. 'It seems we must take our places at the table. The time is now.'

They are placed around the circular table draped with velvet cloths: male then female then male. There are ten of them in total. Five men: Karlsson, Helgi the theatre manager, Torfi with the golden moustache, Kári, June's husband, and Olga's cousin Jón. Anna sits next to him, Helgi on the other side. Daphne had supposed that they would be given seats outside the circle but it appears they are to be active participants. Neither of them will be able to make notes. She must pay close attention.

The maid dims the lamp and draws curtains that separate this area from the formal parlour, sealing them all in. Daphne slides her legs under the tablecloth and tries not to fidget, but tension is creeping up her spine.

The only illumination comes from an elegant candelabra on the table. It has six candles but only one is lit. Some minute signal passes between Karlsson and their hostess, who stands and lights the remaining five. They are purple. Daphne knows candle colours have their own correspondences: blue for protection, white for purity. But purple, particularly this deep shade? She is unsure what it signifies. Something that guides the dead?

The shipping magnate, Torfi, is on her right. On her left sits Karlsson. Before him on the table is a wooden box. With corners embossed in gold, it looks antique.

Torfi whispers in her ear, 'That candelabra is a gift from me. It comes from the great opera house in Vienna. Have you been? So ornate. Stately architecture. Admirable. Phantoms always attach themselves to such places, though that building has two, I hear. I hope the candelabra hasn't brought one of them back.'

Daphne stares at it. Now that all six candles are burning it has taken on a sinister, gothic aspect. A golden cherub supports the central column. Twining leaves and vines embellish the others. The smell of cedar permeates the air.

Beside her Karlsson sits up tall in his chair. 'I know most of you are accomplished in this field, but for the benefit of tonight's new guests,' he nods at Anna then smiles, sickeningly, at Daphne, 'I shall remind you of the preparations we must make to pave the way for the spirits of the departed, to enable their passage to this place.' He swallows loudly. 'Rid your minds of the woes and distractions of this mundane life. Look into the flames.'

They flicker and bob above the candles' waxy stems. The room has become very quiet. The curtains have insulated them from the rest of the world. She cannot hear any sounds from the street, just the breathing of those in the circle.

Bowing his head, Karlsson moves his hands to the box. He

uses a key to unlock it. There is a contraption within that he removes. Closing the lid, he places it on top of the box. It is a peculiar sight. A miniature gallows-like structure, made of wood, but from which hangs not a body, but a bell.

'The night is clear tonight,' says Karlsson. 'I feel conditions for contact are good.'

To Daphne's other side, Torfi twitches. 'How many do you think we will see here,' he asks.

Minutely Karlsson shrugs. 'Perhaps two. I don't know. If we are lucky, three or more. It is not in our control. We must be as open as we can be.'

He pauses and it seems to Daphne that the room grows darker as he addresses the circle. 'Most of you gathered here tonight are aware that death is just a transition, the beginning of another journey. Please,' he says, 'join hands so we might meet those who are travelling.'

Torfi takes Daphne's right hand tightly, then loosens it. His palm is moist. Again, she feels the urge to pull away but banishes the impulse.

To her left she feels Karlsson's limp fingers. They twitch as he speaks up. 'The spirits may announce themselves by ringing the bell. But first, I have a request for you all: although you may be shocked by what happens tonight, you must not,' he stops for a moment to underline his command, 'you *must not* break the circle.'

A mild flutter of fear runs through Daphne. She remembers a similar instruction given while she held hands in a circle, back in summer, on a night that ended in destruction and a panorama of hell. Staring into the flame dancing atop a purple candle, she cannot block out memories of devastation: blackened trees, burning like people with their hair on fire. The image prompts a shudder. Torfi tightens his grip on her hand. She darts a glance at him and sees him smile as if to comfort.

But she does not wish to appear weak so straightens her spine and lifts her chin, then sees the others at the table have bowed their heads, so follows suit.

'Spirits,' calls out Karlsson, 'are you with us tonight?'

Nothing.

Tension crawls across her shoulders like a black spider. She is aware of the darkness behind her, quivering with shadows cast against the curtains and walls.

Again, the medium speaks. 'One ring for yes, two for no.'

And again there is no response.

Only the beating of her heart, which has accelerated.

Is it her imagination or has the temperature dropped?

No, it must be that she is sitting still. They have all stopped talking and moving.

The velvet plush of the tablecloth makes the soft undersides of her wrists tingle.

She hears a sigh: female, quiet. Greta? Olga? June sits over on the other side of Torfi. Perhaps it came from her. Daphne does not think it would have been Anna, who will be doing her best to blend into the background.

Someone sniffs.

Karlsson's breathing has become audible. He sucks in the thick air.

Suddenly the bell rings.

Everyone at the table starts. Daphne looks up and sees the bell is still trembling. Beyond it she can see Kári's face: eyes wide, mouth open. He looks towards Karlsson, as does she, and they see that his head is thrown back.

'Spirit, are you there?' he asks, eyes rolling to the ceiling.

The bell rings again.

Though these are evidently seasoned séance attendees, she hears gasps echo around the circle.

Karlsson's head jerks forward and flops onto his chest. He

wheezes, coughs, then his arms tense and his frame stiffens. His head comes up, with a clicking noise. The eyes stare over Olga's head.

A gurgling sound, then, 'Mamma.'

The voice is high-pitched, strangulated.

Over on the other side of the table Greta jumps. She raises her left hand, which is just as quickly pulled down again by Helgi. 'Einar!' she says, though it is more like a wail.

'Mamma. I see you.' Karlsson's eyebrows twitch. His mouth forms a weak smile. Sweat dampens his upper lip.

Greta leans in. 'Einar, is that you?' Her voice is as fragile as a glass bell.

'Angels,' Karlsson says, in a higher pitch still. 'Angels all around me.'

Torfi tightens his grip on Daphne's hand. 'Is that you, boy?' he asks.

The medium's head slowly rotates towards him. 'Don't be unhappy, Papa. Everything is all right.' It is a melancholic expression that carries with it a woeful intonation.

Torfi breathes out heavily. He tries to speak but his voice catches. Daphne knows if she looks at him she will find his cheeks are moist.

His hand trembles in hers.

'I . . .' says Karlsson, then his neck sags. 'I . . .' His head flops back onto his chest.

'Einar?' Greta calls out.

But Karlsson remains mute. His shoulders slump forward. For a moment he seems to sway then his head straightens once more. 'The connection is diminishing.' It is his own voice this time. 'The spirit has withdrawn. Greta,' he says, turning his face to hers, 'I felt great peace. The dead often wish the living to know that they are still with them. "I see you," is what he meant to say. That is the phrase I hear from them.'

'Is there any more from him?' she asks. Her face is lined with pain.

'Not that I can feel,' he says. 'But wait. Look into the flames.'

Daphne feels prickly. Unnerved. The air weighs down upon her.

'I see, I see,' says Karlsson, and they all turn their focus upon him.

This time his eyes are wide.

Torfi's hand slides against hers. It is so clammy.

'There,' says Karlsson. 'In a place. North. I see a book. Precious. I hear the words – wait, wait. I hear: "Land of Sorcery". The book is opening. I hear a voice: "Here, affirmation sought by the winged man." Is that what he is saying? There are pages within. Poetry. No, great prophecy. "Upon speaking of wars, the United Isle will hold him in contempt. Through tyranny in the isle esteem changing."'

'Dash it,' says Jón. 'Isn't that Nostradamus? That's Nostradamus!'

'I have heard you, spirit. There are pages, words that have been lost to us. Now found. For years unseen. A vanished vision . . .'

The doctor, Jón, is rigid. His hands grip Anna's and Olga's so tightly his knuckles show through the skin. 'Where is it, Sindri? Where is the book?'

For a moment Karlsson's eyelids flutter uncontrollably. 'I see a great fjord. An ogre in stone . . . I see . . .'

'Ouch!' Daphne does not mean to say it out loud: Karlsson's fingers have contracted round hers like a vice, crushing them together so hard it hurts. Her hand is pulled back towards him. His shoulders, abruptly, begin to jerk.

A great whistling comes out of his mouth. Fast but clogged, congested. He is struggling to breathe. His neck is not right. She cannot tell how she knows this, but she can see the muscles rippling within, like little serpents wriggling under the skin. A gagging sound. Daphne's hand is yanked towards his chest. She is not sure what to do and looks at Anna.

Olga's voice is stern. 'Do not break the circle.'

But Daphne cannot sit still. She rises. 'He's choking.'

Torfi grips her other hand. 'Sit!' And he pulls her back down.

On the table the bell starts to ring, not once or twice, but back and forth, back and forth, without stopping.

Karlsson's shoulders spasm violently.

His mouth opens. 'Euayaymichayeal . . .'

It is nonsense. Or is it Icelandic? She is beginning to panic. The man is clearly in trouble, his mouth opening and closing like a fish on a bank, lips turning blue. The pupils of his eyes have rolled back into his head.

'Someone needs to do something,' she begins.

He jerks forward. His face snaps up.

The sight is shocking. 'Dear God.'

Karlsson's eyes are completely white, his skin glistens. Words and saliva fly out of his mouth. 'The hand of death is on your shoulder.' His voice is gravel.

For a moment she is paralysed by fear. Then the whole of Karlsson's upper body jerks. His head moves up and down with unnatural speed, as quickly as a bird's wing.

'Hvað er þetta?' It is June's voice. Daphne can tell from the pitch that the woman is alarmed too. This is not normal.

As Karlsson shudders, a sound that has started low in his chest erupts like the howl of a wolf. 'The mountain shakes.' The words come with such force they snuff out two of the candle flames.

Someone whimpers.

'See her fear,' says Karlsson, twisting and turning as if he was in a fight. In the struggle he releases Daphne's hand. 'Quick!' His voice becomes a scream. 'Brace, brace, brace—'

Then it is as if he is discharged roughly from the grip of an unseen foe. His body seems to empty like a balloon leaking air.

A blast of cold air blows through the room, extinguishing the remaining light, and they are plunged into darkness.

For a moment there is silence.

Then Karlsson cries out in great pain.

The legs of his chair screech back violently. There is a thud: the medium has been thrown to the floor.

Sounds all around: scuffling, shrieks, footsteps, orders barked in the native tongue.

A light comes on.

Though she does not know how she got there, Daphne is on her feet by the wall.

On the floor Karlsson is convulsing.

Helgi shouts, 'Jón, Jón!'

Torfi calls for the maid.

Then the doctor is at Karlsson's side. 'A seizure! Help me.'

'Out!' screams Olga. Then something in Icelandic that Daphne nevertheless understands. 'Everybody leave now!'

Someone grabs her arm and she is rushed out of the room.

CHAPTER TWELVE

'Það eru mörg undur í höfuðkúpu!' Anna shakes her head. The words have come out in a hurry, all under her breath, straight from the part of her throat that is beneath her chin.

'God, God, God help us!' says Daphne, panting. 'What *was* that?' Her own breathing has not yet slowed.

'I don't know. I don't know.'

'Was it meant to happen?'

The pair of them are walking down the street as fast as they can. Without communicating, both have acknowledged the need to put as much distance as possible between themselves and the scene of chaos at Olga Jónsdóttir's house.

'I don't know, I don't know,' says Anna again. Daphne notes a quickening in the delivery.

It is dark. Daphne cannot see past the shadows covering her friend but thinks she is wringing her hands.

Stress is contracting her own muscles, hunching her over as she hurries along.

'Will he be all right?' she asks.

Anna stops walking. 'I don't know. Stop asking me. I have only as much information as you.'

'Yes, sorry,' says Daphne. Anna may be her guide to this new landscape she has arrived in, but not to the stranger one that Karlsson and his kind inhabit. 'At least the doctor is there with him,' she says, more or less to herself.

'I am shocked.' Anna's statement is customarily bald, and yet Daphne is surprised to hear her state it, as if the aloof journalist has given away some secret part of herself.

'Me too,' says Daphne. 'I wasn't expecting that. I'm not sure it was part of the performance. But you can never tell.'

'To hurt oneself like he did? No.'

'Though if he's paid?'

Anna says something that sounds like 'Gah'. 'It is too . . .' She searches for a word. 'Is not comely. It lacks elegance.' She goes on, 'I thought he had his eye on you. That you had caught his fancy. Pride is there. He wishes you to think well of him and would not humiliate himself so.'

Daphne contemplates this and concludes that her friend's observation may well be true. 'So was it real?' She does not really want to know the answer.

Anna says again, 'I don't know.' It is the phrase of the evening. Then she huffs, 'We should not talk about this here.'

And Daphne realises they are standing in the street. The moon emerges from behind a bank of clouds. The air is crisp, cold coming through her gloves.

'Follow me,' says Anna. Or rather commands. 'My home is not far. We can speak there. You must be quiet though: my mother will be asleep.'

Nodding, Daphne quickens her step to catch up with her friend.

Her loaded heels slide.

There is frost on the pavement.

Anna has a notepad on her lap and looks more complete with it. 'Unsettling,' she says.

Daphne couldn't agree more.

The fire in the hearth has been built up from dying cinders and the parlour is becoming warmer. Almost cosy. She pulls her chair closer. Anna has given her a fleecy blanket, which is wrapped loosely around her shoulders.

The décor must be Anna's mother's choice for there is lots of lace in this room: a coverlet on the chair where her head might rest, fringing on the curtains and mantel over the fireplace, a doily on the small table on which her cup of coffee stands. Anna has stirred in sugar and something which tastes like cognac but is not. Her friend has assured her she would never touch Black Death.

They are un-numbing themselves from both the cold and the shock of the evening. The sweetness of the hot drink helps. And the liquor too.

Now Anna's fingers are warm enough, she is making as many notes as she can before the memory fades.

Daphne watches as her friend stops writing and frowns. 'What?' she says.

'Why did the ghost child speak in English?' asks Anna.

That is not what is bothering Daphne, but she drags her mind back to it and says, 'I don't know.'

'Greta and Torfi would speak Icelandic to their son, I'm sure. Though he may have been learning English.'

'One explanation could be that the words are filtered through Karlsson's consciousness, which was tuned into English tonight on my account,' Daphne says, and thinks back. 'In fact, everyone spoke English to me.'

'To you, yes,' says Anna. The lines on her forehead have not diminished. 'Not to me.'

Out of everything that has happened, Daphne regards this as a minor point to fixate upon, and so brushes it aside, eager to discuss more pertinent concerns: '"The hand of death is on your shoulder"? He said that, didn't he?' Repeating the words sends another chill down her back. She pulls the blanket firmly around her.

'He was looking in your direction.' Anna's eyes narrow as she summons to mind the seating arrangements. Daphne can see her picturing it in her mind's eye. 'Though Torfi and June were close to you. Karlsson might have addressed the remark to either of them.'

'I am quite sure he was looking at me.' Daphne tries to summon the image but it is lost amidst the more dramatic memories.

'Really? You are certain?' Anna tilts her head to the side.

Daphne is being observed. It is important to be as accurate as possible so she casts her mind back with greater effort and the ghastly image rears up. His eyes were pure white, the pupils had rolled so far back in his head. And yet she had felt he was looking at her. Or beyond her? Now she can't be sure. She shrugs.

The end of the pen has found its way to Anna's mouth and she sucks on it like a cigarette. 'Could it have been a threat: if you continue, you will find danger – death?'

Daphne does not answer. She is remembering his last words. '"The mountain shakes,"' she says. '"See her fear. Quick! Brace, brace."' It makes no sense.'

'Oh, that is apparent to me.' says Anna flatly. 'Karlsson is the mountain. I have heard him compare himself before. "I am the summit!" or something similar. When he said it, he was . . .' She extends her arms and shakes them. 'He had fierce tremors going through his person, like so.' Her body trembles dramatically as she points to Daphne. Then she lowers her arms and sits back. 'Perhaps he looked at your face and read in your expression that you were feeling great alarm and distress for him. And so when he said, "See her fear," that was what he was observing at that time – your fear.'

'He said it out loud,' Daphne agrees. 'You're right, I was frightened that he might have a seizure. So when he saw my fear, it prompted him to, "Brace, brace, brace." Before his chair went back and the convulsions came upon him. He was warning *himself.*' Now it makes sense. And yet, and yet, there is still unease coiling and uncoiling in the pit of her stomach, like a snake that wishes to rise.

Satisfied, Anna moves on. 'His answer to Torfi's question – how many tonight?' She takes the pen from her mouth and runs it over her notebook, quoting from it: 'Perhaps two. If we are lucky, three or more.'

'Oh, yes,' says Daphne, as the familiarity of the phrase strikes her. 'That was the same at the picture house. Well, very similar.'

'That is my feeling too,' says Anna. 'So, if this *is* a code to indicate information of use to the enemy, "perhaps two" might signal that the message will come through the second spirit who appears.'

In her mind Daphne sees Karlsson's eyes fixed somewhere above Olga's head. 'Though he saw the book then, on the second turn, didn't he? Somewhere in the north?'

'Muttered something that Jon identified as "Nostradamus". Who is he? A mage?'

'Nostradamus?' asks Daphne. 'He lived in the sixteenth century.' Anna's eyebrows are high on her forehead; she is evidently surprised by Daphne's knowledge. 'My boss Jonty – I mean, The Grand Mystique – thought about doing a trick along the lines of Nostradamus's famous prophecies,' she explains. 'We went to the British Library and did some research. But the texts were too difficult, too wordy, for our audience. So we didn't follow it up.'

'He was a fake?' asks Anna.

'Oh, no,' says Daphne, almost defensively. 'Nostradamus was a learned man, a seer. His first almanac of predictions was so successful, he was appointed to advise influential people. He used astrology, if I recall, and was also a healer. Many of his prophecies have come true.'

'Have they?' Anna's scepticism is evident. 'He is respected then?'

'Oh, yes.' Daphne nods her head vigorously. 'Some say he predicted this war.'

Anna's reaction is muted: a minute nod of acknowledgement then she goes back to her notes. 'I have recorded Sindri's words as accurately as I could: "Affirmation sought by the winged man." Then, "Of wars, the United Isle holds him in contempt. Through tyranny in the isle esteem changes."'

Daphne tries to think but can't summon the detail. 'As far as I can recall. The point is this – he was quoting a section that has probably been interpreted widely as relevant to this war. If you assume "The United Isle" is the United Kingdom, which is a name we in Britain are also known by, then you can assume that the "him" they hold in contempt is Hitler. Is he the winged man too?' She pauses to let her brain catch up with her mouth and remembers once more the woman in the theatre – *his wings . . . they smoke.* There are connections here. 'Is it a message to someone else? A flag? A clue for some recipient to pass on?'

Anna shrugs. 'We cannot know one way or the other. We are not enemy spies. Or higher-ups,' she finishes with evident bitterness.

In the grate the fire spits. Daphne jumps. Anna rises from her chair and puts another log on the coals.

Once it has caught, she replaces the poker in its holder by the hearth and takes her seat again. 'So Sindri says these prophecies were "lost". But now, because of his vision, has he "found" them? In the north?' She waits for her friend to respond.

Daphne's eyes are glassy.

'Daphne!' Anna calls out. 'Are you quite well?

The colour has drained from her cheeks. Slowly she says, 'I have read a document. Back at the—' Then stops herself. She would have said 'prison' but remembers the location of Section W must be closely guarded. 'Back home. I read a document, back home. The High Command in Germany – many of them are interested in such things.' She thinks back to the tatty notes she Roneoed a lifetime ago. 'Astrology,' she says. In her mind she sees again the words that she glimpsed. The initials that related to the obsessions of those in the enemy government. 'Parapsychology, clairvoyance, occultism, something called psychokinesis and . . .' her pulse quickens. 'And Nostradamus.'

Anna swallows hard. 'Are you suggesting that they would be keen to get their hands on such a book?'

Daphne finds herself shivering. Why do those words still linger in her mind? Why do they have such power to frighten her? Even after all she has been through. No, she thinks, it is *because* of all she has been through. Answering she says, 'I should think so. Hitler stormed the Kunsthistorisches Museum when he unified Austria. He ordered the Imperial Regalia to be removed. It contains the Spear of Destiny. Such items are of great significance to him and the party leaders. The population over there already considers him some kind of Messianic figure. In their minds these religious objects add credence to his claims and ignite more passion, excite the belief that Germany will be victorious.'

Anna angles her head to the hearth and takes the poker again. She pushes it against the coal with more force than necessary. 'I have heard this,' she says. 'It is not rational.'

A small laugh escapes Daphne's lips. It is coloured with cynicism. 'The spirit of their nationalism is extreme. Hitler's phony rhetoric has driven out all reason. And that isn't a metaphor. Moderation, moderates and intellectuals, have been annihilated. Who can challenge him, when challenge means a death sentence?'

The words hang in the air for a moment.

Anna throws the poker on the floor. Her shoulders are rigid. 'How did we get to this?' she asks the fire. Then moving so that she faces Daphne, she leans across and touches her knee. Daphne starts at this unexpected touch. It is the first time any physical contact has been exchanged between them.

'I am so grateful,' says Anna, looking into Daphne's face, 'that it is you who has come, and not them.'

Me? thinks Daphne. Or us, the British? Though it doesn't matter, she appreciates the sentiment.

Removing her hand, Anna sits back in her chair. She takes her coffee and sips it. 'Strandasýsla is in the north,' she says, her eyes becoming focussed. 'It is known as the Land of Sorcery.'

This is new information. It contextualises Karlsson's prophecy. And something else rears up in the back of Daphne's mind. A memory. 'Hang on. Didn't your friend Kolbrún, when we met her at Hotel Borg, didn't she say that Karlsson has a grimoire? In the north?'

Anna's eyes stray to the drawn curtains behind Daphne's back. 'If I remember rightly, she said there are rumours of such.'

Sitting up, Daphne feels like she is following a thread. 'And now it seems that there may be this book with prophecies. He has alerted us to it.'

'Yes,' says Anna. 'And possibly German agents.'

'Do you think so?' asks Daphne, her mind going over the personalities gathered at the séance.'

Anna is pacing back and forth in front of the fire. 'With all we have discovered, it would be reckless not to alert your seniors. Or I can, through my contacts, though it will take longer. We don't know if Sindri Karlsson is leaking information, weather forecasts and the rest. We don't know if there is a convoy approaching.' She stops and stands in front of the fire and puts her hands on her hips. 'But if there is an artefact, like a grimoire of the prophecies of this Nostradamus, which may fire up the German people, then he's let everyone gathered at Olga's tonight hear of it. There could be an as yet unidentified person there with links to the Nazis. And *that* might well interest your superiors.'

The fresh revelation releases a surge of adrenaline in Daphne also. 'I will report this at once.'

'And if Major Spike is not there?' Anna bites a fingernail while she waits for a reply.

Daphne thinks back to her previous message. 'I won't go to him. I'll telegraph London directly.'

Anna has already retrieved Daphne's coat. 'No delay.'

She agrees. 'Me? I've left already.'

## CHAPTER THIRTEEN

Caught up as she was in the clamour of her internal voice, which stressed haste, it did not occur to Daphne to change into her washerwoman's clothes.

It was an error she did not realise she had committed until she came upon the sentry post once again.

The same soldier was manning it. 'Miss Essex,' he said, by way of greeting. And again she chided herself – what good was a disguise if she didn't mask her accent?

'Here for the signals again, Corporal Yorkshire.'

His gruff laugh reminded her of the men who clustered round the bar in some of the less salubrious salons of Soho frequented by Jonty. So she pressed on with the password, in no mood to make idle chit-chat or entertain him. 'The king has done well today.'

'That he has,' said the sentry and admitted her, lifting a wooden beam that had been hung across the small opening.

She wasted no time in getting to the Signals hut.

The soldier she had talked to previously was on the headsets. Another man, whom she had not come across before, took her message.

'Further enquiries made. Coat fits better. On previous fitting tailor reported stock. Imported from west. His fitting guide, in north, previews new fashions. From . . .' She paused then and wondered what word could be used to camouflage 'Nostradamus'.

Pressured by the need for haste, she gave up and wrote it down. 'From Nostradamus.'

The soldier took it and sighed.

This time, however, she urged him, 'It is important. Please transmit as soon as possible.' Then as an afterthought added to the message: 'Couturier's attendees: Jón Jakobson, Olga Jónsdóttir, Kári Abelsson + wife June, Torfi Birgisson + wife Greta, picture house manager Helgi.' She did not know his surname.

'Permission slip?' the signalman asked when she handed it over. 'From Major Spike?'

She had prepared her answer. 'It's being organised. You'll have to do it retrospectively.' He frowned his disapproval but she pressed on. 'Look, would you rather get ragged on by the higher-ups when they find out you delayed this communication for the sake of keeping up your paperwork, or will you believe me when I say lives may be at risk here? British lives. Take my word for it – this is urgent.' *Could* be urgent, she thought, but kept her nerve and held steady.

She saw him weigh it up in his mind, eyebrows creased. But then he had complied.

It is only now as she walks back to her lodgings that the reality of what she has done hits her. What will Major Spike say when he finds she has gone behind his back? It does not bear thinking about. And what of Septimus? He has been so quick to dismiss her concerns. She wonders if it is because of her youth, or because of her sex, or both. But that is of little significance – she has wilfully gone against orders.

The realisation forces a shudder. Is it possible she will be disciplined? Court-martialled?

Oh, goodness. Everything she has worked for in this new, strange career might come crashing down around her. And her mother has not yet been released from detention in the Isle of

Man. Has Daphne jeopardised that? How could she? Her mother's life is just as important as those on the convoy.

Or is it?

Carabella cannot hold a rifle or steer a boat. She cannot make any difference to the war effort.

Daphne's thoughts scramble like rats escaping a sinking ship.

No, she thinks. Stop it. Because what if she's right? What if her disobedient action does save lives? Or somehow skews the Nazi war machine? Then perhaps Hugh Devereaux will weigh in on her side. Though does he have influence over army higher-ups?

The click-clacking of her heels on the frosted pavement is adding to her irritation. Why can't the ingenious minds who dreamed up weaponised shoes cushion the sound they make? They must have been designed by men. Everything is made for men then customised for women, like they are an add-on. But this is very unwise – the city is quiet – she is like a siren sending out morse code with each step: I am here. Come and get me.

As if confirming this, she hears a harsh exhalation behind her.

At first shivers bristle down her spine. It is late. She is alone. Then she remembers the incident two nights since: the false alarm she experienced. Other people move around the city. Not everyone is part of this game of war. And so another paranoid thought is dismissed.

Now she breathes out more freely. Her breath forms clouds again. The night is clear. Clear and starry.

The footsteps, she thinks, have gone. Or perhaps they have fallen into time with her own.

Her nose is pinched with cold. She is glad she is not far from home. The pavements are now silky-white with ice. They glisten wildly. That is a strange way to describe their Arctic coating, but she thinks it is right. For each crystal seems as though it is dancing a reel: moving with elegant undulations while simultaneously changing, shifting colour from silver, to gold, now green.

It is as if someone has plucked the mundane lens from her eye and replaced it with one that perceives another spectrum.

She blinks in case her vision is playing tricks on her but sees the illuminated frost shine again in a wave of colour.

What is this? she thinks. Am I mad? And stops walking and lifts her gaze to look around.

The landscape has become utterly alien.

A stationary frost-covered vehicle reflects the colours: gold, azure, emerald green. The greenest of greens. Green like the boat in which the owl and the pussycat sailed.

Her gaze moves higher and . . . oh, my!

The universe is upon her.

Up above the rooftops there are planks of light. Great stripes of peacock green, as if God has cleft open the sky and let heaven shine down upon the city.

Light is all around.

Above her and reflected on the ground.

Shapes. Patterns.

Vibrant, shimmering colours – the essence of nature – fringed with the metallic hue of gold.

Unearthly.

Spectral.

The whole sky is shimmering with light.

Captivated, she can do no more than stare. It is a little scary.

Then fear is replaced by awe, and a phrase from her briefing passes through her head.

'Aurora borealis,' she says to no one.

The beauty of it, the beauty is so . . .

Surging through her bosom is the wish that Jack might be here, to share this with her.

A stipple effect, gem-bright, changes into waving piano keys before her eyes. Then a host of angels, outlined with God-gold, spreading their wings before morphing into a curtain of celestial light. And now a phoenix diving to earth, and now the wing of a moth.

The moon is no longer a dead planet, but an aperture – an eye watching from the other side of the sky.

It winks.

Can this all be real?

If she had not seen it, she would not believe it.

She feels an impulse, so strong, to remain still, unmoving in this magic, so as not to break the spell. She must soak it up, record it in her head so she may remember the way she feels now, the all-encompassing sensation of ethereal brilliance, of things in the universe that cannot always be seen but which have appeared tonight . . . let this never end. Let this—

—a tug at her waist. Two arms come down over her shoulders and clamp around her body, like a vice, shocking her from her reverie. She lets out a sharp breath.

For a moment she thinks one of the Huldufólk has come to whisk her away: she has glimpsed their kingdom and must pay the price. Her mouth opens and a surprised 'huh' comes out.

Then, in her ear, a voice: 'Æ þegiðu!'

A male voice.

The aroma of liquor and stale breath hits her: the scent of danger.

Her senses snap together so that she is instantly back down on earth, her brain functioning at full capacity.

What? Man.

Who? Unknown.

Intent? Malicious.

Arms pinned to her sides, she is jerked into the air. The assailant takes a step forward, then staggers under her weight and she falls to the ground feet first. Her heels screech as they connect with the icy pavement.

His grip momentarily loosens. She breathes out, makes

herself bigger, occupies more space, and then tenses all her muscles. At the same time her synapses flare, retrieving instructions, memories of training. Her right foot slides up and down her left heel in quick precise movements.

A deep grunt, his hands groping for her coat buttons.

Just in time, she hears a click in one heel. Both feet find firm ground. She tenses, changes her centre of gravity, pushes herself up full force. He stumbles forward and she kicks back.

Swish-slice-rip. There goes the fabric of his trousers.

Slash. She makes contact with his calf, though he has not yet felt it.

As instructed, she hunches, leans into the weightbearing arms, then with as much force as she can muster, throws back her head so that the hardest part of her skull cracks his chin, maybe splits a tooth.

'Hup.' It is her, not him, the sound coming out of her mouth at the same time as she hops and jerks the blade that has sprung out at a right angle from her armed heel, up the inside of his lower leg, carving a jagged crevice through his flesh.

*Now* he feels it – and screams loudly.

If she is not careful someone will come out of the houses.

He has let go of her, hands flailing to staunch the wound. Bending over his wounded leg, he howls. Her coat is already unbuttoned, allowing her fingers to slip inside and unfasten her belt. It is all done so quickly that even before she can fully process her actions, consider any potential repercussions, she has plunged the second concealed knife between his shoulder blades.

The threat is neutralised for the time being.

She must exit this place of danger as soon as possible.

With a nudge, she pushes the man over and leaves him sprawling in a mess at the side of the road.

Click-clack, click-clack: run-run! Run-run!

All the way home.

## CHAPTER FOURTEEN

What to do?

First: wash.

She removes her clothes, then stockings and shoes. Soaps her body thoroughly. Wrings out her hair. Puts on nightwear. Examines her suit, which is not too bad. Her stockings are drenched. She rinses them. A few russet stains remain.

Her coat, however: though it is black, she can see blood has splashed across the back. Spatters, only a few, discolour the sleeves as well.

In the lining of her suitcase there is a small vial which contains Section W-issued powder. She sprinkles it over the fabric and watches it form into a jelly. Once it has hardened, she scrapes it off, then repeats the process on the sleeves. The stockings ladder when she scrapes them. They will have to be taken out of the house and destroyed.

She sits on the bed. The process of eradicating evidence has regulated her heartbeat but she finds that she is shivering and pulls the blankets around her.

Who *was* that man?

A random attacker? Someone who merely happened upon a woman out alone at night and seized his opportunity?

Or could it be more sinister? Are there German spies out there who have seen through her cover? Is she now exposed?

The sound, the feeling, the vibration of her heel-blade as it tore through flesh runs through her again and unleashes disgust.

There have been moments in the past when she has been violent. But never with weapons. How could she have done that?

Then her trainer's voice echoes through her head: 'You are more useful to us alive than dead.'

It is wasteful to give into her feelings now.

Instead she must take action: Septimus should know what has happened. All of it. She must wake him.

Quietly she slips out of her room and pads across the landing. Knocking gently on his door, she waits then bends her ear to it.

The house is dark and full of furious silence.

Again, she knocks.

No answer.

Creeping back into her room, she finds her notepad and writes on a page: 'Wake me when you are up. I need to speak to you.' Then she tears it out, folds it and goes back to his room. With care, she slides the message beneath Septimus's door.

There is nothing else to do now but return to bed, try to sleep. Or wait in dread until morning.

Transcript: 00917

Security Service HQ
02.18 a.m., 27/10/1940

P.O.: Sorry to wake you at this early hour, Mr Devereaux.
H.D.: Wait a minute.
(receiver falls. H.D. retrieves)
H.D.: Speak.
P.O.: We have received a communication from SNOWDROP in R——
H.D.: Yes?
P.O.: Marked Urgent, sir.
H.D.: Right.
P.O.: Concerning the 'tailor'.
H.D.: Go on.
P.O.: It appears he has alluded to stock, supplies, coming from the west.
H.D.: Is that it?
P.O.: No, there is more. His 'fitting guide', located in the north, I assume of the island, contains predictions of Nostradamus.
H.D.: I see. (rustling of paper) Has she mentioned any other names?
P.O.: She has included those who attended the meeting.
H.D.: Run the names past B——. And send a copy to H——. If any intelligence comes up, let me know.

P.O.: Affirmative, sir.
H.D.: Oh, and P—.
P.O.: Yes, sir?
H.D.: Do not ring back if there are no hits. I'm seeing W— at the club tomorrow evening. We can mull this over then.
P.O.: Understood, sir. Would you like me to reply?
H.D.: (disconnects call)

## CHAPTER FIFTEEN

Why has he not come?

It is eight o'clock in the morning and already Daphne has knocked another three times on Septimus's door.

Spiralling anxiety has kept her awake all night.

It is unusual for military personnel to rise so late. Though, she reminds herself, she slept in past her usual hour on her first morning here. The sun did not appear till after nine. It is disorientating.

By today's sunrise she has decided to seek help and goes downstairs to the dining room. Septimus is not there. She finds only Captain Armstrong, who is reading a news-sheet. He puts it down when he hears her and greets her with a smile, which is dashed when he distinguishes her expression.

'Is everything quite all right, Daphne?' He is already on his feet coming round the table towards her.

She shakes her head. 'I can't wake Septimus and must speak with him. Can you go into his room?'

He is surprised by the request, she can see, though nods and follows her out.

Up the stairs, along the landing, then to Septimus's room.

'Have you knocked?' the captain asks.

Of course she has! He is being polite, she tells herself. 'Five times.'

'Right,' he says and looks at the door. He rubs his chin.

'The handle is there.' Daphne points to it.

'Yes,' he says. 'Yes.'

'I can't go in,' she explains.

'No,' he answers. 'That would be quite improper.'

She wants to shake him, take hold of his hand and put it on the door handle. Why is he waiting? 'But you can,' she says and pushes his arm.

Enlivened by her touch, he at last makes a move. The handle turns easily and the door opens.

The room is empty, the bed made.

'Oh,' they both say.

'It looks like he hasn't come home,' says Captain Armstrong.

Daphne goes to the bed and touches the sheets, which are cold. Her concern dials up a notch. Where is Septimus? What has happened? Has she done something to jeopardise his safety too?

Beneath, from the hall, they hear the tinkle of the doorbell.

They look at each other, then Daphne flies to the top of the stairs.

Down one flight, then as she rounds the corner, she sees in the porch a man in a cap.

Guðrún has already answered the bell and is standing before him. 'For you,' she says as Daphne hurries to the visitor.

The man in the cap executes a stiff bow. 'Message for Miss Dione-Smith. From *The Times*.' He hands over an envelope. Across the top someone has written 'Eyes Only'.

'Thank you,' she says.

They are standing there, each of them looking at the envelope, when the uncommon sound of a powerful engine rushes through the open door. The man on the doorstep turns to look down the road. Daphne brushes past him and sees a car swinging round the corner. It screeches to a halt outside. The driver, a woman, gets out. 'Quick,' she says to them. 'He is unwell.' Her face is twisted with anxiety.

Already Daphne can see Septimus in the backseat. He is unconscious.

Though it is not decorous, she runs over and wrenches open the door. 'Wake up!' she says urgently, stuffing the telegram in her pocket. 'Septimus!'

His eyes open briefly but they are fuzzy and unfocussed. He moans and his jacket slips open, revealing his braces. *Brace, brace, brace. Is this it?* she thinks. *Karlsson's prophecy?* And darts a look at the woman who is getting back in the driver's seat. She seems afraid, for sure.

The messenger is there, nudging Daphne's side, Guðrún behind him shouting orders.

The three of them try to pull Septimus's limp body from the car. Captain Armstrong marches out, his gait fast but unhurried. 'Clear the way. Take his arms,' he barks at the messenger. 'Now, pull.'

He leans in and hooks his hand under one armpit. The messenger grabs hold of the other.

It is an awkward manoeuvre, but they manage to slide Septimus along the seat. The captain puts his shoulder underneath the limp body and carries him into the house. Something falls from Septimus's coat. When Daphne picks it up she sees it is a small drum with strange symbols inked into the skin. What is he doing with that?

As she follows the group into Guðrún's she hears the engine rev up. The car is already motoring off down the road. At the bottom it takes the corner sharply then disappears from view. She stops for a moment, wonders if she can remember the registration, fails to, goes into the house.

On the landlady's instructions they lay Septimus on the chaise-longue. Guðrún goes to fetch blankets.

'I must go,' says the messenger and quietly slips away. Though Daphne and the captain do not notice him leave. They are both lost for words. Armstrong kneels down and raises one of Septimus's eyelids. 'He's quite out of it,' he says. Then takes a flaccid hand in his and feels the wrist. 'Pulse is fine.'

'Are you sure?' asks Daphne. 'He's not going to die?'

'No, he's not going to die. I would suggest, however, that we get a medic to look him over.'

An enormous sense of relief floods through her. Guðrún returns with blankets. She sniffs the prone form. 'Bonfire,' she says. And now Daphne can smell it too. She panics.

Seeing her expression, Guðrún raises a hand – stop. 'He is not burned,' she says, allaying Daphne's fear. 'Look: his clothes undamaged. Perhaps too long outside.'

What was he doing outside overnight? Daphne asks herself. And where was he?

Guðrún gives a little chuckle, intended to lighten the mood. 'Or maybe Black Death,' she says.

Captain Armstrong joins with a 'Humph' laced with mirth, then says to Daphne, 'Your cable. Hadn't you better . . .?'

'Oh, yes,' she says. She dashes a glance at Septimus and puts the drum on the floor next to him. Colour is beginning to return to his cheeks.

'I'll take care of him,' says Armstrong. 'Don't worry. He's in capable hands.'

In her bedroom she closes the door. Her heart, she realises, is beating hard.

She does not want to open the missive but knows she must. Gingerly she unfolds the paper.

'Order: Fitting guide must be located,' it reads. 'And also N. papers. AT ONCE. Imperative. You and Septimus to use all available resources. Utmost importance. Make contact once secured.'

It is not what she expected.

Though at least it presents a reprieve of sorts: her orders are clear. Her message has been read and responded to. She is glad that she sent it and feels she made the right decision.

Throwing everything into her suitcase, including her ruined stockings, she carries it back to the dining room.

'Guðrún,' she says, as she enters, 'I have to leave for a few days. Can you keep my room? I'll be back. Is it—'

But there is another man in the room. She had not heard the bell ring.

The captain is at Septimus's side, preparing some kind of tincture in a glass. Though now he stops, eyes fixed on the new arrival.

Guðrún too comes to a standstill in the middle of the room, as if she was halfway to somewhere. In her hands she holds a damp flannel, which she is now twisting. Her attention is fastened on the visitor, who is young, perhaps in his twenties, with a downy beard that won't grow long. His face is notably tense: lips pursed, forehead contracted into lines that should not be so deep in someone his age. He lowers his eyes and brushes snow from his sleeves.

When did it start snowing? She looks out of the window. Thick flakes are whirling by, settling on the bare branches of the tree opposite.

She thinks her entrance has interrupted something for the young man speaks, addressing the landlady in Icelandic. Daphne cannot understand the words. Yet the tone of his voice, the speed of his delivery, speak of gravity and another emotion. Something like fear, or perhaps dread.

It is not good news for Guðrún shrieks and throws her hands up in the air. The flannel falls to the floor with a damp thud.

Captain Armstrong retrieves it and walks over to their landlady, his arms outstretched as if to comfort her. She is already on the move, spitting out staccato sentences punctuated by small sobs. Captain Armstrong places the flannel on the tray by Septimus then leaves the room. Guðrún scurries to the kitchen, changes her mind before she reaches the door, pivots round.

The young man says something else, stamps the cold from his feet, shivers, points to the window.

Then Armstrong is back, holding Guðrún's coat and bag. He says something in the native tongue, helps the landlady into her outerwear, then she and the young man leave together.

It has happened so quickly.

Daphne stares at her fellow lodger.

It is not the first thought that comes into her head, and yet she finds herself saying, 'You speak Icelandic?'

'A little,' he says. He does not smile.

'What's going on?'

Captain Armstrong rubs his chin. It is a tic that betrays restlessness. Unease. 'Her son was injured. Last night. Grabbed and stabbed in the back. Cowards! He is unconscious. In the hospital.'

The world slows.

Daphne's vision shrinks to a tiny perimeter. She can hear the worms in the wooden beams chewing their way through the timbers; the thump of a log of wood in the stove as it burns through and drops onto the embers below, the pulse of her heart in her ears. Light, coming in at the window, catches a nail in the floorboards and twinkles. The smell of smoke on Septimus's clothes is distinguished by the hairs of her nostrils and then processed by her brain as originating from pinewood and dried moss.

Deeper within – a whirlwind of feeling. Too much to understand.

She hears her heartbeat pause and then accelerate into rapid thumping.

Slowly she realises Armstrong is talking to her. Though it is as if his words come through water. '. . . not be concerned,' he bubbles. 'I will oversee his care. Personally.'

'What?' says Daphne, and with this is sucked back into the room. The world quickens around her once more. 'What?'

She is speaking like a machine, her brain whirring, taking stock of what he has said: the horrible implication. And she understands, right then, that she has stepped over a threshold into a place where expediency is all and the normal rules of conduct do not apply. There is iron in her heart that she had never suspected was there.

How quickly we adapt when the Fates cast again and weave a new destiny for us.

'I say,' says the captain. 'If you could possibly become paler, then I think you just did.'

Her head tilts up and she sees in his face both benevolence and anguish.

'Right, you listen to me,' he is saying. 'I'll look after Septimus. You need to go.'

She does not thank him. In fact, she says nothing.

Merely opens the front door and goes out into the snow.

## CHAPTER SIXTEEN

How do you adjust to harm? Not done to you, but imposed by you on another human being. And perhaps, ultimately, on yourself as well when you come to terms with your own actions. The process of adaptation, which would take hundreds of pages to describe, is achieved, within oneself, in a second. Perceptions change, memories alter. And of course self-justification has its role.

Daphne reminds herself that she was in a perilous situation and forced to strike or be struck. Or worse. It was a matter of survival. But these are thoughts to be unpicked after the dust has settled. After the war. And may not need to be examined at all, if she does not make it through.

Guilt is a luxury reserved for survivors.

If unfairly so.

I can never tell, she thinks. I should not speak of it. No one else need ever know. Only he and I. And he is dead to the world.

She marches on. There are spectres in the misty snowfall, which is becoming a storm: men in chains, the unlucky dead. Calling to her from every corner. Shrieking into the wind. Lamenting their choices – if only they had waited, if only they had moved sooner.

Who is she in all this confusion?

Someone approaches her. A woman, wrapped up in so many clothes Daphne can barely see her face.

She shakes her head and moves on.

I am a puppet, Daphne thinks, the burden of her actions weighing heavily on her. An instrument of war. A grim reaper with painted lips. I am danger.

'What is it?' asks Anna when Daphne arrives at her office.

She has forged through the fierce weather in clothes that are far too thin. Her hair has frozen into Medusa-like wisps, scattered with snowflakes. Her lips, downturned, are blue.

'For goodness' sake, get to the fire.' Anna does not wait for acknowledgement but takes Daphne by the shoulders and propels her into the warmth. 'This is not how we do things in Iceland,' she tells her.

Daphne's teeth are chattering. She is aware of dripping. I am made of wax and melting, she thinks.

Then there is something hot and ceramic in her hands and Anna is telling her to drink. She puts the coffee cup to her lips but then sees in her head the rust-coloured bowl of water in which she washed her stockings last night. It is Björn, she thinks. I have brought death to this island, to Guðrún's house. Though, she remembers, he is not dead but wounded. Mortally? If she had known who it was, would she have been as severe?

What was he doing? Was it play? Or something more malevolent?

'I don't know,' says Anna. Those words have been said too often. And yet they are so true. What does either of them know for sure? 'What are you meant to tell me?'

'Pardon?' asks Daphne. 'What do you mean?'

'You keep saying you have to tell me something.'

It is too difficult to explain. Words are beyond her grasp. They are uncontrollable and keep slipping out of her mind, like steel heels on ice. Instead, her fingers delve into her pocket and pull out the telegram.

Her gaze is on Anna's face, watching her reaction, though with only half her mind on the task. The other is racing through possibilities: has the landlady's son been following her? If not, who else could it be?

Then Anna says, 'Let me call my cousin.' Her expression is far from happy.

Can she tell? wonders Daphne. Does she know I have blood on my hands? She looks at them to see if there is any evidence left there and begins to rub at her fingers.

Anna makes a telephone call. Daphne has not yet noticed the large black cabinet in the corner of the office. While Anna speaks in Icelandic, Daphne inspects her overcoat. There is nothing suspicious that she can see. However, the puddle on the floor beneath her, where the snow has thawed from the fibres, is tainted with a faint streak of pink. She pushes her boot into it and distributes it across the floorboards so that it is diluted and not noticeable.

'Where is this Septimus?' asks Anna. She is back by Daphne's side, taking her wet coat from her. 'Does he still not believe us?'

I must let this go, thinks Daphne. I must enter into the now, like a proper agent. *You are more good to us alive than dead.* There are other things at play here. War is dirty. It takes from everyone it touches. It can destroy the heart, the mind and the soul if it is allowed to. 'No,' says Daphne and brings the whole of her mind into the present.

Anna thinks this a simple response. She does not appreciate the enormity of Daphne's answer.

Raising herself from her seat, Daphne tells her, 'Septimus is poorly.' And adds, 'Sick,' when Anna's face remains blank.

They cross the office and settle at the desk.

Anna pulls out a seat for Daphne and tells her, 'Tomorrow Karlsson will go to church. He always does on a Sunday. My cousin Rafn is in the new military police division.'

This sends a shudder through Daphne. The police will be investigating the crime she committed. Will this Rafn know she is the perpetrator?

'Sindri will come with us,' says Anna. 'Then we will find the grimoire and the predictions from the mage.'

'Tomorrow?' Daphne asks. She wants to leave this city of blood as quickly as possible. And not with a policeman.

'Yes.' Anna inclines her head to the window. 'No chance of driving in this. We can only hope it will be a short storm. But we must go tomorrow. We cannot leave it any later. The roads will become impassable – the snow season is coming.'

Daphne looks at the world outside the window – varying shades of white, moving in flurries. 'We should go at once,' she says. 'That is the order.'

But Anna shakes her head. 'You are not going anywhere in those clothes. They are inadequate. Tonight, you stay with me. I will find you more appropriate dressings. Or else you may die out there.'

Daphne bows her head. She does not wish to die from exposure – of all things – and so takes the defeat. For now.

**34 Killed by Torpedoes**

The sinking of the liner Eurymedon (6,222 tonnes) was disclosed at Ottawa with the announcement by the Canadian naval minister, Mr MacDonald, that one of their fleet, a destroyer, had rescued her survivors.

MacDonald revealed she had managed to stay afloat for three days after she was struck by two enemy torpedoes resulting in 34 fatalities. The same destroyer was also able to rescue survivors from the *S.S. Sulairia* (5,800 tonnes) despite it going down in 12 minutes.

A telegram from New York reports the sinking in the Atlantic of the Brocklebank liner *Matheran* (7,650 tonnes), a Dundee trader which was carrying iron, zinc, grain, machinery and general cargo. Its convoy passed through waters with a heavy concentration of enemy U-boats and came under attack. Six crew members were killed in the explosion. The remaining men had no option but to abandon ship and were picked up by another convoy vessel, the *Loch Lomond*.

We are now receiving reports, as yet unconfirmed, that the *Loch Lomond* herself has been torpedoed.

## CHAPTER SEVENTEEN

They are ready by seven o'clock in the navy-blue morning. Daphne sits in a pair of boots donated by Anna's mother. They are made of oiled sheepskin with fleece on the inside. She has not put on the coat, also loaned, as it is too thick to wear inside the house.

In her suitcase is a knitted jumper, another pair of woollen stockings and a vest, which are entirely unbecoming but practical. A shawl rests in her lap, along with a pair of gloves, made from the same material as her boots, though thinner to allow more dexterity. Now she has seen how the natives armour themselves against the winter, she wonders why her Section W-issued wardrobe is so lacking.

On her face she also wears a borrowed expression. One of neutrality, which she has copied from her friend, a version of her own blank stage smile. It is a mask to hide behind while Rafn sits opposite her in the kitchen and listens to his cousin Anna explaining their theory about Karlsson and the mission they must now pursue. Daphne is not sure if she is breaking the rules by taking this man into her confidence, but she has run roughshod over so many that she doesn't really care. Ironically, it was rule-breaking that prompted her recruitment in the first place.

She thinks back to the gentlemen's club where she first met Hugh Devereaux, recalling his grim face as they talked in the blackout gloom. 'There are those who cling on to their idea of a "noble war". It no longer exists,' he had told her, in his deep, purpose-filled voice. 'We need people who are not afraid to think differently.' And then he had paused for emphasis and added, 'Wickedly even. To come up with solutions, ideas, strategies, actions, which our regular operatives cannot conceive of.'

Well, she has been wicked. And now she is thinking very differently, developing a plan unsanctioned by higher ranks, and working with an Icelandic military policeman.

Needs must.

Anna's cousin is taller than her. His shoulders are much broader and brawny. He has similarly flaxen hair, but with strong curls running through it, which he brushes back over the top of his head. The sides and back are kept short and neat. His eyebrows are darker and define very light, hazel eyes, which keep straying to Daphne. He is not in uniform but exudes an air of good health and an authoritative presence, both of which are keenly felt.

Daphne puts him at a few years older than her.

Intuition tells her he does not suspect her of anything. At least he has given no sign. Not yet. Though if he is a good detective, he may well conceal his suspicions. She thinks, at present, he merely views her as curious: a petite woman with long dark hair in this country of statuesque blondes. And, of course, she is wearing his aunt's well-padded but dowdy winter clothes, which make her look like a bolt of cloth on legs. She would laugh were the situation not so dire.

It is interesting to see how he speaks with Anna. She'd thought he might be protective of his female cousin but he treats her as an equal in competence and intelligence.

Anna, she realises, is concluding their story. Gesturing to Daphne for the telegram, she hands it to Rafn.

There is a long moment of silence, in which the two women watch the man's face.

Daphne's heart is thumping again. Now she worries that they have disclosed too much. That this man will think them silly like other men do, that he will tell them to leave it to him and report the plan to the police.

He looks at his wristwatch. 'The service will end soon,' he says. 'I'll bring the car round.'

It is the same church where she briefly sat when she had trailed Karlsson to his meeting with the two men. The one in the trilby, whom she now knows is Helgi the stage manager. The other, the communist Sigmundur Gunnarsson.

Now Daphne thinks about it, it seems very possible that both of them could have been feeding the medium information. Helgi would be privy to the identity of those who had bought tickets to the performance. Reykjavík, as Anna has often mentioned, is small. People know each other. Advance knowledge of the audience and something of their situations would be like gold dust for someone who professed to be a psychic and a stranger to them. This Sigmundur, if he does work at the Reykjavík airfield as Anna has told her, well, it is likely he would hear talk from the British there. Snippets of information. Everybody knows how important news from home is to the troops stationed here. Any comment dropped about mail on its way will alert listeners to vessels and convoys due to arrive soon. And this of course would be invaluable to the Germans. Along with any advance information on the meteorological fronts sweeping in.

She experiences a moment of relief as she sits in the back of the car considering what they know: they may have embarked on a rogue mission but it is the right thing to do.

The windows have steamed up with the three of them in here. She sweeps her glove across the glass and looks through the clear patch she has made.

The church, she sees now, is not as small as she had first

thought. Or perhaps she has become more accustomed to the size of Reykjavík and contracted her sense of perspective accordingly. It cannot hold many people though, she knows that from being inside. Perhaps a couple of hundred. Which, if it is full, could make their plan rather difficult. They have fine-tuned it whilst sitting in the truck, which Rafn calls a car. It is not a robust strategy but things are moving at pace now and they must rely on their wits and quick thinking. They are all more resourceful than they realise. Though Daphne is partially aware of her own resilience, she has no idea of the tremendous challenges that lie ahead. None of them do.

It will go like this: Daphne and Anna will intercept Karlsson on his way out and ask if he might agree to have his photo taken for the London *Times*. As he will no doubt be in his Sunday best, she will flatter his appearance. It must be today, they will say, as she has wired her copy to the newspaper: they are delighted with it and wish to go to print as soon as possible but will require a photograph to accompany the piece.

They would like to go somewhere picturesque with their 'photographer', Rafn. Somewhere with a backdrop of Reykjavík where readers can also be awed by the majesty of the bold Icelandic scenery. Their photographer has a vehicle waiting across the street. The unmarked truck Rafn has borrowed from the police for the night is functional but not as salubrious as she had hoped. A stubby carriage with a larger boot but enough room inside for the four of them. Anna has told her it is sturdy, and this is apparently the most important factor. The journey will be long and the terrain unkind.

Daphne hopes the medium has recovered enough from his fit to attend the Sunday sermon.

'There!' says Rafn.

The church doors have opened and the minister has come outside. They watch as the trickle of parishioners begins to pass out into the light, blinking at the azure sky. It is bitingly cold yet the sunshine dazzles. Rafn has told them they must be quick with their manoeuvres: more snow is due. The roads may become impassable if they delay.

Anna slips from the car. Daphne follows. They take up position on the pavement outside the church.

Unlike the congregations at home where the number of males is much diminished, there are lots of families present here. With both parents. Young men too. The children are the same: boisterous and eager to unleash the energy that has been bottled up whilst attending the service. Groups gather on the pavement to exchange greetings. Some set off in the same direction. She wonders if they have a tradition of Sunday lunch. It has been so long since she sat down with her parents and broke bread. Shame comes over her as she remembers the reluctance with which she would catch the train from the bright lights of London back down to Essex, which seemed so parochial and dull by contrast. Now, the image of her father carving, her mother passing the gravy boat, has gathered an aura of comfort and stability for which she suddenly yearns. How could she have taken such love and care for granted?

With a jolt she realises that Anna is moving. Karlsson has appeared. He is speaking to the minister. When he sights Anna, his eyes spark. He stops short and bows quickly to the reverend then speaks to an older woman at his side, perhaps his mother.

Karlsson greets the journalist like a friend. Daphne is pleased to see he has recovered from his seizure. If indeed that is what it was, and not a part of the performance. They have a long journey ahead and she would be reluctant to take him if he were in a poor physical condition. But his eyes are bright, his skin pale, though she thinks that is his regular colour. Deftly she unbuttons her coat and removes the shawl. She feels the cold immediately; however, this outerwear is unflattering and she wishes the medium to see her suit, which is flimsy but feminine and à la mode.

It works.

When the medium sights Daphne he begins to nod and smile. He calls over his shoulder to his mother, who waves a dismissive hand at him. As Daphne approaches, she sees Anna hook her arm through Karlsson's and guide him to her. Smiling widely, she shows her teeth, dips her head coquettishly. The effect is instantaneous: his chest puffs out, he draws himself up and pushes back his shoulders to impress. For a moment she feels sorry for him, for the fraud he is about to discover. But then she remembers, she is merely a pawn and must do what she has been tasked with for the greater good. Whatever that is.

And he is a traitor.

That thought causes her jaw to tense as she goes through the motions that they have plotted. But he does not notice and follows them obediently to the car. Rafn has stepped out and opens the rear door for the medium to settle onto the back seat. In a display of solicitude, he also offers him a thick blanket to cover his legs. As Daphne gets in beside the evidently delighted Karlsson, he spreads it over her legs too. It is a gentlemanly gesture but makes her feel queasy. She does not want to get close to him.

As they drive out of the city Karlsson peppers her with questions: what did her editor say? Did they think him a man of unusual gifts? When will the article be published? Can he have a copy? Perhaps he can pick the photo to be used?

She answers him as best as she can. However, her eyes are on the landscape opening up to one side of the road. The hilltops tower overhead. There is no softness here. Only craggy, black volcanic rock pushing itself skyward, shedding the sparse vegetation that clings to its lower levels. Lava has come to rest in layers, so there are ledges of compacted ash and molten rock like a giant's staircase stretching to the sky. These inky mountains are tough, hard-faced and brutal, like the Vikings of old. You would have to be such to stay alive out here, she thinks.

To the other side, brilliant open water glistens greyly like the back of a great seal. Frills of white break across its surface. Waves. Though the firth should by rights be sheltered by this crescent of mountains, it feels more menacing here than in the harbour. Dangerous and untamed and vast. Sulking like a pike.

Never had she thought she would come to this land of ice and fire. A thrill of excitement runs through her. How wonderful, she thinks, despite herself, despite the present situation, to be out here now in this strange wilderness with its unfamiliar palette of colours, to be seeing such things.

Karlsson, who has been prattling to Anna in Icelandic, suddenly realises where they are and asks, so that Daphne can understand, if they are to be much longer.

From the front, Rafn calls over his shoulder that he wishes to get a sense of perspective. 'Just a little higher,' he says.

Sitting back, Karlsson looks at the sea, then at Daphne, who smiles. Over his shoulder she sees the great peaks in the distance are snow-capped. 'More than majestic,' she breathes.

The medium laughs and touches his hair. Oh, surely not? thinks Daphne and turns away to look out of her window, concealing her cruel smile. Vanity, thy name is not woman.

Rafn has turned off the main road, with a skill born of years navigating this terrain, and down a lonely track strewn with rocks, which ping against the undercarriage and bodywork. The sound is loud, like a machine gun firing off rounds. Daphne, who is not used to unmade roads, begins to feel uneasy. The car must not be harmed. It has work to do.

None of the Icelanders display any sign of consternation.

At the end there is a small shack used for fishing. Beyond it, a cliff top with a view of the city in the distance.

'Here,' says Rafn. 'If we hurry, we will benefit from good light.'

They disembark. He points to a cluster of rocks and suggests this would make an excellent composition. His English is impeccable.

The secret plan about to be played out briefly becomes a burden that speeds her heartbeat.

They begin the climb to the rocks.

This is it.

Karlsson sits on the central rock and arranges himself so that he is facing out to sea, head slightly inclined, in a proud and haughty pose.

'Good,' says Rafn. 'Good.' He has brought with him a bag, which lies at his feet. 'Hold it just there,' he says.

Then in the quietness they all hear a click. Karlsson relaxes and smiles as he rounds to face them.

The sound has not come from the camera's shutter but a police revolver. It is pointing at Karlsson's head.

For a moment he stares, stupefied, then defaults into outrage. 'What is this? How dare you bring me out here on false pretences?'

Anna and Rafn remain silent. They are waiting for Daphne to speak.

Her voice shakes as she says, 'You have been giving out secrets.' She has rehearsed this but it is coming out wrong. Her voice leaks fear.

Karlsson laughs with bitterness. 'It is my job to relay the secrets of the dead.'

It is not a good feeling knowing that she holds his life in the palm of her hand, though it lends her now a smoothness, a power which enables her to stand firm. 'But not those that may be of use to the Germans.' The words come out bolder now.

He hears the strength in her voice and tries to adapt. 'You are mistaken, my dear.' Karlsson has decided to placate. 'I am . . .'

he flourishes his hand in the air '. . . like my country was once upon a time – neutral.'

She catches the thread of his argument and answers back. 'But now you are occupied, anyone found collaborating with the enemy, in whatever *medium*,' she says, emphasising the word, 'will be dealt with by the authorities most severely.'

For a moment he drops his gaze to the ground and Daphne can see he is weighing his options. Then he bolsters himself, stands up and performs a display of blustery outrage. 'I will go to the highest authorities with my complaint.' And with that he turns on his heel and marches past her, past Anna. 'And I am very well connected. This is preposterous.'

Rafn stands in his way, gun still pointed, but Karlsson knocks it aside and strides ahead.

For a moment she sees uncertainty flash across the policeman's face. Anna falters then begins to run after the medium, who is gaining ground. Rafn turns towards them. There is a moment of confusion.

A loud crack echoes across the clearing.

Three people duck and freeze.

Daphne's pistol is hot in her hand. She should reload it but feels there is no real need.

The shot has flown several feet over Karlsson's head but submission is written over his features.

Across Anna's she sees surprise. On Rafn's concern.

None of them can know the chamber is now empty.

Slowly she walks up to Karlsson and aims the Kiss of Death at his heart.

'I'm afraid that won't work for me.' She is surprised by how calm she sounds. How calm and cold and lethal. Her words effect a change in the others. Anna shakes her head at Karlsson. Rafn realigns the sights of his revolver on the medium's head.

Seeing the two guns and the steely expressions on his audience of three, the medium's face takes on a caved-in look. 'It was Torfi Birgisson,' he says. 'Wasn't it? All his talk of the Viennese opera house. I feared someone would . . . of course, spending time in Austria, that could easily alert . . .' He stops talking and pulls himself up straighter.

Ah, thinks Daphne. That makes sense. Of course she is not privy to the reasons why Hugh Devereaux has sent her north in search of the grimoire. But now it is becoming clear that one of the names she included in her telegram must have set alarm bells ringing in Section W. Vienna has been under Nazi control since the annexation of Austria two years ago. Entry into all Nazi-occupied territories is highly controlled: travellers must pass through several layers of security. If Torfi Birgisson has been in Vienna recently, then his visit was officially approved. He is doing something that benefits the Nazi regime.

Her attention returns to Karlsson who puts his hands on his hips and raises his head to her. 'What is it to be then? I can't think you would bring me out here to turn me in?' He takes a step towards them.

Rafn cocks the hammer on his weapon. 'The grimoire,' he says.

'With the prophecies of Nostradamus,' Daphne adds.

This takes the medium by surprise. Then he gathers his wits and she sees the real man step forth. 'For a price, I can give you the location.'

Inside, she feels the iron hardening and does not answer his question but says, 'You will take us to it.'

Turning his head to the sea, Karlsson has the look of a man who is stalling for time, allowing his brain to catch up with this sudden reversal of fortune, assessing the hand he has been dealt, calculating outcomes. 'And then what?' he asks.

'And then we will see,' she says.

She thinks he is going to yield and follow Rafn's instructions to get back into the car. But the medium has started to chuckle. It is a low, phlegmy sound. Unpleasant. Anna darts her a glance – what's going on?

Rafn goes over to him and takes him by the shoulder. 'Come on,' he says, and pushes him towards the path. But Karlsson cannot stop laughing.

'What is it?' Daphne growls.

When he has calmed down, he looks her square in the face. 'You're right about one thing,' he says between ragged breaths. 'The grimoire contains secrets. Ones the Germans are prepared to pay a good price for.'

Daphne looks at Anna and they exchange a smile: their actions are justified. They were right.

'You seem to forget,' he says, wiping spittle from the corners of his mouth, 'I announced it two nights ago.'

For a moment Daphne doesn't see the relevance.

Then he says, 'They've got a head start on you, to Hólmavik.'

Unwittingly, he has just revealed the location of the grimoire. They knew it was Strandasýsla, though not exactly where.

But then he says, 'Yes, a very good lead. By my calculations, at least a day and a half.'

And so he went north, blessing the land as he passed through it, until he reached a place known by all local people to be wicked. Nothing grew there. When men from nearby villages, driven by famine, went to pick eggs and hunt birds, they fell to their deaths, leaving many widows. If a newly married couple travelled to set up home, after twenty years the wife would simply disappear. So, it was to there the bishop journeyed, intending to bless the cursed land.

When he reached the despicable place, he began to sprinkle holy water across it. But no sooner had he begun than he and his men heard a roar and a rumbling. A huge hairy fist on the end of a huge hairy arm thrust out of the cliff. The gathered men fell to their knees shaking.

'No,' yelled the troll from within the mountain. 'Evil needs some place to live.'

So Bishop Guðmundur stopped and declared that place a sanctuary for evil.

And, they say, still it may be.

Guðmundar Saga (1314–44)

## CHAPTER EIGHTEEN

They have made the decision not to tie Karlsson's hands. Where would he escape to anyway? No vehicle has passed them for an hour and signs of habitation are few and far between.

Night is on its way now and the temperature is dropping quickly. Outside, the land folds in on itself: the valleys narrow, the plains thin and the mountains grow ever higher. Snow stretches down their sides.

Karlsson appears to have accepted his fate and lies passive in the backseat. At least that is the impression he is giving. But Daphne knows appearances are deceiving. He must be watched at all times. She notes a slight tremble to his hands and remembers his prediction: 'The mountain shakes.' Well, now he is.

Though what of the rest: 'See her fear.'

While Daphne and Anna are far from fearful, they could not be described as breezy.

They have discussed the implications of Karlsson's new disclosure before getting back on the road. Rafn had wanted to return to Reykjavík and involve his superiors. If enemy agents were in their midst then they ought to notify his CO. Daphne had argued against that: not only would they lose time, and the acquisition of the grimoire is imperative (for reasons she cannot explain), but: 'I have acted without informing Major Spike, the Chief of Intelligence on the island, and fear he would not allow me to continue the mission once the police alert him to it. Which they will be obliged to do.'

She has no doubt Rafn is reconfiguring his assessment of her. The appearance of her weapon has tipped the scales of this working dynamic off balance. Whilst they are now more potent as a unit, she has become his equal in fire power. Or a formidable opponent. His eyes have grown darker. There is more depth to them. However, she finds she doesn't mind the way he looks at her and discerns a new emotion there. Perhaps respect. Anna, seemingly unphased by Daphne's pistol, has sided with her British friend and so, with two out of three votes in favour, they have pressed on. A fresh urgency tenses their hands.

Thrust into her pockets, Daphne's fingers fray the seams of Anna's mother's coat.

It has started to snow and they are losing visibility. She cannot see much out of the window, just the ominous outlines of jagged black rocks. Their speed has reduced too.

'Can't we go any faster?' she asks Rafn. The idea that German agents may get there before her is unbearable. She *must* reach the grimoire first. To return empty-handed would be the worst outcome. If she proves ineffective, Hugh Devereaux and the Security Service will not leap to her defence. That is not to say they won't sort her out eventually, but if she is of limited use to them, she will not be a priority. The thought of spending time in a military prison makes her shiver.

'Too dangerous,' says Rafn, gripping the steering wheel. 'This road has sheer drops and bends. We can only go as fast as is safe.'

'But what about the grimoire?'

Neither he nor Anna answers.

Anna has her eyes fixed on a point ahead. Her fingers, gloved, drum on her lap.

They are arriving at the entrance to a wide fjord. Daphne follows Anna's gaze to a checkpoint, just visible in the arc of light projected from their headlamps. A shabby hut from which two shadows have emerged.

Cold does not improve the temperament. It sharpens the edges of whatever mood one is in. These soldiers are disgruntled. She cannot see this in their faces but it is evident in the gruff manner they shout instructions as they approach, demanding identity papers. The arrival of a truck with four passengers is clearly an interruption. Above the hut smoke funnels up from a small chimney. It will be warmer in there.

They are waved over and pull into a bay. Rafn gets out to talk to them.

The wind has got up and is blowing the soldiers' scarves around their helmets, like bothersome snakes. It clearly adds to their sense of grievance: one of them shakes his head and points north.

Beside her Karlsson stirs. Registering that they have stopped, his mouth opens and he sits up straight. When he sees the British soldiers he slumps back: he will get no assistance here.

'You may need to get out and speak with them,' says Anna from the front seat. 'Some trouble?'

There is another man coming out of the hut.

Daphne opens the door, quickly shuts it when protestations come from Karlsson. Walks over to the two soldiers. Her legs are stiff from the journey. The wind is biting and she can taste snow in the air.

'Hello,' she shouts above the wind. There are three of them now, clustered round Rafn. 'Can I help?'

'Stone the crows!' says the third man, who is fingering Rafn's identity papers. His face barely shows between his scarf and helmet. 'Is that Miss Essex? You get everywhere, you do.'

It is the sentry from the Reykjavík camp. 'I might say the same of you, Corporal Yorkshire. Posted you up here now, have they?'

'Not my favourite place, "Whale-fjord-jur",' he says. 'Had whales here.'

Rafn winces and pronounces under his breath, 'Hvalfjörður.'

The soldier from Scarborough doesn't notice. 'I'll be back down in the city in a few days. Never thought I'd say it, but I can't wait. This ain't the Ritz.'

She looks at the hut and commiserates. 'I can see that.'

The other two soldiers and Rafn regard her with mild surprise.

'Look,' calls Corporal Yorkshire. 'Can I have a word?' And he leads her into the hut.

Wind screams through cracks in the flimsy building. Even the oil lamp flickers. It is slightly warmer inside. A stove in the corner is pumping out heat though much of it is lost through the poorly insulated walls. Three chairs are angled around it. On each stands a steaming mug of tea. By the far wall is a camp bed heaped with blankets and a table laid with dominoes.

'I don't know what you're doing, and I probably shouldn't ask,' he says, removing his helmet. The hair beneath it is slicked down but the bits around his temples poke out at odd angles. He is younger than she'd supposed him. 'There's a storm on its way and we've been told to strongly dissuade anyone from travelling north tonight.'

She shakes her head. 'I've got orders too, I'm afraid.'

He pauses and unwraps the scarf from his chin, which is lightly coated with a five o'clock shadow and errant bits of fluff. 'Your superiors will be up to date with the forecast. They'll understand if you hunker down for the night.'

Her superiors know nothing about this trip. Only those in London, who will not be apprised of the weather, nor the debilitating impact it has on those who live on this rock. For a moment she thinks about returning to the car and discussing this news with Anna and Rafn. Then she remembers what lies back in Reykjavík – an irate Major Spike and a wounded man, the reckoning she must face. Then there are the Germans. Are the recipients of Karlsson's intelligence really racing to the prize right now, as he suggested? It is not a chance she should take.

'No,' she says. 'We cannot afford any delay.'

The soldier nods then, after a moment's pause, says, 'I'll ring to the next checkpoint. It's the other side of the fjord. They'll let you through.'

She thanks him and heads for the door. Just as she opens it, he shouts, 'Wait!'

For a moment she panics. But he is holding out a blanket from the bed. 'Take this. It's going to drop below freezing point.'

It would be churlish to refuse so she accepts it, feeling guilty: they too will suffer the cold tonight. He follows her out and signals to the remaining two men, who waste no time in returning to the hut. 'Good luck,' he says, as she gets into the vehicle. 'Don't die, will you?'

She hopes not to.

He waves them on and they move back onto the road.

'It's going to snow,' she says.

'We can tell,' says Rafn grimly. He puts his foot down hard on the accelerator. The pebbles on the road recommence their rat-a-tat-tat on the car.

The journey round the fjord takes a good hour. There are battleships moored in it, their shadows like whales.

The pistol is back in her pocket. Karlsson keeps one eye on her at all times. As well he might. It must be something of a shock to realise that the bright young thing who had captured his heart is a spy who has now captured him. She is embarrassed for the foolish man with all his preening. He should have paid more attention at church. All good Christians know pride comes before a fall.

By the time they reach the next checkpoint the land is shrouded in darkness. Above them thick clouds have gathered, obscuring the stars. The night is dark and dense as charcoal and they are climbing into it.

In the great mountains, the wind is stronger, battering at the car doors, clamouring to come in.

At one point her ears pop from the altitude. She stares ahead between Anna's and Rafn's shoulders. The headlights' beam reveals a narrow sloping road. On one side the incline is steep. Boulders that look like they might topple down at any moment fringe the wayside. On the other side there is nothing.

A mist is seeping onto the road.

'Are we in the clouds?' Daphne jokes.

'Yes,' says Anna, but she does not laugh.

Despite her confidence in Rafn's driving skills Daphne begins to worry.

The angle of the car alters and it feels like they are descending, though the mist is thickening, becoming clotted with mothlike creatures.

'Snow,' announces Karlsson. The first word he has spoken since he got back into the car. 'How far are we from Borðeyri?'

It isn't a place she has heard of.

'Three hours at least,' says Rafn. 'Perhaps more.'

Karlsson leans forward and says, 'We won't make it.'

'What?' Daphne looks at him aghast. There is no light inside the truck, only the reflection of the car's lights on the road. His face, from what she can make out, is twisted with maniacal glee. He is trying to spook them. Of course he is.

Ten minutes more, then they pull off the road at a passing spot. Rafn gets out and goes to the boot. She hears a clinking, rustling sound. Then Karlsson opens the door on his side. 'I'll help,' he says.

With mercurial speed Anna also jumps out. She has a torch in her hand, which she shines at the ground.

Now Daphne is the only person inside the car. She does not want to go out into the freezing air – the blanket Corporal Yorkshire has given her is large and thick – but at the same time she is worried about her safety. What if there is a rockfall and the car is swept away? What if Karlsson stupidly makes a dash for it? The thought propels her out to join the others.

Anna has the torch trained on the men who are attaching lines of metal to the tyres. 'Snow chains,' she says to Daphne, who has never heard of such a thing and does not know what to make of it.

In fact, there *is* snow on the ground. At least a good inch or two. She peers into the near distance. All she can see is the road ahead dusted with white, heavy flakes. On their fall to earth they dance in the headlights. The land is flatter here. The mountains around are vague outlines pushing against a smoky haze. She cannot see the tops – the sky has come down to claim them.

While outside the wind becomes faster, lashing at their faces. It is the storm, she thinks. Will we be stranded? She puts her tongue out to catch a snowflake, but the air is too cold for it. She returns to the car, aware of her grumbling stomach.

Anna has shared the bread, cheese and dried fish that her mother packed for her, but that was hours ago. Daphne wonders if she has done the right thing, not heeding the warnings. Night is pressing into everything.

After a while Karlsson gets in. He does not offer to share the blanket, as he had back in the city, but wraps it round himself, eyeing her with disdain. 'Too good to be true,' he says.

It is on the tip of her tongue to answer him back, 'Well, what did you think?' but this will only incite him. His ego is woefully damaged. Men in this state can become irrational. She prefers to keep him where she can control him, so says, 'These present circumstances constrain us all. The world is a darker place. I'm sorry.'

It placates enough for him to ask, after a moment, 'Are you even a writer for *The Times?*'

She considers her answer then says, 'Yes and no. I may be able to publish a piece about you yet.' He will be more co-operative this way —

The driver's door squeaks and the car sags as Rafn lurches in. He is shivering. 'Anna!' he shouts and then she is in too. He turns on the engine. It starts then splutters.

Karlsson sits up straight. Anna's neck has become rigid. She sends a look to Rafn.

No one says anything.

But they are all thinking the same thing: they will not survive the night out here.

Rafn turns the key again.

The engine makes a sound like a dog dying.

Daphne holds her breath for a long minute.

Then it sputters into life.

Thank God, they all think. And they turn back onto the road.

It has been a slow journey on roads that have twisted and curled. Twice the car's engine stalled. Twice Daphne's heart climbed into her mouth. But now there are lights visible in the distance. Pinpricks of life.

She hopes they will make it, for the swirl of snow has become a blanket.

## CHAPTER NINETEEN

The car gave out a quarter of a mile outside Borðeyri.

Not far, but the walk of four hundred odd yards has probably been the hardest of her life. Every cell in her brain was focussed on the road. Visibility, poor in the extreme, was limited to perhaps six or eight feet. The wind, erratic, often blew in gusts that made them all stop and hold onto each other, battling to remain upright.

Their bedraggled group waded through a good foot of snow. Some drifts were three or four feet higher. Exhaustion threatened to overwhelm.

Eventually a cluster of houses became visible on the lower side of the road. Rafn pointed down the hill. 'That house at the end by the water. British soldiers posted there. Do you need to speak with them?'

Daphne was unsure. Did she? On balance, considering the mess she had left in Reykjavík, she thought not. Unwise.

Communicating this to Rafn, he had shrugged and gestured to a red-boarded house, half covered in snow, that was much closer. Thank goodness.

Down they went. Karlsson, in his city shoes, slipped and skated all over the ground. At one point both women had an arm around his waist to steady him. He cursed in Icelandic: hard consonants softened by the wind. Perhaps to counter the emasculation. She felt him shiver and experienced a sudden pang of sympathy. Then smashed it.

They pressed on, leaning into the wind, which whipped at their faces punishingly as if they were the ones who were traitors.

A lamp had been lit outside by the door, a beacon in the storm, which they made their way to. There was water further down, not smooth and glassy like a lake but storm-tossed. She could hear it hissing. The gulls, geese and seabirds had wisely gone to ground – protecting their nestlings in safer places.

Rafn forged on ahead and knocked on the door. When they arrived at the porch, they were hurriedly shown into a side room by a concerned young woman.

The relief of being inside, out of the raging weather, was immense. There were only three wooden chairs in the room, but they sank into them at once. Rafn briefly lay down on the floor to rest.

For a while no one spoke as they tried to recover from their ordeal.

But now Daphne has collected herself.

After goodness knows how long – seventy seconds, three minutes, ten minutes? It is too difficult to gauge the time – Daphne asks, 'Where are we?'

Rafn, continuing to lie on the floor, answers, 'Axel's place. He was a policeman in Reykjavík. He has moved up here to be with his family again. He will help us.'

The young woman comes in again and begins to make up the stove in the corner of the room.

Struggling to his feet, Rafn speaks to her. Daphne is watching, trying to work out what they are saying. It is too difficult, Icelandic doesn't sound like the other languages she's familiar with: neither Italian nor German. The door opens again and a man enters. He is large, with a thick beard and a long nose. He greets Rafn heartily. The two converse in Icelandic.

Anna rouses herself when Rafn mentions her name. She gets up and greets the man, who must be Axel.

Rafn says 'Daphne' and she smiles at their host and waves. It is such an odd gesture to make, as if they are being introduced at a birthday party, not a refuge in a storm, and she suddenly feels like a silly little girl. Though the man just nods before switching his gaze to Karlsson. She doesn't hear Rafn mention the medium's name but Karlsson's eyes dart towards him from under hooded lids and he nods a greeting. Axel returns the gesture.

They begin a conversation that includes Anna. There is more nodding.

Axel calls out to the young girl. She stops laying the fire and begins to remove the wood and coals and put them into an empty tin bucket by the stove.

Anna translates. 'We can stay in Borðeyri for the night.'

'But we must go on tonight,' says Daphne. Even as the words come out of her mouth, she knows it is impossible. The storm is howling outside. Though her resolution remains firm, she does not want to go back into it. She doubts anyone will be travelling tonight. Not even Germans.

'No one will take us further north. Not now,' says Anna. 'It would be more than reckless. It would be self-destruction. The car needs attention. We can leave it here. Axel says he will tow it in tomorrow and look it over.'

'Can we borrow another one?' Daphne presses her.

Anna has been brushing her coat but now she looks at Daphne, surprised. 'Another car?'

'Yes. To get to Hólmavík.'

Then she laughs. 'I am sorry, I thought I told you. There will be no car journey. Tomorrow, if the weather is better, we go by boat.'

No, no one had told her that. A boat! She thinks of the sea they passed on the way here. Icy black and leaping against the shore. They have to go into that? And again, Jonah and the

Whale swim across her mind. She shudders as she visualises the jaws of a huge creature looming before them and engulfing them in one gulp. Then the words of Corporal Yorkshire visit her once more. She has been told not to journey onwards. However, she has come this far. Now she must heed the warnings. *You're worth more to us alive than dead.*

There is movement. Rafn and Karlsson are making their way to the door.

She looks to Anna for an explanation.

'Axel will take us to his brother's house where we will sleep.'

There is nothing for it but to concede, so she picks up her wet, battered suitcase and follows the men into the night.

Axel leads the way, holding a hurricane lamp high. It is blowing a gale out here and she realises how tired, hungry and thirsty she is. Her body tenses as they forge against the wind, up a hill, to a house that she would have missed if she were on her own.

It has the look of something straight out of a fairytale: apex roof rising to a steep point, with a wooden frontage and a small window either side of the door. Though it is half white with snow and ice, the part that is sheltered from the wind looks as though it is made of grass. This house has been cut out of the hillside with turf for its roof.

Axel opens the door without using a key and lets them in.

The frame is so low they must stoop to gain entry.

Inside it is very dark. All wood and, yes, the walls and ceiling are fashioned from slats of turf. She has never seen anything like it in her life.

Depositing the bucket of firewood and coal, Axel rests his lamp on a surface.

'Here,' he says to her. 'Kitchen. For eating. There,' he points to the interior, too dark for them to see clearly, 'bunks for you.'

Daphne masks confusion with her stage smile and thanks him.

Then Axel is gone.

The wind shrieks like a banshee, crying to get in and claw them all to death.

Daphne shivers.

For a moment her resolve fails her.

Death is on its way, she thinks.

CHAPTER TWENTY

When more lamps are lit the turf house becomes real. Though it is just as strange on the inside as out. Beneath thick clothes Daphne is sweating. She wants to tear off her layers but limits it to the outer ones. Anna has done the same: gathering their garments, she hangs them on hooks near the stove.

Rafn makes the fire.

The temperature begins to rise. Smoke seeps into the room but no one else is concerned by it. In fact, they all seem to find this accommodation quite regular. Only Karlsson, sitting on one of the bunks, notices the expression on her face.

'Many of our ancestors lived in places like this,' he explains. 'Most farmers. No wood for building. We haven't many trees.'

It is true, she hadn't seen many on her journey here before the sun went down.

'Why is that?' she asks.

He looks at her and his stare is like a thousand knives piercing her soul. How could she have thought there might be easy conversation between them? Not now he is their prisoner. Not now that she is his gaoler. For a moment they face each other over an abyss, miles apart, divided by war and ideology, here in this little house.

She shrugs – both of them believe they are doing the right thing – and takes her sodden suitcase further into the dwelling.

The sleeping area is communal. There are bunks to either side of the room. It is such an odd place. Could a family really live here? She chooses the bunk with the thickest blanket and puts her suitcase beside it to stake her claim. Rafn has disappeared. She cannot work out where he went.

A bigger stove for cooking stands at the rear, among cupboards, shelves, a sink. She peers across from it and finds a doorway into a dark passage, emerging at the other end into a second room, wood-panelled and painted a jaunty yellow. Going through, she finds chairs tucked under a table upon which burns a large oil lamp with a patterned glass shade. A love seat, painted green, is set against the far wall. It is all scrupulously clean. Rafn is squatting by a chest and rummaging through its contents.

'Won't they mind you doing that?' asks Daphne.

He jumps, darts a glance at her, returns to his task. 'Axel has given permission. It is necessary. Karlsson needs socks, boots, trousers and a better coat. He may be, as you say, an enemy of the Allies, but I will not let a fellow Icelander perish from the cold.'

That is fair enough, she thinks, and continues inspecting the room. It is brighter and prettier than the one with the bunks. 'Perhaps Anna and I should stay in here?' she suggests.

Rafn kneels back on his heels and answers decisively, 'No. We all stay together. Next door. You can use this parlour to change your clothes.' He adds, 'For privacy.'

It is delivered like a telling off and she begins to pout. He hands her a bundle of assorted garments and says, 'Give them to him, please. He can use this room to change out of his wet trousers. I will stay here.' The 'please' sweetens her temper very slightly.

She takes the pile and returns next door where Anna is brewing a hot drink. Karlsson is in the same position as before, staring at the wall.

'Here,' she says and drops the clothes in his lap. 'These are warmer and dry. You can change next door.'

Without a word he looks down at them, then, after a long sigh, gets up and goes through to the panelled room.

Everyone is doing something useful except for her, so she calls to Anna at the stove. 'Can I help?'

'In the basket,' Anna points to the entrance, 'there is a pot of stew. Fetch it for me, please.'

She does and watches Anna place the casserole over the fire. It does not take long before it is steaming.

Once they are fed and watered Rafn announces that they will take turns keeping watch. Despite Karlsson's taunts, they have no solid knowledge whether there are enemy agents on the hunt for the grimoire or that they have already left the capital. If they were sensible, they might have 'hunkered down' as Corporal Yorkshire had suggested. Which means, if they are indeed on their way, if they exist at all, then the enemy could be behind Daphne's party or up ahead. Or indeed near them now. The policeman is taking no chances.

He gives the revolver to his cousin, then pulls out drawers under the bunks and takes out more blankets.

Daphne feels the cylinder of her own gun weighing down her pocket. She did not think to use it when she was attacked in Reykjavík. Though she couldn't have reached it – her assailant had pinned down her arms. Only the blades were accessible. In a way, the fact she didn't use the pistol was a good thing: the sound, indeed the bullet itself, would quickly have alerted the authorities to a foreign agent in their midst. She has got away in the nick of time.

Karlsson, in fresh trousers and jumper, gets up from a chair by the stove to sit once more on his bunk.

Rafn has also changed his clothes and wears a Fair Isle sweater that clings to his athletic body. He plumps a pillow, which looks thin, puts another jumper over it then pulls the blankets around him like a cocoon and settles in.

Anna is taking two cups of coffee to the chairs by the stove. Daphne follows. She will need the drink to help her stay awake. Though the stew has warmed and satisfied her, it has also made her sleepy. As she sits down a sudden howl fills the room. They all start. For a moment she thinks a wild animal has got in but then she sees the sound is coming from the medium. Rafn has jumped out of bed with a blanket clutched at his waist.

The moan falls and diminishes as Karlsson's lungs empty of air. When he has finished, he gapes blankly. Daphne has seen that look before: the medium has withdrawn into his own inner country. After a minute, he splutters and falls on his side. Rafn is immediately at his shoulder, whispering words into his ear. Karlsson grunts, then the policeman unwraps the blanket he is wearing, drapes it over the stout man and tucks him in like a child. 'He's all right,' he says to Daphne and Anna. 'Anguished. He needs sleep. So do I. When you tire, wake me.'

She can't stop staring at him. His compassion is both unnerving and commendable. The Nazis see it as weakness, but right now she understands it is the very opposite. Rafn's strength pervades every fibre, every sinew. Anna taps her hand and urges her to turn round and face the stove or the window, as if this scene is something they should not witness. She tucks the revolver into one of the large pockets in her cable-knit cardigan. The metal weapon nesting in against the cosy wool is a sight that Daphne finds jarring.

Beckoning her closer, Anna lowers her voice and bends forward to whisper, 'We don't know what he is thinking.'

Daphne is not sure to whom this refers but her mind goes straight back to the medium.

Of course this is true. No one can tell what goes on inside another's brain.

'We know he has sent messages,' Anna continues. 'Messages in code.'

Daphne thinks this is stating the obvious. Then Anna whispers, 'But we do not know why.'

For a moment, Daphne does not know what to make of that statement.

Anna can evidently see it in her face for she says, 'He may have been tempted by promises of riches. Or he may have been blackmailed.'

This has not occurred to Daphne. The fresh possibility hits her so hard she feels winded. Not everyone who collaborates volunteers. She had assumed the obvious – that he was pro-Nazi. But there can be many reasons for an individual's actions. Of course there can. She herself was pressured into this work by the Secret Service dangling the carrot of her mother's release from internment, if she, Daphne, co-operated. They must always make it difficult to say no, and she thinks again of Carabella. Her father has taken up lodgings in the Isle of Man and reports that the camp is not the same or as harsh as those reserved for prisoners-of-war. People may come and go more freely. She pictures her mother with her basket on her arm and wonders if she is still able to shop and cook. She hopes so: fresh food is very important to her. And then, for a moment, she worries that she has abandoned her parents to their predicament. But she swiftly gathers herself. She is doing the very opposite. All of this, *all* of it, is for them. And the country and king. That is why she is here in this strange house made of turf.

Who, she ponders, is Karlsson doing his bit for?

Anna gestures to Daphne she should bring her chair closer to the stove. It is made of iron and appears orange in the tawny light that reflects off the wooden floor and beams. There is something about the way it is wrought that reminds her of Russia. A chimney draws smoke out through the top of the hut, though it is still hazy inside, the smell mixing with the damp, earthy cud of the walls.

Around the window above the stove, curtains not completely drawn flutter in the draft. It feels like this room will never get entirely warm. But at least it is not cold. Somewhere in between.

Out of her pocket Anna produces two small glasses and a hip flask. She fills them both to the brim and offers one to Daphne, who hesitates, unsure whether she should drink when she's already fatigued. About two seconds is all it takes to convince herself she should try the amber liquid. It is like fire in her throat but peculiarly reassuring.

One of the men has begun to snore.

'My brother was a farmer,' says Anna, looking out of the window through the gap in the curtains. 'Stayed on after Father gained his position in Reykjavík.'

'Oh,' says Daphne. Somehow, she had thought that Anna had lived in the city all her life. She has a worldly, cosmopolitan aura about her that other Icelanders do not. 'Do you visit often?'

Anna jerks her head up. 'Visit?'

'Your brother? Is his house like this?'

Taking a long draught of the spirit, Anna directs her gaze once more towards the storm swirling outside. 'No.'

Leaves and debris crack against the glass. Daphne can hear the black waters, close by, seething. 'Did he end up in Reykjavík too?' she asks.

Anna's eyes are vague, absent of their usual acuity. 'Who?'

'Your brother?'

Another slug. She takes out her hip flask and refills the glass. Daphne is not sure that her friend should be drinking this much. Not when they have a journey by boat to make tomorrow. Not when there is so much at stake. But she is not going to caution her. Already she is aware that Anna is her own woman. She will do what she likes, regardless of the counsel of others.

'No,' says Anna.

The word is spoken at high volume and makes Daphne flinch. It is as if she has said something to offend. 'Sorry,' she says, simultaneously noting how English she sounds. However, her unnecessary apology has softened Anna.

'Þór is dead,' she says. 'Killed.'

'Oh, I am sorry,' Daphne says, unaware she is apologising again. It is a default.

'I told you this island trembles a hundred times a year. Sometimes it is nothing. Sometimes it is everything.'

Reading the confusion in Daphne's face, she says, 'Sheep-gathering weekend. He went up to get the flock down from the hills. My brother. But the earth trembled, and it was Something.' Anna's voice is surprisingly steady but her grip on the glass is tight. 'Rocks, earth, all that had been perched upon a precipice, came free. Down the hill they toppled, into the fjord, taking him and a couple of the sheep with them. Though most were found alive, Þór was not. His life was ended.'

This intimate disclosure floors Daphne. She cannot use the word 'sorry' again. To do so would be trite. However, she finds herself floundering for a response and does not know how she might make her grieving friend feel better, ease the pain evident in the furrows of her brow, the tense, knotted muscles of her throat and jaw.

Eventually Daphne tells her, 'That is an awful tragedy. It must have devastated you and your family.'

Anna throws back her head and gulps down more brandy (if that is what it is). Feeling the need to do the same, Daphne coughs and splutters as the spirit burns her gullet. Her obvious inexperience with strong liquor raises a smile from Anna as she refills the glasses. 'Skál,' she toasts Daphne.

'But tomorrow?' she bleats.

Anna shrugs. 'We can never know what tomorrow will bring.' She leans over and clinks her glass.

Daphne understands she is not talking about this moment. No one professes to know what the future holds. Although they have one in their midst who says he does – and her mind goes back to Karlsson's séance: *The hand of death is on your shoulder.* Is everything he says a hoax? All the messages some kind of code for the enemy? Or is some of it . . . is it genuine foresight?

She shivers and swallows a large measure of the drink. This time it is not so harsh on her throat.

The woman before her, she sees, has risked a lot to accompany them here: returning to the countryside has brought back painful memories. Daphne feels a surge of gratitude and wonders how it has come about that the journalist is willing to take on such a task. 'Why are you doing this?' she asks.

'You get used to it,' Anna replies with a smile. 'Eventually you end up liking it,' she says, and raises the glass to her lips once more.

'No,' says Daphne, correcting her. 'I meant, all of this.' She gestures to Karlsson and Rafn now sleeping in their bunks. 'Helping me. Assisting the British.'

'Oh,' says Anna. 'I had a friend. In Germany. I studied there,' she explains to Daphne's puzzled expression. 'He was a dissident and sent to Dachau, a work camp, last year. We think he is dead.'

Her language is blunt. Her tone entirely devoid of emotion. But Daphne watches Anna's eyes blinking rapidly as she drains her drink and the empty glass trembles momentarily in her hand.

'They must be stopped,' her friend says. 'A true democracy needs all opinions to be heard. Not *some* of them. Germany is no longer a democracy.'

Daphne is about to agree when there is a loud crash on the other side of the window. Anna is already up. Daphne grabs her coat and the two of them run out into the night. It is hard to see anything in the storm.

'Someone was here,' shouts Daphne and points to footprints in the snow, already being covered by fresh flakes.

Anna looks around for a moment more, but the wind is tearing at her hair. She clutches her arms around herself. 'They're not here now,' she says and goes back inside, teeth chattering.

Daphne follows. Anna bolts the door after her.

'Could it be the Germans?' Daphne asks as she rehangs her coat and goes straight back to the fire to warm her hands. The shock of the outside temperature has brought on involuntary shivers.

'I don't know.'

'Or maybe they are already there. Maybe they have beaten us to the grimoire.' Her voice is morose.

'Unless there have been some communications that we are not privy to, the only person who knows *exactly* where the book is hidden in Hólmavík is Sindri,' says Anna and Daphne marvels at her logical deduction. 'The spies may be there, but they will have to wait for him. They may know the region. They may know the town. But they do not know the specific hiding place. Or else, and I hope to God this is not the case,' she says, and casts her eyes out towards the storm again, 'they are following us, watching us even now.'

The gusts and drafts are developing into a wild frenzy. No one could be out in that, Daphne thinks. But the prospect of someone watching them feels very real.

She breathes out heavily.

'You're exhausted,' says Anna. 'Get some rest for a few hours. I have found a book I can read.'

Daphne would like to object, to stay awake with her till Rafn takes over, but her friend is right: forty winks will keep her going.

'An hour is all I need,' she says and gets in the bunk fully dressed.

'The night will be long,' says Anna. 'I will wake you, perhaps in two. Is that all right?'

But Daphne is already asleep.

**PM's Memorandum**

W.C. wishes you to send a letter immediately to Major the Hon. J. J. Astor.

---

~~Amidst this terrible plague of war,~~ You and your staff must be ~~so~~ very highly commended for the honourable manner in which you ~~have kept up your spirits and~~ continued in your duties and commitment to the country despite the awful destruction and disturbance you experienced when you were bombed yesterday at Printing House Square.

~~I didn't~~ Nobody, ~~not I,~~ at least none of your readers, would ever be able to tell from reading the latest edition of The Times that your editorial and management offices have been utterly devastated. I hope there were no casualties.

Your ~~strength~~ dedication and high values of professionalism are beyond compare.

This is the spirit with which war is won! Well done.

*At once please!*

CHAPTER TWENTY-ONE

It is still dark when she awakes. Sleep has been fitful. She was hot in the night, as if she was burning. Memories of the bombing in Christchurch had seeped once more into her dreams – the hole in the ground, a flaming crater, smouldering leafless trees. For a brief second she detects smoke in the room and throws back the blankets, expecting flames. Then she sees where she is, and her brain revolves and places her in the current chronology. That's right, she is in Iceland now. In a hut full of fumes from a wood-burning stove.

The room is unexpectedly warm. She stretches and hears the vertebrae in her neck crack. Time to get up.

When she reaches the stove by the window, she finds Rafn there.

'Oh,' she says. 'I'm sorry. How long have I been out?'

He shrugs. 'Anna woke me at three.'

Oh, no, that means Daphne has had a good few hours.

There is a solitary candle alight on a shelf by the window. The flame flickers in the draft so she cannot properly see his face and isn't able to ascertain whether he is disapproving of her lengthy slumber. Daphne herself feels guilty but also simultaneously refreshed and much better for it.

'Do you want coffee?' he asks and points to a steaming pot.

She accepts and he pads down the centre of the room and returns with a mug, which he fills and presents to her. No milk or sugar but she will have it any which way. Her mouth is parched.

'What's the time?' she yawns.

'Close to seven. I will rouse the others soon. But we cannot go out before dawn. And only then if there are fishermen willing to take us.'

'Willing? We can pay good money.'

'The storm has abated but the water is still rough. Few will venture out in it, for good money or bad. And,' he says, contracting his brow as he looks at the window and moves closer to the glass, 'this village is one of the smallest in the country. Not many people.'

When he relaxes back into his chair, she catches a whiff of his scent, which is musky and very male. Like wood and resolve and vigour.

'I will go out and see if Axel has had any luck,' says Rafn but doesn't move.

The thought of staying here another day is intolerable. 'Right,' she is still absorbing everything he has said, 'I see.'

Thinking she had better get on and dress for whatever the day brings, she is about to ask where she might wash when Rafn suddenly says, 'You look attractive in this light.'

At first, she is unsure that she has heard correctly and swivels her head to face him. He is regarding her with those pale hazel eyes, which are alert and large and full of energy, though the rest of his person is motionless, perfectly still, composed.

For a moment she wonders if he means that she looks unattractive in other lights. But the thought scatters when he says, 'We will go for a meal at a restaurant when we are back in Reykjavík. You and I.'

It is a statement, not a question as is usual when making overtures to the opposite sex. She does not mind too much: his directness seems appropriate in this turf hut that resembles a Viking longhouse. 'Don't you have a girlfriend?' she asks him. After all he is good-looking and athletic. As soon as she has said it, however, she worries that she has been too forward.

His reply confuses her. 'I don't know,' he says.

When they were walking to the picture house on the first night that they saw Karlsson, Anna told her that sometimes young Icelandic couples will live with each other before they marry, to see if they like it. Or if they don't. Perhaps Rafn has tried it and not liked it. Or perhaps his girlfriend did not like it.

She thinks briefly of Jack and wonders if he is walking out with other pretty girls who populate his neck of the wood – wherever that is – and suspects, in a moment of clarity, that if the opportunity presents itself then he will probably take it. So why shouldn't she? 'A drink would be nice,' she says, and then something catches in her throat and she begins to cough.

Rafn gets to his feet and goes to fetch a glass of water. When he passes her, he puts his hand on her shoulder. It is like a shock. As he removes it, she feels as if his fingers have showered electric particles across her skin and is stunned by her reaction.

Is that all it takes, she wonders, for you to find someone attractive, Daphne? For them to tell you they like you first? Is that all it takes, you fickle, fair-weather friend?

No, she thinks. It can't be that.

It is easy to be undone by the senses. Smell and touch can be as powerfully persuasive as sight and sound. You simply don't notice how much influence they exert until your body reacts. It is instinctive.

*Now* she is fully aware of him, of his position in the hut, of the way he moves, of his natural dexterity, as if he is in full command of his body. Unlike her.

When she takes the glass off him, she can't help but smile. He does too.

And it lights her up.

'Gaaah.' Someone in the bunks is waking. Which is a shame as she would have liked more time to see what would happen. If anything. She is still not sure if they have understood each other correctly. Though there is definitely something there. A charge in the air between their bodies.

'Hvar er . . .?'

It is Karlsson moving about in the dimness of the sleeping area, bumping into the other bunks. He makes a low noise as he yawns. Then female sounds: a light sneeze and a grunt. A match flares and an oil lamp is lit.

'I need to wash,' says Daphne, becoming aware of her messy hair and crinkled clothes: how does she *really* look in this light? Is her face dirty?

Rafn's eyes flicker over her for a second longer than is absolutely necessary before he says, 'Heat some water on the stove then take it through to the other room. There is a jug and bowl on the windowsill.'

Anna jogs her as she moves through the hut. 'I will use the water after you,' she says. 'Don't throw it away.'

Daphne nods and fills a saucepan.

# Vindgapi

Take the head of a ling and carve the stave on it and with a raven's feather apply blood from the right foot into the stave. Put the head on a pole and raise it where land meets sea. Point the mouth in the direction the wind should blow from. The greater the height the mouth points at, the more forceful the wind call will be.

CHAPTER TWENTY-TWO

The water had been calmer when they set sail from Borðeyri.

However, the boat is not what she had imagined. Little more than a dinghy with two sails, they are to be rowed into the next fjord where a larger vessel will take them on to Hólmavík. Of course, she objected. To which Anna replied, 'It's either this or we walk.'

A persuasive argument.

Sitting on a plank across the boat, her feet in a puddle, Daphne raises her eyes to the receding land and sees the mountains that cradle the fjord, shining bone-white like the smooth plane of a skull. Three black rocks rising through the snow give the impression of empty eye sockets, a nose cavity. Beneath those the bank juts out, like a jaw twisted in warning. Low clouds seep down over houses on the slopes, like jealous ghosts reclaiming their old homes.

It does not take long to reach the next fjord. They change onto a fishing vessel with a small crew who eye their group with suspicion. She knows from home that there are those in remote villages who view outsiders in the same way. So she ignores their stares and soon adjusts to the ebb and flow, the slap of the waves that sends spray over the sides. The stink of fish on the decks is strong. Scales are everywhere. The wind in her hair blows out any cobwebs that still cling to her brain, and despite the odour, she feels as if she is being given an air bath, washed clean all over, inside and out.

For a while they make good speed. But soon she sees that what started as a mist curling up from the waves has met the clouds descending the mountainsides and become a thicker fog, creeping across the boat like a wraith's fingers searching out something to squeeze.

It forces them to weigh anchor closer to shore. On deck there is much consternation. The fishermen are uneasy and fractious. Their voices rise like an angry flock of gulls squabbling over food until one man, in middle age with rough chapped skin, approaches Rafn and Karlsson, assuming that they are in charge of this odd expedition.

An older fisherman, with a dark-grey, fluffy beard, trails him but will not talk. He eyes Anna and Daphne and shakes his head. Rafn remonstrates, hands held in front of him, gesticulating in small, sharp movements.

Across the deck Anna leans into Daphne. 'They want us to go below,' she whispers.

'Why?'

'They think we have brought bad luck on them. And fishermen, I'm sorry to say, are very superstitious.'

Daphne rolls her eyes. 'Because we are women?' she asks. This fallacy exists back home amongst the sailors and fishermen of Leigh-on-Sea. Though she had thought it irrational, not credible, and supposed it was a good excuse to keep their wives and daughters in the house, hard at work and out of their way.

Anna does not confirm or deny it but says, 'One of them recognised Karlsson from the newspaper. Same as Kolbrún did. These fishers have also heard the rumours she mentioned to us that night. About the book from which he draws his power. They have put two and two together and think he is going to consult it.'

'Goodness, news spreads fast here,' Daphne says, unnerved by this revelation.

Her friend shrugs and dislodges some of the dewdrops covering her hair. 'The issue is that, where we are heading – deeper into Strandir – it is a region of magic and sorcery. And of witch-hunts. In the past men have been flogged or worse – burned alive – if found with a grimoire in their possession.'

'But centuries ago, surely?' says Daphne.

'Time works differently out here. Seasons are longer – and shorter too. The darkness of winter means much time spent inside where there is not much to do but tell tales. Events are narrated as stories and held onto, retold as lessons. We remember our ancestors. Their stories live in us. They are not buried in the distant past.'

'So,' concludes Daphne, 'the fishermen are worried about the grimoire. Is it the magic it contains? Or is it the fear of retribution from the Church? Perhaps it is of Karlsson himself? Though they have no trouble talking to him now.'

'A strange clairvoyant seeking advice from a grimoire might alarm them as much as two women aboard their vessel. Probably it is a combination of both. Anyway see – Rafn is reasoning with them,' Anna interprets as her cousin nods, hands on hips, listening to the red-faced fisherman. 'Yet reason is not a fish they catch regularly in their nets.'

It is an apt allegory. As Daphne watches the men talking, her eyes stray past them to the strange symbols carved into the wood of the prow. They are similar to staves painted onto The Grand Mystique's Mystery Box, which can, in front of an audience, produce flowers, scarves, animals. The sigils engraved here, however, are clearly no trivial ornamentation. They are functional, warding something off, evocative of real magic and as powerfully pagan as the landscape. For a moment she has a sense that above her the old gods are looking down on them, observing how they will navigate this impasse, considering intervention.

'Come on,' says Anna. 'Let's go down below for a bit. We can listen from the step.' She slips her arm through Daphne's and they go into the wheelhouse and climb down the ladder. A cabin, presumably the skipper's, has its door open – an invitation. Daphne is about to go in, but Anna tugs on her sleeve and puts a finger to her lips. They stand at the bottom, listening.

'What are they saying?' she asks.

'I can't hear everything. Someone is talking of trolls.'

A few weeks ago, Daphne would have laughed at such a statement. However, since she has been in Iceland she has seen faces everywhere. Yesterday there was one high up in a mountain that looked so real a jolt of fear went through her. 'The boulders and indentations in the mountains,' she says, as if in answer, 'they look like the facial features of great giants.'

'And if you gaze at them for long enough,' says a voice from above, 'they move.'

It is Rafn, hands on the rail at the top of the hatch, leaning over them and grinning.

She laughs longer than she should and feels silly. Then she wishes that he hadn't told her she was attractive. Then she is pleased that he has. *Not now, Daphne!* she scolds herself, irritated by the lack of discipline her brain is showing. *No time for girlish dizziness.* Not in the middle of Iceland. In the middle of a fjord. On a boat with a mutinous crew.

'We seem to have reached a compromise,' says Rafn, staring down. His hair hangs forward, surrounding his face, a blond halo. 'They want Karlsson to cast a magic circle round the boat for protection.'

Anna nods as if this is perfectly normal. Daphne says, 'Oh. Will he do that?'

'Yes,' says Rafn. 'But you must come and join in.'

Daphne is surprised that the medium is obliging but then she supposes he is also stuck, half adrift, in the cold. This situation works for no one.

Rafn lends her a hand as she reaches the top of the ladder and pulls her out. She thanks him and sees only the nick of a smile on his lips. All his features are carefully composed so she too adopts a solemn expression.

The three of them join a circle the fishermen and medium have created. It spans the deck. Nets have been pushed aside, machinery tacked to the pulleys and winches.

Now no one is speaking she notices a stagnant silence. The water is still, the fog soundlessly gliding over them, wetting their hair with tiny diamonds. Within it, Daphne thinks for a moment that she can see faces, ghost Valkyries developing like photographs on light-sensitive paper. She stares and then blinks. They lose their form and separate, swirling into the mist.

The medium throws his hands high. This time his words are Icelandic, rhythmic, rising and falling. She hears 'Baldur' and somehow knows he is the god of light and radiance. Then 'Odin', the sage and supreme one-eyed god who hung himself upside down on the Tree of Life to gain wisdom. Though she remembers, as Karlsson and the men lift their chins to the hazy heavens, he is also the god of war and death. Should they really be calling on him?

Karlsson pauses for a moment, his recitation echoing across the fjord, as if an infinite number of mediums are repeating his prayer. And then she hears the most extraordinary sound. A wail. No, not a wail, a note like a bell. It is a sea creature singing. A mermaid. High-pitched, like a violin, then sonorous, booming like the beat of a huge drum. The hairs on the back of her neck prickle to attention and a shiver goes all the way through her. She swivels her head to the source and sees that the fishermen are approving of this development. Sindri nods gravely then bows his head. The ceremony is over. One of the fishermen claps. The circle breaks up.

Daphne grabs at Anna. 'What is that? It sounds like a sea monster.'

Anna grins. 'It is, in a way. A whale. But this is good. The men think it has heard the prayer and will protect them.'

Rafn takes her to the starboard side of the boat. 'It is coming from over there,' he says and points into the mist.

Again, the noise comes. Lighter than before: entrancing but simultaneously alarming, a siren calling them onto the rocks. 'I haven't heard a whale before.'

'They are beautiful singers, no?'

She considers this for a moment. Is the sound beautiful? It is certainly like nothing she has ever heard, timeless – at once ancient and new. 'They are,' she agrees.

An enormous splash. As if one of the trolls has thrown a log into the water. And she sees the fuzzy outline of a shape: darkness emerging as a rotating crescent sawing through the surface. Mottled skin is patterned by white markings on its flippers and underside, oddly similar to their runes that stain the prow. A fin is followed by a wide and powerful tail, which rises and then thumps down like a huge oar. The wave it creates jogs the boat and fleetingly she thinks of Jonah again.

The whale exhales forcefully through its blowhole, creating a spout of mist that rises into the air, like a gun discharging or a volcano's sudden eruption, and for an instant she is frightened by its massive frame, aware of her own human fragility. And in this moment she understands too that she is Jonah. The whale is the war swallowing them up whole. She hopes, prays, in fact sends up a plea to the heavens, that she too will be vomited up on a safe shore one day when all of this is over.

The cries begin again. Its song is uncanny, haunting, summoning memories of rituals in summer, Sunday school, fire and brimstone, barracking priests: Archangel Israfil blowing his horn signalling Judgement Day.

Celestial echoes, she thinks. Deep and resonant, they reverberate throughout the entire fjord.

'Is it happy or sad?' she asks Rafn.

'I don't know,' he says.

They watch the beast swim and turn, making for the horizon. She is unaware for how long it keeps them mesmerised, though when Rafn tugs her back from the rail and says, 'We're moving,' she sees that the fog is lifting. The mountains are visible again.

'Karlsson's ritual has worked,' says Rafn. 'The men are pleased. But they would still like you to use the mess. Perhaps you can be ship's cook and make coffee?'

Magician's assistant, occultist, writer, spy. She has played so many roles already, what is one more?

'Fine,' she says and goes below, still listening to the colossus' chorus looping in her head, wondering what it all means, what will happen next, when the journey will end.

But if she knew, she would not be so compliant. She would turn the boat right round and go straight back to England.

## CHAPTER TWENTY-THREE

Little twinkling town. Tucked in, under a pristine white blanket. Hólmavík is as pretty as an alpine village and could be miniaturised perfectly for a Christmas snow globe. Though it is not snowing here. Perhaps it is too cold for it. Back home, when there were icicles on the windowsills and breath-frosting air, her father would tell her it was 'too chilly for snow'. Though Daphne knew his theory did not stand up to scientific scrutiny, she would nod along with him, intuitively recognising what he meant – the conditions were not right for it. On this alien planet, she has no sense of whether it will snow again or if they have seen the worst of it. The climate here is unpredictable. Arctic storms one minute, gales the next, fog, mist, then sunshine. She cannot make head nor tail of it. The fact that the sun has passed behind a mountain peak to the west adds to a general feeling of discombobulation. They are in a strange passing dusk and the world feels very unsteady and transient to Daphne. Though she is pleased to set foot once again on solid ground.

The fishermen have dropped anchor and will sleep on the boat while they wait for the shore party. However, there will be no return tonight. 'Too much danger,' Rafn tells her.

She accepts this without further question and takes his hand as he leads her down the small rocky outcrop to the harbourside. The path is slippery and wet. They intend to stay at the house of another cousin, more distant, who lives here.

Karlsson drags his feet. He is not nimble and leans on Anna. But Daphne thinks it is not just the uneven surface that slows him down. A scarf has been looped tightly over his head, protection from the wind, but what she can glimpse of his face is tense, almost stricken. There is fear in his eyes: the moment is nearing when he will have to give up his secret. If it has not been pillaged already. And then what will happen to him once his Nazi paymasters discover his compromise? They do not treat their own countrymen with dignity, so goodness knows what will befall the Icelander. Karlsson may well be safer in custody than free in Reykjavík.

She has not spoken to him about the methods by which he has passed on information. It is not necessary. The medium is a means to an end. Rafn, however, has grilled him. Anna overheard the conversation on the boat and translated. He wanted to know about the forecasts. As she and Anna had worked out, there is a leak at the army base where the ground for the Reykjavík airfield is being cleared. Whether intentionally or accidentally, the troops are giving out information about convoys – when they can expect supplies and what date their letters must be posted by. It is background noise to most of the native workers but some recognise its value to enemy ears. On the grimoire Karlsson has been more cagey, professing ignorance of who is interested in it. Rafn has declared he doesn't believe him, but Anna isn't sure. 'I wouldn't be surprised if he doesn't know who it will go to. Why should he? The German spies are no more than a cog in a wheel. Like you.' Which sounded rude to Daphne but then Anna said, 'You do not know why you must get the book either.'

She cannot disagree.

Anna shook her head slowly. 'There is something else going on there,' she said. 'For sure he is not telling Rafn everything.'

This Daphne thinks is certain. She would do the same in his situation. He is trapped and thinking through his options, biding his time, waiting to reveal his hand.

The fake bravado is gone now and all she sees is a lumpish, overweight man, pasty and unfit to tackle the territory before them.

As they make their way up the road away from the water, Rafn points to a house and they head for it.

When they enter she sees that, though it is a dwelling, it is populated with a handful of people sitting at tables drinking coffee.

Rafn goes to a makeshift counter as the rest of them take chairs by the fire, which is hearty and welcoming.

It takes her a few moments to realise that everyone inside is looking at them. They seem to be the source of mild amusement. She reaches over to tell Anna but she says 'Shh!' and minutely inclines her head in the direction of two old men sitting at a table by the window, smoking and talking in low voices. Anna is tuning into the conversation. She eyes Karlsson who, in turn, shakes his head, 'Ég veit ekki.' Somehow Daphne understands this means 'I don't know.'

Bending her head to Daphne's ear, Anna murmurs, 'They say Hólmavík is busy this week. "With these four strangers today and those two yesterday."'

'Oh,' says Daphne. 'Were the strangers German?'

Anna shrugs. 'They need not be. German sympathisers and operatives might also have Icelandic nationality.' She nods at Karlsson and Daphne sees her point. Despite the warmth in the room, her mood chills and she shivers.

She pictures the two strangers with the grimoire and fire rips through her veins. It cannot be snatched away from her now. Not after all of this. The thought is appalling and before she knows what she is doing, she has grabbed Karlsson's wrist.

He yelps as she snarls, 'Where is it?' Even she is surprised by the venom in her voice. '*Where?*'

Both Anna and the medium stare at her, appalled. When Karlsson jerks his hand away she sees her fingernails have cut into the soft flesh below his palm. And yet, his response is what she was after.

'Not far,' he says and his head dips, as if shame is sitting heavily across his shoulders. 'But the light is going,' he says. 'We can't get there.'

No! Daphne snaps her gaze to Anna. 'How much of the day is left before sunset?'

Her friend's brow is furrowed, lips easing out of a twist of disgust. 'Night comes sooner up north. Up here.'

That is no help to Daphne and again her tone reveals a coarse urgency that appears to disturb both Icelanders, 'How *much* longer do we have?'

Anna grimaces and gazes out at the white sky. 'Ninety minutes. Maybe less.'

'Then we go at once,' says Daphne. The resolution in her voice brooks no argument.

'It is dangerous,' says Karlsson.

She is not sure she believes him and thinks it is more likely that he does not want them to find the book. Perhaps he is stalling so that the strangers, whoever they are, might come to his assistance. Whatever the reason she will not be put off. She has too much to lose, so purses her lips and shakes her head.

When Rafn sets down a tray of steaming mugs, he does not notice the change of atmosphere at the table. Both Anna and Karlsson are more guarded now they have glimpsed Daphne's violent heart. If only they knew what else she has done, what she *will* do.

Directly she turns to Rafn, informing him that there have been other strangers in the town.

Eyebrows prick up as he digests the news and works through its implications, but then he sits down and takes a sip of his coffee. It irritates Daphne.

Though there is nothing to be done about it: Rafn will do what Rafn wants to do and when *he* decides. He is like his cousin in that way.

After a long minute he puts the drink down and heads for the door.

'Wait!' says Karlsson, and Rafn pauses. 'We will need ponies,' he says.

Rafn takes this on board with a nod and leaves.

The three of them wait.

This sign you should carve on oak.

Colour it with blood from the toe of your foot and the thumb of your left hand, lay the sign on the grave and then walk three times clockwise and three times widdershins around the church. Three surges of earth will then spew from the grave. At the last one the sorcerer must be prepared to receive the dead. Grab the ghost by his neck and squeeze until he asks for mercy. Only then you must instruct the ghost to the tasks he must do. If these be great and much more preparation needed, the sorcerer must be firm and strong.

# CHAPTER TWENTY-FOUR

It is a hard climb up the hills beyond the town. Every so often Karlsson whimpers. He is worried, he says, that in the darkness they will get lost.

Daphne ignores him. She finds his behaviour unmasculine.

When he lets out a high moan for a third time, she titters, then considers if it *is* unmasculine to show fear? She does not think this is necessarily the case. A great many women she knows curb such instincts. It is just Karlsson's way. People are different. And will become more so as the war strains them. Without a doubt it has changed her. Though she is too caught up in the present to consider how. Presently she must direct all her concentration to riding the pony.

While Rafn and the medium seem to have taken to the horses naturally, Daphne, who has only been on such a creature fewer than a handful of times, is sliding off her saddle and finding it hard to balance. Icelandic horses, or 'ponies' as the locals call them, are small. But the ground still looks a long way down and she does not want to fall off. Her backside keeps slapping against the saddle and she cannot find the pony's rhythm.

'How much further?' she shouts to Karlsson.

'Beyond the next peak. On the downward slope.'

Now she sees why he was reluctant to leave the safety of Hólmavík. The track is narrow and peat-brown, snow and boulders all around. Should a storm come in, they could easily find themselves trapped. And the sprays of clouds do seem to be getting lower. At least her pony is sure-footed and does not seem to have much trouble with the rough terrain.

Anna has taken their luggage to the cousin's house. Daphne is pleased she is not with them: the weight of her friend's displeasure at her conduct in the café, or whatever the house was, is uncomfortable. However, she knows better than her friend that war brings out both good and bad in those it touches. There are things she has done she is not proud of, but which were required. One must subsume one's own nature and niceties for the sake of the task. Hard decisions must be made. Anna will find out, she thinks, soon enough. But for the time being she has the luxury of reproof and judgement. Daphne does not begrudge her that. She knows, deep inside herself, that she now exists on a different moral plane.

'There!' yells Karlsson as they crest the summit and she can see in the distance something that looks like a ruin.

'What is it?' says Daphne squinting into the shadows. It is about two hundred yards down on the western slope.

The sun's rays have not grazed this hillside for a while and the snow here is crisp with ice. The horse's hooves punch into it as she leans forward. 'Hurry up,' she whispers in its ears. Though she doubts it understands English so taps it with her foot as well. It tosses its head and moves faster.

When she catches up with Karlsson, he turns to her. 'It's a farmhouse,' he says. 'No longer used.'

He is right about that. The place looks more like an outhouse on a farm back home than a main building. Dereliction and disrepair have taken their toll. The corrugated iron that covers it is orange with rust and sagging. All its windows are broken, most entirely glassless. It is a ghost of its former self.

Rafn reaches it, dismounts and ties his horse to a fence post that has pitched sideways.

They arrive only minutes later and tether the horses.

It is in a worse state inside. Beams poke up from the ground at odd angles. The roof has fallen in and snow drifts against the shadowy south wall. Whoever lived here abandoned their home in haste. A wheelbarrow lies on its side next to a loose wheel. Chairs look like they have been knocked over and left. Though shelves remain up on a wall, the items on them – two tins, a ball of old string and a jar – have gathered a great deal of dust.

Rafn is already at the other end, busy with a freestanding cupboard that has been clogged up by rocks and earth. His head is down and he is pulling at a fallen beam that blocks it.

Karlsson cries out, 'There!'

And she realises what Rafn is doing. 'Is that where it is?'

The medium nods. 'Inside the larder. Hidden in a tin box.'

How did Rafn know? Had they talked about it? *Without her?*

Racing up to him, she sees he has pushed the beam away, scraped the soil with his gloved fingers.

When Karlsson reaches them, he is panting.

'Help me,' Rafn says to the medium and gestures for him to use his weight on a rock that has fallen against the cupboard door.

But instead Daphne puts her shoulder to it and they push and push until it is dislodged. Rafn returns to the cupboard door and pulls hard. The fact that it still has a handle is a miracle.

It sticks.

The policeman puts his foot against the frame and tries again.

This time, with a shudder, it opens.

He drops to his knees. His head goes into the dark place at the bottom.

'Is it there?' she asks, louder than intended.

He doesn't answer so she bends down and peers in. Rafn pulls away a length of lino and hesitates. His teeth press into his lower lip. When Daphne looks down she finds one of the saddest sights she thinks she has ever seen. A small white fox is curled up in a layer of cloth. The tiny thing must have found a way in through one of the holes in the floor. It has frost on its claws. As Rafn lifts it out a section of fabric clings to it. She extends her arm and helps pull it free. Some of the fur comes away.

'Must have crawled in to escape the storm,' says Rafn.

'And succumbed, poor dear,' she says.

Rafn hands it to her. At first she does not want to take the desolate creature, which seems, at that precise moment, to embody everything that is wrong with the world. Then she wonders if it is diseased and may contaminate her? But she has gloves on, so takes it from him and carries it, like a baby, back to the door, looking for somewhere to make a small grave. It barely weighs a thing. Icy and hard. But it leadens her heart.

She opts for the snowdrift and lays the fox gently on the ground, scoops out a small hollow, then wraps the fabric around the little creature. It cannot lie in its shallow grave unprotected, cold and alone. She sends it a kiss through the air then pats the bundle and piles snow on top.

Behind her, she hears Rafn speaking – no, not speaking, exclaiming, in Icelandic.

'What is it?' she calls.

'Gone,' says Karlsson.

Then she is there, at his shoulder, staring into a box of boxes, like a Russian doll. Newspaper has been wrapped round a suitcase. Within it is a rectangular tin. The tarnished gold lining glints. It makes no sense.

It is unthinkable.

It is empty.

Her stomach pitches. They are too late. The Germans have beaten them.

Reading her expression as dismay, Rafn shakes his head. 'They cannot have been already. The snow and earth out here

– untouched.' He waves his hand in the direction of the wooden beam he has shifted. 'The fox, frozen solid.'

And she understands what he is saying. It has not been disturbed for a while. At least days, maybe weeks, months.

'But if not them, then who?' she asks facing Karlsson.

His high forehead is stitched full of frowns. 'What is that?' He pokes a stubby finger at one corner of the tin.

They peer inside.

Something is there. A tiny square of parchment that has been folded and folded till it looks like a crumb. Rafn scrapes it away from the sides with a fingernail, then gently opens it out. He scowls, asks, 'What is this?' and shows it to the medium.

The effect on Karlsson is immediate. He jerks back and gasps. 'A curse!'

All Daphne can see is a circle, intersected by lines and garlanded by the runic symbols she has seen on the boat.

'Death,' says Karlsson. 'Don't touch it!'

And she witnesses a tremor run through the medium. *The mountain shakes.*

But none of this seems to affect Rafn. He is peering closely at the scrap. Daphne too can see it more clearly and recognises it is dried animal skin. 'Just words and patterns,' he says, turning it over. 'There is something on the other side.' He shows it to Karlsson. Who blanches.

'A spell,' says the medium, reading the odd sun-shaped symbol with a rudimentary face carved into it. '"To see the shadow of he who has stolen from me."'

Suddenly, he seems to buckle and stagger, grabbing hold of Daphne for support. As she grips his coat, she senses that this message is intended for him. '*You* stole it,' she says. 'You stole the grimoire. Who from?'

His voice falters as he bleats, 'I borrowed it. From a farmer. With a family line of sorcerers.'

Rafn snorts. 'You borrowed it and were selling it on to the Germans? That is stealing, my friend.'

Karlsson's lips move as if he is composing a defence but can't find the words.

Daphne's anger is mounting. She shakes his arm roughly. 'So you swiped it?' She laughs with a bitterness that makes her mouth taste sour. 'But the farmer has played you. He has got it back! Where is this *sorcerer*? Where does he live?'

The medium totters. She wonders if he is going to faint, but then he says, 'In Hólmavík,' his voice sounds as if it comes from far away. 'Not far from the town.'

'The light is going,' says Rafn. 'We must hurry.'

CHAPTER TWENTY-FIVE

It is pitch-black when they reach the cousin's house. Their hosts are uneasy, eyeing the newcomers with both curiosity and apprehension, whispering to each other in low, fraught voices.

They have been allotted a place on the ground floor, a cross between a boot room and a storage space. Three beds have been made up. Karlsson has collapsed into one of them. Pale and sweating, he shivers beneath blankets and the coats they have piled on top. It is clear he is in no fit state to venture out again.

A fresh plan is hastily convened. Anna will take the revolver and nurse Karlsson, while Daphne and Rafn proceed to the Magnússon farmstead, home of Viktor, from whom Karlsson stole the grimoire.

They have lanterns but so far there is no sign of snow.

In fact, the moon is high and clear tonight. Approaching its fullest aspect, it lights the way so there is no need to use the lantern yet. The stars are out, scrutinising them coldly, blinking in astonishment at the two little figures moving over the planet's surface. Their restless energy bounces off them.

Although Daphne was uncomfortable at first walking at night, Rafn has reassured her that it is a regular occurrence here. So far north, the islanders are accustomed to going out in the dark. There is so much of it, both in terms of daytime spent with the sun out of sight, and of the darkness itself: with very few streetlights or landmarks, the horizon merges with the black belly of the sky so that it seems that there is just a yawning chasm ahead, ready to gobble them up whole.

Thankfully it doesn't take long for her night vision to kick in and then contours in the land show themselves, shades of black against navy, grey on brown.

'But how will we convince them to give it up?' Daphne asks.

Rafn laughs. It is a nice sound. She is not sure she has heard it before. 'You know the answer to that,' he says.

'I do?'

'If they don't hand it over to us, there are others on their way here who will not be so pleasant.'

'The Germans. Or their sympathisers,' she concludes.

'We are all aware that they are playing this war game unlike any other. The British, at least, have integrity. They are known for their honour.'

She nods but is not as convinced. She has experienced this 'honour'. It comes with strings attached and thinly veiled threats. However, she thinks she is best placed to persuade the farmer to co-operate. And failing that, she has her gun.

The way is hard going. Uphill. When they turn a corner and crest the mountain, she sees the farmstead glittering in the distance. A weatherboarded house that gets bigger and more expansive the closer they come.

Before they reach the front door it opens. A man stands there, tall, sturdily built and imposing, backlit by the light in the hallway. She cannot make out his features but his pose is unmistakable: he is a human barrier, a rigid column, blocking their entry.

They have been quiet, yet he has heard them approaching. Perhaps the stirring animals gave them away.

He takes a step forward and light glints on something shiny in his hands. A shotgun. The farmer is taking no chances. 'Þekkja sjálfan þig,' he shouts at them.

Rafn answers with his name and that of the cousin.

The man nods. 'Og konan?'

Touching her arm, Rafn says, 'He wants to know who you are.'

Daphne steps forward into the light. 'My name is Daphne Dione-Smith. I am a reporter for the London *Times*.' The lie feels useless now. What good is a journalist up here? Why would she be on a farm?

For a moment she thinks he is going to wave them off, but he takes a step down and beckons them closer. 'A prestigious English newspaper. Come in.' His voice has changed.

Waiting for them to pass over the threshold he points the gun down at the floor, which is something of a relief.

He follows and locks the door behind them with three turns of the key. 'In there,' he says, pointing to a door off the hall.

It is a living area with a few chairs and a table like other reception rooms she has seen in Icelandic homes. Although there are two suitcases in the middle of this one.

The man pulls out chairs for them and tells them to sit. Now she can see he is maybe fifty, quite old, with a black beard showing signs of grey at the sides and cropped hair. He is dressed from head to toe in brown. When they sit down, he leaves the room. Daphne looks at Rafn for an explanation. He shrugs.

'At least he hasn't shot us,' she whispers.

He doesn't laugh.

Then the man is back again. At his side is a mild-faced woman with greying hair. She looks drawn and tired.

Daphne decides it is time to clear up any misunderstandings. 'Are you Viktor Magnússon? We have been told—'

Raising one hand, he cuts her off. 'How is your newspaper, Daphne?'

The question wrongfoots her, as does his easy use of her first name. 'It's fine, thank you,' she says, and unwilling to be sidetracked adds, 'Look—'

But once more he stops her with, 'I know what you want.'

She does not think he does and continues to explain. 'I'm not sure that can be the case,' she begins as he reaches down to an armchair and picks up a package.

'My grimoire,' he says and throws it on the table. 'That scoundrel Karlsson did not return it when he promised. I watched then followed him to the old farm and took it once he had gone. And left him a present that will repay him for his actions.'

She thinks of the curse that Karlsson did not touch, but which Rafn opened. She wants to ask about it but now the package is in her hands, she must check it *is* the spell book she has been charged with finding. This is her priority, so she begins to unwrap the paper and sees inside a small leather-bound tome. When she opens it, she finds the weird runic hieroglyphs that are carved into everything on the island scrawled across its pages together with diagrams and sigils. At a loss, she says simply, 'Thank you.' Then, 'How did you know? That this is what we seek?'

'We are not so cut off as you think we are,' Viktor says.

The woman, presumably his wife, whispers something to him. He holds up a hand , a gesture for her to be quiet.

But now she has it before her, Daphne wants to conclude their business as soon as possible and get away. 'How much do you want for it?'

He shakes his head. 'You can have it.'

This surprises both her and Rafn.

'But,' Viktor says, and she thinks *aha, here it comes*, 'I go with it,' he says. 'And my wife.'

For a moment she is not sure what he means. When she works it out, she feels blind-sided.

Rafn is also confused. 'You want to go with it?'

'The whole town knows there are enemies in our midst. The British have arrived first. Our loyalty lies with them,' he says.

Astonished by this, she remembers the hostility she has encountered in certain quarters. Though Viktor is echoing the sentiment Anna expressed when they first met. Yes, there are dissenting voices, but the majority of islanders are grateful that the Allies seized their chance when they did.

'It is precious.' Viktor's voice is like a hammer, hitting a wall. 'Its value lies in its power.' He looks out of the window behind them, into the dark mountains.

Rafn has also been wrong-footed. His blond head nods up and down, eyes widening as he stares at the older man. 'How . . .?' he starts to say.

Viktor shakes his head. 'Newcomers stand out here.' His words come more slowly. 'Then you and your cousin and the famous clairvoyant, Sindri Karlsson, who broke his promise to return my book, appear in Hólmavík. We can draw our own conclusions. Are they right?'

It is not really a question but Daphne and Rafn exchange a glance and confirm his suspicions.

'I thought so,' says Viktor. Then to Daphne, 'You're not a reporter, are you?'

This time she does not speak. It is forbidden to reveal the nature of her true work to anyone outside her circle of contacts.

He pulls up a chair. It squeaks against the floor. His face is not unreadable: there is a steeliness in the set of the jaw beneath the wild beard. 'We have read that the offices of *The Times* were bombed days ago. Your prime minister has commended the newspaper for continuing to print.'

Trying hard to keep the blush at bay, and inwardly cursing the fact that no one has told her, she says, 'I know that but . . .' then peters out. It is pointless to keep up the façade when she needs him to trust her.

'I demand safe passage to Britain for me and my wife. Then you can have what you came for.'

She is not of a rank to guarantee this but must take the grimoire. 'I agree,' she says, feeling a twist of guilt in her stomach.

Rafn narrows his eyes and tilts his head. He knows this is a flimsy contract.

'When do you leave?' Viktor asks him.

'Tomorrow at dawn,' he says.

'Then we shall see you at the quay.' He gestures to the book in Daphne's hands. 'Take it. It may be safer with you.'

She can't believe he is simply giving it to her and agrees eagerly. She wraps it up again, putting it under her arm. It is lighter than she expected. A magic book! For a moment her mind pulls back and she sees herself from above, from the perspective of a bird: a little girl in a wooden house on a mountainside. I am in a fairytale, she thinks. Can this be real?

Then Viktor smiles. 'But the prophecies of the sage Nostradamus are packed away in a secret compartment you will not be able to find. Insurance,' he says. 'You can have them once I set foot in England.'

And she is back down to earth again.

## CHAPTER TWENTY-SIX

'But how did he know we were coming?' asks Daphne.

Rafn says, 'Certain communities keep abreast of any new development.'

'Yes,' she says, thinking Viktor Magnússon is more clued up than she is.

Panting on the steep incline, she drops her head so that its weight propels her forward. It is the last hillock before the descent to the town.

'Will you manage to get Viktor and his wife back?' asks Rafn.

'I don't honestly know,' she says. She must speak to Hugh or someone at the department and apprise them of the situation.

'Though you promised,' he said. 'That they could . . .'

This is war, she wants to say. War is callous, does not care for people's feelings or individual safety. Not here, down amongst the little people. There is more at stake than the fate of two farmers. Expendability is not an abstract concept: it is part of the balancing act that must work towards the greater good. You too may come to understand this in time.

However, what she says is, 'I did.' The firmness of her voice dictates she is not going to be drawn on this. Details are for later. First they must get home.

She pushes her feet into the track.

The effort of walking is making her sweat. As they finally crest the summit of the hill, she pauses for a moment to take off her glove and wipe her forehead.

Rafn has stopped too, to take in the view. Hólmavík glints beneath them, cradled by rocky white peaks. Ahead the fjord opens. She can hear the waves crashing on the shore.

'So pretty,' she says, and just at that moment the sky shudders. A whip of light opens a crack into the greater universe. Both of them look up. Turquoise waves appear out of nothingness and ripple silently across the heavens, veiling the stars.

Under this stippled heaven, the mountains around them seem to move.

An Arctic fox, white and sleek, darts across the track and barks, and Daphne is plunged into a deep rapture.

Rafn stands close to her. She hears his breathing quicken and, without thinking, takes his hand. Eyes locked onto the light, she experiences a sudden connection to this land, and this man made by it. And she thinks that she may kiss him, this foreign boy, under the silky moonlight and the swelling sky that blankets the fjord.

Rafn's fingers tighten. When he raises her wrist to his lips she finds they are cold, but they burn her skin. A tingling sensation erupts within her, a volcano that has lain dormant and not moved before. His eyes dance as he smiles.

And so she gives in to the feeling and leans towards him. It is quite unlike her to be so forward, to make the first move, which is not what a lady does. But the landscape and aurora have ignited something feral in her. Something feral which does not feel wrong.

When her lips touch his there is a moment of shock and then a pulling apart, then pulling in again, and everything else disappears.

She is no longer aware of the world around her but only of sensation, of yearning, under the gaze of the mountain giants.

She likes all of him, his closeness and scent and the noises he makes.

It is gloriously sensual and delicious. Then, needing air, she breaks off and he stands back and looks at her, letting hot laughter spill out of his throat. He draws her closer again and puts his arms round her and looks down and says, 'You are not like any English girl I have met.'

'I don't think I'm like any English girl I've met either,' she says because it is true now.

And he kisses her again.

She gives into it and feels the rekindling of desire.

The stars reflect in his eyes. She runs a forefinger over his brow and then down his nose, onto his lips, then reaches up to kiss them again.

'You are lovely,' he says. And for the first time in a very long while she feels lovely too.

When she looks out at the fjord, she realises that the light show has stopped and asks him when that was.

'Don't know,' he says and shrugs. 'My mind was elsewhere.' Then he lets her go and wraps the thick scarf closer around his neck. 'Come on.' He adjusts her jumper, fastens the belt around her coat, which has come undone. 'We'll freeze out here.'

She realises she did not feel the cold and marvels at the power of the mind to blot out discomfort. Though that could be fatal, so she promises herself she will pay more attention to her body next time.

Next time, she thinks, and feels suddenly, delightfully, warm.

Minutes later they are returning to the house, arm in arm. There is such lightness to her step. But her head is whirling, making her dizzy, so she leans into him and breathes in his scent, which is utterly alien but mustily delicious.

And he squeezes her briefly in his arms and says, 'You go in before me.'

She finds herself saying, 'One kiss more.' And he gives it to her, and it is impossible to tell where he ends and she begins.

It takes a while for them to pull apart. Then he says again, 'You go.' And she thinks that is wise.

With one last look back at Rafn, silhouetted by the moon and stars and peaks, proud and dazzling, she goes inside, knowing that image will be burned onto her retina.

Anna is asleep on the floor beside Karlsson's bed, the revolver next to her hand.

The medium is snoring again.

Daphne steps over her friend then takes off her coat. While she is removing her boots, Rafn comes in. Taking in the sleeping Anna and Karlsson, he picks up the revolver and returns to the hard wooden chair by the stove. Once seated he lifts his head and smiles at Daphne.

She cannot help herself but goes over and kisses his hair. It smells of air and mountains.

He strokes her leg. In this light his eyes look bottomless and very warm. 'You should sleep now.'

So wise, she thinks, and obediently returns to the bed, wishing he might fall into it with her.

But this is not the time. They have things to do. Perhaps in Reykjavík . . .

CHAPTER TWENTY-SEVEN

It is not yet dawn but already the ducks are waking. Their song is piercing. Such feathered friends have issued a warning before and Daphne had not heeded it then either.

One day she will be able to perceive the difference between regular and fearful. She will learn to break down the symphony of the natural world into its component parts, to listen to the wind.

But not today.

'Where is Rafn?' she asks Anna, who is shaking gently, despite her thick coat and scarf. They are all tired, though two of them have hormones whizzing through their veins that make them feel alive and vibrant.

'He has gone to fetch food and milk for the journey and make a telephone call. He was expected back in Reykjavík today. He will not make it.'

A telephone call, thinks Daphne. Someone here has a telephone! She has been so immersed in her instructions and various codes, the signals and comms requirements, that the idea of simply lifting the phone and dialling London had entirely escaped her. Hugh's instructions were to make contact once she was in possession of the grimoire. Well, she has it now. And its appendages.

She eyes them, sitting on crates by the boat, suitcases at their feet. Viktor's wife is talking to one of the crew. The engine is running and the rest of the men are scrubbing the decks, running the ropes, preparing for departure.

'And the fishermen?' she asks Anna. 'Have they agreed to take Viktor and his wife?'

'The first mate knows Kristjana Jónsdóttir.'

'Who?'

'Viktor's wife.' Anna points to her.

The Icelandic surnames are so confusing. Married couples do not share the same name.

Kristjana's jaw has lost some of its rigidity; she does not hold herself together as if she may fall apart, like she did last night. Her conversation with the sailor seems easy and fluid. As she sits there, looking up at him, Daphne notices what a beautiful white neck she has.

'There is a cost to it, of course,' Anna continues, and Daphne looks back. Her friend seems to have soaked up Kristjana's former tension. Her eyes are tight, bluish patches underneath. 'You must pay them before we leave.'

Daphne doesn't mind doing that. She still has money sewn into her underwear. It will be a relief to get rid of some of it.

'And they want us to keep below deck.'

For a moment Daphne wonders who she means by 'us'. 'You and me?'

'You, me and Kristjana. Rafn has told them we will cook Kjötsúpa.'

Assuming this is a native dish, she nods. It is a smaller price to pay than she had expected.

'Meat stew,' Anna explains. 'It has sugared them.'

'But first things first,' Daphne says. 'Where is the telephone?'

'You can probably use the one at the blue house.' Anna points to a building at the foot of a hill, painted turquoise. It can't be more than two hundred yards away.

Seeing Daphne start towards it, Anna calls, 'Don't be long. They want to leave as soon as Rafn gets back.'

After some painful negotiation during which she has to mime putting her finger into the telephone dial and saying 'hello', Daphne is escorted into a small room. The telephone is not one of the modern Bakelite models they have in London but an ornate wooden box with two bells, an earpiece and speaking piece, one handle at the side. It sits on the sideboard atop a lace runner. Her host, a man in a thick hand-knitted jumper, with the look of a fisherman but the hands of a clerk, asks in stilted English who she wants to connect to.

She gapes at the phone. It is not prudent to telephone HQ: the international call will have to be routed via the telephone exchange.

Instead, she tells him to connect to a London number. He winds the handle several times, speaks to the telephone exchange, waits, speaks to another telephonist, then hands Daphne the two pieces and withdraws, leaving her to it.

This is a gamble, she thinks, as she listens to the clicks and whirs coming down the line. Will he be there?

After a few moments, a voice answers. 'Mayfair six-four-six-four?'

A muscle in her heart tears. She had not realised how much she has missed him until she hears his crackly voice.

'Jonty!'

'Daphne, is that you?' He sounds slightly befuddled. It is probably too early for him. However, she can hear the affection in his words and imagines him standing in the hallway of his townhouse smiling.

'Of course it is!' She too has broken into a broad grin.

'How the devil are you, dear one?'

'All fine. Are you keeping well? In good spirits?'

He hesitates. In the pause she hears the strains of Tchaikovsky playing somewhere in the house. The drawing room probably, with the long chintz drapes and chaise-longue by the windows where Mrs Trevelyan would hum along softly to the tunes on the gramophone in the months before she died.

'Well,' he says. 'You know how it is here.'

And she realises she doesn't, so says nothing.

'Bombs,' he says, 'every night now. London has been badly hit.'

'I thought you might be at . . .' she can't say Farnham for fear of giving the location away '. . . in the country.'

'Back tomorrow,' he says. She can feel his restlessness across the miles. 'Not performing at the moment. Onstage,' he adds. 'I seem to have mislaid my assistant.'

She laughs and wants to say 'I miss you, my friend,' and ask about the theatre folk at the Oriental, find out about the love affairs and disputes, the rivalry and new acts. Oh, how wonderful would it be to submerge oneself in such tittle-tattle and gossip! But all of that is gone for her. A pastime of a former life.

'I've got to be quick,' she says, thinking of the waiting boat. 'I need you to get a message through to Hugh. Can you do that?'

Another pause. 'Hugh?'

'Who you went to school with,' she adds, though does not for a moment believe Jonty has forgotten their recruiter. More likely he is surprised she is contacting the boss through him.

'I'll try my best,' he says. 'What is it? Do I need a pen?'

'Just tell him I have the tailor's guide. But it comes with the previous owners. Two of them. Who will bring it over. I'll apprise him of more details when I am back in Reykjavík.'

'Where?' he says then. 'Iceland! Good Lord! Are you safe? They have polar bears there, you know.'

'They don't actually,' she says, 'so you have nothing to fear. I won't be eaten up by one.'

'Reykjavík, eh?' he says. 'Have you seen the Northern Lights? Meant to be splendid.'

'Just last night, in fact,' she says. 'But not in the city. I'm further north. They are even better here.'

'Be careful, Daphne, I don't like the sound of you out at night in the wild.'

'Don't worry, I'm on my way back.' She laughs lightly to reassure him. 'Have you got the message down?'

'I have. Will deliver it today, old bean.'

'Thanks so much.'

'And you're quite all right?' he adds.

'I am.'

'Good.'

'When will you be safely back in the city? Shall I tell him when he can expect to hear from you?'

'Probably tonight,' she says. 'But I have to go now: the boat is leaving.'

'A boat! Marvellous. It sounds quite the adventure. I look forward to hearing all about it when you're back.'

'Ciao, Jonty. Many thanks.'

# KJÖTSÚPA

INGREDIENTS

A boned shoulder of mutton or lamb with fat on the meat. Plus one or two necks.

2 large swedes

10 good-sized carrots

6 parsnips

12 potatoes

Two handfuls of peas

2 onions

METHOD

Separate meat from the bone. Keep the bones. Then slice meat into rough pieces. Season meat with salt.

Place lamb or mutton into a large soup pot with the bones.

Fill it with enough water to cover.

Bring to the boil then simmer for at least an hour.

Then remove the bones. Use tongs – they will be hot.

Skim the top until broth is clear.

Chop vegetables into chunks and throw into the pot for a further 15 minutes.

Next add the peas and cook for 5 minutes more or until everything is soft.

Serve up steaming Kjötsúpa to hungry crew.

# CHAPTER TWENTY-EIGHT

She is grappling with a large swede, of the vegetable variety, when Rafn finds her. The other women seem to know exactly what must be done and are moving about the small galley with ease, chopping meat and veg without conferring. Daphne however keeps asking what to do next. In some strange way this makes her feel unwomanly. As if she has never cooked before. Which of course she has. Just not this type of food.

As she applies pressure to a blade to slice through this dense root vegetable, part of it shoots off and hits the wall. Rafn hoots with laughter. She has liked the sound before but this time it makes her feel inferior, as if her culinary skills are being judged. And found to be comically wanting. Though Anna remains stoic, attending to the carrots, Kristjana giggles. Daphne purses her lips. It's not fair, she has only a small knife. The other two claimed the bigger ones before she could reach them. She is determined not to think of it as being outplayed.

Handing her the rogue chunk of swede, Rafn asks, 'I believe this is yours, Miss Dione-Smith.'

She takes it and pokes out her tongue at him.

He grins. 'Can you come up on deck?'

When she gets over the excitement of his unexpected appearance, she remembers why the women have been consigned to the galley. 'But the fishermen?'

He shrugs. 'I told them you would put fish into the broth. They have caught some.'

Fish, she thinks, with mutton? That will never do.

Wiping her hands on her apron and hooking it up on the back of the door, she is glad to be rid of the smelly thing. It is not so much protecting her clothes as coating them in a scaly sheen.

'Where did you go?' Rafn asks when they reach the prow.

The waves ahead are choppy and silver-grey, the fjord narrowing, mountains sloping down to its shores. Above, the sky is descending: clouds thickening, full of dark weather. Below decks the atmosphere is one of silent conviviality and joint enterprise. Up here tension permeates the air, as if the land, the boat, the crew, are waiting for something to happen.

Behind them gulls squawk and dive over the wake. Lots of them. They seem to be playing. As she watches she notices a strange thing attached to the rail there: the head of an ugly fish stuck upon a pole. It looks out to the sea behind them. The jaws hang open. A piece of wood has been wedged into its mouth. There is such a sense of evil radiating from the queer object that she finds herself shuddering.

Rafn's voice is full of concern. 'Cold? Here, take my scarf.'

She shakes her head. 'No, it's that,' and points to the skull.

'Oh,' he says. 'Just superstition. For a good wind.'

'A good one!' She is surprised that something so malignant can bring luck.

'Ling,' he says, with a chuckle, 'is a very tasty fish. I will serve it sometime so you can taste for yourself.'

A tiny flame of desire is dancing in Rafn's eyes. His lips are trying hard not to smile. 'You should not be so fearful of this.' But his tone is only mildly chiding: he is amused by her reaction. 'You who have commanded us up here,' he says, 'who have driven us on through darkness and wind and snow to fetch a grimoire. Which we carry on this boat, right now.'

He looks over his shoulder at Viktor and the men who are

smoking in a huddle. A couple of the crew are working on a pile of fish, gutting them and chucking the heads back into the sea.

Yes, Rafn has a point. She has been fearless and bold. Yet the grimoire has provoked a curious feeling in her since its acquisition. Set her on edge, if you will.

She leafed through its odd, patterned pages this morning. The peculiar spindly diagrams and cursive Icelandic script mean nothing to her. Whilst some staves resemble runes, not all of them do. Others are spear-like or feathered, pointed like leaf skeletons. Though she has long performed as a practitioner of magic in the theatre, 'fluent' in telepathy and mesmerism, she has never been so close to such arcane darkness before. At least not in book form. Her experience in the summer just past has taught her to keep an open mind on such matters. Not to judge, if she can.

Yet she cannot shake the idea that the spells in the grimoire are full of devastation and blood, secrets from another age when the world was wilder, less sophisticated, more truthful. Brutal. Before men had learned to twist words, rather than daggers, or needed to. When the force of will was all. It is fascinating but simultaneously repulsive. It is dirty, pagan, obscene. And as much as she tells herself it is just a book, she knows it is not. Nothing is ever 'just' one thing. Not anymore. The dial has shifted so that everything in this strange new world has multiple meanings and values.

She does not ask, nor want to know, why it is worth sending her and a pocketful of gold to north Iceland. But she understands it is not 'just' paper and leather. It is power and knowledge and must be protected until it reaches its destination.

Safe in the hold now, she can picture exactly where it is and imagines it glowing like sulphur. Since last night she has been constantly aware of it, like a stone in the gut. Part of her senses that it is also aware of her and follows her movements like a flickering shadow.

'I can put a hat on it, if it bothers you so much.' Rafn grins.

She is glad of his intervention; so caught up in her thoughts she had forgotten momentarily the horrible fish skull.

Sending a rueful smile, she says, 'No, Rafn. It doesn't really scare me. It's just so revolting. I wouldn't want it in my workplace.' Though she thinks the fishermen would be just as appalled if they saw her onstage, about her regular business, tied up, sawn in half or fastened into a target for flying knives.

Rafn laughs. 'What is that?' he asks. 'When you're not in the war.'

How strange, she thinks, that they have been intimate and yet are unfamiliar with each other. Rafn doesn't even know her real name.

'A stage magician's assistant,' she says. And he nods, as if that is an ordinary and commonplace job. Then his eyes dart to the deck, and she knows his thoughts have returned to the other passenger who also treads the boards. Karlsson is downstairs in one of the bunks, under a mound of blankets, getting over his fever.

'That's why,' he says, putting two and two together but leaving 'they sent you' unsaid.

'Amongst a great many exceptional skills. And of course my sterling character,' she says and then winks at him.

He seems to find this unusual and tilts his head but then his grin broadens.

She likes that smile, feels an urge to reach out and touch his lips, but knows it is improper. Indeed, she isn't *absolutely* sure if he would welcome it. That is the thing with desire: although it is a strong driver, it can be tamed. Perhaps Rafn has conquered his. She would like to ask him how he feels about last night? Was it a welcome conclusion? Or a brief encounter relegated already to the transience of war-time?

The way he is looking at her now makes her more certain that passion is still there.

But how does she herself feel about it? What does she want? An image of Jack briefly flashes across her mind but she dispels it. How pointless to dwell on what could be when all anyone can ever attend to in this time of conflict and upheaval is the 'now'.

'You came aboard at the last minute,' Rafn says, inching closer.

The statement sparks defiance in her. Is he accusing her of something? Gallivanting? He knows she is not a tourist. It was *important* for her to make that call. 'I paid the fishermen before we left,' she says, hearing a faint ring of petulance in her voice. Touching the steel of the rail, she adds, 'They are fine with the arrangement, I understand.'

He keeps his body facing her and leans against the steel. His pose is casual. This is not an interrogation. 'I looked for you. Where did you go?'

The wind tosses her hair. She must look like a harpy and wants to pat her tresses down but resists. 'To the Blue House. The postmaster's, I think?'

'Oh,' he says, eyebrows soaring. 'Yes?'

'To make a telephone call.'

At once the internal light in him is snuffed out. His features harden. 'To whom did you place the call?'

'I spoke to my old boss.' Reading his expression she is appalled. Anxiety and disappointment have crept into the lines around his eyes and mouth.

But she is not sure why – she has given nothing away to Jonty. The call, the message, was dressed up in loose language so as not to leak information. 'I told him we had the tailor's guide and were returning to Reykjavík.'

'What?' He straightens and immediately her throat becomes tight. 'What else did you say?'

She is frightened by his tone, which is harsh and contains desperate anger. Selecting the right words, she bleats, 'I said we would arrive in Reykjavík tomorrow.'

His hand goes to his lips. 'Did you say where you were?'

She thinks back. No, she didn't – shakes her head. 'I had to ring off quickly, to catch the boat.'

'You didn't say that, did you?' He stands and looms over her. His fists are clenched. A vein in his neck is bulging.

Now Daphne is worried. 'Why? It's true.'

Rafn takes in a long breath of air that whistles over his teeth. 'You weren't to know,' he says, as if defending her in an argument, and jerks his head to the side.

'What?' she says. 'Know what?'

He sighs. 'The telephone lines in each fjord, the rural lines, are linked to each other.'

She doesn't understand why that is significant.

'Anyone', he continues, 'can hear the phone calls that are made in their area. They just need to pick up the phone and listen.'

It takes a moment for her to process the information, to apply it to their current circumstance.

As he walks away and speaks to the crew, she realises what she has done.

The boat is the only route to Reykjavík. She has announced they are taking it to anyone intrigued enough to listen in to what a stranger, an Englishwoman who has unexpectedly appeared in the north-west fjords, might have to say. And to whom she is saying it: Mayfair 6464. London.

How long will it take for the news to be passed on?

How long will it take for the enemy to catch up with them?

A shudder goes through the boat as it accelerates sharply, causing the engine to scream.

For a moment Daphne thinks the noise is coming from her.

CHAPTER TWENTY-NINE

There is no time to rest at Borðeyri. No pause to use facilities or say goodbye. They must get on their way as soon as they can. It is her fault.

Her fault!

She cannot look Anna in the eye as they get into the truck. Though her blushes have diminished, shame still burns inside.

Daphne busies herself with laying out a rug across the long seat that they will share. The vehicle has been repaired and is roadworthy, though Axel has told them snow is in the air and urged them to stay overnight: the road out of Borðeyri is fraught with dangers on good days. On bad ones, without luck, it can prove fatal.

Urgency possesses her. They must move on, away from the unseen figures on their scent. How *could* she have been so stupid?

Neither she nor Rafn has divulged this fresh peril to the others. However, it is not long before their fellow passengers become attuned to the atmosphere pervading the truck. It is, in fact, difficult to escape it, squeezed in tightly as they are like sardines in a tin. The women have been assigned the back seat. Of course they have: Kristjana, Viktor's wife, is lodged between Daphne and Anna. Occupying the front seat are the men. Of course they are. Viktor, then Karlsson. Rafn in the driving seat.

Their luggage is in the boot and fastened onto the roof by ropes, a tarpaulin stretched over the top. Though Daphne has refused to let go of the grimoire. It rests in the suitcase which she grips tightly on her lap.

Before them the road inclines steeply, twisting its way to the heavens. Rafn has changed gear several times. The engine protests as they climb higher into the mountain pass.

There is nobody around. Not a single person for miles and miles. They have not encountered a vehicle since they left Borðeyri.

Outside, the landscape glowers: patches of black age-hardened rock pierce the snow. There are precarious wedges overhanging the slopes, which make Daphne wince. A slight tremor, a loud noise, and any one might break off and come tumbling down on top of them.

'Do not fear.' It is Kristjana whispering into her ear.

Daphne twists to face her. She can feel the heat of the woman's thigh through her coat. 'Fear?'

Kristjana bends closer so that her breath touches Daphne's cheek as she says, 'Viktor has put one into place.'

What is she is talking about?

Reading her confusion, the woman swivels her eyes to the suitcase. 'He has invoked a spell. We are protected,' she says with great conviction.

'Oh,' says Daphne. A prickle starts at the back of her neck, runs down past her shoulder blades and settles in her belly.

'To protect us,' says Kristjana again.

Good, she thinks. Someone needs to. This road is narrow and unmade. Full of ruts that bump and jolt their vehicle.

Ahead of them the mountains never end. As soon as they crest one, more appear. In the distance their peaks are pale triangles with dark ridges, white pyramids carved eons ago not by men but prehistoric glaciers on their journey to the ocean. She saw nothing of this on their way here: the view was obscured by night and snow. To her left, the land slopes down past gigantic stones that give way onto heart-stoppingly sheer drops, dark caverns and canyons, at the bottom a foaming river of white water. Its banks are steep, littered with ragged boulders, like black teeth protruding from snow-heavy ground.

The road has no barriers, and they are so close to the edge she is afraid to lean towards the river in case her weight further unsteadies the vehicle. Her ears popped a way back and yet still they drive higher and higher.

When she returns her gaze to the interior of the truck it is dim. The light outside has faded too. With her focus elsewhere, she had not noticed the sky deepening. It has been filled with low, dark-bellied clouds seeping along the mountain tops, spreading above them like a canopy blocking out what little of the sun's watery light persists into this late afternoon. The lilac-greyness soaks everything in a creeping alien light. It is hard to believe that humans are tolerated out here at all.

Rafn switches on the headlights and she sees that the clouds have let go of more mist, which is rolling down the slopes. On the windows droplets of moisture have appeared.

Karlsson mutters something under his breath. As does Kristjana. Daphne darts a glance at her and sees her easiness has vanished. She is hugging herself again as she did last night, her body taut. Leaning forward, she hisses at Viktor, 'Þetta er ekki gott.'

Her husband does not turn to answer but raises his hand to quieten her.

Daphne can't work out what is going on, but senses all is not well. She grips the strap above her head.

Rafn slows. The mist has become a dense fog and, in the headlights, taken on a yellowish glow.

Tension in the truck is also thickening.

Anna has bent towards him. 'The birds,' she says, and Daphne sees small shadows flutter in the mist, hears muffled flapping over the noise of the engine. And squawking too.

Anna breathes out loudly. 'They are making strange noises.'

And then, as Daphne is just about to respond to her friend, the earth rumbles.

A vibration goes through the truck. The windows rattle in their frames.

Rocks ping against the chassis.

Karlsson's voice is a growling gargle, but Daphne can make out his words. She has heard them before: 'The mountain shakes.'

Anna's eyes are fixed out through the window on the mountainside. Daphne has not observed such a queer expression on her friend's face before: her forehead is a labyrinth of furrows, eyebrows pulled together, jaw dropped and open, eyes so very wide the whites dwarf her pupils. And before she can select the right word to describe it, Daphne's mind has already summoned a phrase. *The* phrase.

For a fraction of a second she is back in the dark of the candle-lit séance room, the clairvoyant jerking in his chair. The memory explodes across her brain: 'See her fear.'

As Viktor groans, Daphne strains to recall. What came next? What did the possessed medium say?

She is thinking hard as the headlights latch onto something in the mist and she sees . . . what? It cannot be.

The fuzzy shadow forms into the shape of a small child. A boy, peat-brown, is standing in the dead-centre of the road. Unmoving, even as Rafn blows the horn.

Someone shouts, 'Móri!' Another, 'Nei!'

Karlsson screams, Kristjana whimpers.

Rafn slams on the brakes. But it is too late to stop.

The truck swerves violently towards the open side of the road.

Tyres squeal as they lose purchase on the surface and skid towards the cliff edge.

Daphne is thrown against Kristjana.

Her eyes clamp shut as she grips the front seat, then yells out the warning already on her tongue: 'Quick! Brace, brace, brace.'

And completes the prophecy.

The road beneath them vanishes.

For one long moment they are suspended in mid-air.

Not on earth.

Not in heaven.

Yet.

## CHAPTER THIRTY

Daphne holds her breath for five heartbeats.

One. The bumper scrapes the top of a boulder. Sparks fly across windows, a shower of tiny comets presaging disaster. Simultaneously the friction of steel and rock combine to emit a shrill screech. Off balance, the truck's trajectory changes.

Two. On it hurtles, tilting left, pointing down engine-first. Skimming the surface of a bog, it veers sideways. The front wheels slip deeper, sending slews of grey water over the windows, reminding Daphne of washing the family car with a hose. Father! she thinks in a micro-second that will not be remembered until the time comes, soon, for her to die.

Three. Dragged by the suction of the bog and offset by the rotation of the bodywork, speed decreases.

Four. Impact. The truck slams into a slab of ancient magma that has lain untouched for centuries. Smash. Clang.

The bonnet absorbs the initial shock, then crumples. Bodies lurch, crash, decelerate. Violent shudders run through the vehicle, puckering its sides, ripping the seats free, tearing the panels: windows and mirrors shatter, spraying the occupants with thousands of tiny stars. The bodywork concertinas in–out, in–out at awkward angles.

Five. Rebounding in a shallow arc, what is left of the truck bounces. Once, twice, four times, six. Then comes to rest in a shelf of snow. Dislodged, chunks of it fall upon the roof with dull thuds. The engine begins to steam.

Seven lives,

Six lives,

Five lives left.

## CHAPTER THIRTY-ONE

Her head has a sound in it. A 'shhh' noise, like a hum. Deafening, yet she is still able to tune into the beat of her heart battering away like a machine gun taking down the enemy.

It takes a moment for her to realise she is moving, being pulled by something, someone. Strong arms are grabbing for her. Instinctively, during the crash she has held onto something – a strap or a piece of upholstery – to stop herself slipping. But now she understands she must surrender and give in to the tugs. So, she lets go and slides across the seat, away from the window. Which is no longer a window, but an open expanse of white. Her other hand is still gripping the handle of the suitcase which has taken much of the force of the collision and ruptured at one end. Though, thank God, it has protected her head – then immediately she worries about the state of the book. Is it intact?

The first thing she does when she is clear of the smoking vehicle is check the grimoire. When she finds it still cushioned in its layers of newspaper, she relaxes and only then examines herself. Kristjana and Rafn let go of her to return to the vehicle. Her legs are wobbly but still attached to her body and able to hold her up. Her neck is sore, her midriff bruised where she was thrown against the case, the ceiling, the door. Small scratches mark both hands. But that is it.

If it weren't for the dizziness she would shake herself and brush off her clothes. But it is too soon. She leans against a boulder and takes stock of the situation.

An eerie quiet pervades the bank they have come to rest upon. Though she can hear the hiss of the engine and the river as it ripples around fresh boulders, absorbing them in its course quickly then continuing down.

Nature simply carries on, she thinks, readjusts effortlessly no matter what happens.

But what *has* just happened?

The mountain shook. Yes.

As Anna told her, Iceland trembles a hundred times a year. 'Sometimes it is nothing. Sometimes it is everything.' Well, what was that? Something or nothing? She casts her eyes around. The land is almost as it was before except the birds have gone to ground or flown away to safer territory. The mist is lifting very slightly. Through it she can see Karlsson sitting on a rock staring straight ahead, eyes unfocussed. He has a scrape on his forehead which is bleeding, but otherwise appears unharmed.

Bent over, Anna supports herself with her hands on her knees. It looks like she is trying to regulate her breathing: Daphne watches as she blows out for a length of time, golden hair hanging forward, obscuring her eyes. Then, through lips that have formed a tight 'O', Anna inhales deeply, filling her lungs. At this sight, a net of concern meshes Daphne and prompts her to stagger over and put her hand on her friend's back.

'Don't!' Anna snaps, at her touch. 'Give me space. I will be fine.'

Her friend's fiery courage and demeanour is admirable. Anna is strong, birthed from this land of rock and lava: she will not brook weakness, will not disgrace herself by showing it. Noble.

Which, thinks Daphne, makes it all the more peculiar that she revealed a less stoic reaction minutes before the crash.

Never before had she seen Anna's face so unguarded, so open. So *vulnerable*.

Just as Karlsson had predicted all those days ago. The mountain did shake, Anna did take fright.

The experience was bewildering and frightening for Daphne too, but she remembers that for Anna it contained a greater darkness: it was how her brother, Þór, was killed. Of course, such a twist of fate as his sister following him would have been so cruel and callous as to be unthinkable. And yet, this is how the world is now. The unthinkable, the very worst, is happening to people all over Europe. Death is on street corners, in ghettos, at the hands of mobs, falling from the sky into East End warehouses, gashing open holds so that sailors cannot do anything but breathe in the sea.

Fear is omnipresent. Yet the sight of Anna's, in plain sight, is what prompted Daphne to shout out the once-cryptic warning – to brace, brace, brace.

And thank God they did. The truck, she sees now, is badly wrecked. Crushed in snow, the front grille is twisted and shattered, one headlight hanging loose from a tangle of wires. Tyres poke at odd angles. The bonnet is wrinkled like an accordion, revealing the damaged engine beneath, which fizzles. The front bumper bends almost to the ground, while the windshield is a web of smashed glass. Shards of it litter the dashboard and seats. A small trail of oil leaks from the engine, pooling on the ground then carving out a course in the snow.

Rafn is half inside, stretching over to the passenger seat, Kristjana beside him. They are doing their best to extricate Viktor. When he emerges through the battered door Daphne sees he too has cuts on his head and glass over his coat. When she looks down, she finds the same diamonds pattern her own, so shakes the splinters and fragments out of her clothes.

'Is everyone all right?' Rafn asks.

She is pleased to see that he is. The others groan or grunt affirmatives.

Goodness, she thinks, it is really something of a miracle that none of them have been seriously hurt.

Then she stops herself. Miracles do not exist. Life is savage. Then, once more, her mind doubles back – Karlsson's message. *Not now*, Daphne tells herself. This is not the time to pause and consider the nature of the universe! She will note it all down and speak to Septimus about it. But, she thinks, as Karlsson gets to his feet, if his prophecy was not simply coincidence then what is this man? Again, she tells herself, it is of no consequence now.

There is a heated discussion taking place. Viktor is pointing ahead, back onto the road, which seems to upset Kristjana.

She can't tell exactly what they are saying but has an idea it may be about the boy on the road, whom she had forgotten about in all of this chaos. She is sure that Rafn swerved in time to avoid hitting the child but of course they must see if he is there and has any injuries. What such a young lad is doing out here, unaccompanied in this wilderness, is anybody's guess. It is unconscionable that a parent should let them wander here. Surely, they must be lost.

As soon as the bags are unpacked from the roof and what is left of those in the boot are salvaged as best as they can, the small group walk, limp and stumble back to the road.

It is hard to see where to put your feet. Daphne tries to tread on grey rocks but her boots slip through the snow and skate across the ice beneath it. Several times she comes close to falling – arms flailing, dropping her bags, coating herself in snow and mud. It is inelegant, but of more concern is the chill. As she moves her body temperature increases, warms her coat, melts the snow and this dampens the cloth. She imagines the crimson welts she will find where the thick wet fabric of her coat rubs:

that soft spot underneath her armpits, over the top of her brassiere, against her ribcage.

The landslide has coated the road in a new layer of rocks and stones, which makes it hard to see if there are any fresh footprints. Though the light is dimmer still, she tries to search in the place where the boy was standing. There are no tracks visible.

She feels Rafn's presence before he places his hand, once again, on her shoulder. When she greets his handsome face, there are lines of exhaustion carved into the soft skin around his cheeks. 'Are you fine, Daphne?'

'I am fine, Rafn. Anna is . . .' Her eyes drift to her friend, but she seems to have collected both herself and her belongings and is trudging up the road alongside the medium, who, although white-faced and breathless, is at least making some effort to talk. She is pleased he has come to no harm and is starting to reappraise him.

'The mountains are not her preferred place,' says Rafn, jerking Daphne away from those thoughts and back into the warmth of his smile. Oh, look at him, she thinks, still trying to shine through all this catastrophe. She wants to bathe in his gaze for a while. But he says, 'We must get away from here at once. You know that.'

And she does. Although loose rubble from the mountain has peppered the road, any decent farm truck with good tyres will be able to navigate over it. The gap that exists between them and the enemy agents must be contracting rapidly. Their advantage is gone and the prospect of attack is becoming an inevitability.

Out here they will be easy pickings.

'Viktor tells me there is a skýli, a weather house, further up.' Rafn says this not just to her but to Anna and Karlsson who have caught up with them.

Anna rephrases it for Daphne. 'He means a shelter. In case of such an episode as this.'

Rafn looks south-easterly into an area of peaks and black wastes, as behind them the sorcerer and his wife begin to shout.

'But first,' Daphne says, holding onto Rafn's attention for as long as she can, 'we should look for the boy.'

Beside her he tuts. When she inspects his face, she sees annoyance there. 'What?'

'Can you hear her?' He gestures to Kristjana, who stands about thirty feet away, her hands on her hips. Though Daphne can't understand the words, she *can* tell she is arguing with her husband, refusing to cross the road to him. Viktor shouts something back. There is pleading in his voice.

'I can hear her,' Daphne confirms. 'But I don't know what she's saying?'

'She saw it too,' Rafn says.

'It?' Daphne asks. 'The boy? Yes, we must make sure he is not injured.'

'It was not a boy,' Rafn says firmly, meeting her gaze with a strange look that is at once both entirely open and yet hiding something.

'I thought it *was*.' Daphne directs her gaze to Anna, who points one single finger in the air and shakes her head.

'It came rolling down the hill – an odd-shaped mess of boulders,' Anna says. 'I saw them.' She pauses to wince then shakes the image from her head. 'They can do much damage. Shifted by the mountain. Too heavy for men to move.'

'But it was brown, not black like the rocks.' Daphne is not sure why Anna is denying there was a child.

'The headlights are – were yellow.' Anna thumbs over her shoulder to the smoking wreckage. 'Softens the appearance and colour of the thing. We should be going.'

Daphne agrees with the latter but not the former statement.

'It was a boy, but not a child,' says Karlsson. His voice, Daphne hears, is firm, almost insistent. 'That's what she's saying.' And he switches his gaze to Kristjana, continuing to stand her ground on the other side of the road.

Rafn calls out something to Viktor, who turns and looks at Daphne.

'I don't understand,' she replies to the medium. 'How can a boy not be a child? Is this a riddle?'

Viktor takes two, three steps towards her and motions for the suitcase.

Daphne holds it up, her expression conveying – this?

He nods. Points into it.

The grimoire.

No, she cannot hand it over to him and so leans away from his approach.

But then Anna is at her elbow, nudging her forward. 'Give him the book. He needs to calm Kristjana.'

'Why?' Daphne asks but is already handing the case to him: if Anna thinks this is wise, then it probably is. She watches Viktor fumble inside, then remove the grimoire and take it to his wife.

'Because she is frightened. I saw rocks but she says it was a móri,' says Anna.

Before Daphne has to ask, Karlsson is already explaining: 'The boy. He was likely a ghost. They frequent these places,' he says. 'In hard times, famine, parents brought their children here and left them so they would die.'

Dear God, Daphne thinks, the simple brutality of it. But she does not react to his words and makes an effort to keep her face free from emotion.

'Kristjana will not walk where she saw it,' he continues, 'for fear of its revenge. Viktor is showing her the spell he has used to protect us.'

Protect us, she scoffs. It is utter insanity to believe this dishevelled group of crash survivors has had luck conferred on them. But as that thought is processed, she remembers Karlsson's fulfilled prophecy again. Then, just as quickly, snuffs it out and re-examines the image of the boy on her retina – mouth open in a silent howl. But no, it cannot be: Anna, Rafn and the others – all of them but she and Kristjana – saw only boulders. What is more likely to be true after an earth tremor – boy or boulder? Then she laughs at herself, out loud, even as she is considering it. Of all the people here, Daphne Devine, assistant to The Grand Mystique, really should know better. Didn't Jonty always tell her, 'The entirety of perception takes place in the mind. The magician is only as guilty of its manipulation as much as we, with all of our subjectivities, hopes and fears, are ourselves.' Only, magicians are aware that they are doing it.

'Seeing is not always believing,' is the cumulative thought that manifests into a statement, which she finds herself calling out across the road to Kristjana. It is clear to Daphne that the farmer's wife has dug herself into a spot. But they are losing time, and it is imperative that they get off to the shelter before they are found. If they did not now possess the grimoire and the prophecies, she would have no hesitation in leaving them here at the side of the road. But they do and her mission is unequivocal.

Kristjana's eyebrows rise. Even Viktor becomes wary as Daphne approaches the pair.

'You think you know what is real. There,' says Daphne, waving her hands at Kristjana, palms up, demonstrating they are empty. 'Or out here.' She gestures at the stretch of road she will not cross. 'But it is in here,' she takes a step closer and taps Kristjana's forehead, 'that we really see.'

As Kristjana flinches her eyes latch on to Daphne's hand. In her fingers, seemingly plucked from behind Kristjana's own ear,

Daphne has produced a gold coin. The farmer's wife cannot stifle a cry of shock.

'Sometimes we see what we want to see,' says Daphne. 'Sometimes only our fear.'

She holds out the coin to Kristjana. 'Our brain enjoys playing tricks. Just as we do.'

Kristjana is not a stupid woman. After a long moment, she nods at Daphne, takes the offered coin then walks with great dignity into the road.

It starts to snow.

Again.

## CHAPTER THIRTY-TWO

It has become another blizzard by the time they sight the shelter. The journey has been arduous – pushing, pulling, trudging, wading. Progress slows when one must lift one's feet high over the snow rather than step out in front. It takes much more effort. And Daphne is dressed so cumbersomely – for protection against the elements – her agility is severely limited. But they have finally made it.

And not a moment too soon. For the mountainside is silting up with snowdrifts. The flakes that started as large, dusty petals have contracted into gravelly pellets that dash at their faces and cluster on the track, the slight dip between stretches of brush that they have followed. The fresh layer means their footsteps will show. Unless the storm continues.

Daphne does not want it to continue though. They have passed from twilight into night and the wind has become more severe, faster, coming at her horizontally, blowing her scarf and her hat away. Its sound has become a scream from the mountains, whistling loudly in her ears. All over her body hairs are standing on end, giving her goosebumps, and she has started shivering violently.

The slopes and hillocks are white now. If not for the sparse vegetation she might think they were on the mountains of the moon. The small, cloaked bushes and shrubs shiver and nod in the turbulence, like the necks of her father's collection of plaster dogs that once stood on the mantelpiece at home. Until her mother discovered that they were made in Germany and threw them in the bin. Nod, nod, nod. She knows it is peculiar to think of them now and wonders if cold and exhaustion are fraying her nerves. Her briefing included notes on problematic thermoregulation and adverse effects that can be suffered when the body's ability to adapt to temperature variation becomes impaired. It makes you feel hot. Parts of her feel hot.

Not long now, she tells herself, as she sees Rafn, the fittest and strongest of them, disappear around the side of a low building.

The shelter is half concealed under snow that has blown down from the north. If she were here on her own, she would have missed it. Fashioned from smaller rocks and cobbles, its turf-covered roof is only visible above the central gable over the door.

It takes the weight of all the men, pushing against it, to force this open. When it is done, they stand back to let the women inside before following them in.

Two bunks against two walls, not nearly enough for the six of them, but in the corner a stove. Resting on its lid an oil lamp. Next to it a pile of dry wood. Viktor makes for the lamp, lights it, then they all throw themselves down onto the bunks for a moment, gathering their energy, enjoying the break. By chance the men have piled onto one, the women on the other. For a moment Daphne imagines they are at a dance, waiting to choose their partners and take to the floor.

No one speaks but the air is full of laboured panting. The lamplight flickers over them, casting tall shadows against the stony walls: black ogres sitting on their shoulders. With a groan, Karlsson leans back. The journey has stretched him to the limits of his endurance. He is not a robust man and struggles to undo his coat. Rafn watches him but does not help.

'Safe,' says Viktor to his wife.

'For the present,' she says.

Anna rolls off the bunk and crawls over to the fire. Daphne watches her pull out matches from her pocket and open the stove door. There is a small wigwam of paper and kindling already set up inside. Her heart jumps when Anna lights it and flames tear through the newspaper. Warmth. At last.

Rafn pushes up from the bunk and goes to help.

Slowly the rest of them come back to life. Kristjana gets up and inspects a cupboard. 'Yah,' she says and produces a saucepan. 'Tea or supper?'

'Tea then supper,' Viktor tells her.

It seems absurd to be discussing such domestic rituals in this situation. But then Viktor looks at Daphne and says, 'We must warm up inside, huh?' and pats his chest, and she realises this is likely to be an Icelandic practice developed from the experience of long and bitter winters.

He fetches an empty pail from beside the door and disappears outside.

'Where's he going?' Daphne asks his wife.

'To fetch water,' she says, then corrects herself. 'Snow. It melts.'

Kristjana comes back to the bunk and heaves her knapsack onto it. 'Here,' she says and hands Daphne a smaller sack. 'In there is tea and powdered milk. When you find them, bring to me.'

Daphne glances at the stove. The flames have accepted one of the smaller logs and are lapping around it. Anna and Rafn are counting the rest of them, assessing how much they have and how long the fuel will last.

Inside the haversack her fingers grope around a hard object wrapped in newspaper which, when she unfolds it, she discovers is a bundle of dried fish. How pragmatic, she thinks, that they have packed all of this. How lucky.

She is still ruminating upon the idea of luck when she reaches the tin of powdered milk and another which contains tea leaves.

Kristjana takes them from her as Viktor returns with the pail of snow. He is covered from head to foot in the stuff, though he was only out for minutes. The weather is worsening. What are they going to do?

The question is asked almost formally, once they have returned to their bunks with steaming mugs. There are not enough to go round so she is sharing one with Anna. Because of its small dimensions and being insulated, she thinks by the turf, the hut has warmed up quickly.

Viktor speaks first. 'When the storm calms, there is a farmstead over the way. I know the farmer. He is a good man. He will let us stay with him and perhaps we can borrow a car to take us to Borgarnes where there are British soldiers stationed.'

Reluctant as she is to involve the British army, Daphne sees there are no other options available to her. Hopefully she will be able to make a secure call and get Hugh Devereaux to facilitate their journey onwards.

Rafn is asking how far the next farm is and although Viktor answers in their native language Daphne understands. 'Sjö mílur.' Seven miles.

On flat land in temperate weather, not a long journey at all.

But across awful mountains on rugged terrain, in these winds . . .?

'When will the storm die down?' she asks, and everybody snorts.

She knows why even before Rafn says, 'There are no rules.'

It was a daft question and to save face she says, 'We can't wait it out if this goes on for days. We haven't enough food.'

Kristjana eyes her and says, 'We'll manage.' And Daphne remembers her knapsack is testament to a woman who knows the fickle nature of the land.

'That's not . . .' She stops and rephrases what she was going to say. 'We . . . *I* . . . am worried that there are others on their way. Searching for the grimoire.'

Nobody says anything but they all stare at her. She senses Rafn's disapproval though his face is impassive.

'They cannot know we are here!' Kristjana declares. 'Our neighbours are loyal. We have told no one of our destination.'

'But some have seen us leave in a boat. If they hazard a guess,' says Daphne, feeling her cheeks grow hotter than the rest of her, 'and come this way, then they will find the car and work it out.' None of them ask further questions. Silence returns to add to the gloom.

Eventually Rafn says, 'We do it like this: eat, sleep, take turns to keep watch, stoke the fire.'

'Eat?' asks Karlsson, perking up a little.

Viktor smiles. 'I have a good wife who is well equipped. We have fish.'

'There is a tin of potatoes in the cupboard,' Kristjana adds.

'Fish soup!' says Karlsson. 'You'll think you're at the Ritz, won't you, Daphne?'

His sarcasm grates on her. Refusing to acknowledge it, she says, 'If everyone agrees, I will nap now then take the first shift.'

Rafn nods. 'Good idea,' he says.

Outside something screams in the snow.

Kristjana jumps. She looks at Viktor, eyebrows curved into high arches.

With a minute half-nod, he shakes his head. 'A fox.'

His wife holds his gaze for a moment more, then releases it, or at least allows him to look away. With a stiff sigh, she gets up to tend the supper. But Daphne can tell Kristjana isn't convinced.

She isn't either.

A feeling of great foreboding is rising within her.

CHAPTER THIRTY-THREE

'Come outside,' whispers Rafn, his hand on her shoulder once more.

'What?' Is she awake or dreaming?

No, she's cold. That means awake.

Though it is dark around her. A faint glow from the stove is the only illumination.

How in heaven's name could she have fallen asleep in this position – bolt upright?

But she has.

Kristjana's head lies near Daphne's hips. Her body is covered by coats and some kind of sacking, and she is curled into the remaining space on the bunk they are both occupying. Opposite, Karlsson slumbers deeply. Anna has taken the floor. Viktor, on watch, sits by the door, hands clutching a narrow plank – a rafter from the ceiling? – chin resting on his chest. He is snoring.

She can hardly blame him, can she?

'I'm sorry,' she says and rubs the sleep out of her eyes.

'Come now,' Rafn says again and offers his other hand.

They step over the bodies and push the door open. Rafn waits for her to go out first. She has lost her hat and scarf to the wind and clenches her muscles hard against the expected raging elements, but when she sets foot outside she is shocked.

The snow has stopped. Above them the sun glistens brightly. Is it morning? Hold up – she blinks and looks again. No, it is not the sun, but the moon. Against this midnight sky, painted a spectrum of azures and indigos, it looks so full and radiant and golden it might be taken for its larger celestial sister. Only its tell-tale craters give it away.

Before her stretches a blue Sahara. Covered by snow, the sharp angles of the slopes and peaks are softened, rising and falling around them like desert dunes or waves caught in a moment. Tiny sparkles make her think of precious gems. They are reflections of the glittering infinity above. What glory.

'Everything is exceedingly quiet,' she says, and sees her breath form into crystals and fade away.

After the riot of the storm, the wind everywhere, the rattling of anything not fastened to the ground, this silence and stillness is strange and unreal.

'It's beautiful.' Like a picture. Or a postcard. Or a Christmas landscape. She would not be surprised if she looked up and saw a sleigh flying over the mountain to traverse the sky, seven reindeer pulling it.

Rafn raises her hand to his lips and kisses it. The gesture is becoming a habit. 'There is so much more,' he says.

'What do you mean?' she asks, wondering if he is talking of the mountain range and the miles to the farmstead, which suddenly makes her weary, tired for the journey yet to come.

But he says, 'These are not all the wonders this island has to show.'

'No?' she says and wants to look at him, but she is spellbound by the sight. A milky strip of a thousand constellations has opened like a canyon in the sky above them. It is incredible. So many pricks of light – stars, suns, planetary bodies – froth within, as if one of the Icelandic giantesses had taken her hoard of diamonds and jewel dust and thrown it up into the sky. She has never seen the galaxy before but there it is: a shimmering stream of light stretching in an arc from horizon to horizon.

'In the south we have a geyser,' he says. But she does not want to hear words in this moment. She wants to celebrate it with a kiss and pulls him against her body.

'Stop talking,' she says.

And he laughs so loudly she worries he will wake the others, even though they are yards away in the hut.

As her lips touch his, she feels herself blossoming like an alpine flower. She tastes him and runs her fingers through his hair. She can feel his heat. It is as if he is soaking into her.

When she breaks off and looks over his shoulder, she is giddy. Despite its man-made horrors, the world still contains wonder, she thinks. We need to cherish it more. I will remember this brilliance, she resolves. I will not let it go.

She does not want to let go of Rafn either. But she does not wish the embrace to become fiercer. Though her passion has been ignited, she doesn't fancy any horseplay out on this Arctic surface. And she must be practical now – there are miles to cover and missions to complete.

As she wrests herself away, his eyes search her face. 'We will have some time together in Reykjavík perhaps?'

'I hope so,' she says and means it. 'Though I imagine they'll want me to return with the grimoire. But maybe a rest day or two before. Heaven knows, I've earned it.'

'Good,' he says. 'You rest with me. I will take care of you.'

She can take care of herself, thank you very much, she thinks, but the idea is not at all unappealing. There are so many things she has learned in this land already. Now, she thinks, she will learn about love. And this man before her will be a good teacher: solid, strong, handsome, kind. For a moment she thinks this is why she is here – not sent by Section W on an earthly mission but propelled by the finger of Fate to find her true love. She breathes in and feels a flutter of butterflies in her stomach. It is Hope making itself felt, along with its sister Joy.

'In the morning,' Rafn continues, only half aware of the deep feeling he has stirred in the pretty girl beside him, 'we will head to the farm. It won't take long, now the snow is gone.'

She smiles and nods (she can't *stop* smiling). 'Thank goodness.'

'Go back in, I'll keep watch here. You may wake Viktor if you wish to sleep.'

'It's fine,' she says. 'I feel suddenly full of energy.'

Another shared smile and then she goes back in, full of optimism.

It is ill founded.

The weather has changed but they are in the eye of another storm.

CHAPTER THIRTY-FOUR

She starts.

That was a noise.

For a moment she remains motionless, listening, and holds her breath, eyes flicking around the room. No movement in here. It must have come from outside.

Carefully, so as not to wake Kristjana, she stands up. And waits.

The wind has got up again and is whistling through the cracks in the walls.

Then – bang! Something hits the door.

She is on her feet and over to the entrance in seconds. Has the wind hurled a loose piece of debris?

A cry from the other side.

No, not the wind.

With one fast shove the door is open.

For a moment she is so taken aback by the scene she encounters, she wonders if she has dreamed the interlude with Rafn.

Clouds have swallowed the moon and dense blackness has returned. The air turbulent, mad, shrieks in gusts. She feels it blast at her, sending her hair up into the air, tightening her skin.

Where is he?

'Rafn!' she calls, squinting against the chaos.

Crack! Where? What was that?

And now a yell, some feet ahead of her.

She pushes through the snow and undergrowth, fighting against the gale, narrowing her eyes. But she cannot see far. There is no light. She curses herself for not bringing the lamp.

Her ankle twists in a hole she hasn't seen, and she falls forward, headfirst, into a drift. Pushes herself up and out of it in three moves. 'Rafn?'

Behind her the hut door bangs open, letting light spill out. Now she can see more of the terrain. Ahead she spies his blond hair. No hat. He is on the ground. Why is he lying down?

'Daphne!' It is Viktor standing in the doorway.

'Here!' she says and waves her hand in the air.

Ting. Something whistles past her and hits a hinge, pings diagonally out again and makes the snow sizzle as it plunges through.

A bullet.

Someone out here has a revolver!

'Rafn!' She crawls to him on knees and elbows; snakes over the next mound.

She hears Viktor wading through the snow behind her.

On she goes, spitting ice out of her mouth, clawing her way to him. Should have worn gloves.

Rat-a-tat-tat. Three shots. A gasp. Flashes in the distance, one black shape moving. Another behind it. Perhaps one more. She rolls over, turns and sees Viktor staggering, falling to the ground. Or has he ducked? 'We're under attack,' she shouts uselessly, clambers back, pushes herself on.

Closer now.

Over a bump in the ground, then she is there beside Rafn.

He is conscious, though breathing stutteringly, clutching at his stomach. Dark liquid stains the snow around him.

'Germans,' he rasps. 'Must have been the smoke.'

She doesn't know what he means. Doesn't care. Grabs him. He yelps in pain. She lets go.

'Here.' He pushes something into her hands. Tubular, metallic, hot. It is the revolver.

No, she thinks. She has a weapon. Digs into her pocket. There is the lipstick.

Turns back to Viktor, who is struggling to right himself. 'Can you fire?'

A grunt. She tosses the revolver towards him and sees, silhouetted in the doorway, Anna squatting down, peering outside.

Past the threshold, Kristjana is standing, arms outstretched, eyes rolling to the heavens, muttering. Or is it chanting?

But Rafn! 'I need to get you back inside.'

'No time,' he says. 'They will be upon us.'

Torn for a moment between staying by his side, helping him, or facing the foe, she knows he is right and makes the decision to wriggle forward in the enemy's direction. Feels the ground slanting down. Fingers, numbing, meet something hard: a snow-covered boulder. She crawls onto her knees. Runs her hands up its sides. Leans against it, peeps up over the top.

An undulation of white hillocks then the road. A new vehicle on it. Before that, shapes – men, moving like shadows.

There are at least two of them. One, crouch-walking towards the hut, only yards away. She can hear the other but cannot see him.

Damn. She drops back down behind the boulder. Breathes.

Frozen fingers push into her pocket. Feel-find the lipstick.

Out it comes. Cold, heartless, magical thing of lethal power. At least, she hopes it will be.

Training, training. What did they say? Yes, that's right. Hold the base, twist the outer shell. Done. The barrel springs out. Click. Next the thumb latch. Click. Manipulate the hammer spur disguised as the cosmetic logo. Whirr. Put your eye to a jewelled golden bump that contains the rear sight.

The range is limited. Which means she will not have much time. If she misses, the assailant will make it to Viktor.

The man's bulk creeps closer.

She steadies one hand on the rock, though shivers run through it. Lines her right eye up to the sight. The man is there. Hard to see, dressed all in black. But right in the frame. Quick, pull, release.

Pop. Flash. Whine. A stifled scream. Not hers. His.

She lifts her head. He stumbles back, off balance, then to the side, clutching his shoulder. Injured, but not neutralised.

Behind her, another shot.

Viktor too has fired.

She snaps her head back. The man in black is going over.

Another gunshot from further away, ahead of her. The air splits as it finds its target.

Viktor howls. He has been hit.

Anna's voice, firm, measured: 'Gefðu mér byssuna.'

She is taking the gun.

Kristjana's mutters becoming a shrill incantation. 'Rísa upp, rísa upp.' Beneath it Karlsson's reed-thin wail: 'Hier. Ich bin hier drin.'

The treacherous villain is calling to them.

No time for recriminations.

Back.

Focussed once more on the remaining attacker in the middle distance.

A small explosion. A high-pitched mechanical buzz. The bullet hits her boulder, sends splinters of stone up into her face, over her hair.

She ducks, twists round, back against the rock. In her pocket fumbles for the second bullet, the last bullet.

Freezing fingers hurt.

But she locates it, shakily. Loads it up.

Beside Viktor, propped on her elbows, Anna fires.

No sounds from the approaching men. She must have missed.

Just as Daphne is about to turn back, she sees a shadow, tall and spindly, come out from behind the hut. He takes two, three soundless steps and bends towards her friend on the ground.

'Anna!' she screams out in warning.

But it is too late: he has used his pistol to crack her over the head. Anna goes down.

No, no, no. Now, Daphne calculates, it is only her and the farmer's wife left unwounded. But Kristjana is just standing there in the hut shouting out bizarre words.

Anna's assailant, alerted to Daphne's position by her shout, starts towards her.

But she needs to stop the other man, the other *men*, reaching the hut.

Which to do?

Think!

Fumbles with the bullet. Looks up.

Oh, God, Anna's attacker is three yards away.

Bullet drops in.

Pulls back the hammer.

Now he is two yards away.

Concentrate!

Raises the sight to her eye.

One yard – whack!

He smacks the gun out of her hands. She sees it arc across the snow, hit the side of the hut, fall. Before she looks back at him the first blow hits her cheek. Her head smashes into the boulder.

For a moment her vision goes. Then white light inside her eyes.

Forces them open.

He shuffles forward so that he is astride her. She thinks he is going to raise his fist again.

Still stunned and floored by pain she shuts her eyes, braces for the blow, but fingers begin to squeeze her throat.

An unearthly roar sounds across the land like a great horn. Guttural, low. Too loud for an animal. Too deep for a human. Lonely, deadly, bestial.

Opens her eyes, without breath, confused. For a moment the pressure on her neck slackens. The man has paused and struggled up to look towards the source of the growl. His hands fleetingly let go of her neck.

She wastes no time. Raises her boot, steadies it, swings back then brings it up hard, into the soft part between his legs.

Another moan – his. Beyond it, that howl again.

He doubles over and crouches, hands to groin.

She is dizzy and disorientated but all that combat training is surging to the fore, automating her responses: part of her is reacting like a machine. The drills have conditioned her for such a scenario. She must act quickly before he recovers.

Using her feet, as she has done so many times before to escape magician's boxes and cutting cases, she pushes her back up against the boulder.

He sees her and struggles to straighten.

On her feet, though swaying, she lunges. Her foot connects with his ribs, knocking the wind out of him.

Behind her a man has started shrieking in German. Words pitched high with raw terror and pain. There is grunting, a guttural roar, the sound of clothes tearing. Staccato gunshots, a chaos of noise.

But her assailant is forcing himself up. She must too and balances to centre herself.

Now – she delivers an elbow into the side of his head. He flails back and slumps into the snow, flounders, straightens and sits up. Behind him she sees Kristjana, in her hands Viktor's plank of wood, which she brings down hard on the man's head.

There is a hideous splintering sound as it breaks around him. He blinks for a moment then plunges sideways into the snow.

The screaming intensifies.

Kristjana points behind her. 'There are at least two more. The draugur contends with one, but another still has gun.'

She doesn't understand everything but enough to know the fight is not over yet.

And she has lost her pistol.

'Down,' she orders. Drops, hauls her weary body to the boulder. Kristjana obeys her command. The rock provides just enough cover for both of them.

Another bone-chilling howl. Primal in its despair.

If she allowed it to, this one would fill her with dread: there is something out there that is not human. And it is killing the German. The fight is going on by the side of the hut. Two combatants involved, she guesses. Lifts her head above the rock to see.

A gun nearby rings out.

She ducks.

But the shots aren't aimed at them. They hit the hut near the fight and ricochet around.

A final scream that is cut off by a ripping, splitting sound.

She reaches up again to peer into the landscape.

Blinks.

Two beams of light have appeared over a hillock maybe thirty yards away. They bounce then sweep down over the land as the oncoming vehicle crests the hill.

Caught in the light, just yards away, a white face turns to her. A man dressed all in black silhouetted with gun in hand.

Her face drains of colour.

Has he seen them?

Yes, he has.

He starts towards them and breaks into a run, speeding stealthily over the ground, raising his gun, pulling back the hammer.

What to do? Lunge forward and throw herself against him with all her might? Or retreat? Run away? She experiences a moment of paralysis.

Then crack, more gunshots fired into the air across the mountain panorama. The man flies forward unnaturally, arms out at his sides, lands face down in the snow.

The vehicle stops. Activity around it.

She begins to stand.

The man is on the ground shuddering, his fight over for the time being.

Soldiers run towards them.

Recognising the Allied uniform she shouts out, 'There are two more down by the hut,' and points over.

Three of the soldiers make their way there but one of them remains on course towards her.

She brushes the hair out of her eyes. Bruises are already forming on her face and smart underneath her icy fingertips.

The Canadian stops a few feet away.

Though the headlights are unbearably bright, she can see who it is. She'd recognise that confident gait anywhere.

'I was told you might need some assistance,' says Jack.

## CHAPTER THIRTY-FIVE

She still doesn't understand how he found them. But right now, there are more pressing issues at hand.

The man she and Kristjana felled is not German but a native Icelander, sympathetic to the enemy cause.

'He'll live,' said one of Jack's men as they trussed him up and handcuffed him to a bunk inside the hut. The other two *are* enemy agents. Or were. One of them, the man shot en route to Daphne, is injured but not critical. His head wounds will be dressed once the civilians have been attended to. In the meantime, he too is handcuffed and bound in the hut. A final set of cuffs has been administered to Karlsson, who lies crying on his bunk. 'It's my cousin,' he weeps. 'They have my cousin in Denmark. He'll be executed if I don't cooperate.'

The third man, another German, or what is left of him, is apparently 'in shreds' outside. Mauled by some wild animal, the medic has suggested. 'A polar bear maybe.'

'That's not right,' says Daphne, asserting her local knowledge. 'They do not have them here.'

No one listens.

Kristjana wears a strange expression on her face and, when she is not attending to Viktor, glances at Daphne as though they have a shared secret. Her husband has taken a gunshot wound to his leg. It is not fatal but needs more expert attention, as does Rafn.

The medic has done the best he can, but it is vital that they get him to Reykjavík now.

Daphne and Anna walk alongside the stretcher that bears his poor, bleeding body.

Jack is talking to her, asking questions, but she can't answer, only keeps her eyes on Rafn.

The Canadian senses something has happened with this man, she can tell by the slight lift of his brows, though his manner is efficient, helpful and appropriately concerned. She realises he has the same colour hair as Rafn and wonders if she had noticed that before. Cannot spend further time speculating as the patient moans when they slide him onto the floor at the rear of the truck. 'I'll stay with him,' says Anna, who is concussed with a gash on the back of her head, but otherwise all right.

'Me too,' says Daphne and climbs in behind her. She takes the blankets offered by a medic, who sits on the bench to one side, and covers Rafn with them as gently as she can.

Recognising the voices of Viktor and Kristjana, who must be getting into the front, she feels the truck dip. Then the doors slam shut and the engine starts.

She curls her body around Rafn's.

'You are nice and warm,' he says.

'That's more than can be said for you, old bean.' And even though there are others present, she reaches up and kisses his chin.

The journey is long. They bump and roll. She acts as a buffer, protecting him from the motion of the truck as best as she can. But he still groans when they lurch and take the pass's many, many hairpin bends. So, to distract him, she whispers about home, her parents, her work on the boards. And he tells her he will come and visit, but before that, when they are in Reykjavík, she must see the geyser. 'It is like you – unstoppable,' he says.

At some point the truck slows and they pull in for a break. The medic moves her out of the way to check on the patient. The doors of the truck open and she sees Jack there with a flask of hot tea and two cups.

Fatigue is overcoming her now but she gets up, sways slightly as she goes to greet him.

'You should come into the front,' he says, face furrowed and taut. 'It is warmer and you need to sleep.'

Behind her Anna yelps. Daphne does not turn to see what is going on but feels a push on her shoulder as her friend climbs out of the truck.

She does not think to wonder why as she is considering her answer to Jack. In the end, she shakes her head. 'I will be all right,' she says and goes back to the patient.

A short conversation between the medic and Jack, then the doors are drawn to and they are off again.

'I see you,' says Rafn.


Next, she is being shaken awake. There are more people in the truck. The doors are open and the thin grey light of morning is seeping in.

An army camp. Beyond it the tops of buildings, then low, distant mountains, with rain clouds coasting down their slopes. They must be back in the city at last.

'It's time to go,' the medic says as she tries to sit up.

'We're here?'

'Yes,' he says.

His eyes are kind, she thinks, but reveal a depressed heart.

'Good,' she says. 'We must get Rafn to the hospital at once.'

He puts his arm round her shoulders and helps her up. 'That won't do any good now.'

She scrunches her forehead. What does that mean? Has he got better?

Then she reels back to the figure on the floor.

His body is rigid, eyes open, staring at the roof of the truck. One of his hands lies across the blanket which is stained a burnt orange-red.

She hears the medic's words but can't understand them.

'When we got to Bifröst he had already passed,' he is saying.

But the man is confused surely. She has been talking to Rafn.

Dulled by the news, her mind a confusion of impossibilities, she allows him to direct her to the bench at the side so the others can lift the stretcher and take Rafn out.

His body rocks inelegantly like it is a hard thing, unresponsive, not reacting to the men bearing him away.

They are too rough with him, she thinks, they will hurt him. And as he is carried off, she puts out a hand and touches his cheek.

It is cold. Like a stone. Like death.

So often it is like that. When the mind cannot absorb the shock of the real, it is the body that feels the truth.

The crush of understanding leadens her at once. A heaviness moves through her limbs as her cheeks begin to burn.

She watches him leave her.

'Are you all right?' asks the medic.

But she has no words. None of her own. All that come to her are the lines of a Greek play she learned once at school.

'"You have seen strange things,"' she whispers to him, though she is talking to the world.

'"The awful hand of death, fresh shapes of despair,
Unspeakable sufferings,
And all that you have seen
Is God."'

The medic puts his hand to her forehead and frowns.

## CHAPTER THIRTY-SIX

So numb is she, Major Spike's barracking barely registers. Though it seems to go on and on and last forever. Afterwards she is put into a car and sent back to her lodgings with instructions to be ready at 0800 hours the following morning.

She has a vague sense that she should be feeling lucky about something. No charges. That Hugh has used his diplomacy, or rank, to smooth it all over. But her mind cannot hold any detail. It is like a sieve – as soon as one thing goes into it, another five fall out.

The door is opened by Björn, the landlady's son, which is enough of a surprise that it makes Daphne speak again.

'Oh,' she says, her voice rusty with disuse. 'I thought you were dead.'

He thinks she is joking and is tickled by this, smirking as he lets her in. 'No,' he says and takes her bag. 'A disagreement with a motorcar.' He points at a stick he is using to get about.

Shakily she takes her bag back off him. He is crippled and she, in body at least, is still competent. 'I can't let you carry this.'

He submits cheerfully and she walks into the house, grateful that she hasn't injured him after all. Just some other man. 'But someone was stabbed?' she says aloud. 'The messenger who came here said so.'

'Yes, another Björn. Not me. Though both of us were hurt on the same night and they mixed up our surnames. Björn

Magnússon is a bad person. Criminal. Not long out of prison and drinking too much. Black Death changes people into beasts. Björn Magnússon is always brawling. He cannot remember what happened, but we all think another drunken fight.'

So this must be her attacker and he is still alive.

There is some consolation in the idea that she did not kill the landlady's son, at least.

Then she flinches. Did she kill Rafn?

And Karlsson's prediction comes back at her like a punch to the gut. Not his prophecy about the mountain but the other one that she has not thought of since: 'The hand of Death is on your shoulder.' And she remembers how Rafn touched her there.

Oh, God, she thinks, it *is* me.

If Rafn hadn't come with them to Hólmavík he would still be alive. This glorious man who was to be her lover has been cut down before he could begin. Before *they* could begin. And all the moments she has hoped for, all the flutterings of joy, disappear into a vacuum within.

*He is dead. Rafn has died. He is gone.*

*He did not deserve this.*

It is her fault.

Plucked from the world when he was so much finer, so much *better* than all of them.

And then something rips in her heart and she feels the weight of his absence sink in.

A bitter loneliness bleeds into her veins.

*He has left me.*

*I am alone. Without love. Without him.*

She will never be the same again.

And suddenly she experiences a desperate urge to punch something or, worse still, break down and cry.

'Can I get you coffee?' asks Björn. 'You are not looking well.'

And she realises she is still standing in the hallway, staring at the floor. Although she does not answer – she does not know if she wants coffee or not – it seems cruel when Rafn cannot taste it anymore – the landlady's son gently takes her arm and guides her into the dining room.

The table is already set for tomorrow's breakfast. Nothing has changed at all. At the end by the wall is the table with the waiting porridge tureen, bowls, a dozen glasses.

Björn hobbles into the kitchen and returns with an enamel jug and two mugs, which he fills, adding two large spoonfuls of sugar to Daphne's. It is a thoughtful gesture but makes her feel a jagged sting internally as if he has stabbed her with kindness. The pain forces her to breathe in sharply, but as she breathes out, a sob finds its way too. Then suddenly she is shuddering and crying as if she is a little girl again.

*He is dead. He is lost to me.*

And as if she is a little girl again, Björn takes her hand and pats the back of it gently while she weeps. Tenderness is brutal. He doesn't say anything and neither does she. There is too much, too many words, but none can be spoken.

*Oh, Rafn, how I grieve for you. It will take forever. It will take . . .*

They stay like that for nearly an hour until there is nothing left inside her anymore, then she picks up her bag, and with a nod at her host, climbs the stairs to bed.

## CHAPTER THIRTY-SEVEN

'Quite extraordinary,' Septimus is saying, 'that it revealed itself to me in such a fashion. The clairvoyant was delivering something more than messages.'

Daphne nods. 'Yes,' she says. She has tried telling her story to her superior but he is in love with his experience of what he calls 'a shamanic tribe'. Which is something she has not seen on her own travels in Iceland. Sorcerers – yes. Shamans – no. Perhaps they have travelled down from Greenland. Or perhaps Septimus has been 'had'. He taps his souvenir: the drum with the symbols inked into its skin.

'I will speak to Major Spike,' he says, brimming with enthusiasm now he is back to full health, 'when we get to the camp and suggest Karlsson is taken into custody.'

At this, she is able to offer some inside knowledge. 'He is already in custody, sir.'

'Oh?' says Septimus, and for the first time since they got into the car, trails his gaze over her. 'You know that for a fact, do you?'

'I do,' she says, and looks away from him out of the window. They are approaching the centre with its little shops and cafés. The few people who are on the streets are buttoned up tightly into winter clothes. Everything is grey and black. It is as if the city has gone into mourning for Him.

'Well, you're better informed than I,' Septimus sniffs. 'Let us hope they lock the cell door and throw away the key. Or have him up in front of a firing squad. The Atlantic is a battleground. U-boats are hunting us like wolves in a pack and winning too. Who knows how many lives have been lost because of that conspirator?'

She has had similar thoughts but this morning cannot bear the spectre of death touching anyone else. Though she is not sure she believes anything Karlsson says in his defence, especially while handcuffed to a bunk by Allied soldiers, she is also aware the Germans use dirty tricks and could well have kidnapped his cousin in order to exert pressure. She recalls he offered to sell them the location of the grimoire for a price, but that may have been a tactic to buy himself time. However, there has been too much bloodshed already.

'I don't think many people know that he has been incarcerated,' she says to Septimus, tearing her eyes away from the cityscape. 'It feels like weeks have gone by, but it has only been days. Karlsson's loyalties to the enemy are not set in stone. With a little persuasion and sensitive handling, we could put him to good use.'

Septimus points his chin at her. His eyebrows arch. 'What do you mean?'

'Should the charges against him remain pending, then I think he could be convinced to work with us. If he continues his séances and performances the way he has been conducting them, *false* weather reports leaked out in code might throw off the Germans.'

'Oh, I see,' says Septimus, directing his eyes away from her to the road ahead. 'Disinformation.'

Disinformation, distraction, dazzle, deception – she is adept at all of them.

'Precisely,' she says.

He breaks into a smile. 'Cracking idea. I might suggest that to Spike.'

She wishes he would. She herself is persona non grata. Nothing that comes out of her lips will be taken seriously. 'And he is worth investigating in other ways. Some of his predictions came true.'

'They did?' Septimus is only half surprised, she thinks. 'Which ones?'

She swallows hard before she can say, 'He foresaw a minor earthquake.'

'Hmm,' says Septimus. 'In a place like this, not difficult. What else?'

*The hand of Death is on your shoulder. He is dead. He is lost to me.*

'It doesn't matter,' she says. *It matters so much, I can't tell you.* Her voice breaks as she plasters her stage mask over her face and slaps on her performative smile. 'If, ahem, you don't mind me saying so, you can be charming, sir.' She sends him a plump-cheeked grin that she does not feel. 'Misinformation is as important as the real stuff, in certain hands. I'm sure someone of your standing can bring the major round to a tactical strategy such as this.'

'Yes, I could do that, I'm sure,' he says and taps his chin.

Already he is asserting ownership over the notion, obediently following the trail of breadcrumbs she has sprinkled with her words. Young women with sharp minds must work laterally through limitations. Though she loathed it at the time, she sees that all her childhood and adolescent schooling by older women with a keen eye on the marriage market has given her an appreciation of the male's whims and caprices. It is odd, how Englishmen act as if women know nothing of them at all.

Septimus's eyes glitter. Though he looks at her, she can tell he is already picturing the splendid reception of 'his' proposal. 'A medium,' he mutters aloud, 'who the Germans think is their own. Their preoccupation with this kind of thing can be exploited to our advantage.'

She releases a very small sigh that Septimus does not register. Karlsson is a weak man and an enemy, but he is a valuable fool, and better alive than dead in terms of her own moral burden.

The car slows down, pulls into the pavement but keeps its engine running.

'Right,' says Septimus with brisk efficiency, jerked back into the present by the driver's polite cough. 'Daphne, I'll see you aboard. We have two Icelanders to escort to old Blighty, I understand?'

'That's right.'

'I'll get the rest of these bags stowed. Don't be late, young lady.'

'I won't, Septimus. Thank you, sir.'

She waves him off, lets the smile slide from her face and forces her feet over the threshold into the newspaper building.

'I'm so sorry,' she says when she pulls out of Anna's stiff embrace.

'I know,' her friend returns. Her once clear eyes are threaded with tiny red veins, bags visible beneath them.

With typical understatement, her friend has addressed Daphne's feelings for her cousin, acknowledged the relationship and accepted her condolences. All without judgement.

Gulping down her rising emotion, it takes effort for Daphne to speak. 'If I could ever have known that such a terrible thing would . . .' But she can't bear to finish the sentence, or the thought, or revisit the images. 'I never would have . . .'

Anna nods, her shoulders hard like a coat hanger upon which her clothes droop. 'Me neither,' she says and raises her gaze to meet Daphne's.

As she looks into her friend's watery eyes, Daphne understands she is not the only one staggering under the weight of guilt. Anna too has played her part. If any of this was predictable, and some of it seemed to be, it is irrelevant now. The only thing she can think of, in this moment, is the fleeting nature of chance and the horrendous sorrows that the war has brought down upon them, the unfairness of it all, the waste of a life. Of lives. Despite her bitterness she understands that there are German mothers and wives who are grieving their boys too. It is more than a squandering, it is a sacrilege that the miracle of life, of *lives* created, can be done away with in a second, because of another man's ambition. If all of this is part of God's plan then she doesn't like Him, doesn't believe in Him anymore. Perhaps the Germans have tipped the balance and indeed brought Lucifer in to reign. Perhaps this is what they all deserve.

Certainly, she feels like she's in hell.

Anna bends down and brings Daphne's old, battered suitcase, burst at one end and with dark patches in the corners, onto the desk. With everything that had happened yesterday when they arrived, she had lost her focus, given no thought to the grimoire and abandoned it in the truck. Only Anna had the remarkable presence of mind to retrieve the thing.

Daphne glares at it. She hates it, wants to rip apart the book and throw it into the sea to rot.

But Anna says, 'You must get this safely to London. If it doesn't reach its destination then all of this . . .' She shrugs and then coughs into her hand, composes herself. 'Then the sacrifices that we and Rafn made – they will be for nothing.'

It is true. So Daphne takes it and feels the grimoire glowing darkly in its wrappings. How she can feel that she doesn't know. But not much makes sense anymore. She is learning to adapt to this new way of living like a river around fresh boulders.

'Thank you,' Daphne says. 'For everything. I will make sure I acknowledge your sterling support in my report. You are an exceptional woman, Anna Tómasdóttir.'

'I know,' she says with a weak smile. 'You must come back here when the war is done.'

'Yes,' says Daphne and leans towards her. With her free hand, she takes Anna's. 'I will. I would like to visit you again.'

'You must come to the great geyser,' says her friend and squeezes Daphne's hand. 'I know he wanted that.'

Daphne turns abruptly to the door so Anna cannot see her face.

'And I was here anyway, instructing men on the new tech.' Jack pauses and rewords his sentence for discretion's sake. 'Training the Signals in the Royal Regiment.'

'Ah,' she says as if this explains everything and pulls her coat tighter. The wind is coming across the harbour from the north. This path alongside the water is exposed to it.

In fact, Jack has to raise his voice to be heard. 'Then, I presume,' he half shouts in her ear, 'your Brigadier Harkness had a word with my Brigadier Page and the next thing I know I'm dispatched to the north of the island urgently on a priority search and rescue. When I saw your name, I realised why I'd been selected. Glad we got there in time, Daphne. Very glad indeed.'

'Uh-huh.' She nods, not really listening. Her mind has reached back to the time she delivered a message to the Signals unit at camp, and the coded words she gave to gain access: 'It is a fine night for a promenade on the harbour, under the stars.' She had thought of Jack then, pictured the two of them strolling along this quay, laughing fondly with each other.

There is no laughter in her now and, while she is grateful to Jack, she feels numb towards him.

'Look,' he says as they reach the gangplank where marines are carrying chests aboard the ship.

She stops and faces him. Objectively he is an attractive man. Running his fingers through his fringe, he sweeps it away from his eyes and adjusts his cap. His features are smooth and flawless, well-groomed, but cannot compare with the heroic honesty of Rafn's face.

But she should not be making comparisons – they are entirely different men.

'... when I get back?' he is asking her.

She didn't catch all of what he has said but knows she will appear rude if she asks him to repeat himself. So she nods vigorously and says, 'Oh, yes, of course.'

He brightens. 'Splendid! And it may be earlier than we think. There are rumours we'll be recalled to England by the end of the month! I'll look you up then.'

Has she committed to seeing him? The idea of it appals. It is disloyal when she feels as if Rafn is still here, scattered across this island with all the beautiful things. His voice remains in her head. In fact, she hears it now: 'Don't worry, you need to live,' he says.

She disagrees. The future is bleak unless *he* is in it.

Jack is fidgeting restlessly by her side. She senses another question in him. 'Right,' she says, unwilling to engage, and looks meaningfully at the gangplank. 'I'd really better get aboard.'

'Yes, yes, of course,' says Jack. Then, as if he too is aware of his rival's presence, 'I truly am sorry about your, er, friend.'

She can't look him in the eye. Puts her gloved hand on the rail and whispers, 'Thank you.'

Then, to her surprise, she feels a soft touch, a smudge on the cheek as he plants a kiss there. She jerks her head to look at him, unsure if she is offended. He has stepped back and is waving, a sunny beam spreading across his face.

'Let it go,' says Rafn.

'Goodbye, Jack,' she says.

'Bon voyage, Daphne,' the Canadian calls as she mounts the ramp. 'I'll see you back in the Smoke.'

Her stomach contracts.

How everything changes.

Aboard the ship introductions are made. Septimus is fascinated by Viktor and expresses a wish to talk to him when they have settled down. The farmer–sorcerer's beard has been trimmed so that he looks younger and neater. He is happy to accommodate this request and Septimus takes his leave with a promise to return once he has located his sleeping quarters.

'I see it has found you.' Viktor directs his gaze purposefully to Daphne's suitcase, which sits once more upon her lap.

'Or I have found it,' she says, avoiding any discussion of why she left it and the great tragedy that prompted her brief lapse.

'You may think that,' says Viktor. 'But you'd be wrong.'

She begins to unclasp the straps at the side of the case. 'I want to know what it says.' If it is important and Rafn has lost his life for it, she needs to know why.

'I have been waiting for you to ask,' says Viktor as the departure horn blows on deck.

At the noise, Kristjana gets to her feet. 'I'm going up to wave goodbye to the island. Do you want to come?' she asks her husband.

'No,' he says. 'I'll be fine here. Too much.' And gestures to his bandaged leg.

'Back in a while,' she says to her husband. Then to Daphne, 'I should leave the sorcerer to his apprentice.'

When she has gone, Daphne takes out the heavy book. 'I don't believe in any of this,' she says.

Viktor nods, unphased. 'Belief is not necessary.'

'The idea that this . . .' She holds the book up. 'That we can exert control over the unknowable, over our lives . . . Well, it's a deception. Life is unpredictable and meaningless and chaotic.'

Viktor does not react, but says quietly, 'And yet, many would say such an attitude is the greatest deception of all. I have a strong conviction that events in the future may well change your mind.'

She frowns but opens the pages and points. 'This one. What is this?' Her fingers skate across the paper.

'Ah,' says Viktor with a smile. 'A good choice for a beginner such as you.'

'Me?' she exclaims with indignation.

'Yes, you,' says Viktor. 'This spell is for vengeance.'

*The convoy sails south past the barrage of mines into the open Atlantic unaware that, miles above, a surveillance plane with a belly almost empty of bombs has sighted its wake. The pilot is tired. It has been a long day. His finger is itchy upon the trigger. But fatigue forces a yawn and his hand comes up to his mouth. Daphne is safe. At least for a few more months.*

*Nearly fifteen hundred miles away, as the crow flies in a south-easterly direction, a man enters an office in Berlin. He does not wish to impart the news he ought to relay. But it is his job. He must obey.*

*'The mission was unsuccessful, I'm afraid, sir,' he begins.*

*His superior sits back in his chair and considers this.*

*It seems to the man that his commander's uniform is shimmering. Perhaps it is the power that radiates from within? The eagle insignia on his lapel moves with each breath. Heavy eyebrows lend him a saturnine aspect that makes the ministerial official feel clammy. Saturn again, he thinks. He has a background in law and facts; all this talk of astrology and magic does not sit well with him.*

*'I see,' says his superior after a while. 'Though I still want it. Do what you can.'*

*The official is not sure what response he was expecting but this surprises him. How can he obtain something that has fallen into enemy hands?*

*'Dismissed,' barks his superior. 'Do not return until you have located it.'*

*The man salutes and turns on his heel.*

*Outside he takes a moment to calm the panic of blood in his veins. As his brain restores itself, he sees he must come up with a new plan. The time for negotiation and bribery is over. He must sully his own hands now.*

## ACKNOWLEDGEMENTS

Only half of this book would have been written without the assistance of Quentin Bates, a fellow crime writer, who has a fantastic track record in both translation and his own very excellent Icelandic crime novels (https://graskeggur.com/). Quentin gave me a lot of help and many pointers as to where I should begin my research. When you begin delving into an idea with just a vague notion of who to talk to and where to go, advice from a native (or naturalised native) is invaluable. I owe him a huge debt.

Also at my request, Quentin thoughtfully made a literal translation of the leaflet entitled 'Tilkynning', which was handed out on the docks to Icelanders while the British invaders walked into the capital city. As he told me, 'It's pretty cock-eyed. Looks like it was written by someone with an imperfect and rather stilted command of Icelandic. And yes, it is quite funny. But a sterling effort by the poor guy who had to write it in a hurry back in 1940.' In addition, Quentin generously translated some of the newspaper excerpts that I have adapted and used in this book.

The inestimable Mr Bates enlisted the help of his daughter Sylvia who, in true family style, helpfully guided me to online resources and the National Library of Iceland. The Bates family are welcome around my place any time. I owe you.

## Reykjavík

I have a number of people to acknowledge here. First, Ragnheidur Tryggvadóttir, Podrunn and the Writers' Union for facilitating my residencies at the stunning Gunnarshús, from where I was able to conduct extensive research into the invasion and occupation of Iceland.

Örn Hrafnkelsson, Director for National Collections and Digital Conversion at the National and University Library of Iceland, aided me in locating specific newspaper coverage of the invasion circa 1940. As those of you who have made it to this section can see – it was put to good use. Arnaldur Sigurðsson, at the Reading Room of the library, tracked down the book *Iceland Invaded* by Páll Baldvin Baldvinsson, which I was able to purchase and bring back home to digest. Many thanks to both of you.

I am constantly telling my students that there is no better research than visiting the places that you intend to write about. This is for many reasons – how else would I know the water in Reykjavík smelled of eggs (sulphur) or been made to feel like a dot of humanity in the great arms of the wilderness? Nor would I have been able see at first hand one of the most detailed and impressive accounts of the invasion that I have been able to source, in the Reading Room of the National Library. As far as I am aware, there are two copies of it in existence: one at the University of Missouri and one in Reykjavík. Written by Donald Francis Bittner as his PhD thesis, this work is testament to scholarly rigour and comprehensive research. Not to mention one of the most impressive PhDs I have ever read. Huge gratitude must be expressed to Mr Bittner for his exceptional contribution to the subject.

I met Thor Fjalar Hallgrímsson at the National Museum of Iceland on my second research trip. Thor helpfully determined which newspaper Anna was likely to work for, *and* its address in 1940. Armed with this information it didn't take long for me to find the former offices of *Morgunblaðið*. Though I would not have been able to pinpoint them without the help of two congenial members of the Reykjavík police (Lögreglan), to whom I am also indebted.

Emil Hrafn Hildarson at the National Museum of Photography facilitated a viewing of original photographs that chronicle the actual day of invasion (!) from the albums of Skafti Guðjónsson, alongside his documentation of Reykjavík in 1940, 1941 and 1942. Thus I was able to get a sense of the clothes and uniforms worn by both civilians and British and Canadian military personnel. These artefacts really brought to life this fascinating period of history and helped me to navigate the city and its people after an interval of eighty-four years.

The Hotel Borg is a real place: beautiful and pretty much the same, structurally, as it was in the 1940s. Like many of the Icelandic establishments I visited it also has wonderful staff who happily accommodated my requests to view the premises. Rita Tekete showed me round what was once the bar and restaurant, where British officers were able to drink locally brewed beer during the period of prohibition. It took a great deal of sleuthing to find out if there were tiles in the porch in 1940 and I am grateful to be able to say that Daphne was indeed likely to have click-clacked over the floor. A little detail, I know, but authenticity is so important. Thank you, Rita, for bearing with me.

And last but by no means least, I am HUGELY indebted to Gestur Páll Reynisson. A random meeting on a bus proved so fortuitous. Gestur has been a great source of wisdom and advice, able to tell me about Reykjavík, cobbled streets, churches, cinemas and political allegiances in Iceland in 1940. His knowledge, drawing on his family's experience, has helped to shape this book into an accurate portrayal of Reykjavík in 1940. Not only ALL OF THAT but he also facilitated my visit to the Alþingi (parliament), where I became immersed in the environment and history of the place where so many decisions relevant to the invasion were taken. Our guide round the Alþingi was Kristján Sveinsson, who was also very well informed and enthusiastic. And calm – I can testify to the fact that the security of the Icelandic government is very efficient. I could not have wished for a better tour. And I'd hazard a guess that Kristján would be great to have by your side in a crisis.

To all of the above, my gratitude is owed.

## Hvalfjörður

The War and Peace Museum in Hvalfjörður was started by Guðjón Sigmundsson, its CEO. Guðjón most graciously opened up his museum for me to visit off-season. He also permitted me to roam around, spending more time than I think he anticipated in the rooms that are testament to a keen collector with a commitment to commemorating the invasion. If you visit, you will find areas dedicated to all the Allied forces, and the Germans who were shipwrecked. Guðjón also displayed immense patience as I plagued him with questions about the occupation and was a most welcoming host.

## Hólmavík

I spent four days in Strandir, the land of sorcerers, and was hosted by Anna Björg Þórarinsdóttir, manager of the Museum of Witchcraft and Sorcery. Anna and the staff at the museum are all commendably committed to challenging preconceptions about witchcraft and sorcery in Iceland, something my readers will know that I feel passionately about with regards to Essex.

Anna told me about the magical talisman that is not only their emblem/coat-of-arms but which has been used as a protective sigil for the Icelandic people.

The subject of witchcraft has been a lifelong fascination and I could have spent a week there. Possibly a month, when Anna introduced me to Magnús Rafnsson. Magnús is an expert on grimoires and the Icelandic witch trials. I am so appreciative of him coming to see me on the weekend when the 'sheep gathering' was taking place. This is an event that involves the whole community. Family members come from all over to help herd the flocks down from the mountains. It is not only a communal activity but a celebration and so I was very privileged that Magnús made time out of his busy schedule to visit this writer.

Our conversations were extraordinary, as is the case when like-minds meet, and I am indebted to this intelligent and gracious man for his wisdom and unselfish sharing of his immense knowledge. Not only did Magnús answer all my grimoire- and sorcery-related queries, he talked about the history of Hólmavík and directed me to another venue that the museum has created – The Sorcerer's Cottage. I found it the following day at the end of a rainbow. An extraordinary site that boasts a re-creation of the kind of dwelling in which people lived during the time of the witch-hunts, it also has a geothermal pool, blessed by Bishop Guðmundur, alongside a troll's chair. Incidentally, Magnús informed me that the bishop blessed lots of waterholes including the one I have referred to in the book.

Magnús and Gestur must also be thanked for providing beta-reader feedback on my first draft of this manuscript and delicately correcting some of my gaffes.

I am obliged to Tóta at the museum for solving my problem with the abandoned church and transforming it into a derelict farmhouse, and Anna and Magnús for recounting stories of the ghost children.

When they were unable to provide me with answers, Jón Jonsson was called upon. Jón is an academic, local historian and folklorist, and it was during my initial conversation with him that the latter part of the plot for this novel coalesced in my mind. Jón's knowledge of Hólmavík, like Magnús's, is phenomenal and through our discussions I discovered the golden nugget of information about the local telephone system in the fjords in 1940. His familiarity with the tracks and roads, what is/was passable at certain times of year and what was/is not, the detours and alternative routes available, the boats that serviced Iceland at that time and local meteorological phenomena, has been priceless. Jón also helped pinpoint the location of the shelter erected near the highest point on the Borðeyri pass.

When I asked Jón and Magnús, 'What do you call these people who used the grimoires?' they both laughed and replied, 'Farmers!' Of course, I was searching for the term 'sorcerer' but the point they made was that, in Iceland, magical ways were ordinary ways: the lore was used by the working classes to protect them against the destructive power of the rich and the rulers. That applies just as much to my own country.

I can't remember who told me the anecdote about Hitler punching the desk globe when he heard about the British invasion of Iceland. Could have been Tóta, Anna, Jón or Magnús. Of course, as Gestur pointed out when he read my draft, it was unlikely to have happened: the German High Command had already written off any possible occupation of Iceland due to logistics. But it's a great story, and as a novelist, when I heard it, I thought: That's going in. Many thanks to whoever it was.

## The Museum of Sorcery and Witchcraft

If you want to learn more about Icelandic witchcraft and see the spells in context please visit the museum's homepage sorcerymuseum.is or pay them a visit in Hólmavík.

## England

I am very lucky to have a creative family. My sister, the artist Josie Moore, produces much of the artwork that goes into my books and the T-shirts for The Essex Girls Liberation Front. Josie painted the poster 'Loose Lips', combining two war slogans into one. As always, my heartfelt appreciation, dear sis. Cheque's in the post.

Thanks must also go to Wayne Hemingway for his speedy advice on hat etiquette in the 1940s and to Joshua Goodyear for his wise insights on séances versus private consultations (and all the film recommendations that came too).

Once again, I have benefitted from studying at the Combined Armed Military Services Museum in Maldon and gained much from perusing the Peter and Prue Mason Collection. This features espionage equipment, suits and shoes laden with blades, as well as Prue's (code name Zoe) 'Kiss of Death' Lipstick Pistol. I have taken liberties with the timeline – the weapon was originally produced by the KGB and Prue's was a single-shot 4.5mm.

My forever thanks, as always, go to Sandra Sawicka at Marjacq, without whom this trilogy would never have seen the light of day. And to Wayne Brookes, my editor, who from the very first has been a phenomenal cheerleader for *The Grand Illusion* and *The Great Deception*. Julian Ball is the most brilliant sales director (and a pretty good DJ too). Margot Weale has been with me from the very beginning of my relationship with

Oneworld, is super fun and a joy to work with, not to mention a magnificent PR guru. Thanks must also go to Anne Bihan, Jenny Parrott, Mark Rusher, Paul Nash, Laura McFarlane and of course the captains at the helm of the good ship Oneworld, Juliet and Novin.

Continuing that metaphor, a book might launch but will not sail far unless it has good winds speeding it. These have come in the form of reviews from Laura Wilson and Nigel Robert Wilson to whom I am much obliged. A special mention goes to Georgia Smith of Starburst Magazine for her beautifully written review and for picking up every nuance that I had intended in *The Grand Illusion*.

Crime writers and fellow authors are inundated with books all the time, so I must express my thanks to Sophia Bennett, Erin Kelly, Barbara Nadel, Olivia Isaac-Henry, Roz Watkins, Anna Mazzola, Rachael Blok, Paddy Magrane and Emma Haughton for their fabulous endorsements. Avid readers and bloggers must also be acknowledged for their importance and support in getting word out to the reading public. Thank you to Jackson van Uden, Budget Tales Book Blog, Lynda's Book Reviews, Big Blue Balloon, Faery Jess, Fat Guy Reading, One More Chapter, Dr Alice Violett, Cheryl M-M's Book Blog, Melanie's Reads, The Book Trail, Tays Book Corner, Travelling-Pageturner, Atomic Books, A Cottage Full of Books, Laura Patricia Rose Reads, Fully Booked 2017 and lovely Thanhmai Bui-Van. Caroline Maston of the UK Crime Book Club has been a great supporter of my work for which I am also hugely appreciative. To all of you, Daphne sends her very best wishes with thanks.

*The Great Deception* was developed as a back story to an idea I wrote for *The Twelve Strange Days of Christmas*. Fans will, no doubt, already know which one, but for those of you who may be new to my work, and who are curious, it is entitled 'Septimus and the Shaman'.

And finally, when Daphne reaches for words upon seeing the dead body of Rafn, she is summoning the last lines from *Women of Trachis* by Sophocles.

## Bibliography

By far the most extensive account of the invasion and occupation of Iceland has been produced by Donald F. Bittner in his PhD thesis, which can be found in the Reading Room of the National Library of Iceland. The author did produce a book based on his PhD, *The Lion and the White Falcon: Britain and Iceland in the World War II Era*, which is sadly out of print but still available online. The quality of Bittner's doctoral thesis, the breadth and detail, is outstanding.

On my visits to Iceland I was able to purchase books that are not available in the UK. One of these, *Iceland in World War II: A Blessed War* by G. Jökull Gíslason, is an illustrated publication full of interesting detail, with some lovely personal accounts from veterans. Gíslason also runs a Facebook site of the same title. I contacted him to find out about the black out in Reykjavík. It was mentioned in one of my primary sources and I needed to know when it ended. He was very quickly able to tell me – it never happened (though it was debated hotly) thus saving me from hours and hours of trawling through books and websites in search of a date that didn't exist. Thank you so much.

Another book available for purchase in Reykjavík bookstores is *Iceland Invaded: The Allied Occupation in World War II* by Páll Baldvin Baldvinsson which is also illustrated and an excellent read.

Available in the UK is *The British Occupation of Iceland* by Philip A. Coggin. The author is British and spent almost a year in the country as a sergeant in the Intelligence Corps working under MI5.

For those interested in Icelandic grimoires I must recommend Magnús's books: *Two Icelandic Books of Magic*, *Angurgapi: The Witch-hunts in Iceland* and *Rún: a magic grimoire*. All of these are available to buy online at the Museum of Icelandic Sorcery and Witchcraft: sorcerymuseum.is

SYD MOORE is currently the first Author in Residence for Essex Libraries. She is best known for her Essex Witch Museum Mysteries. The series was shortlisted for the Good Reader Holmes and Watson Award in 2018 and 2019. Syd founded the Essex Girls' Liberation Front and successfully got the term 'Essex girl' removed from the Oxford dictionary in 2020. She lives in Essex.